# DEATH OF A CURATOR

## SOAR CHRONICLES: BOOK TWO

By

MALORY

# TABLE OF CONTENTS


~~Prologue~~ Omnilogue   7

Chapter One – The Price of Glass and Dust   8

Chapter Two – The Cost of Obfuscation   15

Chapter Three – Barbarians at the Gate   19

Chapter Four – Through the Looking Glass of Lies   24

Chapter Five – Of Gold, Flesh, and Stone   30

Chapter Six – Memory Wiped, Guilt Intact   36

Chapter Seven – Echoes in the Eaves   42

Chapter Eight – A dark and stormy night   47

Chapter Nine – "Fuck me no fucks"   52

Chapter Ten – A Slime Too Far   57

Chapter Eleven – A Museum That Devours   60

Chapter Twelve – Promises in Blood   64

Chapter Thirteen – Wrestling with a Spider   68

Chapter Fourteen – The Weight of Bullshit and Blood   71

Chapter Fifteen – Whispers in the Wreckage   75

Chapter Sixteen – The Truth Twists Twice   80

Chapter Seventeen – The Bard's Swan Song   83

Chapter Eighteen – No Song Left to Sing   87

Chapter Nineteen – Dead Men Don't Charm   91

Chapter Twenty – What the Curator saw   95

Chapter Twenty One – Where the Walls Bleed   99

Chapter Twenty Two – One Gone, Five Watching   103

Chapter Twenty Three – Streets Like Blades   107

Chapter Twenty Four – The Mind's Edge   110

Chapter Twenty Five – Reflections in a Cracked Shield   114

Chapter Twenty Six – No Glow, No Mercy   117

Chapter Twenty Seven – What They Left Behind   121

Chapter Twenty Eight – Silent Witnesses   124

Chapter Twenty Nine – What the Armour Consumes ........ 128

Chapter Thirty – Control the Pieces, Ignore the Noise ........ 133

Chapter Thirty One – The Shifting of Soar ........ 137

Chapter Thirty Two - Dungeon Etiquette ........ 141

Chapter Thirty Three – Arachnophobia ........ 145

Chapter Thirty Four – The Folly of Ambitious Men ........ 148

Chapter Thirty Five – A fortunate chance to gear up ........ 152

Chapter Thirty Six – Fire and Bourbon ........ 156

Chapter Thirty Seven – No Reward Comes Free ........ 160

Chapter Thirty Eight – Fragments of Genius ........ 163

Chapter Thirty Nine – No Way In ........ 166

Chapter Forty – Charades in the Dark ........ 169

Chapter Forty One – Memories of Classtration ........ 173

Chapter Forty Two – No Honour Among Delvers ........ 176

Chapter Forty Three – When the Rules Don't Apply ........ 180

Chapter Forty Four – Blood of the Phoenix ........ 184

Chapter Forty Five – Plans within Plans ........ 188

Chapter Forty Six – In the Grip of the Dreadnaught ........ 192

Chapter Forty Seven: Knights have no meaning in this game. It wasn't a game for Knights. ........ 196

Chapter Forty Eight - Resurrection Is a Hell of a Wake-Up Call ........ 200

Chapter Forty Nine - When Titans Bleed ........ 203

Chapter Fifty - Catastrophic Unmined Mana Explosion ........ 207

Chapter Fifty One: Blood on the Ledger, Smoke in the Air ........ 212

Epilogue ........ 217

Thank you ........ 221

THE CUCKOOS LAST CALL ........ 222

JOURNEY TO THE DARK TOWER ........ 223

RISE OF MANKIND 6 : AGE OF GLASS ........ 224

THEFT OF DECKS ........ 225

QUEST ACADEMY ........ 226

WANDERING WARRIOR ........ 227

KNIGHTS OF ETERNITY ........ 228

SCARLET CITADEL                                       229

LITRPG!                                               230

FACEBOOK                                              231

                                                      232

MALORY

*For Josiah,*

# ~~Prologue~~ Omnilogue

*It's terribly challenging, you know, finding precisely the right words when you're floating free from the tedious grasp of linearity. Ordinarily, one would call this sort of thing a prologue—something neat and polite and tucked comfortably at the start. But seeing as I already know what has happened, what is happening, and what's lurking smugly around the temporal corner, 'prologue' simply won't do. Far too narrow. Far too mortal.*

*So, we'll settle instead for an Omnilogue, shall we? Arkola's Omnilogue, no less. Lucky you. A narrative spanning all conceivable timelines at once—past, present, future, and those awkward in-between bits nobody likes mentioning at parties. How tremendously honoured you must feel. Or perhaps not. Honestly, when one exists beyond the constraints of time itself, mortal enthusiasm becomes dreadfully dull. I really can't bring myself to care either way.*

*When last you found yourself in Soar, you were treated—or perhaps subjected—to the downfall of Commander Cenorth. Brought low by... well, Lowe. A touch of divine irony there, crafted especially for you. Laugh if you must; refrain if you'd rather. My self-esteem isn't exactly on the line here. Jana Lowe is one of my better jokes, after all. Consider him my small gift to chaos, neatly wrapped and dangerously clever.*

*Lowe strides the twisted streets of Soar as a man who is not himself twisted, who carries no stain he didn't earn, and fears no shadow he didn't cast himself. He is not a hero, but is every inch the man required for the time. He's a man of 'honour,' if such a tired phrase can still bear the weight.*

*Your second arrival in Soar occurs at an opportune time. This will be the tale of Lowe's quest for a truth hidden beneath lies, blades, and worse things besides. An adventure meant only for a man built precisely for adventure. It strikes me that if more men were cut from Lowe's particular cloth, then Soar would grow safer without ever becoming too tedious to tolerate.*

*But before the investigation must come the murder. Several of them in fact . . .*

# CHAPTER ONE – THE PRICE OF GLASS AND DUST

On the morning of the first murder, Grackle Nuroon stalked his museum in a complete and utter funk.

Those staff members who had arrived on shift early—unlucky souls bound either by relentless ambition or the cruel betrayal of faulty alarm clocks—did their best to shrink into the shadows and keep well out of his way. But there was seemingly no hiding from a man whose very gaze was capable of carving resignation letters directly from their souls.

Grackle didn't shout; that would have been almost merciful.

No, the Director of Soar Museum wielded his displeasure like a toddler handed a flamethrower—wildly, haphazardly, and with all the reckless joy of having just discovered no one was saying 'no more ice cream' ever again.

Anyone unfortunate enough to accidentally cross his path as he swept from one exhibit to the next, was soon reduced to a sobbing wreck. On his best day, Grackle Nuroon was a curmudgeonly bastard—a Level 56 tyrannical menace wrapped in the shell of rabid wolverine and blessed with all the charm of recurring syphilis.

And today was not one of his better days.

"Which fucking genius mislabelled this piece?" he hissed at a Cleaner who hadn't heard him coming in time to scamper away. The words ricochet off the stone walls like solidified spite, causing the Cleaner to freeze, caught mid-step, clutching his mop like a shield.

Receiving no satisfactory response, the Director stepped forward, glare intensifying on the poor young man. "I asked you a question. Who mislabelled this exhibit?"

"I . . . I . . . I don't know, sir," the Cleaner, barely into Level 6, managed to squeak out. "I just clean them."

"You just *clean* them? You *just* clean them!" The Director's eyes were two pools of fire now that he had locked down on his next victim. "You have been granted access to the single greatest collection of artefacts in the whole of Soar and you *just clean them*! You just *clean* them? You are being allowed into the presence of the stuff of legends! Material that has not seen the light of day since the time before the gods and instead of revelling in a moment of rapture at your proximity to history you instead *just fucking clean them!* Get the fuck out of my sight you pathetic, ungrateful philistine!"

The Cleaner put his head down and ran. As one of his other jobs was sterilising the bathroom at one of the brothels in the undercity, this was hardly his worst interaction of the day. The girls in there didn't come to play. Within that context, being berated by a small, spidery-looking man was almost uplifting . . .

Grackle watched the man run and span around for his next victim, continuing to seethe.

Four decades in the Director's chair had cemented his unwavering disdain for the teeming hordes of plebians who dared to set foot in *his* museum. "Dull-eyed troglodytes," he called them - often to their faces - and lamented the way they "oozed their uncultured stupidity across his floors like slime trails."

Their lack of intellect offended him as much as their sticky fingers on glass cases, their inane questions about the history of artefacts they couldn't begin to comprehend, or their gawping, stupid faces as they stood in awe of things of worth they would never grasp.

His museum was not a place for the masses to parasitically feed on his brilliance. To him, this temple to all he had achieved was sullied daily by the shambling, brainless rabble who thought a guided tour and a latte from the gift shop somehow elevated them to the realms of the 'cultured'.

"They should be stripped of the ability to speak before they enter," he'd once sneered to an underling. "If I could charge the public a stupidity tax, the museum would have its funding forever."

If the throngs of daily visitors were incapable of appreciating his curated treasures, of even attempting to rise above their festering ignorance, then what right did they have to pollute his air with their toxic presence? They weren't patrons— they were an infestation of the mindless, and their very existence in his domain was an affront to the grandeur of his life's work.

His theoretical irritation with humanity was, right now, focused on the offending exhibit he had plucked free from its display cabinet. "'Third Aeon Hunting Knife,' my haemorrhoided arse," Grackle growled, activating on his most levelled Skills, *Artifact Appraisal,* with a click of his fingers. The knife glimmered under the spell's scrutiny, the faint outline of its true origin emerging like a ghost. "Fifth Aeon, at best," he said as the Skill did its work.

"Bloody Khrichen," Nuroon spat. "That pustulent boil masquerading as a scholar wouldn't know an artefact if it crawled up his arse and spelled its provenance on his colon walls. Calling that proficient wanker a 'Senior Curator' is like handing a lunatic a lute and calling him a Maestro—no sense of rhythm, no talent, and everyone's worse off for having heard the noise. Every time he mislabels a relic, I feel the collective intellect of Soar haemorrhage a little more. Fifth Aeon, at best," he growled, turning the knife over in his hands. "Third Aeon? That'd be like calling a glory hole the arse of the Goddess of Beauty."

He ran his fingers over the blade as if seeking to purge it of Khrichen's aura. "Might as well replace him with a paederast with a fetish for licking glass cases. At least they'd have the decency to misclassify things in sacrificial virgin blood. But Khrichen? Oh no, he'll scribble 'Third Aeon' on a Fifth Aeon blade and call it a day, all while masturbating himself into a frenzy of self-regard for doing Soar's 'cultural heritage a favour. This is the tragedy of academia in action. One mislabelling at a time, these mouth-breathing fuckwits are dragging us back to the fucking Age of Reason."

When the *ding,* confirmation of the error came through, Nuroon's grin spread across his face like grease on a slick road. He glanced around, searching for some hapless nonentity to soak up the overflow of his irritation. But the halls had already emptied, word spreading fast that the Director was on the prowl in the Exhibition Hall.

Denied a living target, his wrath fixated on the mislabelled knife.

It lay in his hand, an affront to his very existence.

Didn't these cretins understand? One error, one mislabelled artifact, and the museum's credibility could collapse faster than a whore's virtue during a gold rush. *Idiots!* The thought of their carelessness made his teeth itch.

He threw the knife to the floor. "I swear, I'll gut every last one of you incompetents with this and label *that* an exhibit!"

Because this museum wasn't just bricks and mortar; it was his reputation made manifest.

For decades, Grackle Nuroon had dragged this crumbling pisshole into greatness with the sheer force of his own genius. *His name* was the museum's integrity, its one saving grace, and the thought of that name tarnished by some half-witted cretin's blunder made his stomach churn.

Mistakes like this weren't just stupidity—they were an act of war.

In a fit of incandescent rage, Nuroon's *Cultural Appropriation* Skill surged. The knife quivered, then crumbled to ash. A spectral stream of ancient XP bled from the ruins, flowing into Nuroon's Core and starting a stream of notifications.

He exhaled sharply, satisfaction flickering across his face as the familiar surge of power settled in his veins. He dismissed the messages hovering in his vision. At his age and stage, what did he care for *more* power?

The knife, mislabelled and mismanaged, was no longer a problem. It was now a part of something greater—him.

For a fleeting moment, guilt brushed against Nuroon's conscience—a faint whisper reminding him that this wasn't the conduct befitting a professional of his stature. Once, perhaps, back in the wild days when he'd been just another low-levelled, ambitious Archaeologist scraping through the Pits of Panthen, such impulsive actions would have been his stock-in-trade.

It was how he came to prominence, after all. A Skill by which you could absorb the power of ages past was quite a handy one for someone who regularly found himself balls deep in the collected detritus of lost civilisations . . .

But now? Now he was a figure of respect. A man of standing. Such feasting should be beneath him.

The moment passed.

Then the anger that had simmered since the previous night's insult roared back to life, scorching away any pangs of remorse. The Trustees, with their tone-deaf directives and backhanded disrespect, were lucky he wasn't storming through the museum, reducing all of their priceless exhibits to ash and siphoning their essence into his Core.

They thought he was a 'suffocating presence' now, did they? Wait until he had several millennia of XP on board. Then they'd see of what he was capable! His hand rested on the skeleton of some terrible lizard from the past and half of it crumbled away to nothing before another mountain of notifications caused him to step away.

The thought of absorbing the entire institution ran through his mind, as it always did at moments of high tension. Who, or what, could stand in his way then?

But no.

He had long decided that was not to be his role in life. He would rather be lord and master of all he surveyed in the Museum than a more . . . active presence in the wider world. Starting to calm, he let his charged Skills fade away. Around Soar, several gods that had powered up their own abilities in response to the burgeoning threat, took a sigh of relief.

Slightly calmer now, the Director thought back to his conversation of the previous evening. The one that had put him in such a mood. The one where he was told an auditor would be presenting themselves at the Museum this morning.

He had not taken the news well.

***

"Grackle, I do think you're overreacting just a touch," Liando Verlan had ventured, her watery blue eyes flicking to the door of her office as if gauging the distance to safety. Delivering bad news to this man was a task no one relished, least of all Liando, who had been handed the job like a live mana grenade. Nuroon's temper was the stuff of whispered legend, and she had no desire to become another cautionary tale to future Chairs of the Museum Board.

"It's not that the Trustees are implying you have done anything untoward," she continued. "It's just... well, you know how it is. Our Articles of Association are quite clear on this point. An annual audit of the exhibits is standard procedure to remain compliant with our insurance. Checks and balances, Grackle. Checks and balances. Nothing more sinister at play here."

Her fingers tightened around the edge of the report she'd brought with her, a flimsy shield against the firestorm to follow. "And... well... from our records, it seems it's been some time since—"

But Nuroon wasn't listening. He rarely did when his temper was in full swing.

"Interference," he snapped. "Plain and simple. What you're suggesting is the very betrayal I was assured would never happen when I agreed to take on this role so many years ago. Do you know what a museum is without the independence of its leadership? A circus. A sideshow. A political instrument. And, with your actions, you are threatening to turn this institution into precisely that."

He didn't stop to let her interject—his anger rolled on, building in momentum. "What's next, I wonder? Will one of the Trustees suggest we turn over the Minaron Wing to showcase their personal histories? Shall we swap out the Hall of Kings for an exhibit of the art of their latest whores and mistresses? This is a travesty, Liando. A travesty!" His hands slammed down on her desk for emphasis, sending a stack of documents skittering to the floor.

"I have tolerated much in my tenure here, but up with this sort of thing, I will not put!" The Director's voice echoed in the room like the final gavel in a courtroom, daring her to argue.

Grimacing at the Director's tone, Verlan raised her hands in a gesture of *what can I do?* "I hear your concerns, Grackle. Truly, I do. But I must be clear—the Trustees are united on this matter. The Auditor is already booked, and she will be here first thing tomorrow morning."

Her voice softened, though it was more out of self-preservation than sympathy. "We, of course, expect you to extend them every courtesy. There's no reason—none whatsoever—that this audit cannot be resolved swiftly and without fuss. By the supper bell, it'll all be over. You let them in, walk them through the exhibits they wish to inspect, and if everything is in order - as I'm sure it will be - you won't have to deal with this again for another year."

She paused, offering a carefully practised smile. "This is just a routine formality, Grackle. Nothing more. I'm sure you'll handle it... impeccably."

It was a challenge to sustain the full heat of his indignation in the face of Verlan's calm, reasonable tone, but Nuroon gave it his best shot.

"And that," he said, jabbing a finger toward her for emphasis, "is yet another outrage. Why am I only hearing about this inspection now? We had a Board meeting last week—last week, Liando! An event of this magnitude should have been front and centre on that agenda. Not snuck in like this!" His voice rose, echoing off the offices's polished walls. "It is scandalous—absolutely scandalous—that I've only been informed of this inspection on the eve of its occurrence. The Trustees, it seems, have decided that humiliating me is their new pastime!"

Nuroon's words dripped with theatrical venom, his eyes narrowing as if daring Verlan to contradict him. "Is this what my decades of service have earned me? To be blindsided like some novice Curator in charge of a backwater artefact swapmeet?"

Verlan privately reflected that a significant factor in the Director's prickly personality was likely the fact that he hadn't been humiliated nearly enough during his long and self-important life.

Of course, now didn't seem like the moment to offer that observation.

"I can assure you, Grackle, there's no conspiracy at play here. Tomorrow is simply the first available date we could secure. That's all. "Frankly," she continued, "we must also consider our responsibilities. I'm sure I don't need to explain this to someone with your experience, but Soar Museum houses some of the most priceless artefacts in the region. In the event of fire, flood, or an act of the gods themselves, the Trustees must be certain we're in full compliance with insurance requirements." Her gaze became steady, almost challenging. "You understand, of course, that such oversight is not only prudent but essential to safeguarding our collection—and, by extension, your *impeccable reputation.*"

Of course, the deliberately short notice of the inspection also ensured that Nuroon would have little time to make their lives a living hell in the interim.

And that was the whole point.

The Trustees had learned long ago that giving the Director too much lead time meant he'd have the chance to unearth a host of old skeletons—metaphorical and otherwise—and use them to drag anyone standing in his way into the muck.

There had been countless occasions during his lengthy tenure when the former Archaeologist's Skills had not been confined to the excavation of ancient artefacts. No, Grackle Nuroon had a particular knack for unearthing the kind of inconvenient truths that others desperately hoped would stay buried.

Take, for instance, the now-infamous "Goat, Gallon, and Melon Incident"—a debacle that still haunted certain members of the Board. Nuroon had stumbled upon it during what he liked to call "routine diligence" and what everyone else would call "a targeted campaign of blackmail."

It turned out that a former Chair had been moonlighting as a particularly enthusiastic supporter of the local Fruit Growers' Guild. This would have been harmless enough, except for an after-hours event in the Museum's Hall of Mythic Agriculture that had somehow involved a goat, a gallon of lube, and twelve exquisitely carved melons. The details were mercifully lost to history—something about an interpretive performance art piece gone horribly wrong—but the few grainy Mana-Captured images that survived were more than enough to bend the will of the most obstinate Trustee.

"I don't need to know why the goat was on a wheeled platform," Nuroon had said at the time, lounging back in his chair as the Chairperson's face turned an increasingly impressive shade of scarlet. "I don't need to know why the melons were hollowed out. And I *certainly* don't need to know what the lube was for. What I *do* need is for you to approve my budget proposal. Otherwise, I might find myself inspired to mount a new exhibit on 'Unusual Rituals of the Late Fourth Aeon.' Can you imagine the public interest? The *scholarly* debate?"

Suffice it to say, the funding was approved in record time, and the Chairperson quietly resigned a week later.

It was one of Nuroon's prouder moments—not because of the leverage, but because it so perfectly encapsulated the fundamental truth of his philosophy: there was no closet without a skeleton, and no skeleton without a story to be told at just the right moment.

This time, however, the Trustees were determined to avoid such a bloodbath. They had learned from past mistakes, and they had made sure the cards were stacked against the Director.

No dirty laundry to air, no whispered deals to be put in place and no desperate alliances to be formed.

This time, they were playing it smart—keeping things tight, contained, and most importantly, keeping Nuroon's arsenal of secrets just a little out of reach. All of them had 'gone away to the country' the moment Liandro had sat down with the spidery little tyrant.

"And if I were to offer my resignation?" Nuroon said, skinny nostrils flaring. "Would that make a difference?"

Verlan stiffened. Rising to the Chairwomanship of Soar Museum, the beating heart of the city's cultural life, was no small feat. One didn't get there without learning how to wield sharp elbows and an even sharper mind.

As a Level 40 Captain of Industry, she had recently been granted an unusual threshold bonus by her patron god, and while she wasn't exactly itching to bend Grackle *fucking* Nuroon to her will, she was also done indulging his petty tantrums over a relatively minor request.

"Of course, Grackle," she said, "that would be a matter of considerable regret to the Trustees. We wouldn't want you to feel that was your only option." She leaned forward slightly, just enough to let him know she wasn't going to back down. "However, on behalf of the Trustees, I have been empowered to accept... should you insist that to be your wish."

If Nuroon wanted to escalate this into something personal, she'd play that game. But it would be on her terms, not his. The ball, for once, was not in his court.

Verlan raised a hand, summoning Nuroon's contract into it in a puff of theatrically satisfying smoke—entirely unnecessary, but it served its purpose. She glanced down at the document, her fingers tracing its edges as if contemplating the weight of its words.

"We extended the term of your Directorship just last year," she said. "It would indeed be disappointing to see your long career at Soar Museum come to an end over a matter as trifling as this. But make no mistake, Grackle—while you may regard this as a minor inconvenience, the Trustees cannot afford to compromise on the matter of compliance with our constitutional rules."

She let the silence hang between them. "This audit will proceed, whether you like it or not. And if you choose to obstruct it, we will find a way forward regardless. The reputation of this institution, and the legal standing of its operations, cannot—and will not—be jeopardized over personal grievances."

Despite a little more back-and-forth, there was nothing left to say, not after the stakes had been laid bare.

***

Now, this morning, here he stood, watching the hands of the clock tick towards the arrival of an Auditor—one who might be poised to unravel everything he'd spent years carefully constructing.

His carefully built empire, each piece of the museum's intricate operations a fragile card stacked upon the next, could very well come crashing down around him. And that was quite without mentioning the astonishing find even now being explored in the Great Hall . . .

This had the potential to be a truly disastrous day.

Nuroon let the remaining ash from the desiccated knife fall from his fingers.

Well, there was little to be done about it now, in any event.

It wasn't like he could have the fucking Auditor killed, was it?

# CHAPTER TWO – THE COST OF OBFUSCATION

In a grudging surrender to the relentless shrieking of her alarm, Karolen Mehin pried her eyes open, every fibre of her being screaming to just vaporise the fucking thing and slip back into the oblivion of sleep.

Today was going to be tough, and it took an effort of colossal will to not just yank the sheets back over her head and consign the whole damn thing to the rubbish heap.

Audits were dangerous enough things at the best of times. So how on earth had she allowed herself to be dragged into the middle of a powerplay between Liando Verlan and Grackle Nuroon?

It was one thing, in theory, to be an entirely independent Auditor—free from the tug of alliances, untouched by the politics of the day. But it was a whole other beast when you found yourself caught in the crossfire between one of Soar's genuine up-and-coming business power players and, well, Grackle *fucking* Nuroon.

Today was likely to be the defining moment of her career thus far. The stakes couldn't be higher. She was going to be forced to pick a side, and - when she did that - she would incur the wrath of the other.

Whatever way she played this, someone with *pull* was going to be gunning for her by the end of the day.

The Museum Director was an institution in Soar—or at least, as the joke went, he ought to be locked up in one. And preferably heavily medicated to stop him from breaking free.

From the moment, nearly fifty years ago, when Grackle Nuroon first claimed the keys to that monolithic monstrosity in the heart of the Cultural Quarter, he had deflected every attempt to rein him in with a level of obstinacy typically reserved for feral mules. Trustees, auditors, and meddling bureaucrats alike had thrown themselves against the impenetrable wall of his ego, only to bounce off like rubber balls lobbed at a fortress.

The fact that the Trustees had been reduced to playing their last card—seeking an indictment for tax fraud—spoke volumes. It said as much about Nuroon's Teflon-like ability to avoid any stain on his career as it did about Verlan's growing desperation to finally bring the matter to a head.

And she was allowing herself to be the instrument by which they were attempting his downfall . . .

Man. Was she *fuuuuuuucked*.

It didn't help Karolen's mood that every other Auditor who'd tried to investigate the museum's accounts in the last twenty years had come out of it rather worse than simply having a bit of a shitty day. There had been three unexplained deaths and two inexplicable disappearances—and those were just the incidents that she had managed to pry from the lips of suddenly very unchatty colleagues.

Who knew how many other 'accidents' had been quietly swept under the rug?

Of course, in the brutal world of financial investigation, just making it home with all your fingers and toes was considered a good day's work. However, even Karolen's courage had its limits and, as she sat on the edge of her bed, thinking about the day ahead, she kind of thought Grackle Nuroon might be it.

Despite the polished assurances of Liando Verlan and the explicit backing of the rest of the museum Board, Karolen couldn't shake the sense that there was no outcome here where anything short of handing Nuroon the cleanest, most glowing bill of health wouldn't be her death knell.

The moment she signed off on anything less, that spidery vulture would start circling. Should she uncover irregularities and Liando *didn't* use her report to take the Director down, her career - fuck it, her life - would be pretty much over.

Swinging her legs off the side of the bed, Karolen stood up, her mind returning to the words of her best friend, Arebella Telut, from the wine bar the night before.

"How the hell do you get yourself into these situations, K?" Arebella had asked. "This case is the very definition of lose-lose."

Karolen had almost choked on her drink at the time, half laughing, half wincing at the truth of it. The whole thing stunk of inevitability. No matter how she sliced it, this was going to end in disaster—either Nuroon would chew her up and spit her out, or Verlan would throw her under the bus the moment the ink was dry on her audit.

"You think I don't know that?"

"It's the biggest open secret in Soar that Grackle Nuroon's been fiddling the museum's books since Arkola was in short trousers," Arebella had said. "There's a reason the Trustees haven't found anyone willing to sign off on those accounts in years. Hell, it's a miracle they've kept the whole operation afloat this long. But then again, that's Nuroon's real talent—making things look *just* clean enough to keep the wolves at bay while quietly stacking the deck behind everyone's backs."

Karolen had taken a long sip of wine, considering the truth of it. Nuroon had the kind of pull that didn't just smooth over the cracks; it made them invisible, even to those who should know better. But everyone in the city knew. They just turned a blind eye. In a place like Soar, even the most outrageous secrets were as common as cobblestones.

"I know," she had said again. Somewhat more resignedly this time.

"Best case scenario," Arebella had said, "you manage to spin anything untoward you find as an accident. A clerical error, maybe. A simple failure to carry the one, or whatever it is you're supposed to watch for in those spreadsheets of yours. But even then, there will be red faces all around when the truth comes out. That blood-sucking spider will find a way to make your life hell for making him look stupid. And the Trustees? They'll never forgive you for making it look like they were asleep at the wheel. *That's* the best case, K. I can't even imagine the shitstorm you'll wade through if you actually uncover enough evidence of wrongdoing to kick off a prosecution."

"You'll have *every* one of them gunning for you—from Nuroon's cronies to the Trustees who will backpedal faster than a drowning monkey. You'll be the one left holding the bag, K, and that bag's full of *every* dirty secret Soar has been sweeping under the rug for decades."

"Bella, I know!"

"I know you know," Arebella said. "And that's what makes you accepting this job such a colossally stupid thing to do. You're damned if you do, and you're damned if you don't. Either way, you're stuck in a no-win situation. You need to find a way to recuse yourself before it blows up in your face."

"It's too late for that," she replied, rubbing her temples as though trying to ward off the headache she could already feel coming on. "Verlan's telling the Director tonight that he's to cooperate fully with me. Even if I wanted to, I couldn't pull out now. The trap's already set, and I'm the damn bait."

"Shit!" Arebella had sat back then, the gold irises of her eyes shining in sympathy. "You're seriously going to go through with this? Tell me at least the money is insanely good."

"Enough to keep me in Chardonnay," Karolen said, swirling her glass. "But that's not the point, and you know it. Unless some of us are willing to stand up to the way things have always been, we're just going to keep circling the drain. Relics like Nuroon... Well, justice needs to be done, Arebella. And it needs to be seen to be done. You, of all people, should respect the hustle of trying to disrupt the status quo."

She took a sip, her lips curling into a grimace. "I mean, hell, if we don't stir the pot, we'll all just keep living in the same old sleazy script, watching the same assholes come out on top all the time. And who knows? Maybe one day, we'll all be so numb we won't even notice when they start locking the doors."

Arebella had smiled at that. "True. But it would be ideal if a few of us could live to see the sunlit uplands."

"Of course. But you're forgetting I have another option other than clerical error or wholesale fraud..."

"You do?"

"Yes, of course," Karolen said, "I can just turn off all my Skills and pretend I don't see a damn thing wrong. That's what the last Auditor did when they sent someone to investigate. You should see the report they came up with—it's the work of an evil, maniacal genius. You can practically feel the sweat on his brow as he uncovers a mountain of dirt but stops just short of actually *saying* anything you can pin him down for. It's a masterclass in dodging responsibility. I could play it that way, sure, I could tell the truth, but do it in such a way that no one can touch me. You know, obfuscate. Obfuscate. Obfuscate. But hey, at least Nuroon won't come after me with a meat cleaver." Karolen could still see her friend's disgusted expression at that suggestion.

"I mean, sure. But you're not going to do that, are you?"

There had been a tense silence before she had taken another massive gulp of wine and shaken her head. "No. I'm not. Of course, I'm not. What a fucking shambles."

Other than 'don't touch it with a bargepole', Arebella hadn't had much more advice of use to offer, and she'd made her excuses soon after.

Her friend had recently got back together with that loose cannon of an Inspector of hers and had been spending nearly every waking moment at his apartment. In fact, their impromptu glass (or five) last night had been the first time they'd got together in over a month.

Karolen conjured up a cup of strong coffee and rolled the hot bitterness of it around her mouth as she continued to slowly wake up. No matter how you looked at it, this job was a ridiculously unnecessary risk to take with a career that, since hitting Level 20, was starting to show evidence of going places.

She had chosen *Forensic Dissection* as her Threshold Reward and used all her savings to immediately raise it to the Epic tier. At this stage, she could temporarily reduce a target's stats by 20% and also reveal all hidden Skills and vulnerabilities. As a bonus, she would likewise gain a 10% damage boost against the analysed target. She wasn't exactly 'kick ass' yet, but she could certainly 'prod buttock' of someone five, maybe even ten levels above her.

At University, it had come as something of a surprise to her how often an Auditor found themselves in hand-to-hand combat with their clients, but she was certainly glad to have ground her way to a Skill that gave her a bit more survivability.

And now this job had come up.

All her painstaking progress up the slippery career pole would be wasted if she were crushed between the two nightmare pillars of the Soar Museum's Trustees and its implacable Director.

Minutes ticked by. The coffee was consumed.

Well, she decided, it was too late to worry about such things. She had signed the contract - and accepted the exorbitant fee - and was expected to present herself for Grackle Nuroon's tender ministrations within the hour.

Her flat in the 'emerging district' - as the slimy Estate Agent had described it, although what precisely was emerging remained to be seen - was a short walk from a Portal Stone that would deliver her, literally, at the gates of Soar Museum.

It wasn't exactly like living in Jewel Town, but she was starting to become comfortable with life's little luxuries and was damned if she was going to allow fear of repercussions from a dried-up bundle of malevolent energy to get in the way of that.

Pulling her long, fiery red hair into a tight bun, Karolen regarded her reflection with satisfaction. Moving with more purpose, she crossed to the neatly laid-out clothes she had prepared the night before, as though the very act of dressing was a ritual she could control in a world gone haywire.

Her finely tailored tunic, crafted with an eye for elegance and function, was expensively cut, hugging her frame just right, and its silver buttons more than just decoration: they significantly enhanced both her Dexterity and Concentration.

Her trousers, a recent purchase from one of the more exclusive boutiques in the Commercial District, didn't just look good—they *worked*. A 10% boost to her Endurance and Resilience was a subtle advantage that only the truly discerning would understand.

Over the top of all that, she pulled on her Inspector's Mantle, a cloak of deep, shifting colours that practically melted into the shadows. The cloak had a stealth bonus that made her nearly invisible and now, with her recent crossing of her Level 20 Threshold, the aura it exuded had grown stronger.

It clung to her like a second skin, sharpening her edges, amplifying her every move.

Taking a final look at herself in the mirror, she was pretty happy with what she saw: the very definition of a professional preparing for the most significant case of her career.

She was an Auditor.

If anyone had told her that she was on her way to witness a murder, she would have assumed they were speaking metaphorically.

And in that, she would have been wrong.

# CHAPTER THREE – BARBARIANS AT THE GATE

Despite Karolen living so close to her district's Portal Stone, the inauspiciously driving rain added considerably to her journey to the museum.

As she locked her front door, water poured down in sheets, turning the streets into a network of muddy rivers. All of those commuters who might usually have enjoyed a leisurely early morning stroll to work had instead decided a short, wet queue for mana transportation was preferable to a much longer mobile soaking.

Thus, when she arrived, there was an irritatingly large scrum of humanity waiting around the Portal Stone, all in various degrees of poor humour.

Karolen groaned in frustration as she joined the serpentine queue which wound its way down More-In-Expectation-Than-Hope Avenue and back up towards the street on which she lived, Contemplation Drive.

Of all the things she thought might go wrong with her assignment today, turning up both late and wet had not been in the top ten . . .

But there was nothing to be done about that now.

Having little else to occupy herself with until it was her turn to activate the Stone, Karolen spent the time amusing herself at the eclectic mix of professionals and . . . the less gainfully employed who were now huddled together under whatever ramshackle cover they could find.

At the front of the line stood a Level 18 Cloud Weaver looking particularly embarrassed at this state of affairs. The short, dark-haired woman was muttering incantations to ward off the rain that was, technically, part of their job description and ignoring the glares of everyone else who was getting soaked.

Beside her, a Level 7 Minor Drug Runner tried to shield his wares with an oversized raincoat, regularly checking the deluge wasn't ruining the carefully organised powders. It was very much in keeping with the vibe of this part of town that he was doing a roaring trade with those who needed a 'little something' to cope with the wait.

Indeed, in a display of the entrepreneurial spirit for which Soar was so famed, he had teamed up with a Barista, smelling faintly of espresso and caramel, to offer an outrageously good value '2-4-1' deal. Thus, all the way down the line, people were balancing steaming cups of coffee in one hand and surreptitiously snorting something eye-opening off the wrist of the other.

There are going to be some buzzing people at their desks this morning, Karolen thought . . .

A little further back, a Level 24 Elemental Enforcer stood with their arms crossed, electricity crackling around their fingers whenever someone jostled them and repeatedly shocking themselves whenever rain fell on them. Call it an Auditor's instincts, but Karolen did not think there was much chance of the guy making it to Level 25.

Behind his ongoing suicide attempt, and repeatedly bumping into them, a Dog Walker wrangled a leash holding a pack of invisible, presumably wet, spectral hounds.

Or, Karolen supposed, it could just be they were an early-morning mentalist gearing up for some high-quality chicanery . . .

Watching the man with the leads collide with the shins of the sparking Elemental Enforcer again and again with the lead, Karolen thought it might be too early to make that call.

And all of this was set to the tune of a Level 11 Street Busker playing a melancholic little tune on a waterlogged violin, adding a touch of musical whimsy to the dreary scene.

Despite herself, Karolen's lips twitched upward as she took in the patchwork scene before her. Young professionals—bright-eyed, overworked, and underpaid—crammed into spaces barely big enough to swing a Cat Familiar, their mismatched furniture and hopeful potted plants visible through uncurtained windows. It wasn't hard to see herself reflected in them: striving, pragmatic, and just barely scraping by in a city that never paused long enough to let anyone catch their breath.

Among them, the more traditional residents moved with a stubborn permanence, their routines etched into the fabric of the streets like weathered carvings on ancient stone. It was a haphazard symphony of cultures, ambitions, and survival.

This was Soar at its finest, Karolen thought: a roiling, vibrant mess of humanity that defied logic and thrived in the chaos. It was the heartbeat of the city she wanted to protect, the reason she'd thrown herself into her latest jobs.

Taking down Grackle Nuroon wasn't just about the ledger books or the whispers of corruption—it was about safeguarding *this*. The city's drive. Its diversity. Its soul.

And then it was finally her turn. Pouring mana into stone and thinking 'Soar Museum', Karolen stepped through the shimmering portal and vanished.

***

Karolen had, of course, done her homework.

Her inventory was a tangle of page-upon-page of notes, questions, and outright accusations, a haphazard collection of potential bombs she intended to drop on the Museum Director once her investigation officially kicked off.

Every angle she had explored, every lead she had followed, was dutifully documented—except, of course, the nagging suspicion that it might all be little more than smoke and mirrors.

It had been so long since anyone remotely competent had been allowed to touch the museum's accounts, let alone investigate them properly, that Karolen had to wonder if what she'd uncovered during her long, painstaking hours of preparation was nothing more than dust-covered relics of an old, rotting scandal.

But she couldn't afford to back down now.

She had read enough to know that somewhere in the tangled mess of financial records, buried beneath layers of bureaucracy and decades of misdirection, there was something rotten—and it was going to be her job this day to dig it up, no matter how deep she had to go.

The level of 'creative' accounting, quadruple-entry bollocks, and general numerical sleaze she had unearthed in the previous audit was far from the kind of thing that could be brushed under the rug with a wink and a nod.

What she suspected was going on wasn't a simple clerical mix-up or a couple of misplaced decimal points.

No, this was the kind of skullduggery that left fingerprints all over the books and a trail of smoke that would be hard to ignore. The sheer scale of the manipulation was enough to make her wonder if the museum's entire financial structure actually existed.

Whatever it was, it was *not* something that could be neatly resolved with a couple of hasty adjustments. Whoever was behind this knew exactly what they were doing— and Karolen had no intention of letting them get away with it.

From what she could tell, Director Nuroon was being a very naughty boy indeed.

There was a familiar rush of pressure, like a deep breath held too long, and then Karolen stepped out of the portal, her boots hitting the cobblestones just outside the grand entrance to Soar Museum.

To her left, was a guard's station and to the right, was a dilapidated smoker's hut. Beneath its rusted eaves, five or six museum employees huddled together, trying to shield themselves from the relentless downpour whilst they sparked up.

Karolen couldn't help but smile at that.

There was something deeply satisfying about the sight. Widespread, wholesale financial fraud, it seemed, was one thing—an art form, almost—but even Grackle Nuroon had his limits when it came to Health and Safety legislation.

A long queue had already formed in front of the museum's grand doors, a throng of impatient bodies braving the rain, most of them apparently made up by the members of a school trip gone wild. A clutch of harried Supply Teachers stood at the front of the increasingly impatient horde, clutching clipboards as they tried—and failed—to maintain order.

Without missing a beat, Karolen activated the camouflage function of her cloak, watching as the fabric shimmered and blended seamlessly with the background. The cacophony of the crowd of bored children faded into the distance as she slipped past them, unnoticed.

The noise became a dull hum as she neared the guard at the gates. He was a giant of a man, but his focus was lax, his attention scattered, only half-engaged with the crowd. He stood in his uniform like a piece of furniture, imposing in stature but entirely ineffective in presence. His eyes flicked back and forth, but they never really settled—more concerned with the occasional flicker of movement than any real threat.

The words Level 14 Unaffiliated Security floated above his head, of which Karolen made a mental note. Buried in the last set of accounts was a stream of payments for expensive, bespoke Museum Guardians. It may well be, of course, that some cost-saving measures had recently been instituted. However, she thought it more *on-brand* for what she suspected that Nuroon was working with one of Soar's Gangmasters to invoice for one Class and receive another, splitting the considerable gold difference between them.

"Fuck off," the guard intoned as she switched off her camouflage. "There's a fucking queue."

"I'm Auditor Mehin. You should be expecting me."

"Are you deaf? Fuck off. There's a queue." He jerked his thumb towards the school parties, his attention already back on his half-hearted duty.

Karolen glanced over just in time to see one of the groups enthusiastically constructing a makeshift crucifix with whatever they could scrounge up—sticks, bits of string, and a suspiciously large pile of discarded lunchboxes. They were in the process of nailing their hapless teacher to it.

"I tell you what, why don't we try all this again," Karolen said, triggering *Mandatory Review* and focusing it on the man blocking her way.

This Skill forced its target to undergo a thorough and invasive review of their abilities and actions, disrupting their concentration and reducing their resolve. It also silenced the man and prevented all spell-casting and ability use for a five-minute duration. In theory, Karolen would also gain increased power for each ability the target was unable to use, but it did not seem that this poor chump had many Skills at all to call on.

"My name is Karolen Mehin," she said, "and I was asked to attend a meeting this morning with Director Nuroon. It may well be that this message has not made its way down to you, for which I'm sure the Director will offer a most *profuse* apology when I mention it to him later." She let the implication linger for a few moments. "However, that doesn't exactly help you out right now, does it, sir? Because, as of one minute ago, you made the poor life choice to obstruct an Auditor in the course of their lawful business."

She took a slow, deliberate step closer. "I'm sure you're familiar with your responsibilities—having no doubt undergone *thorough* training in your role of standing still and looking menacing. What I'm certain you are *less* familiar with, however, is the fact that your little obstruction is now classified as a Stage Nine offence. A serious one. The kind that carries all manner of unpleasant consequences."

She let him consider her words for a moment before continuing. "These penalties are up to, and including, immediate incarceration for thirty years in the deepest, smelliest dungeon my office can find. And believe me," she added, "we tend to get *very* creative about such things when people get in our way."

The guard opened his mouth to speak, but, of course, being 'silenced', no sound came out. His eyes bugged out pleasantly, though, Karolen thought.

"However," Karolen continued, "it's first thing in the morning, and I'm sure we're all not quite at our best..." The dying screams of a teacher—whose cross had just been set ablaze by the kids—served as an impromptu soundtrack to her broader point. "Now, if you would like to reconsider the advisability of your current position—standing there, blocking my way and being generally obstructive—I'd be more than happy to start this exchange again. You know, in a *polite* manner that means we both probably come out of this alive."

She waited a beat, her eyes locking onto his, her posture still, every inch of her the picture of controlled authority. "So, nod if you think that would be a simply *splendid* idea."

A meaty neck bobbed enthusiastically up and down.

"Excellent," Karolen said, extending her hand, watching as the big man recoiled just a fraction. After a beat, he hesitated, then awkwardly extended his own hand to meet hers in what could barely be called a shake.

Karolen's grip was firm, but the gesture was all business. She held his hand for a moment longer than necessary, her gaze never leaving his face. "I am Auditor

Mehin," she said, "And I would very much like you to inform Director Nuroon that I have arrived and am ready to begin today's audit."

"As impressive as your little show of dominance is, my dear, perhaps we can stop intimidating the help and get down to business?"

Karolen whipped around, as the scratchy, insidious voice of Grackle Nuroon slithered into her ear. It was like the man had somehow materialised out of thin air. Her body reacted instinctively—every muscle tensed, and before her mind could even fully process the threat, she activated all her defensive Skills.

The air around her rippled in a quicksilver display of energy. A low hum filled the space, as her cloak shone, and her aura flared with sudden, raw power. Even the teenagers—still distracted by their little sacrificial slaughter—paused mid-swing, momentarily subdued in awe.

The full arsenal of an Auditor was unveiled.

Grackle Nuroon, though, merely stepped back with an almost theatrical slowness, as he raised a single, ironic eyebrow at her. Karolen's attempt to blast him away—every Skill she'd summoned in a rush of raw power—washed over him like an errant breeze. His expression remained unchanged, the same thin, amused smirk playing on his lips as though he had all the time in the world to watch her flail.

"I am sure my Secretary can find you a Mana Potion to replace all of… *that*," he said, the disdain dripping from his words like venom from a fang. "But, would you perhaps like a moment to freshen up before we begin? I do find discussions tend to be much more profitable without the stink of impotent Skill usage clogging up one's senses."

He stood there, waiting as though daring her to react. Karolen refused to let him see even a flicker of irritation, but inside, she was seething.

Grackle Nuroon was everything she had expected. His arrogance now a living, breathing thing between them. But she wouldn't give him the satisfaction of showing her discomfort.

Not yet.

Without wasting a backward glance, Nuroon passed through the now-open gates and into the museum beyond.

Feeling somewhat discouraged to have so manifestly lost the opening skirmish, Karolen moved to follow him.

And with that, a series of unfortunate events were set in motion.

# CHAPTER FOUR – THROUGH THE LOOKING GLASS OF LIES

Even with a Skill that boosted her Stamina to a level that could have rivalled a marathon runner, Karolen found herself struggling to keep pace with the wiry little man ahead of her.

Nuroon moved with surprising urgency, his steps quick and light, skipping effortlessly through the maze of hallways like a shadow weaving through the night. Each time she thought she had him back within her arm's reach, he darted around another corner, pushing through doorways with a speed that defied his advanced age.

Karolen did her best to track their path—conscious of the labyrinthine structure of the Museum—but every twist and turn felt like another knot in the tangled web of corridors. From her research, she felt like she knew the Museum like the back of her hand, but the way Nuroon moved, with such reckless abandon and purpose, made her question whether she'd be able to retrace her steps should he decide to put even more distance between them.

The thought made her stomach tighten with real concern. If Nuroon picked up the pace much more, she'd genuinely be lost. And she had no confidence she could navigate the maze of hallways and hidden rooms on her own.

That thought - coupled with a pertinent memory of those unexplained vanishings of previous Auditors - caused Karolen to find further reserves of speed to keep Nuroon close. She was, thus, moving at quite a pace when turning a blind corner, she was brought to a crashing halt by the sudden, unexpected appearance of a staircase leading up to the first floor.

"Do mind your step, Ms. Mehin," came the sarcastic drawl from above.

Karolen paused, her fingers curling into fists at her sides. She needed a moment to reign in the irritation that was quickly turning into something harder. This was supposed to be a measured investigation, not some chase through the bowels of a dusty old museum.

But Nuroon had a way of making everything feel like a game—his game—and Karolen was already sick of it.

"Director Nuroon!" she called. It came out sharper than she'd intended, but in that moment, she couldn't bring herself to feel sorry for it. Every second wasted chasing after him only stoked the fire of her bad temper. She wasn't in the mood for his games, not when she had a job to do.

Especially this job.

"Yes, Ms. Mehin?" he replied, emphasising the sibilance of 'Ms.' as if he were in the middle of transforming into a giant python. Which, as far as she knew, was something of which he was potentially capable of doing.

To Karolen's mind, there were far too many unanswered questions about the Museum Director's Skillset. All records she'd sought about the previous Director— a woman who had mysteriously vanished in a fire of uncertain origins—had conveniently been destroyed.

No one had ever bothered to look into it, and no one had dared to press the current occupant for any details on his own abilities either. It was an odd, glaring omission, but it fit the picture all too well. A man like Nuroon didn't appear to need to play by the usual rules; he made them up as he went along. The fact that no one had demanded a look at his Stat Sheet only confirmed that.

This lack of transparency, this air of deliberate obfuscation, was precisely why every single person Karolen had consulted about this audit had told her, in no uncertain terms, to pack up and run.

Well, it was too late for that now, wasn't it?

"How about we agree on something right out of the gate, Director Nuroon?" Karolen said. "I'll refer to you by your professional title, and you will afford me the same courtesy."

Nuroon cocked his head, looking every bit the skeletal figure of a defeathered vulture. His smile stretched too wide—and that was a smile Karolen could have easily gone her whole life without ever seeing again. "Ah, so you're one of those young women?"

"One of *what* women, Director?" Karolen asked as she started up the stairs.

By the time she reached the top step and stood next to him, she realised with a jolt that she was looking down at him. It was strange, almost comical, how a man who commanded so much influence in the world could seem so physically small in her presence.

Just one word from him, one whisper, was supposed to make or break lives—but here, in this moment, he felt as small and insignificant as the dust gathering in the corners of the museum.

"Oh, you know," he said, making a complicated gesture with his spidery fingers, "all iron knickers, and affirmative action and having it all until your biological clock explodes, and then it's babies, babies all the time."

Karolen opened her mouth to give an outraged reply but then she closed it, smiling broadly.

Truculent and misanthropic, certainly, but Nuroon was not known for his casual misogyny. That he was choosing to play that card in their first meeting suggested he thought it would benefit him somehow.

Maybe her arrival had him more rattled than he appeared?

Mindful of this, she adopted her most sincere, patient tone. "I think, Director, it would serve us both if we left consideration of my knickers for another occasion. Perhaps our time would be better spent if you were to show me to the office from which I will work during my time with you?"

Something flashed over Nuroon's face, but Karolen was unable to properly read the expression before he turned his back on her and flung open the single door before them. "Quite. I was thinking of putting you in here."

Karolen kept her face meticulously still as she regarded a room that, clearly, the better-quality brooms had already rejected.

In her experience, audits tended to go one of two ways. Either the recipient could not do enough for you - coffee, cake and you were based in the CEO's office - or you were made to feel as unwelcome as a split condom at an orgy.

It appeared Nuroon had decided to go all in on the latter option.

"I might suggest, Director, that most people feel it appropriate to provide me with at least a chair. Some even break the bank and make arrangements for a table?"

"Really? Strange and mysterious are the ways of those of Soar. Are you saying this room will not be suitable for your purposes? In that case, as I am afraid space is at a premium with the new exhibitions due to open shortly. It sounds like it might be best if we reschedule. How are you fixed for this time next year?"

Karolen held Nuroon's reptilian gaze. "No, not at all. I was merely musing aloud," she said. "You see, it's a curious thing about my process: the poorer my working conditions, the slower I tend to work. Why," she added, peering into the tiny cupboard with studied indifference, "I could easily see this inspection stretching out to three, maybe even four weeks, given these circumstances."

*

Funnily enough, a more suitable base of operations opened up almost immediately.

This far bigger office had not only a table and chair but also a running coffee machine and a spectacular view of the inner courtyard. Karolen's gaze swept over the almost magical grandeur of the gardens below, the neatly manicured trees and lush greenery stretching out in a verdant panorama.

A tight knot of suspicion formed in her gut as she considered the glaring omission from the museum's records. There was not a single mention of the gardeners—or any maintenance costs for the upkeep of such an extravagant display.

This was particularly telling, given the generous corporate 'Green' grants available to businesses in Soar, an easy handout from the Mayor's office, where any half-decent promise of sustainable living could win votes. Soar's electorate would likely endorse a scrotum with a moustache painted on it if it came with vague assurances about eco-friendly initiatives.

So, the fact that Nuroon hadn't gone to the trouble of securing such funds to cover the maintenance of his little personal jungle seemed downright suspicious. The museum's lush gardens would be a costly asset to maintain, and yet here they were, flourishing without a single penny accounted for in the books.

Where was the man finding the money?

However, before she had a chance to think much about that, two new faces appeared at her door, accompanied by the Director, and insisted she accompany them on a 'tour of the facility'.

The younger of the two, Martha Culloden, was the Senior Preservationist, the member of staff charged with safeguarding and restoring the museum's exhibits, both magical and mundane.

Karolen knew her by reputation, and judging by the tight smile and brittle laugh Martha greeted her with, the knowledge was undoubtedly mutual.

Martha's role in the workings of Soar Museum was crucial—her hands had touched more priceless artefacts than most could even dream of, using both mana-based and traditional techniques to preserve the treasures. But Karolen could see it in her eyes: the tension, the nervous flick of a gaze that suggested she knew exactly why Karolen was here.

If Soar Museum was the trove it claimed to be, then Martha would be the one responsible for protecting the vaults. But if, as Karolen suspected, the museum had far more relics on paper than it did in actual inventory, Culloden would be the first one standing in the firing line. Her professional life hung by a thread that was tied directly to the audit's outcome, which made her presence here necessary— expected, even.

But that wasn't the case for the second visitor standing beside her.

The older man, older by far, really didn't need to be there. He stood in the back, arms folded, looking less concerned about the audit and more about whether or not he'd need to make room for a nap before the whole thing was over.

His eyes were hidden beneath the shadow of a ridiculous fedora, but Karolen could feel his gaze on her. And something about that gave her the distinct impression that he was no accidental visitor. He was there for a reason—one that she hadn't yet pieced together.

Kelvin Kregg, the museum's Public Relations Bard, was very much an unwelcome addition to proceedings.

Karolen might have expected to have to deal with the smooth-talking man in the cheap suit at the very end of her investigation when there was spinning around her findings to be done, but she couldn't for the life of her see why Nuroon had chosen to put him in her path right now.

The tour, if it could even be called that, was more a forced march than anything resembling a guided experience. Director Nuroon was several paces ahead, his brisk strides punctuated by the occasional hiss of a comment about the exhibits.

The words themselves seemed less like information and more like an effort to dismiss the displays with the same casual contempt he treated everything else. He barely gave her time to take in a full glance before he was off again, moving like a man trying to outrun something he feared, though Karolen couldn't quite figure out what that might be.

Beside her, Martha Culloden did her best to offer the sort of commentary that might temper Nuroon's dismissive commentary. She murmured, her voice soft and almost apologetic, about the provenance of the items, where they'd been acquired from, what steps had been taken to preserve them.

The woman was being professional enough, but there was something off about her behaviour, a sense of rehearsed placidity masking deeper unease. The woman was walking a fine line—clearly trying to prove her worth while staying out of Nuroon's way, all too aware of the storm brewing around the museum's finances.

Then there was Kregg.

The man who'd slipped into the blind spot of her right shoulder, always just a half-step behind, always just present enough to make his presence known. He wasn't contributing anything of substance to the conversation, but, then again, he didn't need to. His occasional 'hmms' of approval whenever they passed a particularly famous or impressive work of art felt more like a reminder that he was there.

Karolen had no doubt that his participation in this little circus had a purpose far beyond simply playing the part of an innocent bystander.

But it wasn't the chatter of Nuroon, Culloden, or Kregg that had her nerves stretched tight.

No, it was the feeling that, with every turn they took down another narrow hallway, with every step they took deeper into the heart of the museum, she was being funneled into some preordained confrontation.

There was something about the way the Director moved, the way Culloden seemed to shrink against the walls, and Kregg's deliberate positioning behind her that made Karolen feel like a prisoner. They were all closing in, the walls narrowing with each step, until the only way out was forward.

"But of course, it is not those minor fripperies that are going to be the focus of your audit, are they?" Nuroon said, pulling up short in front of a giant bronze door and pressing his hand against it, channelling his mana to open the lock. "The Great Hall," Nuroon announced, pushing the heavy door open with a theatrical flourish, his back arched with a kind of self-congratulatory pride, "home to the greatest collection of magical artefacts in the known world."

He paused at the threshold, as if he were revealing some monumental truth. His hands spread wide, as if offering the very essence of history itself to her, and Karolen fought the urge to roll her eyes.

"I flatter myself," the Director continued, "that if the Celestial Temple is the heart of modern Soar, then what lies beyond this door is where the history of our civilisation—and perhaps even our future—may be found."

His gaze lingered on the grand expanse before them, and Karolen, despite herself, couldn't help but be impressed. The room beyond the door was vast, cavernous in a way that could swallow a small army without a second thought. Shelves upon shelves of relics, each glinting under the dim, atmospheric light, beckoned with promises of power, secrets, and lost knowledge.

But there was something *too* grandiose about it all. Something that didn't sit right. The room she was looking into felt like a mausoleum, not a vault of history. Nuroon seemed to bask in that atmosphere, as though he alone held the keys to the past— and maybe even the future, as he claimed.

"Bravo!" Kregg said enthusiastically, clapping his hands in an oddly sealion-like manner. Karolen genuinely could not understand what he was adding here.

But, right now, that didn't matter. What was in this room was what she was here to explore.

"The Trustees haven't been able to access the Great Hall in almost half a year," Liando Verlan had said. "It may well be that the reasons we've been given for rejecting our requests for supervisory visits are legitimate. Structural repairs, for instance. But… there's a part of me that suspects the truth is more complicatied than that. We suspect that Grackle has unearthed something he does not wish us to see."

Verlan was no fool; neither was Karolen, for that matter. Both of them knew that Nuroon had a way of making things *disappear*—both artefacts and the truth— whenever it suited his purposes. If he was keeping something hidden in the Great Hall, then it would be worth finding out what.

"Structural repairs, sure," Verlan continued, "but I wonder… repairs to the building or repairs to something hidden beneath it? Because from where I stand, it seems like the cracks might run a lot deeper than the stonework."

The Captain of Industry had leant forward then, and the intensity of her expression had struck Karolen. "It goes without saying that Grackle Nuroon is corrupt. This is Soar, and none of us are so naive as to believe anything else could possibly be the case. However, whilst - over many years - we have turned a blind eye to his peccadilloes, it is our opinion that something, of late, has changed. And we are certain it has to do with the artefacts within the Great Hall. I couldn't care less if you find he's embezzled a king's ransom in gold to decorate his fucking toilet. But I want to know what is happening with the relics in the Great Hall."

"Are you coming, my dear?"

At the sound of that scratchy voice, Karolen's mind was dragged back to the present, meeting the eyes of the Director, his head cocked in that strange, animalistic way.

There was a sudden, unwelcome pressure on her back, and Karolen felt Kregg's large hand nudge her forward through the door. The man was so close, she could feel the heat of his breath on the back of her neck, his words dripping with forced joviality.

"I hope you know what an honour this is, Auditor Mehin," Kregg said, far too loud in the narrow corridor. "It's a rare thing, indeed, for anyone to get access to the inner sanctum of Soar's Museum. Why, I've heard it said some people would kill just to get a peek at what's behind this door."

The last part of his statement hung in the air a moment too long, the casual threat woven between the lines like a well-worn patch in his cheap suit. Karolen felt a flicker of irritation, but she masked it quickly. She'd learned a long time ago that underestimating people like Kregg only ever led to trouble.

The implication wasn't lost on her.

Further narrative commentary here on the nature of irony and the Law of Sod seems somewhat redundant.

# CHAPTER FIVE – OF GOLD, FLESH, AND STONE

"The collapse of the exhausted Dungeon on the outskirts of Soar has brought with it many opportunities," Director Nuroon said. "This isn't the first time Archaeologists have stumbled upon an untapped goldmine, mind you—unclaimed Loot Table rewards, ripe for the taking and the like. But," he paused, "this is the first time I've had the capital to outbid every other museum on the continent and secure first refusal on what's been uncovered."

He stopped, his eyes flicking briefly to Karolen as though she were just another fly in the ointment. "It's only fitting," he said, his gaze now sweeping the shadows of the vast chamber, "that the finest pieces come to those who can truly appreciate them. Most of what we have unearthed is... mere scraps, really. But for those who understand the finer points of acquisition and curation?" He gave a short laugh. "Well, the treasures we have accumulated here have the potential to reshape the entire cultural landscape of Soar."

Karolen couldn't help but think that, in Nuroon's hands, those "treasures" had likely already been reshaped into something far more lucrative than anyone might guess.

She, like everyone else with a functioning pair of ears, had heard about the destruction of the old Dungeon just beyond the city's walls. The story at the time was that the Mayor was considering expanding Soar in that direction and that empty real estate was required.

But the word 'collapse' had not been part of that narrative. Similarly, while there were rumours that exhausted Dungeons retained the rewards they generated for delvers, to have it so casually confirmed was a bit of a shock.

But any further consideration of the broader implications had to be put on hold, as it was the final part of the Director's monologue which had truly caught the Auditor's attention.

Nuroon obviously saw her 'interest' antennae flare. "Yes, indeed. I thought that might perk you up a bit, my dear. I have been fortunate enough to attract some unanticipated sponsorship from... sources. The largesse of these interested parties has enabled me to secure all of what you see in this room."

With that, Kregg raised his hands and executed some sort of showy, dramatic lighting Skill that suddenly illuminated the sheer scale of the room they were in.

Despite herself, Karolen felt her breath stolen from her by the sight.

As a child, Karolen had often lost herself in the rich, winding stories of Soar's folklore. And the legends of dragons—ancient, terrifying, and awe-inspiring—had always been her favourites.

She'd lie on her bed, staring up at the ceiling, and imagine glittering hoards of treasure guarded by those same mighty creatures. In her mind, vast mounds of gold piled high, chests overflowing with priceless jewels, and rare artefacts from forgotten civilizations lay scattered about, haphazardly yet magnificently, within the deep recesses of the dragons' shadowy lairs.

Now, standing in the heart of this vault—a place that seemed more akin to a myth than reality—Karolen couldn't shake the feeling of déjà vu.

It felt almost as though the grandiose stories of her childhood were bleeding into the present, taking physical form in the space around her.

Nuroon must have a small army of employees Skilled in spatial manipulation, because what she was seeing here was impossibly larger than any structure should be from the outside. The sheer scale of it was dizzying, an architectural contradiction that defied logic.

The cavernous space before her stretched out like an endless sea of shelves and glass cases, each containing what could only be described as a mountain of the extraordinary.

Curators moved in and out of her field of vision, huddled around crates and boxes that were piled high and labelled with a variety of inscriptions: "Enchanted Cloth," "Unsocketed Jewels," "Growth Armour"—each label a tantalising promise of some mystical, otherworldly prize.

It was like stepping into one of her childhood dreams, except this time the dragons had been replaced by men in overalls and tight smiles, their hands carefully handling the relics of an age long past.

If her initial impression had been of a dragon's hoard, now that her eyes had adjusted to the sheer scale of the space, what she was seeing reminded her of nothing so much as a roiling termite mound.

"You received sufficient sponsorship funds to purchase all of this?" Karolen asked, her voice slightly strangled.

Nuroon flicked his hands dismissively, as if the entire matter were beneath him. "Yes, yes, of course. Everything above board, I assure you." His voice was smooth, honeyed. "And I'll be more than happy for you to sift through the receipts, if that will put your busy little mind at rest."

He paused, turning towards the vast expanse of the vault, his arms sweeping out in a grand gesture. "But, just for a moment, my dear, allow your mind to rise above the gutter of numbers and formulae," he said. "Leave the mundane concerns of ledgers and balance sheets behind. Just... *bask* in the glory before you. Let your soul soar, if only for a second. You won't regret it"

It was like he was some kind of high priest inviting her to join him in reverence of something far greater than any mortal concern. There was something off about it, though—something artificial in the way he gestured to the gleaming treasures. It was too rehearsed, too polished, as if he were waiting for her to fall in line with his little performance.

Karolen couldn't help but feel that the only thing soaring here was Nuroon's ego.

Nuroon wasn't just playing to an audience—he was orchestrating a symphony of illusion, and Karolen was far too aware to fall for it.

Kregg appeared to have generated a little background music to come into being as the Director spoke, which actually allowed her to ground herself in reality rather than be carried away with the majesty of the moment.

"Yes, this is all very impressive," she said, looking around and attempting to calculate the emperor's ransom the contents of this vault represented.

Clearly sensing that the moment for awe had passed, the Senior Preservationist cleared her throat. "If I may, Auditor, I would note that it is not just the volume of material the museum has been able to secure from the collapsed Dungeon, but also the *quality* of unusual artefacts. Why, just yesterday we uncovered . . ."

"Yes. Yes. Yes," Nuroon interrupted, sliding effortlessly into Karolen's line of sight, cutting off Culloden mid-sentence. The shift in his tone was immediate—imperious, dismissive, as though he couldn't bear to waste another second indulging in the pleasantries of bureaucracy. "We don't need to waste this young lady's time with any of that, do we?" His gaze flicked back to Culloden with barely concealed annoyance, before he turned to Karolen."Follow me, please."

With that, he spun on his heel, a blur of motion as he made for the far left-hand side of the vault. Karolen, unwilling to let him out of her sight, followed closely, even as her eyes were drawn to a small cluster of Curators huddled around a massive stone sarcophagus.

The instant Nuroon entered their space the Curators froze.

The shift in their body language was unmistakable—three professionals, seasoned enough to handle ancient artefacts with delicate reverence, now paralysed with fear. They didn't acknowledge Karolen or anyone else in the room; instead, they stiffened under the weight of the Museum Director's presence. Their eyes flicked up to Nuroon as if they were caught in the gaze of some predatory beast, trapped, unwilling to move for fear of provoking something far worse than a reprimand.

The sole woman of the three, a slight figure with a nervous habit of tugging at her sleeve, seemed to shrink even further into the shadows, while the two men stood stiffly, like statues.

Nuroon's smile was still there, but it had morphed into something that resembled the satisfaction of a hunter watching his prey squirm in the trap. "Now, what have we here?" he barked, glaring at the man who was awkwardly trying to prise the lid free. "This looks suspiciously like an exhibit that you were expressly forbidden from opening unsupervised."

The Level 14 Curator was wearing heavy overalls that must have been stained with sweat even before he began the difficult work of lifting the top off the heavy stone chest. He was, Karolen realised, older than she would have expected for someone of such a comparatively low Level. A middle-aged change of Class, she wondered? Unusual, but not massively so. He was compact and dark, with just the first signs of grey appearing at his temples.

"We think it might be the pair to the one we uncovered yesterday, Director," the woman in the group, a Level 21, supplied. She stepped forward to lay a hand on Nuroon's forearm - a gesture Karolen found surprisingly disturbing in its intimacy.

Nuroon paled, cocked his head this way and that, as if deciding whether the short, blonde woman was worth devouring, and then abruptly turned to Culloden. "Well? Is she right?"

The Senior Preservationist stepped forward and the female Curator stumbled backward with a yelp, her eyes wide in alarm as she scrambled to avoid being trampled underfoot.

"Really, Isadora," Culloden snapped with barely contained irritation, "I was quite specific that no further explorations should occur without me being present!" She gave the younger woman a withering look, and Isadora's blush deepened.

Martha's gaze snapped to the older man at the sarcophagus. "Preece, put that bloody thing back down!" she barked, her tone leaving no room for argument.

The older man, flustered, did as he was told, fumbling with the heavy stone lid before letting it drop with a deafening crash. The sound of it reverberated through the vaulted space, causing several of the nearby Curators to jump in alarm.

"Is there not one of you with any sense?" Culloden continued. Her eyes narrowed as they fell on the third member of the group, a pale, thin man in green-lensed spectacles, who had been standing in the background. His shoulders stiffened, and his hands twitched nervously at his sides, a hint of guilt flashing across his face at the sharpness of her reproach.

"I'm surprised to see you involved in this, Harker" Culloden said, disappointment thick in her voice.

"I'm sorry, Senior Preservationist. We just didn't think we should wait any longer. The scrolls were clear that time is of the essence when powering these things up. If this really is the pair for the Dreadnaught armour from yesterday, then . . ."

"Be silent!" Grackle boomed.

The room fell into an uncomfortable silence. It was clear to Karolen that this wasn't just about what the sarcophagus contained; this was about something far more delicate—something the Curators were desperately trying to keep hidden.

Even those curators too far away to have seen him enter to stop what they were doing and turn around.

And then the Director really lost his temper.

Over the next few minutes, such was the invective that the Director unleashed on the three Curators that Karolen wondered if she should intervene.

He lambasted their abilities, timekeeping, personal hygiene, and even the lineage of their families. The younger man - Harker, was it? - was almost instantly reduced to tears, with both the woman and the older male Curators left white-faced and stammering apologies.

If the Auditor had any lingering doubts about the veracity of some of the HR reports she had come across, they were now more than dispelled.

However, it wasn't just the vile sting of the Director's verbal assault that struck Karolen the hardest. No, that was the reaction of Kregg—and even more so, the unmistakable submission of Culloden. The gleam in Kregg's eyes as he savoured every moment of the scene played out before him... well, Karolen could practically hear the man's blood rushing to his face in perverse delight. He practically *fed* on it.

It wasn't a surprise to her.

Kregg had a *reputation*. One that had echoed through the murky alleyways of Soar's social circles long before she'd ever laid eyes on him. His name was a staple in the undercurrents of conversation, passed around with that knowing glint in the eyes of the people who had the stomach to listen.

The gossip—what little Karolen had managed to pick up through the cracks— was a constant. Kregg's personal life wasn't exactly a carefully guarded secret. He was notorious for his 'GNWW' label: *Go Nowhere Without Witnesses*. Three of her closest friends had recounted sordid tales were far too chilling for comfort.

But it wasn't just Kregg.

No, Culloden's reaction cut far deeper than Karolen could have expected. The Senior Preservationist, a woman whose professionalism Karolen admired, now stood there, visibly shrinking under the weight of the Director's mockery. Karolen expected better. In fact, if the Senior Preservationist was not going to do something to intervene in this public shaming, then she was certainly going to . . .

However, as if sensing Karolen's tolerance for the performance was at an end, Nuroon suddenly halted his theatrical aural assault and plastered on a sickly smile.

"But, let us say nothing more of it, eh? Mistakes happen, and we were all young and enthusiastic once, weren't we?" His predator's eyes flicked to Curator Preece, "Although, for some of us, it is longer away than others, am I right?"

There was an awkward silence, and then Culloden finally spoke up. "Well, you've broken the seal, so we might as well get on with it." Her hands flared with light—Karolen assumed she had activated a Skill—and then she gestured at the sarcophagus lid. It shivered as if the stone had suddenly become very cold and then rose in the air to hover about ten feet above its base.

"Secure that!" Nuroon said.

A couple of Curators scurried into action at once, pulling ropes and rigging from nowhere, their hands moving quickly as they wrapped them around the levitating lid, holding it in place as though it might spring free at any moment.

"Do you have it?" Culloden asked. A small flicker of light pulsed around the lid, an aura of mana that seemed to hold it steady, just long enough for confirmation to be given and the rigging to be secured against the wall.

"Now, let us see what we have here," Culloden said in a tone Karolen had heard before, usually reserved for things that were meant to be cherished, protected, and preserved. "Isadora, would you care to do the honours?"

The young woman responded as if on cue. She practically *leapt* into the sarcophagus—like a child eager to dive into the depths of something forbidden. Karolen, on the other hand, couldn't imagine anything less likely to interest her than crawling into a stone tomb, and there was something about Isadora's sudden enthusiasm that struck her as both uncanny and absurd.

The sarcophagus was enormous, far too large for one person to stand upright within it without being swallowed up by the sheer size of it. And sure enough, as Isadora dove in, she vanished completely from sight, her form obscured by the depths of the dark, hollow container.

For a moment, the room was silent, the only sounds being the hushed breaths of the Curators and the faint rustling of fabric as they hovered anxiously around the edge.

Karolen felt there was an odd finality to the moment, as if everyone was holding their breath in anticipation, waiting for whatever revelation lay hidden in the stone chamber.

Then, after what felt like an eternity, a voice broke the stillness.

"It's... it's not what I expected," Isadora's voice echoed from within, muffled by the stone carrying a sharp, almost indignant edge. "There's something... *wrong* with it."

Karolen's heart skipped a beat. *Wrong.*

An odd atmosphere settled around the group, punctuated only by Isadora's heavy breathing and - oddly - occasional squeals of pleasure. Whatever she was finding within the massive coffin was apparently making her day.

And then something happened.

Karolen heard the Director give a little gasp, and then he was striding forward, reaching into the massive stone casket as if to pull Isadora out.

The smell hit Karolen first—a pungent, sickly-sweet odour of decay and . . . something else. Something unnatural. Her stomach churned as she watched Nuroon peer into the sarcophagus and then reach down with trembling hands. His fingers closed around strands of hair, and a horrific realisation struck them all as he pulled upwards.

The woman's hair came away too easily, sliding through the Director's grip like wet seaweed. Despite this, or maybe because of it, Nuroon pulled harder, his breath hitching as a sloshing sound filled the chamber, and Isadora's body began to emerge.

Her form was utterly liquified, flesh reduced to a gelatinous mass. Her skin had turned a mottled, bluish-grey, stretched thin over the skeletal remains that floated within a slurry of her melted tissues. Her eyes, wide and glassy, stared vacantly, suspended in the soup of her face.

But, what was worse, she wasn't dead.

Her lips, a thin, ruptured line, spread into a wide smile, leaking viscous fluid as they ripped and tore.

Then Nuroon's hand slipped, sinking into the gelatinous substance that had once been the Curator's head. He gagged as his fingers penetrated the gooey mixture, encountering the sharp resistance of bone fragments, the fibrous remnants of her brain oozing between his fingers.

Karolen didn't know what possessed him, but for some reason, he pulled again, harder this time, and Isadora's upper torso emerged with a squelch. Her ribcage was exposed, bones slick with the same dense material, flexing unnaturally as they were drawn up and freed.

Nuroon staggered back, falling to his knees, dry heaving and leaving Isadora's remains sprawled across the edge of the sarcophagus.

And then there was a terrible tearing sound as the floating lid of the stone casket tore free from the ropes that had secured it in the air and fell, crushing what was left of Isadora under its immense weight.

A shocked silence descended, broken by Kregg clearing his throat. "My word," he said, his magically enhanced voice reaching every corner of the room. "There has been the most terrible of accidents. Can someone please call the healers? Oh, what an appalling tragedy! What a horrendous accident!"

# CHAPTER SIX – MEMORY WIPED, GUILT INTACT

For reasons Karolen couldn't quite put her finger on, she had found herself suddenly in charge of a large, milling mass of utterly bewildered Curators—some with eyes wide, others with mouths gaping—stumbling around, unsure whether to stare at the horrific scene or flee from it entirely.

"Just get them out of here!" Nuroon's voice was strained as he stared at his filthy hand in utter disbelief. He was looking at it as though it were someone else's.

For a brief second, Karolen assumed those instructions were meant for either Culloden or Kregg, the two others standing nearby—after all, they were the ones with the more immediate stake in the situation. But when neither of them budged, she felt the cold pressure of responsibility settle over her shoulders.

The other Curators were panicking. Even seasoned professionals like these weren't immune to the horror unfolding before them. Her instincts kicked in. "All right, listen up!" she barked, putting every ounce of command she could muster into her voice and moving into Big Sister mode. "Move it, people! The staffroom. Now! Quick, no time to waste!"

It wasn't pretty. It wasn't dignified. But with the Curators staring at her like a herd of panicked sheep, it was the best she could do. Nuroon stood off to one side, still cradling his hand as if it were an alien object, too horrified to offer any further direction.

If the scene hadn't been so grim, she might have found some small satisfaction in watching Nuroon struggle to regain even a semblance of his usual authoritarian presence. But for now, the only thing that mattered was keeping the Curators from entirely losing their heads.

"Come on! Move! Now!" she repeated.

And then, as if by magic, the Curators started to shuffle toward the door.

It helped that, other than Preece and Harker—who had somewhat of a ring-side seat to the horror that had unfolded—none of the others really knew what had happened. They had heard the crash of the falling sarcophagus lid and Kregg's subsequent explanation, but they were abuzz with questions Karolen was not anxious to answer.

Harker had, somewhat in a daze, taken the lead toward the 'staffroom.'

Karolen couldn't help but notice, even amidst the lingering nausea and shock from what she'd just witnessed, that the room before her seemed out of place—far too polished, far too grand for a mere functional museum staff space.

The light that filtered through the giant windows glinted off furniture that could have been plucked from some forgotten aristocrat's estate—rich leather armchairs, mahogany tables, and impeccably arranged decor that whispered of wealth and power in subtle, almost insidious ways.

She had seen plenty of the grim, utilitarian spaces that dotted the backrooms of various offices and institutions throughout Soar—places that smelt of stale coffee and frayed uniforms—but this?

This was something else entirely. The luxurious velvet curtains draped across the windows, the gold-rimmed glasses filled with a selection of well-aged liquor, the polished oak shelves lined with rare books and artifacts—it looked more like the parlor of some exclusive Gentleman's Club than a place for overworked, underpaid Curators to take their lunch break.

Of course, Karolen'd never been invited to one of those clubs herself—she wasn't the sort who made the cut for that particular circle. But she'd worked for enough high-profile clients to know the type. The ones who liked to remind you, with a subtle tilt of their chin or an offhand comment, just how much money and influence they had.

"Impressive, isn't it?" Preece mumbled, his voice still shaky, though his eyes were fixed with a strange, distant look. He seemed to have shaken off some of his earlier shock, though Karolen noticed the tremor in his hands as he reached for a glass of something amber-colored, perhaps hoping it would steady him.

Karolen didn't answer immediately. She was too busy mentally cataloguing the absurdity of the situation. Here they were, surrounded by all the trappings of power and excess, while a fellow Curator's mangled remains were still fresh in their minds.

"Yeah, it's very nice," she finally said, her tone flat. "Almost a bit too nice, don't you think?"

Preece's eyes flicked up to her, and for a second, he seemed startled by her words. But then the fog in his mind seemed to lift, and he nodded, though it wasn't in agreement. It was more as if he was trying to convince himself that everything was fine.

"It's relatively recent," he said, though Karolen could hear the unease creeping into his voice. "Since the Director secured enhanced funding. For the dig."

She raised an eyebrow at that, but he didn't comment further.

As Karolen glanced around the room again, the sick feeling from before hadn't quite subsided. If anything, it had deepened, tangled up with her suspicion. There was something too neat about this place. Too well-crafted, too... perfect. As though someone was trying to give the impression that everything was under control, even as the cracks began to show.

How had Grackle Nuroon found access to this much gold?

But then the memory of what had happened to the young, blonde Curator surfaced, and she felt ashamed of the intrusive thought.

The Curators, none of them with a level higher than the mid-teens, had gathered in a tight, nervous knot at the centre of the room. Their eyes flicked between Preece and Harker, the two men who had been closest to the scene, but neither seemed willing to share much, their silence only adding fuel to the simmering tension that hung in the air.

A few muttered snippets of conversation and hesitant glances passed between them, but the unspoken truth was clear: none of them wanted to be the one to speak first.

Karolen, who had been observing the dynamics of the room, could feel the pressure building. Her eyes flicked to the refreshment table, a welcome distraction, and with a forced cheerfulness she didn't feel, she stepped forward.

"I could do with a coffee," she said brightly, forcing a smile. "I don't know about anyone else!"

The effect was immediate.

The room, which had been murmuring in its own little world, suddenly snapped into focus. Every eye turned toward her, as though her voice had been a switch, flicking on the light and forcing the room to acknowledge her presence for the first time since she'd entered.

The Curators' collective gaze seemed to weigh her, like they were sizing up something far less friendly than an Auditor in their midst.

"Coffee? I mean… what? Who are you?" said a squat, dark man with thick lips. He looked more like a bruiser than a museum employee. "What were you doing in the vault?" he added, the accusation hanging unspoken between the words.

She could feel the temperature of the room shift, the suspicion hanging in the air like a fog.

"She's the Auditor, stupid. Can't you read?"

All eyes swung upward, drawn to her stats now glowing above her head in unmistakable clarity—her Level, Class, the power she wielded in this space.

The room stilled like a frozen lake and the conversations died in an instant

Karolen couldn't help but feel a slight twinge of satisfaction. It wasn't every day that she could halt a room full of people with nothing more than the display of her rank.

But instead of the usual power trip, she found herself disarmed by the uncomfortable quiet that followed. These people didn't respect her authority. Not really. She was an outsider here, and even her position in the system couldn't erase the fact that she was now a witness to something ugly—and perhaps dangerous.

"I actually prefer to be known as 'Karolen' rather than 'Auditor,' though. How about the rest of you?"

As they worked their way around the group, each giving her a short introduction, Karolen thought that, by hook or by crook, she seemed to be doing a decent job of calming things down.

Until, that is, they reached the young man with the green spectacles, whose hands were shaking uncontrollably and his face was ashen. He didn't look like a man who had just witnessed a tragedy—he looked like a man who had been irreversibly broken by it.

"It melted her!" he suddenly shrieked, his voice reaching a pitch that made Karolen wince. "It was waiting for her in the sarcophagus! The second Isadora climbed in, it started to eat her!"

There was a terrible, stunned silence that hung in the air for a moment. Then, as if they had all been holding their breath, the voices began to spill out from the clustered Curators.

"Bard Kregg said it was an accident…"

"The lid fell on her. We all saw it happen. One moment it was floating, and the next—*splat*."

"You lot didn't tie it tightly enough. Nuroon will have your hide for this!"

"It wasn't me who brought the ropes, was it? If anything—"

"Stop!"

All turned to look at the older Curator, Preece, who was standing a little distance from the rest of the group. Karolen wondered at that and, again, was interested in the story behind what she assumed must have been a change of Class late in life. However, regardless of what had led him to the decision, she was glad he was there right now. The others seemed to have a natural deference to him.

"I know what Bard Kregg said, but Isadora was dead long before the lid collapsed down upon her. None of you who were involved in holding it up need to worry. You weren't to blame. Both Harker and I will testify to that if need be."

"Testify!" One of the other Curators let out a little burst of laughter, his voice strained, like someone trying too hard to sound casual. "Why should anyone need to testify?"

"You do understand that one of your colleagues has been *killed*?" Karolen said. "Regardless of whether it was crushed to death or... by other means," she added, fighting the bile rising in her throat at the memory of Isadora's liquefied remains. "There will need to be an investigation. And if that doesn't sink in, I'm happy to explain it to you again, slowly."

There was a brief pause before the Curator, the one who'd laughed, shifted uneasily on his feet. But he wasn't the one who spoke next. That fell to a different voice, a little too quick, a little too defensive.

"Oh, I wouldn't have thought so. Old Grackle won't stand for anyone sticking their nose into the workings of the museum. Especially not now," the woman said, almost flippantly, as though she was dismissing the very idea. "It's bad enough that the Trustees have insisted on an audit at this crucial time. Just as we've finally unearthed . . ."

The speaker's voice drifted away to silence as she realised to whom she was speaking. Karolen gave her a small, encouraging smile for them to continue, but it seemed that no more was going to be said about that particular topic.

A few of the other Curators were trying to encourage more details from Harker. None, Karolen noted, were attempting the same with Preece.

"But that's crazy. Why would there have been anything waiting in the casket?" one of the Curators asked, his voice edging toward panic.

"I don't know," Harker replied, "but there *was*! I could feel its presence in there. And it was waiting—waiting for Isadora to climb in before it struck!"

"Don't be ridiculous, Har," a woman snapped. "As if anything would want to harm Isadora!"

"But it wasn't *supposed* to be Isadora who explored the sarcophagus, was it?" Harker said, his green-lensed glasses catching a faint gleam of the overhead light. "Culloden was scheduled to be the one to open it! We—" He hesitated, then pressed on, his words tumbling over themselves. "We jumped the gun because Izzy was so determined to get the first look. Especially after what was found in the first one!"

Karolen had any number of follow-up questions about Harker's words there but sensed now might not be the right time.

"So, what are you saying? That it wasn't an accident, that something wanted to kill Martha Culloden, but that you three blundered in first and interrupted it?!"

Karolen didn't catch who had asked that question, but she felt it was pretty damn on the nose. Especially as, at that precise moment, the door to the staffroom opened, and the Senior Preservationist slipped inside.

"Ladies and gentlemen," she said, her voice oddly flat, Karolen thought, "as I am sure you have all discussed, Curator Isadora passed away a short while ago. There are - " the ashen-faced woman paused, looking over the assembled group as if searching for a particular someone, before pressing on - "questions around what occurred. I am afraid to say that we have determined we will need to speak to Cuckoo House for them to look into what occurred."

The news was greeted with something akin to utter horror. In fact, Karolen thought, this was the most shocked the group of Curators had seemed since the death had occurred.

"But what of the exhibits, Senior Preservationist? What about the armour?"

Culloden offered a wan smile to the questioner, a stick-thin woman with massive black-framed glasses. "Director Nuroon and I have discussed the matter, and I am afraid we have determined that, as we expect any investigation will thoroughly compromise the area, we will need to purge all of the samples."

A murmur of discontent rumbled around the room, but Culloden stopped it with a raised hand. "I understand the disappointment this will cause, but a young woman has lost her life and uncovering what took place must take priority."

Karolen couldn't help but think that the woman's words and tone did not quite match up.

"Thus, I must ask you all to wipe any and all records you have made since we opened the first sarcophagus yesterday morning."

At a further gasp from those in the room, Culloden waved her hand, and a rack of blue vials appeared on a table in the corner. "There are mana potions available - Director Nuroon has paid for these personally - and I must ask that you each perform *Cleansing the Canvas* before the investigators arrive. It would not be appropriate for anything we have uncovered to get into the wrong hands. We can restart our research anew once Cuckoo House closes the case, and all interlopers are removed from the sacred space."

Karolen's eyes widened at the outpouring of mana as the whole room effectively performed a massive memory wipe. Well, not quite the whole room, Karolen thought. There was a certain middle-aged Curator whose gaze was not replaced by a look of incomprehension once the Skill presumably triggered.

"Mana potions, Ladies and Gentlemen. And thank you for your support in this matter," Martha said. "The Director is very grateful. As am I." Her tone carried just enough steel to keep any immediate objections at bay.

The Senior Preservationist then approached Karolen with a faint smile. She placed a hand lightly on Karolen's forearm, her touch a little too familiar for the moment. "We obviously cannot insist you clear your own memory of what you saw in the vault," she began, "but I have said that I will ask you to do so. As one woman to another."

Karolen felt her mouth twist into a grimace of distaste at the appeal, the phrasing far too pointed and manipulative for her liking. She shook her head firmly. "I cannot think that would be appropriate in any circumstances," she replied. "Quite apart from my own professional obligations, there are broader considerations here."

Culloden's hand lingered for a moment before retreating. The Preservationist looked almost hurt, though Karolen doubted the emotion ran deep. "The Investigators from Cuckoo House will need witnesses to what took place. It would not be right for them to hear only from you, Director Nuroon, and Bard Kregg, especially now that the other witnesses have wiped their memories."

Culloden's lips thinned, her gaze flickering toward the group of Curators huddled across the room, most of whom were avoiding her eyes entirely. The decision to erase their recollections of the vault incident hadn't been theirs—Karolen was sure of that. It was another layer of control, another neatly tied bow on whatever narrative Nuroon and his cronies were planning to present to the outside world.

"You must see the necessity," Culloden said quietly. "The artefacts we're dealing with here... they're beyond anything most of the city can imagine. If word of them gets out, the consequences could be catastrophic for everyone."

"Catastrophic for whom?" Karolen asked.

Culloden opened her mouth to respond but seemed to think better of it. Instead, she took a step back, her hands clasping tightly in front of her. "You'll do what you feel is right, of course," she said, her voice brittle. "But I would caution against underestimating the Director's reach."

"I'm well aware of his reach," Karolen replied, her tone leaving no room for misinterpretation. "That's why it's all the more important I maintain a clear record of events."

If Nuroon thought she could be swayed so easily, he had grossly underestimated her resolve. Whatever secrets this place held, Karolen intended to uncover them—and not even a direct appeal to her sense of "sisterhood" was going to get in her way.

"Oh, and please don't misunderstand. It is not just junior colleagues who will be wiping their memories of the work of the last day. All of the Senior Staff will be doing so, too. It is a massive inconvenience, as I am sure you will appreciate. We can hardly afford to lose the work at this sensitive moment. The only reason I have not done so as of yet is simply in order to pass on this message to you. I had suggested to the Director that you would not acquiesce in this matter, thus, can I assume you will be available to greet the investigators when they arrive?"

A light blossomed around the Senior Preservationalist's eyes, and then her expression went wholly slack.

Karolen looked around the staffroom, shocked at what was taking place. All around her, men and women were looking at each other with quiet bafflement about what was happening.

"I'm sorry, should you be here?"

The Auditor turned to look into the eyes of the older Curator, Preece. There was not a flicker of recognition in his expression, even though she was sure he hadn't actually wiped his memory.

"Yes," she smiled back. "It is perfectly okay for me to be here. The Director has asked me to greet some visitors he invited."

Preece nodded, seemingly happy with her reply, and moved off to speak to the green-spectacled Curator, who was obviously much calmer now that any memory of what had occurred had left his mind.

Karolen was horrified to realise that, once the investigators from Cuckoo House arrived, she would be the only person in the building who was even aware a death had taken place.

# CHAPTER SEVEN – ECHOES IN THE EAVES

It was early morning, a long fourteen days since Curator Isadora's death, and up in the far more cramped break room tucked into the eaves of the museum, Preece sat staring at his Sending Stone.

He turned it over in his hand, its dull surface catching the faint, tired light that seeped through the frosted window. It was their custom—his and his wife's—to talk around this time every evening. But tonight, as he sat there with the weight of the last few weeks pressing down on him, he already knew where the conversation would lead.

And he wasn't sure he was up for it right now.

Preece turned over the small white stone in his hand, his fingers tracing its smooth edges. His eyes scanned the room, hunting for some distraction, any excuse to put off yet another inevitable quarrel. But what he saw offered little in the way of refuge.

Other than Harker, brooding silently against the window like some discontented gargoyle, the room was filled with faces he barely recognised, let alone felt inclined to strike up a chat with. And judging by their averted eyes and muttered exchanges, they had no interest in discussing anything as innocuous as the weather.

With no excuses left to cling to, Preece let out a low, resigned sigh and pushed mana into the Sending Stone. A faint hum crackled to life in his palm, and, as always, Braife answered almost immediately.

"Any news?" she asked.

He pinched the bridge of his nose, willing himself to sound steady. "No," he replied, doing his best to bury the weariness under his words. "Nothing new since we last spoke."

"But the Security Services are still there? In the museum?"

"There are a couple of junior officers floating about," Preece said. "But none of them seem particularly keen on talking to us, to tell the truth. They're just going through the motions now, like it's all a formality."

"So, they'll confirm it was an accident then?"

"In the absence of any other evidence, what else can they do?"

Because that was the key, wasn't it? No matter how much noise the Auditor had made about Isadora being dead before the sarcophagus lid had crushed her, there was nothing concrete to back it up. It was all just words, whispers in a building already filled with shadows and secrets.

His thoughts flickered back to the day Inspector Wyst had arrived, all bluster and bravado. The man had filled the museum's reception like a hurricane in a tea shop, booming orders and puffing out his chest as if sheer volume alone could untangle the mystery.

But for all his noise, Wyst had brought no answers—just the same hollow reassurances that this was nothing more than a tragic accident.

Nothing to see here.

Move along.

He had not taken the situation as presented to him all that well. "What the hell do you mean you all wiped your memories!?"

Preece had flinched, but he wasn't alone. The entire staff rippled under the force of Inspector Wyst's roar. If Arkola themself had been perched at the top of the Celestial Temple, they'd likely have heard it.

Preece assumed the vitriol was aimed squarely at Director Nuroon, but at that volume, it hardly mattered. Everyone in the vicinity was getting scorched.

"I would ask you to lower your voice, Inspector," Nuroon had replied. Then, with one hand resting lightly behind Wyst's back, he'd tried to steer the man toward the sanctuary of his office, a smile carved onto his face like it was chiseled from marble.

But Wyst wasn't having it.

He shrugged off Nuroon's guiding hand with the same ease he might flick a bug from his coat and spun to face the assembled staff. His glare was volcanic, hot enough to make even the walls sweat.

"Are you all *trying* to get locked up for obstruction of justice?" he'd yelled. "What on earth possessed you? You don't witness a girl's death and then immediately wipe everything you did for the last twenty-four hours! Who the hell do you think you people are? You're not gods. You're not above the law. I'll have the *lot* of you up on charges for this!"

There it was, out in the open now. Preece glanced toward Harker, who looked like he might actually faint. Even Culloden's practiced calm seemed to falter, her knuckles whitening as she gripped the edge of a nearby table.

But Nuroon? He didn't so much as blink. His hands clasped lightly in front of him, his expression so composed it was almost obscene.

"Inspector," Nuroon said evenly, "I assure you, there was no malice in the decision to utilise *Cleansing the Canvas*. It was a matter of professional necessity, given the volatile nature of the artefacts we were handling. Surely you can appreciate that safeguarding the museum's—"

"Safeguarding the museum's *what*?" Wyst thundered, cutting him off mid-sentence. "Its reputation? Its funding? Because you sure as hell weren't safeguarding *her*, were you? That girl is dead, Nuroon, and your lot just erased any chance we had of figuring out what really happened!"

Preece had tried to melt into the background, but the room had no shadows deep enough to hide in from the Inspector's wrath. His gaze had swept over them, a storm cloud looking for a lightning rod. And when it had landed on him, Preece felt the bottom drop out of his stomach.

There was an entertaining few minutes of bluster before, eventually, the combined efforts of Nuroon, Culloden, and Kregg calmed the Inspector sufficiently for him to be led away to somewhere a little political pressure could be applied.

Preece had no idea what was said to him or - perhaps more pertinently - *who* spoke to him, but when the Inspector finally emerged from Nuroon's office a bell later, he showed much less bombastic frustration about the whole event.

And that, as far as Preece could tell, set the tone for the entire investigation. Auditor Karolen might as well have been shouting into a void with her tale of "a sarcophagus that eats people." No one seemed remotely inclined to take her seriously, let alone acknowledge her accusations of what she clearly suspected was a clumsy, heavy-handed cover-up.

Inspector Wyst, once the roaring bull stomping through the museum's china shop, had deflated faster than a poorly cast *Inflate* spell. His team, predictably, followed his lead, their initial energy fading into the dull, disinterested rhythm of people going through the motions. They made all the right noises—asking questions, jotting notes—but their eyes betrayed them. This was just another tick on a checklist, another task to half-heartedly finish before moving on to less politically sensitive things.

The Security Services agent who'd spoken to Preece hadn't even bothered with the pretense of taking the situation seriously. If anything, their disinterest bordered on outright disdain.

Every word out of their mouth dripped with the implication that this entire investigation was a waste of time. The official museum line—dismissively branding Karolen's claims as "the ravings of a lunatic Auditor with an axe to grind"—seemed to have been accepted wholesale, and no one appeared interested in questioning it.

Preece, for his part, kept his head down. He wasn't about to volunteer anything that might make him the next target of Nuroon's icy glare or the Security Services' apathy. Whatever had really happened to Isadora, it was clear to him that no one in power wanted to dig too deeply.

"Look, just give me something, mate. I know you can't remember the last twenty-four hours, but you have to know *something* about the deceased. Anything. I'll take an anecdote at this stage!"

Preece carefully considered his response. He had always prided himself on being deliberate, and now, with Inspector Wyst's impatient eyes boring into him, that deliberation felt more crucial than ever.

As far as he could tell, he was the only Curator who hadn't followed through on the command to perform *Cleansing the Canvas* when the Senior Preservationist had requested it. He still wasn't entirely sure why he hadn't. If anything, the nightmares that had plagued him since Isadora's gruesome death—terrible, vivid flashes of her final moments—made him long for the oblivion the spell would have brought.

But even in that moment back in the staffroom, he'd hesitated.

Something had snagged at the edges of his conscience, sharp enough to keep him from reciting the incantation. The death of his… well, what had Isadora been to him? She wasn't exactly a friend. An acquaintance? A colleague? Whatever she'd been, Preece had felt—*knew*, even—that her death shouldn't be erased, shouldn't be blurred into the background of the museum's carefully curated facade. It wasn't right.

It wasn't like he was lying about it, either.

No one had directly asked him whether he'd gone through with the memory-wipe. No one had questioned him about what he might have seen or remembered. It said more about the almost cultlike authority Nuroon wielded over his staff that, as far as Preece could tell, he was the only one who had refused the order.

His voice, when he finally spoke, came out even and measured, giving nothing away. "She was… enthusiastic about her work," he said. "Always ready to dive into something headfirst. You know the type—excited about every little discovery, always trying to find the story behind it. A bit too eager for her own good, maybe."

He let the words hang in the air, watching as Wyst scribbled them into his notebook.

And then, right there, had been his big chance to tell someone what he had seen.

One-on-one in a locked room with a member of the Security Services, and all it would have taken was for him to give a quiet word to confirm that what Auditor Karolen had reported was accurate and that there was more to the death of Isadora than a simple workplace accident.

But no.

He'd bottled it.

He just couldn't risk it getting out that he'd disobeyed an explicit instruction: he enjoyed this job too much. "I'm sorry, I don't really know much about anything. Isadora, Harker, and I weren't all that close, and I don't know anything about her that you won't have heard a hundred times over. I wish I could be more help, but I don't know anything."

His interviewer had rolled his eyes, made a few notes, and then excused himself. Preece hadn't seen him again since.

"I just don't understand why you want to keep working in a place that's so patently dangerous!" his wife snapped, her wheedling tone dragging him out of his spiraling thoughts and back to the present.

"It's a museum, Bray," Preece replied. "Not exactly the front lines of a Forlorn Hope. Let's try to keep a little perspective, shall we?"

"It's a museum where the girl you were fucking *died!*" she shot back. "So don't you dare act like I'm making a fuss over nothing!"

Preece flinched, a telltale flush creeping up his neck as he tightened his grip on the Sending Stone. There it was, laid bare in her usual tactless fashion—the accusation she'd been dancing around for weeks now, finally out in the open.

"That's not fair, Bray," he said after a long pause. "You know it wasn't like that."

"Do I?" she countered, her tone icy. "Because from where I'm sitting, it looks like you're putting an awful lot of effort into mourning someone you keep insisting was 'just a colleague.'"

A few of the other Curators in the break room darted eyes towards him at that. Preece shrugged and gave the universal sign for 'bitches be crazy', which drew a few snorts of laughter from the now highly attentive audience.

Turning his back on them and trying to cushion the sound from the stone with his thumb, he once again did his best to reassure his wife.

"Look, I've told you again and again that nothing was going on between Isadora and me. I mean, just on a purely practical level, when do you think we would have had the time or energy? I've told you how busy the Director keeps us. I'm either here or at home, and I'm fucking knackered either way."

"I just think none of this would be an issue if you just went and worked for Daddy."

Ah, there it was.

That spectre of unspoken recriminations hovered over every conversation they'd had for months. If only Preece would stop being so damn stubborn and just play the dutiful little soldier, none of this unpleasantness would have happened—or so his wife seemed to believe. She was clinging to that narrative with a tenacity that bordered on the pathological.

So wedded was she to this viewpoint that Preece was fairly certain Braife thought Curator Isadora might still be alive if he'd simply prostituted his soul to her father's ridiculous Second-Hand Horse empire. In her mind, Isadora's death wasn't just a tragedy; it was a divine judgment—a celestial reprimand for his refusal to shuffle papers and haggle over the price of nags.

The idea was absurd, but then, so was much of Braife's worldview.

The conversation petered out shortly after that, both of them too drained to land any more blows. Preece promised they'd talk at the same time tomorrow. "And tomorrow, and tomorrow, and tomorrow," he muttered under his breath.

Around him, the break room fell silent as several heads turned his way, their faces puzzled by the sudden theatrical declaration. He ignored them, pocketed the Sending Stone, and leaned back in his chair, letting the weight of the day settle onto his shoulders.

A buzzing sound indicated that break was over, and the Curators began to file out and back down the stairs to the Exhibit Hall. Preece waited for them to go, hoping to catch a few words with Harker's still, silent presence.

So strange was the young man's behaviour in the last sevenday or so that Preece had assumed he must have also refused the request to blank his memory and was suffering with the same sort of nighttime horrors as he was.

However, in the few conversations they had had since, it was clear something else was bothering his friend. He just had not been able to figure out what it was.

For a moment, Preece considered pushing the issue—laying it all out, dragging the ugly truths into the light, and seeing if anything could be salvaged from the mess. But his "chat" with Braife had already soured his mood, leaving his nerves frayed and his patience worn thin. The words he might have said dried up in his throat, leaving him with nothing but a bitter taste and a lingering sense of unease.

Instead, he settled for placing a hand on Harker's shoulder, a gesture that was meant to be reassuring but felt hollow even as he did it. "Take care," he mumbled, knowing full well the sentiment would ring as empty as it felt.

Harker didn't respond, his pale, sickly expression frozen in a grimace of silent torment.

Preece hesitated for the briefest of moments, caught between the urge to stay and the pull of the other Curators, who were already moving on. Finally, he turned and left, his footsteps heavy as he followed the others out of the room.

In the days to come, that moment would return to him, unbidden and unrelenting.

Harker's face—drawn, colourless, and etched with an agony he hadn't dared voice—would haunt Preece in the quiet hours of the night.

He would replay the scene over and over in his mind, wondering how much of the horror that followed could have been avoided if he'd just stayed, just spoken, just listened. But by then, it would be too late.

Far too late.

# CHAPTER EIGHT – A DARK AND STORMY NIGHT

The evening shift at Soar Museum was not especially highly prized.

True, you were significantly less likely to fall foul of a Grackle Nuroon tantrum if you started work after he went home, but on the other hand, there was something about the atmosphere of the place after the sun went down that tested the temperaments of all but the most courageous Curator.

Too many long-dead bones. Too many unheard secrets. And far, far too many cursed artefacts.

And on the night of the second death, a furious storm was blowing a tempest across Soar, making those late-night workers even less happy about their lot in life.

The guard on gate duty was particularly unhappy about things, especially as the automatic *Illume* spell on the outer wall had failed, and he had been ordered to set himself up outside to keep an eye on any comings and goings.

Lacking any Skills to protect himself from the storm, Porthern Barth - Level 11 Unaffiliated Security - had swaddled himself in a borrowed Sou'wester and plonked himself down, with as much bad grace as he was capable, on a chair just outside the gatehouse.

It was just as one day surrendered to the next that Porthern was startled awake by the crackling hum of the Portal Stone opposite the museum flaring to life. The sound echoed through the stillness of the night, pulling him from his uneasy doze.

He frowned, leaning forward slightly to peer through the rain-slicked darkness. At this hour? And in this weather? Whoever it was, they'd have to be either desperate or mad. Most likely both.

When no figure materialised from the glowing gateway, his curiosity overcame his reluctance. With a muttered curse about the cold, he grabbed another jacket and trudged across the slick cobblestones toward the stone. The harsh light it emitted threw spikey shadows onto the museum's façade, making the otherwise quiet scene feel faintly menacing.

Porthern stood in front of the portal, hands shoved deep into his pockets, watching the flickering energy ripple across its surface. Minutes dragged by; each one stretching longer than the last, but still, no one emerged. The air seemed to hum with poised tension, but otherwise, there was nothing—no sound, no movement.

Just him, the rain, and the strange, silent glow of the Portal Stone.

He racked his brain, trying to remember the protocols for a dormant activation.

He was sure there had been some tedious training on this, back when he'd started, but for minimum wage and no hazard pay, Porthern couldn't be expected to keep track of every little regulation. He sighed, running a hand through his damp hair.

Maybe he should just head back inside and wake someone more senior? Let them deal with it.

He had just turned on his heel, rain dripping from his hood, when he froze. A faint sound—barely more than a whisper—reached his ears. He spun back toward the portal, half expecting to see some drenched and bedraggled traveller stepping through at last.

But it wasn't the portal.

It was Martha Culloden. "What are you doing?" she asked. Her appearance had been so sudden that it nearly sent him sprawling.

Culloden's tone carried just enough irritation to remind him that she wasn't the sort of person who tolerated dithering from subordinates. Porthern straightened, brushing off his jacket as if the rain had somehow soaked through more thoroughly because of her disapproval.

"I thought someone had activated the portal, Senior Preservationist," he said. "But... nothing's come through. Thought I'd... check, you know, in case it was something important."

Culloden's gaze flicked to the shimmering stone. "And did you find anything?"

"Not yet, ma'am," Porthern replied, his voice faltering slightly under her scrutiny. He hesitated, then added, "I was about to call for backup when you came along."

The Senior Preservationist had obviously invested considerably in some 'quality of life' Skills, as there was a wide cone around her through which no wind or rain was being permitted to cross. Porthern surreptitiously tried to stand as close to her as he could whilst she addressed him.

"Ah," she said. "I thought I heard the Portal Stone activate and came to investigate."

Even Porthern, lacking as he was in brains, smarts or any ability in deductive reasoning whatsoever, could smell bullshit when it was shovelled his way.

He had only noticed the stone coming to life because he was sitting less than ten feet away from the thing when it bloomed into being. Even without the storm trying to blow the museum's doors off, there was no way this woman had heard anything on this side of the street from inside her office.

Seeing scepticism on the man's face, Culloden gathered her coat around her and made to pass through the summoned portal. "Well, if no one is coming through, I might as well make use of it to get off home." However, she had taken no more than a few steps forward when, as if a thought had suddenly occurred to her, she turned, smiling at the guard.

"While I remember, I think the lock to the door of the canteen might be broken. I've cast a temporary *You Shall Not Pass* on it, but that will only hold until the morning. Be a dear and let Mr Levick know, will you?"

Porthen nodded, and for a moment, the two stood awkwardly facing each other before the Unaffiliated Security realised the blasted woman expected him to go and get on the Sending Stone immediately.

Seriously?

It was the middle of the night, the whole museum was locked down, and she'd already secured the door by the sound of it. But no. That wasn't enough. She wanted him to traipse back inside, wake up the famously grizzly Estate Caretaker and have him come and take a look.

Porthern gave a sarcastic salute - if she didn't know his name, she could hardly report him, could she? - and ambled back across the road and into the guard house.

It was just at the end of a robust conversation with Trei Levick that Porthern realised Culloden wouldn't need to know his name to check the rota to see which rude fucker was on duty this night. Yanking his mana out of the stone, abruptly cutting off the spew of bile from Levick coming his way, he quickly went back outside to make amends.

However, not only was the Portal Stone now switched off, but there was no sign of the Senior Preservationist.

"Weird," Porthern murmured before pulling his drenched coat around himself and sitting back down.

***

It was a little after the second bell of the morning that Preece finally finished cataloguing a pile of [Rare] Gauntlets that he knew he had done once before. However, short of admitting he hadn't performed the requested memory wipe, he could not easily argue the point.

He was pretty sure his immediate supervisor, Deputy Chief Curator Thenon, had guessed he was still in full possession of his memories and was giving him a string of pointless tasks to elicit that admission.

Well, this wasn't Preece's first rodeo of dealing with petty tyrants, and he was willing to play the long game. Also, unlike the rest of his Curator peers, he didn't have a string of exciting and athletic social engagements awaiting him and was more than happy to rack up the overtime.

Stretching out his back, he stood and began to return to the staffroom for a quick brew before starting the next of his mundane tasks. He wasn't sure what had come over the Director lately, but the quality and quantity of refreshments had gone through the roof. Even at this time of night—or in the morning, he guessed—there would still be 10% concentration-enhancing green tea available.

He was just at the bottom of the stairway when one of the myriad shadows surrounding him solidified into a hooded figure and tapped him on the shoulder. "Fucking hell, Kelvin. You gave me a start!"

Kregg lowered his hood and glanced somewhat furtively about. "Preece, what are you doing here?"

"Late shift. Thenon has me doing all sorts of crappy tasks, and I could do with the cash. What's your excuse?"

Did the Public Relations Bard blush at that? Surely not, Preece thought. "I'm just making sure everything is as it should be. I was a little worried the storm might have shaken some of the tiles off the Exhibit Hall. But it turns out there was nothing to worry about. Please excuse me. I should check the top of the Chapel."

Preece frowned as the man pulled his hood back up and slipped away down the corridor. Only after his third sip of tea did the oddity of the man responsible for PR checking on roof slates make him frown.

***

Less than half a bell later, in the dark hours when the city held its breath, one of the towering stained-glass windows in the Chapel of Rest shattered inward with a deafening roar.

No one heard it.

The wind had battered against it relentlessly, night after night, as though trying to force its way inside. Tonight, it finally succeeded.

The gale tore through the chapel like a vengeful spirit, howling and feral. Hundreds of books were hurled from their shelves, their pages flapping wildly like the wings of startled birds. Sheaves of paper caught in the maelstrom, spinning upwards in a violent, chaotic dance before scattering like leaves on the cold stone floor.

The door to a cupboard, left ajar by its last, hurried visitor, slammed shut with a resounding thud, the noise reverberating through the empty, cavernous space. It echoed briefly before being swallowed whole by the relentless roar of the wind.

And yet, no alarm was raised. No hurried footsteps came running to investigate. The gale, the shattered glass, the scattered remnants of knowledge—it all went unnoticed.

Within the labyrinthine corridors of Soar Museum, life carried on as though the Chapel of Rest remained untouched, its sanctity unbroken.

But something had shifted, a tremor in the unseen fabric of the place.

It lingered, heavy and unseen, as if the wind had left more than chaos in its wake. A subtle yet palpable sense of foreboding settled over the museum, though none within its walls yet realized it.

***

The sun hung low, a molten coin rising out of the horizon, as Grackle Nuroon strode past the slumped figure of the sleeping Unaffiliated Security guard.

His eyes barely flicked to the man, registering his presence only as one might notice a piece of misplaced furniture. Challenges were for lesser mortals, and Nuroon had long grown accustomed to the unspoken rule that his arrival required no fanfare. No interruptions.

If the guard's stillness and heavy layers conveyed anything, it was the appropriate deference of silence—no idle chatter, no prying questions, just mute acknowledgment of the important figure who walked these grounds.

He swept through the gates without a word, his steps as light as his mood was sour. Waiting just inside, of course, was Estate Caretaker Levick.

Levick, that perennial thorn in his side.

For a moment, Nuroon allowed himself the indulgence of imagining the caretaker reduced to a smouldering pile of ash, a neat little bonfire lighting the grounds he so obsessively maintained.

"I warned you about that fucking door!" the squat man bellowed, barely waiting for Nuroon to take off his coat.

"I'm sure you did, Trei. I'm sure you did," Nuroon said. "If only there were someone like, oh, I don't know, an Estate Caretaker who could address such things. Imagine it—someone with access to a veritable arsenal of Skills, finely honed for the maintenance of aberrant doors and cracked windows. Why, if they'd crossed their Level 50 threshold, that'd be even better, wouldn't it? Truly, a gift from the gods. Now," he added, leaning in ever so slightly, "where do you think we might find someone like that?"

"Fuck you, Grackle!"

"Was there anything in particular, Estate Caretaker?"

"You need to tell that woman of yours to stop putting her fucking cantrips on maintenance issues. It took me longer to dispel *You Shall Not Pass* than it would have done to just fix a fucking broken lock."

"I have no idea of what you speak, Trei. But it sounds fascinating. I shall be certain to give it my full attention at some stage in the near future."

Levick had thrown a report at him as he'd left, and it was a good few hours before Nuroon deigned to glance at it.

"What on earth was Martha up to?" he murmured to himself when he'd finished reading it. It went without saying that senior staff did whatever they could not to wind up the Estate Caretaker. Casting a rather sticky spell on a door was almost calculated to raise his ire.

Deciding to take this up with her—he always liked ensuring the shit rolled firmly downhill—Nuroon slid his chair back under his desk and strode briskly toward the Senior Preservationist's office. The prospect of delivering a sharp reprimand always brought a certain vigor to his step.

When he reached her door, it was unlocked. That much didn't surprise him. Culloden often left it ajar, a misplaced display of openness or perhaps arrogance. But what did surprise him was the fact that she wasn't there when he pushed it open.

Not nearly as much, however, as the sight of the cooling corpse sprawled across the floor.

Curator Harker's body was a tableau of horror. His face, unshielded by its usual green spectacles, bore an expression of sheer agony, his wide-open eyes frozen in a silent, pleading scream. The rest of him—what remained of it—was unrecognisable. The flesh seemed to have melted away, leaving glistening patches of exposed bone and a viscous sludge that soaked into the carpet.

Nuroon took a step closer, his lip curling as the stench of decay and something far fouler struck him. The sight, though nauseating, tickled at the edges of his memory. He'd seen something like this before—hadn't he? A thought scratched at the back of his mind but refused to fully surface.

"Well," he murmured, stepping back and pulling the door shut with a measured calm that belied the scene inside. He twisted the lock, the soft click breaking the heavy silence.

"This," he said to no one in particular, brushing invisible dust from his hands as he turned on his heel, "might be a touch trickier to make go away."

# CHAPTER NINE – "FUCK ME NO FUCKS"

"The Deathcaller is here, sir," a uniformed junior piped up, sticking his head around the door and delivering a jaunty thumbs-up that grated on every last one of Inspector Jana Lowe's nerves.

Lowe didn't bother responding, just fixed the kid with a withering glare that sent him scuttling back into the hall. He pinched the bridge of his nose, exhaling sharply through his teeth.

The scene itself was enough to sour anyone's mood—a shitshow that would linger in the back of his mind long after the formaldehyde stench faded.

But that wasn't all.

It was the arrival of the Deathcaller, of all people, that truly set his teeth on edge. Of the many denizens of Soar Lowe would have preferred to work with, Lant sat comfortably at the very bottom of the list.

He surveyed the scene again with tired, bloodshot eyes, the knot of tension at the base of his skull tightening. The room was swarming with a gaggle of young officers, each looking greener than the last, fumbling with equipment, jotting notes, and doing their best to look competent under his glare.

They weren't bad kids. Not really. But Lowe couldn't shake the feeling that they were playing at being investigators, their eagerness bordering on recklessness.

Maybe it was the gulf of years between them and himself—twenty years, at least, and every one of them weighed heavier in moments like these. Or maybe it was the creeping exhaustion that came from knowing exactly what kind of circus the Deathcaller's presence would turn this into.

Either way, Lowe's mood was foul enough to curdle milk.

"Great," he muttered under his breath, his tone drenched in sarcasm. "Penarth Lant. Just what this nightmare needs. The cherry on top."

He knew he shouldn't complain. The roil of emotions twisting in his gut was unbecoming of someone in his position. He should have been grateful—thanking his lucky stars, or whatever celestial body might tolerate a glance in his direction— to be back in the good graces of Soar's Security Services.

Gainful employment in this city wasn't exactly handed out like sweeties, and the fact that he'd managed to claw his way back in after everything? That was no small feat.

Lowe rubbed at his temple, trying to will away the headache that was building behind his eyes. Sure, he was back on the payroll, wearing the badge, going through the motions—but the hollowness in his chest told him it wasn't the same.

Not really.

And yet, and yet, and yet . . .

"What the fuck did you expect, you moody wanker?" Commander Pernille Staffen had asked him, glaring up from a mountain of paperwork. "That we'd all drop to our knees and genuflect for the return of the great and marvellous fucking Jana Lowe? Maybe you thought we should blow you while we were down there, too? Twat."

"I don't know what I expected," Lowe had said, not for the first time finding Pernille's salty approach to conversation a touch embarrassing.

Such a mouth in the possession of someone who looked like they'd be more at home baking cookies for their phalanx of grandchildren was quite a trip.

However, following the considerable public and private fallout at Commander Cenorth's involvement in any number of crimes, it was felt someone a bit more straightforward and 'plain speaking' would be ideal to take over at Cuckoo House.

Enter Pernille Staffen: five-foot-two of uncompromising grandmotherly severity wrapped in a no-nonsense shawl of authority. She moved like an apocalypse in sensible shoes, her reputation for taking no shit preceding her like the ominous roll of thunder. If you had any doubts about what you saw being exactly what you got with this Level 46 Guardian of the Wall, her choice of patron god would clear that up *fast*.

Blurian the Unimpressed didn't tolerate ambiguity. His doctrine was as straightforward as Pernille herself—unyielding, unapologetic, and deeply skeptical of anyone claiming to know better. In Pernille, Blurian had found the ideal champion, and in return, she carried his ethos of *not being at home for any of your shit* like a badge of honour: steadfast, focused, and utterly intolerant of shenanigans.

"Well whoop-de-fucking-do. Then you can't be disappointed, can you? Keep those expectations low, Lowe. That's the ticket! Now, what can I do for you on this fucking fine afternoon?"

Lowe had held up the file that had been unceremoniously thrown on his desk. "Apparently, I'm up for a suspicious death at Soar Museum."

Pernille raised a bushy grey eyebrow. "And you are making that my fucking problem because?"

"Wyst was all over something similar there a few weeks back. Surely, he needs to at least look at it before passing it on?"

"Fucking hell. Blurian save me from whiny men and their constant dick-measuring. Close the door, Lowe."

He did so, and then took the seat that the Commander pointed towards with an insistently jerking finger.

"No one likes you," she said once he had settled himself down.

"Well, that's just because they haven't got to know me yet."

"No. No, it isn't."

Lowe waited for Pernille to say more, but she just sat back in her chair and continued to glare at him. "Sorry, was there more to this or have I just been treated to another one of your legendary pep talks?"

"And it's because of things like that."

"Like what?"

"The smart-talking. The answering back. The acting like you think you are better than the rest of us."

"I'm not better than the rest of you."

"Too fucking right, you are not. Some of us here are bonafide fucking legends, and I doubt even your massive sense of fucking self-regard misses that. But, for whatever reason, that doesn't stop you acting like your shit doesn't stink. And it pisses people off."

"Well, I'm sorry about that. But I'm not sure how . . . "

"You've managed it *twice*, Jana—*twice*! The kind of colossal clusterfucks that most people don't just fail to come back from; they don't even *try*. First, there was all that unpleasantness last year," Pernille said, "And I can tell you right now, there are plenty who think you got off *lightly* losing your Class over that particular fuck-up."

Lowe opened his mouth to protest—big mistake.

Pernille's hand slammed down on her desk with a crack. "*Shut the fuck up and listen!*" she barked, her glare pinning him to his seat. "Blurian gave you two ears and one mouth for a reason, so use them accordingly. I'm not saying I agree with all those panty-wetters crying foul over what happened. But if you think anyone but a *vanishingly small minority* has your back after the clusterfuck to end all clusterfucks, you're delusional. *Do you get me?*"

Lowe nodded stiffly.

"But oh no," she continued. "One life-changing disaster wasn't enough for the great Jana Lowe, was it? *No.* That absolutely wasn't enough for you. You had to go and bring down a fucking Sentinel of Justice as your encore performance, didn't you!"

She leaned back in her chair, her eyes boring into him. "Do you have *any idea* how impressive that is, Lowe? It takes a *special* kind of screw-up to get the literal avatar of law to eat shit in front of the entire city."

"Commander Cenorth was killed in the line of duty . . . "

"Fuck me no fucks, Lowe. We both know what happened at the top of the Celestial Temple, and I'd ask you not to insult my massive throbbing fucking brain by pretending otherwise."

Lowe wasn't entirely sure how he was supposed to respond to that.

Instead, he held up the file he'd been given and gave it a little wave, like a man drowning in paperwork trying to signal for a lifeboat. "I get all of that, but this case *has* to be linked to the death last month. Wyst should be—"

"*Wyst?*" Pernille cut him off with a bark of laughter. "Inspector Wyst was warned off the case so hard I had to send him on a month's sabbatical. You should've seen him. A grown man sobbing into his coffee. *'Wah, they're going to kill my family, wah.'* It was pathetic."

That gave Lowe pause. "Warned off?" he asked. "I thought he just screwed up the investigation in his signature, blundering fashion."

"Things like that, Lowe, things like that." Pernille stood and padded around to Lowe's side of the desk. He was disconcerted to note she appeared to be wearing massive fluffy slippers as she jumped up to perch on her desk, legs swinging free.

"Don't get me wrong. Wyst could screw up boiling water, but this was different. This wasn't just bumbling incompetence. Someone leaned on him. Hard."

Lowe felt a chill creep up his spine. Wyst might've been an idiot, but he wasn't the type to crumble under pressure—not unless the pressure was very specific and very personal. "And you think whoever leaned on him is tied to this?"

Pernille shrugged, her expression carefully neutral. "I think the world's full of people who don't like messy questions being asked about very tidy secrets. And if there's one thing this case is bound to be, it's messy." She gestured at the file in his hand. "So buckle up, Lowe. You're the lucky bastard who gets to step into the shitstorm Wyst ran screaming from. Try not to fuck it up worse than he did."

"Seriously? That's all I get?"

"Look, I'm going to level with you. I've been told in no uncertain terms that we're not to touch what's happening at Soar Museum with a ten-foot cock. 'Above your pay grade,' is how the Mayor put it when I was summoned for a reaming out this morning. And, boy, does the Mayor give good reamings."

"I'm not being funny, but I've been used in the whole 'put our worst investigator on a case and hope it goes away' game before. I wasn't a fan."

"Oh, fucking get over yourself, you fucking sadsack. There are two dead youngsters over at that museum, and it doesn't work for me that I'm being told to look the other way. But, more importantly, Blurian is fucking unimpressed by the suggestion I can be bullied away from doing what I think is right. The Council gave me this job, and I'll be a monkey's uncle if I don't do my best for as long as I have it."

A pipe appeared in Pernille's hand, and she lit it with a click of her fingers. "So, even though the word on the street is that you are the biggest fucking pain in the arse," she continued, sucking down on it contentedly, "I need you to get on down there and get to the fucking bottom of what is going on."

Lowe stared at her. "So, knowing that, literally, the last two cases I investigated ruffled more feathers than a raptor in a chicken coop, you are purposefully pointing me at a politically sensitive situation?"

"Sounds about right."

"And you're not worried about the fallout? That there will be significant consequences?"

"Fuck no. My pension is secure."

"I meant for me!"

Pernille shrugged with her pipe. "Way I figure it, if they haven't killed you yet, you must be valuable to someone with pull. I might as well get as much use out of you as possible before that changes. And you've got that ridiculous self-heal Skill, haven't you? What you moaning for? Now, if there wasn't anything else?"

Lowe drew a deep breath, summoning every ounce of composure he had left for one last plea. "Commander, there aren't even any witnesses to the first death! The whole damn museum wiped their memories! What exactly do you expect me to do?"

Pernille's expression hardened, shedding any veneer of affable irritation like a discarded coat. Her gaze bored into him, and Lowe suddenly understood why so many violent offenders had seen her face as the last thing they ever did.

They didn't call her the Iron Fist for nothing.

"I am not a stupid woman, Inspector Lowe," she said. "The words above your head might say Level 25, but if I were to petition to examine your stats, I'd wager I'd find a very different story."

Lowe opened his mouth to protest, but Pernille silenced him with a raised hand that could have stopped a runaway carriage.

"Shove it," she snapped. "I don't want to hear it. You're allowed your secrets, Inspector. *Until* I decide I need to know more. Do I need to know more?"

Slowly, deliberately, he shook his head.

"Excellent," Pernille suddenly beamed and jumped off the desk, "I'm glad that's settled. I look forward to reading your thoughts on the case moving forward. Now, run the fuck along and stop bothering me."

*****

There hadn't been much more to say after that.

"The Deathcaller, sir?"

Lowe's thoughts reluctantly snapped back from the unpleasant memory of his meeting with Pernille to the gruesome reality of the scene before him. Or, more precisely, the scene beneath him.

He grimaced as his gaze fell upon the remains of what, he had been assured, was once Curator Harker.

The young man's body was no longer a body at all—just a puddle of liquefied flesh and viscous fluids spreading across an expensive carpet that, despite its craftsmanship, would surely never recover.

What bones hadn't fully dissolved jutted out at unnatural angles, protruding like ghastly signposts.

The stench was overpowering. Not just the reek of decay—although there was plenty of that—but something else. Something vile clung to the back of Lowe's throat like guilt. He fought the rising nausea, his hand twitching toward his pocket where a vial of anti-sickness tonic rested, just in case.

Harker's face—or what was left of it—was still disturbingly recognisable.

That almost made it worse. The tatters of his skin hung in loose shreds, ligaments and muscle tissue blending into the sickening soup pooling beneath him. Lowe had seen his fair share of horror shows in his time, but this? This wasn't just death. It was an obliteration of humanity itself, an insult to the natural order.

"Ah, Newly-Reinstated-Not-Quite-Disgraced-As-Of-Yet Inspector Lowe. We meet again!"

Dragging his eyes away from the smear on the floor, Lowe turned to greet the corpulent form of Penarth Lant.

# CHAPTER TEN – A SLIME TOO FAR

"We really must stop meeting like this!"

"To be honest, I would rather we didn't meet at all, Penarth. But you know how it goes: people will keep killing each other. Although, this particular corpse seems a little below your pay grade. Don't you have an assistant or something like that for this sort of thing?"

"I do, I do. But they seem to quit on me faster than I can break them in, as it were. Or maybe they quit because of me breaking them in. Who can tell the minds of young women nowadays? Just seemed quicker for me to come out here."

Lowe grimaced with disgust. He had heard tales of what those who worked in Penarth's office had to endure from their boss.

If he didn't suspect the goblin-like man would enjoy a kicking, he'd have long since taken it up with him.

Cenorth, his previous boss, had said the long lists of HR complaints were a "price worth paying" for the expertise of someone as good at his job as Penarth. Lowe hoped Cuckoo Houses' new Commander would take a different, more retributive view.

"I must say, though, I'm glad I made the effort for the day out. I rarely get to see anyone killed in as interesting a way as this poor fellow," the Deathcaller said, kneeling over the liquified remains of the Curator. "I will tell you this for nothing, though, this fucking carpet has absolutely had it!"

As Penarth triggered his various Skills, Lowe left him to it and took the opportunity to further inspect the office in which the body had been found.

He thought it was a nicely appointed space, the window opening out onto the museum's inner courtyard. Standing at it and gazing down at the grass below, Lowe could see roving gangs of Security Service personnel exploring the grounds. It seemed Pernielle was sparing no expense in terms of manpower.

Turning back to face the inside of the room, Lowe triggered *Grid View* and let his eyes slide around space. He did not try to focus on anything over much at this stage of things; from experience, it was much better for him to use these initial moments to gather as much evidence as possible and then review things at his leisure once he returned home.

The beauty of his Skill - especially since he had raised his Intelligence and Wisdom to Level 2 - was that it captured not just a visual representation of the crime scene but also the sounds and smells.

When he returned to this memory this evening, it would be as if he was standing here right now, but crucially without the distracting presence of Penarth Lant grunting and squealing like a pig at a trough near him.

"Well, he's dead alright," the Deathcaller said, dismissing his Skills and standing up, running his hands through his thinning hair.

"Thank all the gods that you were here," Lowe said, "I was about to attempt mouth-to-mouth."

"Be my guest, Inspector," Penarth replied, "though I imagine it will not be quite as satisfying an experience as sucking on the face of delectable Ms Telut. I hear the two of you are a hot and heavy item again?"

Ignoring the question, Lowe knelt to get a closer look at the goo himself. " Do you have any idea what might have caused him to . . . is the correct word 'melt'?"

"Of course I do. That is why they pay me the big bags of gold, after all. This young man has been covered in necrotic slime. You know what they say about necrotic slime, don't you?

Necrotic slime, it eats away,
It melts the bones by night, by day,
It turns the flesh to dark decay,
But takes the heart's pure beat away."

"Well, thanks for the little poetical interlude there, Penarth. I'll be sure to pass that on to the lad's family. I've often thought a good rhyme scheme eases the suffering. So, what, it's your professional opinion that he walked in here and, boom, there was a bucket of necrotic slime suspended over the door? This isn't a murder, just one of those classic museum japes gone wrong?"

"Fuck knows, Inspector. Fortunately, I do not get paid to work out the whys and the wherefores of these things. No, my sole domain is the world of the 'what', and I can tell you that this unfortunate gentleman has been covered head to toe in necrotic slime."

"Instantaneous death?" Lowe asked, more in hope than expectation.

"Oh my word, no. In fact, I'll let you into a little secret here," Penarth leant in close, and the fetid smell of his body odour nearly made Lowe gag, "he's actually not technically dead."

"What!" Lowe jumped back, looking down at the body. "He's still alive?!"

"Well, obviously not. I mean, look at the fucker. And yet, well, technically, yes. Necrotic slime has a somewhat unique property that allows it to selectively dissolve organic tissues while temporarily keeping certain critical systems intact. This selective dissolution is governed by the various unpleasant properties infused within the slime, which can be controlled or influenced by the being who created it."

"Being?"

"Well, I don't want to be too leading for your investigation here, but if you were to discover that this lad really pissed off a Necromancer I would not be too surprised. That or, of course, some sort of ancient mythological beast rose from the dead and decided to snack on him. That'd do it too."

Lowe made a mental note. It was pretty annoying when Penarth was actually helpful. It made despising him a touch more difficult.

As if sensing Lowe's internal conflict, the Deathcaller gave a huge sniff and then spat a darkly green globule down onto the body.

And then, helpfully, he did something like that.

"The slime targets the body's structural and superficial tissues—skin, muscle, and non-vital organs—gradually breaking them down into a gelatinous, liquefied state. However, it avoids completely destroying the nervous system and major blood vessels. This allows the heart and brain to continue functioning, though in a highly compromised and, I hope it goes without saying, agonizing state. What we see here is still, I suppose, alive. However, he is more slime now than person. And what little humanness remains is certainly entirely out of its gourd due to the pain."

"Fuck me!" Lowe murmured.

"I will freely admit that in your current shaved, showered and appropriately coiffured state, I find you slightly more attractive than has hitherto been the case, but even so, I will have to decline. Yes, I am afraid it is all sadly true. The necrotic magic within the slime sustains the essential functions of life. The slime can infuse the remaining organs and tissues with necromantic energy, which keeps the victim alive despite the extensive physical destruction. This state is excruciatingly painful, as the victim remains conscious and aware while their body dissolves. The slime has a peculiar affinity for preserving neural tissue. It coats the neurons and synapses with a thin layer of itself, preventing them from being dissolved. This ensures that the victim's brain and spinal cord remain intact, maintaining consciousness and the ability to experience pain."

"But you say he's still not dead?"

"That's the funny thing, really. I mean, not funny 'ha-ha', but perhaps darkly amusing? Whichever, it is certainly noteworthy that this level of decomposition via the application of necrotic slime should take days, if not weeks, to occur. I will, however, assume that it might have been noted if he had been lying here for that length of time."

"Indeed. The Senior Preservationist, whose office this was, left the museum grounds around midnight. Of course, she's apparently missing, too, so we cannot say for certain that the body was not there then, but I think we can assume she might have mentioned it to someone if it were. I guess he could have been moved here after she left?"

Penarth shook his head. "No, this has to have happened in situ. The nature of necrotic slime is that it is essentially unstable. Once active, you wouldn't want to be anywhere near it. Of course, nothing is impossible in the world of Soar, but I cannot conceive of someone applying the slime to their victim and then moving what would be, for all intents and purposes, viciously toxic sludge. I mean, how would you even begin to transport it? I will have to burn through this month's budget to get the little squelcher here back to my lab. No. Whatever happened, it happened here."

Lowe nodded. Well, he supposed that was helpful. "I don't suppose you have a ballpark time frame for me, do you?"

"Nothing I would want to bet my massive set of cock and balls on, but from what I can tell, the slime started to feed no later than eight bells ago and no earlier than twelve. I might know more when I open the blob up, but I doubt it. That's probably the most exact I can be."

About the time the woman who owned this office was last seen, Lowe thought.

Finding Martha Culloden was looking like a reasonably significant priority.

"When you are quite finished gawping, Newly-Reunited-Probably-Eager-To-Get-Home-And-Fuck-Your-Girlfriend Inspector Lowe, I will arrange for this poor chap to be removed back to Cuckoo House. I'm sure there are all sorts of exciting experiments I can do on this much necrotic slime.

"I'm sure," Lowe replied, slipping out of the office and into the corridor beyond.

# CHAPTER ELEVEN – A MUSEUM THAT DEVOURS

Although it felt like he had only taken a few steps away from the crime scene, Lowe appeared to be already lost amongst the museum's winding corridors.

It struck him that there was something rather perverse about Soar's key repository of knowledge being quite so impossible to navigate. Still, then again, anyone who knew Grackle Nuroon would surely introduce the word 'perverse' into the conversation at the earliest possible opportunity.

Determined not to need to call for help and alert his men to his difficulty, Lowe chose to wander onward, his polished boots - Mylaf had developed a special paste that she applied and buffed off each morning - disturbing the thick layer of dust that blanketed the stone floors.

Did the museum not employ any Cleaners? Lowe wondered.

Of course, he recognised the hypocrisy here as he himself had been perfectly comfortable living in utter filth before . . . acquiring a Drudge with Legendary powers during his last case.

However, it felt like Soar Museum should possess slightly higher hygiene standards than a down-on-his-luck disgraced detective.

Riffing on a similar theme, shafts of weak, dusty light filtered through high, grimy windows, casting shadows that seemed to reach for him as he passed. It created the illusion of movement in the corner of his eye as if he were being followed.

Yes. An illusion. That was all it was.

Lowe paused, trying for a moment to regain his bearings. Really, this was all rather stupid. He must only be yards from all sorts of other people, so why did he have this odd feeling of complete isolation? He looked down at the floor, preparing to retrace his footprints in the dust.

But, no. There was nothing there.

With just a trace of embarrassment at having to resort to his using a Skill, he activated Grid View, seeking out the memory of being led from the entrance of the museum to the Senior Preservationist's office and its attendant dead body.

This corridor was not one of the ones he had been escorted down.

Swearing, Lowe turned around and tried to retrace his steps back to Penarth Lant, one eye on his progress and the other on the images on display in Grid View.

Somehow, the museum's layout seemed to defy the constraints of logic and space, passages doubling back on themselves and leading him into increasingly unfamiliar territory.

Lowe paused at a junction, glancing down each of the four possible routes available to him. He was sure he had not been here before.

Grid View was apparently being interfered with by something in a way he did not think was supposed to be possible.

Well, wasn't that just a treat?

Looking down each option in turn, Lowe couldn't make out anything that seemed familiar. The branching corridors stretched out like the insidious tentacles of some aquatic monster, each one promising only more confusion and entrapment.

"Fuck's sake," he muttered, looking back at the way he had come. The last thing he needed was it getting back to Cuckoo House that, minutes after arrival, he became lost at a crime scene.

That would be the final nail in an already heavily studded reputational coffin.

Choosing a path at random, the one on his right, Lowe started walking - almost jogging - his footsteps echoing in the silence, a growing unease at his predicament gnawing at him.

The corridor he had chosen was lined with tall display cases, their glass fronts cracked as if someone - or something - had sought to break in.

Or out.

Well, wasn't that a lovely thought that would not fester at all?

Inside each cabinet, the bizarre and the grotesque vied for his attention: a mummified cat, its shrivelled body contorted in eternal agony; a collection of rusted surgical tools, still stained with the remnants of use and an array of eerie, faceless dolls, their porcelain heads cracked and eyeless sockets staring blankly.

A shiver ran down Lowe's spine, and not just from the cold. Was someone following him?

He turned abruptly, scanning the dancing shadows for any sign of actual movement, but found nothing. The museum was silent, save for the faint creaking of the old building settling around him.

Where the fuck was everyone!

Turning back around, the sensation of being watched persisted, a prickling at the back of his neck that refused to be ignored.

It had been a while since he had activated Slugger - Arebella had been clear that she would prefer it if he could find more effective methods of conflict resolution - but he did so now.

Immediately, the increased weight in his fists calmed his trembling nerves. As Staffen had hinted at earlier, the label above his head might say Level 25, but anyone - or anything - that leapt out at him from the darkness would quickly discover that, thanks to the practical application of Essence Transmutation Theory, he packed a punch equivalent to a Level 50.

Hands swinging with a comforting heaviness at his side, Lowe pressed on, noticing that the musty smell was growing more pungent as if he were descending into the museum's bowels rather than moving towards the exit.

It must be his imagination, but the narrow corridor seemed to be closing in on him, the walls leaning inward as though the building sought to swallow him whole.

Lowe's breath came shallow and rapid. He glanced back again, expecting to see some remorseless hunter in pursuit, but only emptiness was stretching into darkness. Then, he rounded a corner and found himself in a small, circular chamber.

The ceiling rose high above to become lost in darkness, and the walls were lined with strange tapestries, their colours faded, and designs obscured by layers of dust. In the centre of the room stood a pedestal upon which a single, lit candle rested.

For some reason, the sight of it sent a chill through him, an inexplicable sense of foreboding that rooted him to the spot.

Lowe took a moment to steady himself before stepping forward.

The candle, though innocuous, seemed to pulse with a quiet menace. He shivered, the coolness of the room seeping into his bones as his eyes traced the faint patterns etched into the pedestal. If it was in a language spoken in Soar, it certainly was not one he recognised.

He crouched down, his fingers brushing the cold stone base of the pedestal. As he did, a sticky substance clung to his fingertips.

He brought his hand closer for inspection and recoiled slightly—a viscous, dark slime similar to what he had seen covering the body of the Curator.

Then, Lowe's mind was on other things as the burn from the necrotic slime started to consume his fingers.

He stood up abruptly, hastily wiping his fingers on a handkerchief. *Roll with the Punches* activated as Lowe's hand literally began to melt before his eyes, and he manually pushed a trickle of mana—and then a veritable river of the stuff—into the Skill to overwhelm the damage.

The power of this shit was something else!

The candle, the slime, the eerie, expectant silence . . .

Determined to find a way to make sense of all this, Lowe activated *Grid View* again, hoping to overlay his memory with his current location. But the interference persisted, the images flickering and distorted, offering no clear path.

Frustration mingled with unease as he deactivated the Skill.

Lowe's eyes scanned the room, landing this time on the colourful tapestries lining the walls. Moving closer to one, he noticed a tear in the fabric, a narrow slit that had gone unnoticed at first glance.

Peering through, he saw more of the necrotic slime smeared on the wall behind it. He stepped back, but this was not the right atmosphere for revelatory moments of stunning insight. He needed to move, to find his way out of this disorienting maze before the creeping dread overwhelmed him.

However, as Lowe turned to leave, the faint sound of rustling fabric reached his ears again, more pronounced this time, like a whisper of something brushing against the stone walls.

His heart pounding in his chest, Lowe quickened his pace away from the chamber, the sense of being pursued becoming almost tangible. The corridor outside stretched before him, lined with the same macabre exhibits that had greeted him earlier.

As he walked, he noticed more signs—tiny, almost imperceptible patches of necrotic slime smeared on the walls and floor. It felt that they formed a path, guiding him forward, and the realisation sent a shiver through him.

Was whoever had killed the Curator leading him somewhere? And if so, did he have any other choice but to follow?

The patches of necrotic slime became more frequent, their viscous presence now almost covering the walls and floor, and Lowe needed to carefully walk to avoid stepping in it.

Sensing his fists were about to explode with the gathered power of Slugger, Lowe dismissed the Skill and then resummoned it immediately. The drain on his mana was substantial, and he felt a flutter of unease at what would happen should *Roll with the Punches* be needed and the well be dry . . .

Suddenly, a low, sad noise reverberated through the very walls. It was a sound of pain and despair, but before Lowe could react, a presence manifested behind him.

He spun, throwing out an enhanced punch, but his attack landed on nothing.

Lowe took a step back, raising his fists in a defensive posture. His eyes darted around, searching for any sign of the creature he knew must be there.

The mournful sound intensified into a deep rumble that shook dust from the roof. His instincts screamed at him to flee, but his legs felt rooted to the spot.

Then it was in front of him.

Lowe threw out two massive blows with *Slugger*, striking something solid but with no visible sign of impact. No creature revealed itself following being hit by the equivalent of a Level 50.

What the fuck was this thing?

Lowe stumbled back as the noise shifted, becoming softer, almost pleading. It was a resonant agony, and Lowe tried to focus on its meaning - to listen - but the moment's terror made it impossible to think clearly.

Then the presence moved again; the sense of it closing in around him was overwhelming. Lowe threw out another blast of *Slugger*, draining his mana dry before complete desperation overtook him.

Lowe turned and ran, his footsteps echoing hollowly as he fled down the corridor.

But as he did, he noticed something—marks on the walls, smeared in the same dark slime. The marks were crude, almost like writing, forming a pattern that beckoned him closer.

He stumbled into another corridor, the low, sad sound following him, a constant reminder of the unseen presence. It grew louder, more insistent as if urging him to understand. But the terror was too great, the oppressive weight too much to bear.

As he stumbled out of the corridor and ran mindlessly, Lowe could still hear the faint echoes of the creature's cries.

The clues as to what had happened to the Curator were there, somewhere in the darkness, waiting to be deciphered. But for now, Lowe could only run, driven by the desperate need to escape the unseen thing that stalked him through the twisted halls of the Soar Museum.

# CHAPTER TWELVE – PROMISES IN BLOOD

"Are you quite alright, sir?"

Lowe looked up at the solid form of the young man in the uniform of a Security Service Constable. He was happy to testify to that solidity, having just run straight into him as he rounded a corner in a full-blown panic.

Scrambling to his feet, Lowe turned around, peering back down the dark corridor. His relief was almost overwhelming - and a tinge of embarrassment crept in - as he realised no looming threat was stalking behind him.

"Sir?"

The Constable's expression was rapidly changing from 'confused-bemusement-at-being-bumped-into' to 'wishing-there-was-someone-else-around-to-cope-with-a-clearly-hysterical-senior-officer'. In response, Lowe tried to get a handle on his emotions. "Yes, sorry. I just got a little turned around down there. I didn't want to risk getting locked in!"

The young man's eyes were drawn to Lowe's hand, which was conspicuously smoking as an unlaunched *Slugger*, and a thin coating of necrotic slime fought to win the race to disintegrate bones and flesh.

Lowe dismissed his offensive Skill and poured even more mana into *Roll with the Punches* to counteract the extensive damage. "I don't suppose you have a hanky, do you? I seem to have got something on my hand."

Hesitantly, the Constable reached into his pocket and withdrew a reasonably clean square of cloth. "Of course, sir."

The moment Lowe accepted the gift and wiped away the last residues of the necrotic slime, his mind suddenly cleared: it was literally the difference between being trapped in a haunted oubliette and standing in a bright meadow.

He turned to look back at the way he had so recently come and saw only a well-lit, common-or-garden corridor with various rooms leading from it.

Heads were being popped through doorways to know the cause of the shrieking, foot-pounding kerfuffle that had just blundered past.

"Nothing to see here; please go back to your . . . museuming," he said, smiling and absent-mindedly passing the soiled handkerchief back to the Constable.

The young man, in horror, held the blood and slime-soaked thing between thumb and forefinger and triggered a Skill that instantly reduced it to ash.

Lowe's mind, though, was racing.

Had the slime caused his perceptions to become nightmarish? Was what he had just experienced a vivid hallucination rather than reality?

Remembering he had tried to use *Grid View* when being hunted underneath the museum, Lowe tried to bring up his most recent memories.

But no. It was like there was a thick coating of vaseline across the lens of his vision. In fact, he had no clear remembrance of anything since he had stepped out of the room which had held the body.

"Inspector Lowe, I presume?"

He was brought back to the immediate present by the appearance of the outstretched hand of a wizened little man he had read an awful lot about. "Director Nuroon, thank you for taking the time to speak with me."

Lowe shook the proffered hand, trying to style out that *Roll with the Punches* had not entirely managed to recover bone and sinew with skin.

"Constable, I don't suppose you have another spare hanky for the Director, do you?"

***

After cleaning himself down, Nuroon led the way back to his own office, and Lowe could not help but notice that what had seemed like a labyrinth from a horror story was far more navigable than he had just experienced.

As they walked, he saw none of the bizarre or grotesque exhibits that had surrounded him on his solo journey. If, as now seemed likely, the necrotic slime had some sort of psychotropic effect, when exactly had it got on him?

He had initially assumed it was from when he had touched the pedestal on which the candle stood, but he had been seeing some pretty creepy shit sometime before then.

Had Penarth spiked him in some way? And if so, why? And was the answer anything more significant than: 'the man is a colossal twat'?

"I do not wish to be rude, Inspector, but it is quite unusual for people not to pay attention to me when I speak. Have you got somewhere you would rather be?"

"My apologies, Director. I was just thinking back to the state of that young man's body. I understand it was you who first discovered it?"

"Indeed. Indeed. A terrible thing to have happened. And in my museum of all places. Terrible. Simply terrible."

There was something about the way Nuroon said that which made Lowe wonder whether the Director's sorrow was less for the death of the Curator and more at the disruption to the museum's operation.

"What was the cause of you being in the Senior Preservationalist's office?"

A dark frown passed over Nuroon's face. He doesn't like having to account for his actions, Lowe thought. Well, he will love having a murder investigation running around him.

Seeing the momentary fury on the man's face at the benign question, Lowe could quite understand how pressure had been brought on Wyst to drop the original case.

Then, the tumultuous anger cleared, and Nuroon was all sweetness and light again. "There was a small maintenance matter I wished to discuss with Martha. Naturally, I would expect to find her in her office."

"And you did not?"

"Clearly not."

"And you were surprised to find the body there?"

"Extremely."

"So, you opened the door to your senior colleague's office, and instead of her, you saw the melted remains of one of your junior staff members. Is that correct?"

Nuroon pushed back in his chair and held his fingers before his mouth in a steepled gesture Lowe instinctively associated with supreme wankery. "Inspector, I wish to be honest with you. Can I?"

"No. I much prefer it when people tell outrageous lies. It keeps me in business."

The Director pressed on as if Lowe had not spoken. He assumed this was the man's usual way of conversing. "I have spoken to the Mayor about this . . . investigation, and we are both of a mind that it would be best if we treated it as an internal matter. It seems clear to me that what has occurred is a simple matter of a collegiate disagreement that has got out of hand. Martha and . . . I'm sorry, I cannot recall the young man's name."

"Harker. Josap Harker," Lowe supplied brightly. "Son of Geraldine and Horace Harker. He has - or, I suppose, 'had' - worked for you for the last three years."

"Well, a lot of people work for me," Nuroon said airly, "where was I? Ah, yes. As I was saying, it seems clear to me that Martha and this Harker have had an academic disagreement and . . . "

"And she covered him in necrotic slime, murdering him in the most agonising and painful way imaginable? You get a lot of that in academia, do you, Director?"

"You would be surprised, Inspector. You would be surprised." Nuroon suddenly leaned forward, pressing both hands to the side of the desk, and lowered his voice. The effect was quite predatory. "I have to tell you, I am not wild about your tone, Inspector."

"And I'm not cockahoop about yours, Director. A man is dead, and a woman is missing. I cannot conceive why you would think this is an 'internal' matter rather than one that is under the purview of the Security Services. Or are you so used to unexplained deaths in this building that such an event has become somewhat mundane?"

"You are speaking of the unfortunate accident of last month."

"Am I?"

"You will, of course, know I have no memory of that."

"Having wiped your memory just before my colleague arrived to question you."

"A colleague who, I am pleased to say, quickly learned his place in things. An example I would encourage you to follow."

"Oh, I think you are going to find that, in all manner of things, I tend not to follow the crowd. To a fault, actually. You should read my latest appraisal: 'does not do what the fuck he is told.' I had a little plaque made and everything."

The two men stared at each other for a tense moment. Lowe thought the Director triggered a couple of Skills in the silence, but he had no idea what they were intended to do.

Once upon a time, he had been in possession of a handy little Skill of his own that would have identified any active or passive techniques a suspect - because he realised this man was definitely a suspect - happened to use when being questioned.

His Classtration had removed that, of course. He missed it right now.

"Are you going to be a problem, Inspector?"

"I don't know. Director. What I do know is that I'm going to find out who killed Josap Harker, where your Senior Preservationist has gone and - and I'm not bragging here, I really am quite good at this - I'm probably going to unravel what the fuck happened here last month at the same time. Now, you tell me. Would you see any of that as being a problem?"

"How is Arebella Telut?"

Before he even realised what he was doing, Lowe had activated *Slugger* and crashed his hand through the Director's desk, splintering it into kindling.

"Don't even fucking go there with that shit. It's been tried before, and I'm sure you will have heard how that turned out for all concerned. Come for me as much as you like - I'm built for it, and I accept it comes with the territory - but if I even sense you thinking her name again, what happened in the Celestial Temple will feel like an unexpected visit from Oulian the Birthday Fairy compared to what I will bring down on this fucking museum."

Nuroon glanced at the wreckage of his desk and then back up to meet Lowe's steely expression. "It is good to know where we both stand on this matter." He clicked his tongue, and a precisely located spot of time unspooled backwards until the desk was repaired.

"If we are in the 'making threats' stage of our relationship, I feel I should respond in kind. I don't care what happened to Curator Barker . . . "

"Harker," Lowe corrected automatically.

Nuroon simply carried on. "Neither am I much bothered about the whereabouts of Martha Culloden. This is an internationally renowned facility, and I am sure I can replace her with someone of equal, if not higher, competence before the end of the week. But I do care about the efficient running of this museum and, what is more, the Mayor agrees with me on that point. Your . . . investigation, should you insist on progressing, will not interfere with that. I will not threaten you with consequences because I do not make threats. I do, however, promise you that if you are the cause of any disruption whatsoever, you will regret it. And for the rest of your life. Now, do you have any other questions for me, or shall we call it a day?"

# CHAPTER THIRTEEN – WRESTLING WITH A SPIDER

"Tell me, are you capable of speaking to someone in a way that *doesn't* lead to a bounty being taken out on your head, little man?"

"In my defence, it is Grackle Nuroon."

"Good point, well made," Latham glaring at the Waitress, who was proving to be a little slow in bringing him his third plate of sandwiches of the morning. "Are you curing your own fucking meat back there or something? What's the fucking hold up!"

Being shouted at by a giant Temple Warder had not been on the poor girl's 'to-do' list when she woke up this morning, and she turned an even whiter shade of pale. "Let me just go and check on it for you," she said, backing away from their corner table. "Your coffees are on the house!" she added, triggering her *Complimentary* Skill, which she felt was certainly earning its mana this day.

"You know, some people would think it was the height of bad manners to give minimum-gold servers such a hard time," Lowe said, shielding his own sandwich from Latham's predatory gaze.

"And are any of those judgemental fuckers sat at this table?" the big man asked, teeth-baring.

"Nope. Not at all. In fact, if I may add, fuck that undernourished, overworked and clearly underappreciated young lady. I'm sure she absolutely deserves you giving her a hard time. The bitch."

Latham sighed. "I know, I know. I'm just not myself when I'm hungry."

"You don't say!"

A blur in a uniform was suddenly at their side, dropping several plates piled high with steaming food in front of Latham before scurrying away. "You see, all she needed was the right encouragement."

Lowe leaned back in his chair, watching his friend eat. It was funny, he thought, but he did genuinely think of Latham as a friend. He hadn't expected them to stay in touch once the fuss died down around what had occurred in the Celestial Temple, but he'd been pleasantly surprised.

It helped that Hel and Latham were an item, especially since the Wind Tyrant and Arebella had struck up a firm friendship of their own. It had become a Thirrupsday tradition for the four of them to go out and paint Soar, if not red, then a charming shade of off-pink.

Lowe wasn't the type of person who had a best friend. The fact that the last candidate for that position had been actively using him to further his rise to power had left a mark. However, something about Latham encouraged Lowe to begin seeing him that way.

"Come on then, out with it. Explain to Daddy how you've fucked things up with your customary incompetence again and need me to save the day."

Although, Lowe thought, it was still early days . . .

"Well, first of all, 'Daddy' isn't going to happen. But I'm pretty sure Hel will find it hilarious when I mention it to her." Suddenly, their Waitress wasn't the only person looking extremely pale. "Now, having put that to bed, as it were, do you actually want to hear more about the case, or are you going to be a dick?"

"I'm more than capable of being both," Latham said, demolishing the first of the newly arrived plates of sausage sandwiches and moving to the second. "However, in exchange for your silence on my little nickname *faux pas*, I will refrain from colour commentary on your woes for the foreseeable."

"Fair enough. So, despite what everyone is trying to pretend, it's clear to me the two deaths are linked. The fucking Deathcaller won't go out on a limb and formally say the first dead Curator was liquified by necrotic slime before being crushed, but I don't have any doubts. Bella's friends with the Auditor who saw the whole thing, and to hear her tell it, the girl was screaming and melting before the stone came tumbling down." He went on to recite the rest of the facts of both the Curators deaths as he knew them.

Latham listened, nodding along until Lowe had finished. "So let me get this straight. You either have two epically convoluted suicides, one or two bizarre accidents, the first death being murder, but the wrong victim killed, or two distinct murders with two intended victims. Oh, and the Senior Preservationalist, who is either a third victim or the perpetrator of one - or both - murders, has gone missing."

Lowe nodded. "Sounds about right."

Latham took his time on his final sandwich, carefully chewing it over as he thought. "And Nuroon wants to cover the whole thing up?"

"Yep."

"Let him."

Those two words were so unexpected that Lowe was sure he must have misheard. "I'm sorry, what?"

"I said, 'Let him.' That is some murky shit, and you don't want any part of it."

"There are two dead Curators . . . "

Latham leant forward, his voice suddenly lacking any of its customary humour. "Grackle Nuroon is - " Latham paused, casting his eyes around the coffee shop for listeners. The Waitress, misunderstanding the searching glare, hurriedly dived back into the kitchen to hunt for more food- "not to be messed with. And I say this as someone who has to deal with fucking avatars on a daily basis."

"He's the Director of Soar Museum. I hardly think his threat level is on par with what we went through in the Temple. I mean, what's he going to do? Lecture me to death?"

Latham's laugh had no joy in it. "If that's what you think, little man, you need to drop everything right now. Grackle Nuroon is not to be trifled with."

The Temple Warder grimaced at Lowe's sceptical expression and edged his chair closer, voice dropping to a conspiratorial whisper. "You think you know what you're getting into, tangling with Grackle Nuroon, but you don't. That spider fucker doesn't do anything in the open. You've never heard of Mayor Tolliver, have you?"

Latham paused, the name hanging in the air like a death sentence.

Lowe shook his head. "No idea. Must be before my time, Grandaddy."

Latham cocked his head to one side, wincing. "Fuck you. Look, just listen to what I'm saying. Tolliver had a reputation as solid as iron. Brilliant, ambitious, with connections you can only dream about. But Tolliver had one flaw—he believed he was powerful enough to take what he wanted, even if it meant crossing Grackle Nuroon. A simple land dispute, that's all it was. Tolliver wanted to annex a parcel near the city, land that the Soar Museum had been eyeing for years. It was perfect for Tolliver's estate expansion, and he thought Nuroon was just another dusty old man, more concerned with relics than real power."

Latham's lip curled into a bitter smile. "Tolliver pushed his claim through the Council, confident his allies would see it passed. But he didn't know that Nuroon had been preparing for this moment long before Tolliver even set his sights on that land. You see, Nuroon isn't a man who reacts. He anticipates, manipulates, and then, when the time is right, he executes."

Latham leaned even closer, his voice dropping to a near hiss. "The Director started by quietly undermining Tolliver's support base. He dripped poison into the ears of Council members, sowing seeds of doubt and distrust. Subtle rumours about Tolliver's financial dealings began to surface—nothing too overt, just enough to make his backers nervous. Whispers of unpaid debts, of deals that might not be as clean as they seemed. Within weeks, Tolliver's staunchest friends began to distance themselves, not publicly, but in those little ways that matter. Invitations rescinded, meetings 'postponed indefinitely.' And Tolliver, confident in his power base, never saw it coming."

Latham's eyes darkened, his tone taking on a grim intensity. "But Nuroon wasn't satisfied with just isolating Tolliver. He had a lesson to teach—an example to make. Tolliver's wife, Lucinda, was a socialite adored by all. She had some sort of unusual Class that changed water into wine. You can imagine what a hit that made her at parties. Well, Nuroon had her patronages audited by the Treasury, and lo and behold, irregularities were 'discovered' in the charitable funds she managed. Suddenly, Lucinda was under investigation for embezzlement, her name dragged through the courts and the gossip circles alike. She was innocent, of course, but that didn't matter. The stain on her reputation was enough to ruin her. She killed herself in the end.

Latham paused, wetting his lips. "But it didn't stop there. Tolliver's eldest son was a bright young man destined for a career in the Security Service. Nuroon made sure that a scandalous 'cheating' allegation surfaced at his academy—completely fabricated but damning enough to see him expelled in disgrace. Every door that had once been open to him slammed shut, his future annihilated before it even began. His body was found in the river - no one looked into that death too carefully.

Latham's voice took on a steely edge, his eyes locked on Lowe's. "What happened in the Temple was brute force and ignorance. And, the gods help us, but you seem to have a talent for weathering that sort of shitshow. But Nuroon didn't need to draw a sword or challenge Tolliver to a duel. He used the systems Tolliver had once wielded with confidence against him. Within a year, Tolliver was ruined. His reputation in tatters, his family dead, and his fortune gone. The final blow came when Tolliver was quietly removed from the Council—not by a vote, but by a whisper campaign so insidious that it was already done by the time he realized what was happening. He was outmanoeuvred, outclassed, and utterly destroyed."

Latham's expression hardened a grim finality in his words. "And all the while, Nuroon never once raised his voice, never showed a hint of anger. He simply... erased Tolliver. By the end, Tolliver was a ghost, a man whose name no one dared speak for fear of attracting Nuroon's gaze. So, if you think you can take on Grackle Nuroon, think again. The man doesn't fight. He simply waits, watches, and when the moment is right, he ensures you don't just lose—you cease to exist."

# CHAPTER FOURTEEN – THE WEIGHT OF BULLSHIT AND BLOOD

Lowe had arranged to meet the museum's remaining senior staff - *sans* Nuroon - later that afternoon at Cuckoo House.

He'd even booked one of the more unpleasant interview rooms, the one which smelled of damp wood, desperation and just the right amount of spilled blood.

His thinking had been simple: get them off their own turf, away from the Director, and maybe, just maybe, they'd spill something useful about what had happened to the two Curators.

Oh, and if he were lucky, maybe he'd get a lead on where the fucking Senior Preservationist had vanished too. Because right now, with Nuroon refusing to play ball, Lowe had absolutely nothing to go on.

He was being stonewalled by a man so steeped in arrogance and privilege that he was practically dripping in smug. Even without Latham's doom-filled warnings, the little chat the two of them had had—the one where Nuroon all but told him to fuck off with his banal questions and stick to the nice, tidy corners of Soar that didn't ruffle any feathers—was still a raw wound in Lowe's mind. It had been the kind of conversation where every word had put his teeth on edge.

Nuroon hadn't just warned him off; he'd practically shoved him out the door with a pat on the head and the assurance that the adults would resolve the matter and that he should go and play with his toys somewhere else.

It had left Lowe groping in the dark with the miasma of the Director's aura hanging over him, and every attempt Lowe had made in the last twenty-four bells to move the case on was being met with roadblock after roadblock.

Polite but firm 'no's' to every request. Even the Deathcaller had stopped replying to his messages, and Penarth could always be relied upon for at least a hearty 'fuck off'.

Lowe's frustration had clawed at him, leaving a bitter taste in his mouth, but all he could do was grit his teeth and keep moving forward - which was why he had arranged for interviews to take place off museum grounds.

However, just as he left Latham, who was happily munching his way through his fourth plate of sandwiches—seriously, where did the Temple Warder put it all?—his Sending Stone buzzed in his pocket.

He fished it out, expecting the usual—some bullshit update or another complaint from the Mayor's office. Instead, what he read made his blood pressure spike so high that *Roll with the Punches* activated on its own to prevent him from stroking out.

It was a written message from Nuroon's Executive P.A., a polished raptor with an icy smile, informing him that all proposed interviews were off.

And what is more, if he wanted to "interrogate any museum employees, he could only do so in the museum's library—under the supervision of in-house counsel," no less.

"Are you fucking kidding me!"

Lowe's voice bounced off the grimy glass windows of the shopfronts, scattering a flock of Bloodgulls that had been pecking at some unfortunate soul's corpse.

Pernille Staffen, who was unfortunately on the other end of the connection, flinched and turned down the volume on her own Sending Stone, flopping back in her chair like a cat that had decided not to care, but couldn't quite pull it off.

"It's hardly a completely bullshit request, Inspector," she replied.

"Oh really? When was the last time *you* allowed a murder suspect to be interviewed at their place of work? At a time of their choosing. And with their own legal advice! Maybe I should take a picnic with me and a bottle of something chilled? You know, just to play nice! I don't know, Commander, I thought we were the Soar Security Service, not a fucking village newsletter!" He spat out the words like they tasted foul, which they absolutely did.

Staffen's eyes narrowed, and though Lowe couldn't see her - standard Cuckoo House tech didn't have the visual function on the Sending Stones - he felt the weight of her anger settle upon him. He figured she had triggered her *Implacable Stare* Skill, the kind of Epic ability that sent better men than him scrambling for cover.

✳✳✳

In truth, Staffen was just as pissed off as Lowe.

Grackle *fucking* Nuroon was pulling strings like a puppeteer who never intended the show to end. This last-minute interview venue switch was just the latest in a long line of arse-fuckings the Security Services had taken since the second liquefied body had been discovered.

The sudden, colossal interference in hundreds of cases under her purview hadn't been easy to take, but she wasn't about to let Lowe add to the burden.

From the minute Lowe had begun ferreting around, it was like the Mayor had apparently got her on speed Stone; the Council wanted hourly, in-person updates on progress; and dark noises were coming from the Temple that Arkola was displeased their favourite Museum Director was being bothered with such "banal trivialities" as a couple of meaningless slayings.

Oh, and she was reasonably sure someone had broken into her house last night and licked all her teaspoons.

But if anyone in Soar thought any of that would bother her, they'd misjudged their woman. And that included Jana 'Oh Woe is Fucking Me' Lowe.

"Tell me you aren't raising your motherfucking voice at me!"

The power of Staffen's fear-inducing Skill crashed down the connection into Lowe like a Berserker late for lunch. The strength of her displeasure sent him reeling backwards, swerving into a wall, *a -20% Courage* debuff settling on him like a death shroud.

He might have even wet himself a little.

"Because I can tell you this for fucking nothing," Staffen continued, her voice the kind of chilly that burns. "The last wanker who spoke to me like that is still having his fucking arse cheeks stitched back together."

Lowe's angry frustration drained out of him like a gutter run-off. He squeaked an apology, the sound so pitiful he almost didn't recognise it as his own voice.

"That's better," Staffen said. "Look, I don't know what you want from me here, Lowe. There's been a murder. You're a fucking murder investigator. Do I need to hold your dick while you piss too? Suspects won't come to you? Boo-fucking-hoo. What do you want me to do about it? Slap them on the arse and tell them to stop being mean to you? Quit your bleating and do your *fucking* job. Get your backside to the museum and find out who's killing its Curators. It really ain't more fucking difficult than that. I couldn't give Arkola's left ball sack about where you ask your questions. But here's another thing I'll tell you for free; if night falls without some sort of progress for me to pass up the chain, you'll discover why I'm Blurian's chosen bringer of vengeance. Are we on the same motherfucking page?!"

***

Lowe didn't trust himself to answer without gibbering, so he dragged his mana out of the stone and dropped it back in his pocket, the weight of it suddenly much heavier.

Until relatively recently, he had prided himself on his ability to navigate the twisting alleys of Soar's power structure - *I mean, sure*, a little voice chimed in his head, *you can keep telling yourself crap like that. Still, if we're going to start hallucinating bollocks, perhaps we can do so a foot taller and ten pounds lighter?* - but on days like this, he felt like he was wading through a quagmire of bureaucratic bullshit.

Leaning back against the wall, Lowe adjusted his collar, damp with a cold sweat that had nothing to do with the weather and cursed under his breath.

Staffen's words rang in his ears, each syllable laced with disappointment. The kind that didn't wash off. And it was all the worse because she had a point. Since when was his go-to response to difficulty to run to 'mummy' complaining about the unfairness of it all?

Since your Classtration, subsequent betrayal by your best friend and the realisation the gods of Soar really couldn't give a fuck, the little voice in his head added snidely.

Well, there was that . . .

Looking around, Lowe didn't think it was just the residue of Staffen's fear Skill that was making it so the streets of Soar had never felt so menacing, each shadow a potential threat, each cobblestone a trap waiting to trip him up.

He knew he'd been in worse situations before - this wasn't even making the top three after the year he had had - but there was something about this case.

Something rotten.

It was like Soar itself was holding its breath, waiting for the next shoe to drop. And knowing his luck, it'd have a fucking Orc's foot in it.

Maybe it was the fear Skill. Maybe it was the look in Latham's eyes as he had passed on his warning. Or maybe it was the residue of the necrotic slime still freaking him out.

But whatever it was, Lowe couldn't help but feel like his life would be an awful lot easier if he just put a warrant out for the arrest of Martha Culloden on suspicion of murder and filed his report.

73

"You okay, boss?" a wandering Street Vendor asked, eyeing Lowe like a snake that had spotted a wounded animal: he'd sensed a commercial opportunity in Lowe's staggered steps, white face, and general attitude of vulnerability.

The vendor's cart, filled with dubious meats on sticks and bottles of even more questionable liquid, looked like it hadn't seen a health inspection since Arkola was in nappies.

"Just regretting some recent life choices, mate," Lowe muttered, flicking the man a silver coin before steadying himself and crossing the intersection of Triumph and Disaster to join the queue for the Portal Stone.

The vendor watched him go, a sly smile curling on his lips, then pulled his own Sending Stone out of a grubby apron pocket, its surface greasy from too many unwashed fingers. "Yeah," he said into it, his voice low and conspiratorial, "he's just on his way there now."

# CHAPTER FIFTEEN – WHISPERS IN THE WRECKAGE

Lowe was not sure what he had expected from Soar Museum's library.

Certainly, his most recent experience 'behind the scenes' of the massive building had not been pleasant: the ramshackle, dusty corridors and bizarre exhibits had left a lingering effect on Lowe—although he was willing to accept that might have been more to do with the impact of being under the influence of the necrotic slime.

However, he could well imagine Nuroon allowing thousands of books to build up in giant, mouldering piles just because he could.

Nevertheless, he was pleasantly surprised.

The library was a large, high-ceilinged room on the ground floor. Apart from one wall, which opened out onto the green space of the courtyard beyond, the other three had row upon row of books from the floor to the ceiling.

As Lowe watched, the titles shimmered every few seconds, new ones appearing to replace the old. Some sort of version of a bag of holding, he presumed.

He wondered if that was a built-in enchantment or if a captive Librarian was strapped to a rack somewhere in the Museum's bowels and was being forced to revolve the stock.

The very centre of the room was bare, but it was furnished with a giant banqueting table behind which, on one side, were five ornate leather armchairs.

A little group of conspirators sat in these, whose heads turned in one movement at Lowe's entrance. Then, the silence ended abruptly, and the pantomime began.

He had already met one of the men before—Kelvin Kregg, the Bard—and the tall, thin man stood and moved forward with a professional smile.

Lowe did not respond in kind. Even without Arebella giving him the lowdown on a man whose hands were apparently the very definition of 'wandering', there was just something about someone whose life was the definition of illusory which set Lowe's teeth on edge.

Even as he had that thought, Lowe felt a little mental tug of warmth towards Kregg.

"Mr Kregg, I would ask that you please refrain from using any of your Skills on me. If you were not aware, it is an offence to seek to magically influence a member of the Security Services going about their business."

If Kregg was embarrassed at being caught in an act which was, at best, thunderously rude, his smiling face did not show it. He gave a wink, and then Lowe felt the slight pressure on his mind fade, and his dislike of the man increased a hundredfold.

"Can't blame a guy for trying," he smirked.

"Actually," Lowe replied, fixing the man with a glare, "I can. Fair warning, you try that again, and it'll be a while before your hands wander anywhere."

"I am sure you are not threatening my client with physical violence," the second of the men in the room said, standing to approach and damply shake Lowe's hand.

The little figure had a pinched, hollow face with bug eyes that were now frowning with the confusion of a dog that had been shown an especially difficult card trick. His flaxen hair lay in piles on his shoulder and down his back, and it took every ounce of control Lowe had not to reach out and give it a good yank.

"Is it a threat if I absolutely promise I'll do it?" Lowe asked, withdrawing his hand and ostentatiously wiping it dry on the leg of his trousers. "And you are?"

"Felicitous Gral, at your service. The Museum has retained me to ensure that no . . . misunderstandings occur during their employees' interactions with the Security Services."

"In which case, you might want to ensure your clients do not 'misunderstand' the penalties for attempting mental manipulation on an officer in the course of his duties. I *will* be punching him in the face if he tries that bollocks again."

A middle-aged woman in the third of the chairs sighed and waved a hand in frustration.

"Really, can we dispense with the dick measuring? I am sure all three of you have simply imposing members that any young lady would gladly get her hands wrapped around. However, could we get to the reason we have all been summoned here? Some of us have other things we would rather be doing."

Lowe recognised Liando Verlan, the Chair of the Museum's Board and nodded respectfully. "Apologies, ma'am. I just find it helpful for everyone to know where they stand on such things."

"You'll be standing there without any teeth if you 'ma'am' me again," she snapped back, but there was a hint of a smile in her voice.

If what Lowe had heard about Kregg was bad, then the opposite was true of the Captain of Industry. Immensely tough but scrupulously fair was the word on the street. Looking at her now, Lowe could believe it.

"My apologies!" he said, turning his attention to the fourth and final member of the little group. "And you are?"

"Trei Levick," the small, round man replied, showing no sign of getting up in greeting. "And I definitely have things I should be getting on with. The mess you spooks have caused around this place beggars belief."

Lowe nodded, hiding his frustration. He had asked for a meeting with the relevant staff of the Museum, and in response, he had been given access to the Estate Caretaker, their PR manager, the Chair of the Museum Board and a fucking lawyer.

He doubted anyone in this room had anything helpful to tell him about the circumstances that had caused the deaths of two young Curators.

"Shall we get started?" Gral said, moving to sit back down behind the enormous table.

It struck Lowe that the furniture had been configured so he would be forced to stand in front of the interviewees like a naughty schoolboy in the Headmaster's office.

Sure, there was a spare chair for him, but if he sat in that - on the extreme left of the group - he wouldn't be able to see anyone other than the lawyer when he asked his questions.

"It is very nice to meet you in the flesh, Inspector," Gral continued. "I have heard so much about your checkered career. Let us hope that your insistence on continuing to look into this matter when the solution is so manifest does not lead to another . . . sanction."

Lowe was pleased to see Verlan roll her eyes at that. It appeared he was not the only one irked by the strange little man.

"You do not believe there is anything else to uncover here?" he asked.

Gral gave an odd little shrug as if his shoulders were not adequately connected to his spine. "When I hear hooves, Inspector, I think horses, not Minotaurs. What do you actually have here? A Curator crushed to death by a falling exhibit. Awful, awful thing to happen and the girl's family have been very generously compensated. However, other than a rather hysterical Auditor who seems to be having a very public nervous breakdown about the whole thing -" Lowe noted that Verlan shuffled uncomfortably at that description. Arebella has hinted that she had had employed Karolen to look into the Museum's affairs -"there are no witnesses that anything untoward took place. Your own colleague closed the case. An Inspector Wyst? Astute man, I thought."

"Scared man, certainly," Lowe said. A faint pressure had settled into the middle of his forehead as if a storm was coming. He glanced at Kregg, wondering if the Bard was trying another Skill-enforced mental push, but if the slimy man was trying something, there was no obvious sign.

"Scared. Sensible. You say 'potato', and I say 'living long enough to see retirement.' The critical point is that, in the absence of any new evidence, I will be instructing my clients to say nothing whatsoever to you about the death of . . . that young lady." Gral snapped his fingers when reaching for Isadora's name. The casualness ramped up Lowe's irritation to another level. "Do you have anything new to share about that nasty occurrence?"

Frowning under the weight of his growing headache, Lowe was sharper than he intended in his reply. "It's pretty fucking hard to gather new evidence when everyone seems determined not to talk about what happened!"

Trei Levick snorted at that. "It's almost like that was Nuroon's plan, ain't it? Why do you think everyone in the Great Hall wiped their memories!"

Gral turned to the Estate Manager and made a strange growling noise. It was such an odd thing to do, Lowe almost laughed at the incongruity. By the sick look on Levick's face, though, he didn't find it amusing at all.

Gral turned back to Lowe, his giant eyes unblinking. "That brings us to the latest . . . event. To my understanding, you have a dead body in the Senior Preservationist's office, the woman herself is reported to have been seen acting strangely around the time of the murder and then, of course, she has fled the scene. Far be it for me to tell you your business, sir, but is this not the definition of an open and shut case?"

The pressure in Lowe's head was almost too much to bear. He raised a hand and massaged the bridge of his nose. "No. Not to me."

There was a silence. Kregg appeared to find it embarrassing and cleared his throat noisily. "Well, pardon us if we're not wild about that. We have a museum to run here, and we need you Security types offsite. You're scaring the patrons."

"I would have thought, with two unexplained deaths occurring within a month, *everyone* within the environs of the Museum would feel much better having us about. Everyone without a guilty conscience, of course."

Kregg, after carefully ensuring Verlan couldn't see him from her vantage point, gave Lowe the bird in reply.

Gral continued, his voice stripped of any emotion. "As far as the Museum is concerned, Inspector. Neither death is *unexplained*—an unfortunate accident followed by the aftermath of . . . I don't know. It could well have been a love affair gone wrong, could it not? I fail to see any link between the two. And I - and the Museum more generally - am concerned that resources that could be used to locate the murderer, Martha Culloden, are being wasted gawping at our exhibits and intimidating the staff. Essentially, Director Nuroon would like me to ask: 'Is there not something else you all should be doing?'"

Lowe did his best but struggled to focus on the man's words; his head felt like it was about to explode.

Desperate, he manually pushed as much mana as possible to *Roll with the Punches*. The Skill soaked up all the energy offered and returned for more, making Lowe blanch and channel even more its way.

He was no stranger to traumatic injuries, but ever since his recent, unexpected ranking up, he had never come close to running out of mana to feed his healing Skill. But he was pretty close right now. And what the fuck was it healing anyway?

Then his vision blurred at the edges, each pulse of his heart sending shockwaves through his skull. Sweat beaded on Lowe's forehead, trickling down his temples as he clenched his jaw, trying to keep the pain at bay.

But it was relentless, digging claws into his brain.

*Roll with the Punches* wasn't touching it! In fact, it felt like all his mana was being fed into something else—something darker, something that felt like it shouldn't be there.

The cooling warmth he associated with the activity of his Skill twisted, turned cold, and then hot again, a burning, searing heat that lanced through his mind.

With a gasp, Lowe suddenly clutched at his temples and slipped to the floor.

His vision darkened, and the room seemed to warp and twist around him, the walls breathing in and out like some grotesque, living thing.

The faces of the four people in front of him distorted into monstrous faces, dripping with . . . was that necrotic slime.

Lowe's skull felt like it was splitting open, a thousand jagged fractures tearing through bone and tissue.

He could feel his brain, swollen with the pressure, push against the inside of his skull, threatening to burst through. Blood trickled from his nose, a crimson rivulet running over his lips.

And then, with a sickening lurch, *Roll with the Punches* twisted in his Core and . . . branched out.

A new Skill erupted into existence, birthed through his agony and smashing through all the blocks imposed on him.

Mental Fortress.

The name rang out in his mind, but - right now - it brought him no comfort. Lowe's body convulsed, his back arching as the new Skill anchored itself within his Core, breaking through the Council's enforced lock.

His vision was suddenly back, but it was tinted red. He could feel the walls of his new passive Skill slamming into place, protecting him from what on Soar had been attacking him.

The headache was gone, but a deep, throbbing emptiness, a hollow ache, was in its place.

Lowe's hands trembled as he wiped the blood from his nose, his fingers slick with it as he stumbled back to his feet, his legs weak, barely able to support his weight.

There would be a time to consider what had just happened, but that wasn't right now. He glared at the four horrified expressions facing him.

"Okay, so which of you fuckers just tried to mind control me?"

# CHAPTER SIXTEEN – THE TRUTH TWISTS TWICE

"And what happened next?" Arabella asked, her eyes wide and unblinking, curiosity writ large across her face.

"Well, I vaulted the table," Lowe began, his voice casually nonchalant. "Punched Kregg right in the face, wrestled the Estate Caretaker to the floor, kneed that bloody lawyer in the groin, and then, because why not, ravished Liando Verlan right there on the spot."

Silence.

"No, you didn't," Arabella said resignedly.

Lowe chuckled, a grin spreading across his face, stretching wider as if pulled by unseen strings. "Of course I didn't. But you couldn't tell I was lying, could you?" He leaned back, insufferably pleased with himself, the grin settling into approaching smug.

Arabella didn't respond immediately, and in the quiet, Lowe watched the gears turn behind her eyes.

The golden shimmer that had been emanating from her, a manifestation of the mana she was channelling, intensified. It wrapped around her like a shimmering halo, turning her into something more than mortal—like a goddess surveying the battlefield.

Lowe found it pretty hot.

He considered, just for a fleeting moment, acting on that attraction, but then he caught sight of Mylaf, seated across the room, munching contentedly on something that dripped with honey and thought better of it.

Mylaf noticed his glance, and he gestured to the towering plate beside her. "May I?"

The Drudge smiled, her expression one of serene indulgence. "I didn't make them for myself, lovely. Tuck in."

Lowe didn't need to be told twice. He reached for one of the pastries, careful not to let the sticky filling ooze onto his shirt. As he bit into it, his eyes met Arabella's once more, and he couldn't resist. "This is the nastiest thing I've ever tasted in my life."

"Oh, do fuck off, Jana," Arabella shot back, though her eyes betrayed a flicker of amusement. "Do you have any idea what kind of shitstorm it's going to cause when people realise there's a Skill that can defeat a Veritas Assessor?"

Lowe wiped a crumb from his lip with practised nonchalance. "I'm not sure," he replied, his tone breezy. "Is it going to be anything like the complete lack of kerfuffle around the attempted mind control of a Security Services inspector?"

The words were light, but the weight behind them was anything but.

Beneath the veneer of humour, Lowe felt the sting of the bureaucratic indifference that had followed the attack on him. He'd been expecting a reckoning, a fiery wave of retribution.

Instead, he'd received three cold, indifferent words: "No further action."

"What do you mean, 'no further action!'" he had demanded, incredulity giving his voice an uncharacteristic edge.

Staffen had blinked at him, her owlish expression one of almost patronising patience. "It's three words, Lowe. Which one of them are you struggling with?"

"At least one of them tried to mind control me!"

"Oh, boo-fucking-hoo," Staffen had retorted. "You're a big boy, Lowe, and I'm sure worse things have happened to you than a little light fumbling around in your cerebral cortex. And the key thing is the attempt failed."

"But—"

"Shut the fuck up and listen to Mummy," Staffen had snapped, her voice suddenly sharp, the air around them suddenly cool as if the temperature had dropped. "Now, don't get me wrong. If someone had managed to gain control of that walnut you call a brain, I'd be pissed off. I don't want it getting around that my investigators are so lacking in willpower that anyone who fancies turning one of them into a meat puppet can give it a go. But even if such an attempt was made…"

"What do you mean 'if'?" Lowe had interrupted, his voice rising.

"Interrupt me again, and you'll be eating your next month of meals through a fucking straw," Staffen had warned, eyes flashing with a momentary red glow. "Now, where was I? Oh, yes. The 'mind control.' Even if one of those thoroughly upright citizens of Soar—four beings who have no registered mind control Skills whatsoever, I should note—had attempted to own your brain, the fact they couldn't pull it off against a Level 25 Classtrated nonentity like you makes me think we hardly need to make an all-points alarm call. No harm, no fucking foul."

Staffen had leaned forward then, removing the pipe from her mouth and fixing Lowe with a significant look. "Unless, of course, you have something you want to share that makes me able to justify the resources it would take to investigate this properly." She had raised both hands either side of her, mimicking scales, moving them up and down as if weighing her options. "Underpowered Level 25 getting a head owy in the field. Significant mental attack I need to scramble all sorts of serious and expensive units for. Which is it?"

And just like that, Lowe had found his resolve to share the news of his new Skill evaporating faster than mist under the morning sun.

"Are you serious?" Arabella's voice cut through his reverie, sharp and demanding. "To my certain knowledge, there are no registered Skills in Soar that'll let you lie without me knowing. That's pretty much the whole basis of my department's existence!" She ran a hand through her hair, exasperation and disbelief mingling in her expression. "This is a fucking huge deal! Like, epoch-defining."

"Only if people find out."

Both of them turned to look at Mylaf, who had been contentedly nibbling on another pastry, seemingly oblivious to the tension in the room. "I mean, sorry to interrupt, but surely this is only an issue if Mr Lowe registers his new Skill."

Arabella's mouth opened to retort, but the words seemed to die on her tongue. Lowe could almost see the moment the implications of Mylaf's statement hit her.

"Of course he's going to register it!" she finally exclaimed, though her voice lacked the earlier conviction. "To not do so would be in breach of about a hundred regulations and open him up to risk of…" her voice trailed off.

"Classtration?" Lowe supplied, his tone devoid of emotion.

"Amongst other things!" Arabella agreed, her voice rising again, more from nerves than anything else. "Seriously, Jana, first thing tomorrow, you must register this Skill. At the very least, it's fascinating that you've broken through your Council blocking not once but twice in a few months. The University will want to study that. And that's before you tell them about your…" she gestured helplessly, "…your Skill that makes my entire life and career completely redundant."

Lowe reached out then, his hand covering hers. "Bella, I'm not going to be telling anyone about this Skill."

"But—" she began, her voice faltering.

"Mylaf is right," Lowe interrupted gently. "Think about it. The Council was already pushing it when they let me keep three Skills with no Class. What do you think they're going to do to me when it turns out that not only do I have two new ones, but at least one of them is an entirely unheard-of Skill that undermines a significant pillar of the judiciary system. I'll be buried under a mountain of bullshit so heavy I'll be lucky to ever crawl back out again."

"Not to mention that you've somehow got the stats of a Level 50," Mylaf added casually, taking another bite of her cake as if she hadn't just dropped a bombshell into the conversation.

Lowe and Arabella exchanged glances, the tension in the room ratcheting up a notch. "Sorry, Mylaf, what do you mean by that?" Lowe asked carefully.

Mylaf laughed, the sound light and carefree, completely at odds with the prevailing atmosphere. "Don't worry. It's not like I'm going to tell anyone, is it? But if there's one thing I know, it's stats," she said, waving her cake around for emphasis. "And unless I've suddenly got an awful lot better at baking in the last few months— and my Skills are already Legendary, so we can pretty much park that—it would seem to me your numbers have gone through the roof recently. You've been making all sorts of deductive leaps beyond my experience for someone of your… stated Level. Why, you've even taken to putting your dirty clothes in the hamper I've left for you rather than leaving them on the floor next to it. That's at least male Level 40 behaviour. And you've not forgotten to put the toilet seat down once in all the time I've been here. If I didn't know better, I'd be preparing meals for you as if you were a Level 50. And I know my stuff. So, tell me that I'm wrong."

Lowe cleared his throat, suddenly finding it harder to maintain his usual composure. "It's not that I wanted to keep it from you. It's just…"

"Least said soonest mended and all that." Mylaf smiled, a knowing look in her eyes. "It's fine, Mr Lowe. I just wanted you to know that I know, and I won't tell anyone. No more needs to be said about it."

Arabella sighed, the sound heavy with resignation, as she leaned back in her chair. "Okay, look, let's park the wider implications for a moment. You've developed a new *Mental Fortress* Skill. Wonderful. It came into being because someone was trying to influence your mind, and you somehow managed to defeat it. Awesome. But do you know which of them it was?"

Lowe let a slow smile spread across his face, the kind of smile that was all teeth and no warmth. "Now, isn't that an interesting question?"

# CHAPTER SEVENTEEN – THE BARD'S SWAN SONG

Kelvin Kregg was feeling pretty pleased with himself.

Of course, this was not an unfamiliar emotion for the Public Relations Bard, so this particular moment of smug satisfaction did not completely register as especially noteworthy.

Which was a shame because it would be the last time in quite a while he would feel this pleasant background hum of utterly unearned joy at the way his life had worked out.

Kregg fancied himself the sort of man who left a lasting impression. As he sauntered down the cobbled streets of Soar, away from the museum, he imagined that every passerby's gaze lingered on him, their eyes drawn irresistibly to his commanding presence.

Of course, most people's eyes slid right off him like grease, but if there was one thing a Public Relations Bard was good at, it was not letting reality get in the way of perception.

Soar was a city that liked to think of itself as cosmopolitan, but that was just a polite way of saying it had a bit of everything and a lot of nothing.

The streets were an architectural patchwork, with grand old buildings such as the Celestial Temple and the Tower of Law dominating the skyline with newer, uglier modern constructions that didn't so much inspire as they did impose.

The air was thick with the mingled scents of market stalls, damp commuters, and the ever-present scent of discharged mana—a smell that had a knack for clinging to the back of your throat long after you'd left it behind.

It was a city that, like Kregg, was increasingly past its prime but pretending otherwise with all the vigour of a former Beauty Queen who'd learned to compensate for the inevitable ravages of time with liberal makeup application. And murdering her competitors.

Kregg whistled as he walked, utterly unbothered by any examples of the city's poverty he passed, which - on more than one occasion - he literally stepped over.

Truthfully, his personality was ideally suited to his Class, though he would have insisted it was the other way around.

As a Public Relations Bard, he spent his days spinning mundane events into something resembling newsworthy.

In the grand scheme of things, his Skills would be considered mundane, as minor as his god's wider influence, but his little tricks could make a dull story seem slightly less so, like adding a dash of salt to a bland soup.

In his hands, a minor exhibition at the Soar Museum could become "a groundbreaking exploration of the artistic influences that shaped our cultural identity," which was to say that it was still as boring as watching paint dry but with an added layer of pretentiousness that made people feel clever for enduring it.

But since he had obtained access to necrotic slime . . .

As he walked, Kregg held his head high, chin thrust out to best display his jawline, which he considered one of his more admirable features.

His clothes were expensive but worn with careless arrogance, as he considered himself above the need to impress. This was, after all, Soar—where the only currency that truly mattered was power, and, right now, Kregg had plenty of that to spare.

His god, Carvanal, a minor deity of Fascination, was an obscure figure in the pantheon, the sort that most people had never heard of and wouldn't care to worship even if they had.

And that suited Kregg perfectly.

He had no desire to compete with the fervent followers of the more popular gods in the Celestial Temple.

Not for him jostling for the favour of deities who had long since stopped listening. No, Kregg preferred to be a big fish in a tiny, unremarkable pond.

And for that, his god rewarded him with the occasional stroke of good fortune, some eclectic Skills and a talent for the sort of shenanigans that kept Kregg in a comfortable flat with a decent view of the park and ensured his position at the museum - and his use to Director Nuroon - remained unchallenged, even as more talented Bards struggled to find work.

Friends were surprised that Kregg had chosen to work at Soar Museum. Although he fancied himself a man of taste, his idea of culture was more about what could be seen and less about what could be understood.

They understood he saw  himself as a connoisseur of the arts, but they'd sought to explain to him that, because his appreciation was never able to extend beyond the surface—a painting's value, in his eyes, was determined more by the artist's name than by any particular quality of the work itself – it might not be the most sensible of occupations to seek to promote the museum to the wider public.

Unfortunately, this superficiality extended to all areas of his life, including his relationships. And he ignored any and all advice.

This inability to hear 'no' was pretty much why Kregg had developed a reputation in certain circles. His advances toward young women were as subtle as a hand up a dress.

Yet, no matter how many slaps to the face he received, to his mind, they were flattered by his attention; after all, what woman wouldn't be?

He was a catch—a man of standing, intelligence, and an intense charm which was surely irresistible. That all the young women at the museum found a sudden interest in the far corners of the building, their conversations taking on a hushed, hurried tone as he passed by, was taken by him to be a sign of universal adoration.

Although, in truth, Women frustrated him.

They were all too timid, too prudish to appreciate his attention, too blinded by some misguided sense of propriety to recognise his inherent worth.

He had, for example, been certain Martha Culloden would have come his way eventually, she had just needed time to realise what she was missing.

But, no. That wasn't going to happen anymore, was it?

As he walked, Kregg couldn't help but feel a grin spread across his face.

Finding the source of his unexpected good fortune in the Exhibit Hall was working out far better than he could have hoped. Here he was, a man of increased influence in an institution that, while it might not have been the centre of Soar, was still a place of great importance.

The fact that most of the people he passed barely acknowledged him didn't register as an insult; it simply reinforced his belief that they were beneath him, too enmeshed in their dreary little lives to appreciate the quality of the man walking among them.

The streets of Soar were busy this time of day, filled with people going about their business. He liked to imagine that they did notice him, of course, that their eyes lingered just a moment longer as he passed, recognising, even if only subconsciously, that he was someone of consequence.

He passed by a Street Musician, a wiry young man playing a tune that was either very avant-garde or very bad—it was hard to tell the difference. Kregg paused for a moment, considering whether to drop a piece of gold into the hat that lay at the musician's feet, but then thought better of it.

He'd once fancied himself a patron of the arts but, over time, had decided that most of the arts weren't worth patronising.

No, he had a more worthy focus for his attention now.

Kregg's flat was in a district of Soar that had once been fashionable but increasingly had seen better days. His building, a towering block of greying stone with iron railings that were more rust than metal, was a relic from a time when people still cared about how things looked.

Kregg liked to think of it as having character, though others might have called it a bit of an eyesore. He was so looking forward to being able to trade up.

Kregg climbed the steps to his front door, his mind already turning to the evening ahead.

There was a bottle of wine waiting for him, a gift from one of the museum's Trustees, no doubt intended as a subtle bribe to ensure their latest donation received a bit more publicity than it might have otherwise deserved. Kregg had accepted it with a smile and a nod, already planning how to make the bottle last over several evenings.

One didn't need to be extravagant when one was alone.

The lock clicked open with a familiar creak, and Kregg stepped inside, the door closing behind him with a soft thud that echoed through the empty space.

The flat was tidy, almost sterile in its cleanliness; he liked things to be just so, everything in its place, a world where he was the centre and everything revolved around him.

He made his way to the small sitting room, where a comfortable armchair awaited him, positioned so he could gaze out of the window at the city below.

He liked to sit there in the evenings, a wine glass in hand, watching the world go by, content in the knowledge that he was above it all—both literally and figuratively.

With a sigh, Kregg poured himself a glass of wine, watching the liquid swirl in the glass, catching the light from the fading sun. As he took a sip, he allowed himself a small, satisfied smile.

Yes, life was good, he thought. He had a position of influence, a comfortable home, and a god who rewarded his loyalty. And now, he had a whole host of new opportunities opening up for him.

The soft click of his window blowing shut caught his attention, and he half-turned towards it. Then, he completed a full turn when he saw the short, dark woman standing in the shadows.

"Who the fuck are you!"

"Ah," Hel said, hurricanes spinning in her eyes. "A perfectly valid question. But I have some of those, too. How about we start with mine, and if there is enough of you left alive when I'm finished asking, we move on to discussing my biography? Yes? Excellent. Now, first things first," she opened her hand, and a vial of something glittering unpleasantly floated in the air, "where the fuck did a nonentity like you get your hands on necrotic slime?"

# CHAPTER EIGHTEEN – NO SONG LEFT TO SING

"I tell you what, once that fucker started talking, nothing in Soar was going to stop him," Hel said, accepting a piece of Mylaf's best cherry cake and sighing in pleasure at the 20% boost to her HP. "The prick had a lot of words, not much sense, but enough greasy charm to make me want to rip out his throat."

She lounged in the battered armchair, her legs slung over one armrest, chewing like a cat toying with a mouse. Lowe sat across from her, his collar stained with sweat, looking like he'd been born tired and never quite managed to catch up.

"You do know that if ever you get bored of Lowe's trademark hangdogness, I'd hire you like a shot?" she asked the Drudge, only half-joking.

Mylaf smiled. "That's very kind, Ms Hel. But I think I'm very happy here with the master."

"Well, you know," Hel said, spraying crumbs as she did so, "suit yourself. But remember, the offer's there if you ever get tired of playing nursemaid to Mr Sunshine. The same goes for you, too," she added as Arebella returned to Lowe's sitting room.

"Sorry, what did I miss?"

"Just Hel trying to poach Mylaf. And you, apparently," Lowe said, rubbing his temples. "She thinks she can find a use for a Veritas Assessor in her line of work."

"Oh, I'm sure I can come up with something to occupy the long, dark hours," the Wind Tyrant said, smiling wolfishly.

"Let's focus, shall we?" Lowe said, clearing his throat as Arebella blushed bright crimson. "It sounds like you were successful?"

"Well, yes and no." Hel sat up a little straighter, the smile fading from her lips as she produced a vial from her coat. "You were right, he had this hidden in his flat."

They all stared at the glowing liquid. Even seeing it safely encased in a tube of glass, Lowe felt himself shift uncomfortably. He could well remember the clawing to his mind the substance had caused in the bowels of the museum. "Sneaky fucker."

Hel sniffed. "I'm afraid that might be the last of the good news, though. As far as I could tell, he's only really been using it to make his targets more . . . suggestible."

"Targets?" There was a sharp quality to Arebella's voice.

"Yeah, and I'm not going to lie, I'm going to need the longest, hottest shower in the history of Soar when I get back home. That man is one of the creepiest fuckers I've ever come across. And you need to remember, I had a Nightmare Reaver on my squad."

"Oh, and how is Tenia? Have you heard from her?"

"Just last week, actually. Her and Charl have found a little farm to settle down on. Turns out the Skills that make you a good assassin are completely useless when confronted with cows and chickens. They're having a ball."

"How lovely! Do give them my best."

"Ladies!" Lowe couldn't help but feel he was losing his grip on the general direction of the conversation. "Can we get back to Kelvin Kregg?"

"Sure," Hel twisted her wrist, and a small pillar of wind rose to spin the vial end over end above the table. "It is - well, *was* -I suspect he may have learned the error of his way - the wanker's habit of slipping a couple of drops of this into the drinks of anyone he liked the look of. Apparently, having some of that on board made his weak little Charm Skills far more . . . persuasive."

She retrieved a leatherbound book from her other pocket and threw it to Lowe. "And if that wasn't simply lovely, he also kept lengthy notes of his conquests. His prose is unpleasantly explicit."

"Fuck," Lowe caught the book and began flicking through it, brow furrowing as he read.

Hel nodded, a steely light coming to her eyes. "Yes. He did. Regularly. Probably not so much, moving forward, though."

"And he used this to poison Jana?" Arebella asked, staring at the spiralling vial with horrified fascination.

Lowe shook his head, both at what he was reading - Hel wasn't the only one who would need a wash - and the question. "No, I didn't drink anything when I was there."

"Yeah, I wondered about that. I'm assuming, though, he made some sort of ostentatious 'hail fellow well met' greeting with you when you came in?"

Lowe triggered *Grid View*. Yes, he saw, Kregg had come walking towards him, gloved hand outstretched. Concentrating, he paused and zoomed in on Kregg's palm. It glittered unpleasantly. "He had this shit smeared on his hand. Bastard."

"Yep. He was pretty smug about that. At least to start with. Of course, he got all kinds of remorseful as the evening progressed."

So, Lowe had been right. It had been the Public Relations Bard who had sought to mind control him. "Did he say why?"

"No, but this is where shit gets interesting. He says it was because you were being your usual charming self, and he wanted to teach you a lesson. But - " Hel's voice trailed off, and the spinning vial moved in the opposite direction.

"But what?"

"There was clearly another reason. If I had to put gold on it, I would say someone ordered him to do it. But if that was so, he wasn't sharing."

"Perhaps you didn't ask hard enough?"

The temperature in the room dropped through the floor, and Lowe hastily clarified. "Sorry, what I mean is . . . what I was getting at was . . ."

"What Jana meant was 'thank you very much for taking time out of your busy schedule to help him out in this matter." Arebella supplied smoothly.

"Yes. Yes, that's what I meant."

Hel cricked her neck, and the room began to warm back up. "Sorry, I'm more than a little on edge. That man - " she shook her head.

"It was bad? I mean, I've heard rumours," Arebella said. "Everyone knows about Kelvin Kregg."

"I would suggest they don't know the half of it." Lowe closed the - for want of a better word - abuse journal and tapped its cover with his finger. "I'll make sure this gets in front of Staffen first thing."

"Good," Hel said. "Although you may want to warn whoever picks him up that he'll probably be a touch fragile. They may want to take a mop with them."

"Sorry, so is that it? This unpleasant young man is who you were looking for?" With a blink of her eyes, Mylaf swapped out the cherry cake for a celebratory round of mana-regenerating cocktails.

But Lowe was shaking his head. "No. Not at all," he said, holding up the journal. "According to his journal, Kregg has been up to this for years, but it is only in the last few weeks he started introducing necrotic slime to proceedings."

Hel nodded. "He says he 'found' the stuff after the first death. Several vials were left on his desk, apparently. He had no idea who put them there, and he swears he had nothing to do with any murder."

"You believed him?"

"I didn't disbelieve him. But he wasn't telling me the whole story, which was quite impressive considering how I was asking. Someone has put the fear of Soar into him, and he was willing to keep schtum even with me - "

"I don't think I want to know the details," Arebella interrupted.

"Ah, don't knock it until you try it, sweetie. It's amazing how close pleasure and pain can get. Let me know if you fancy a dabble. I don't mind telling you that Latham's *quite* the convert."

"Anyway," Lowe said, clearing his throat, "let's see where this leads us. If we're confident Kregg didn't kill either of the Curators . . . " he looked at Hel, who shrugged back.

"I think so. He was lying about something, but it wasn't that."

"Okay. Well, in lieu of anything else to go with, let's run with that. He's not our guy. What about the missing Senior Preservationist?"

"He definitely knows something about what happened to Culloden. For example, he's clear she's not returning to the museum, but it feels like he's been told that rather than was the cause. But I couldn't get out of him who. Again, I feel the need to stress that if he was more afraid of the hypothetical wrath of whoever was threatening him rather than the very real and actual presence of me, you're going to need to be real careful, Lowe."

Hel paused, and when she met Lowe's eyes, there was no humour in her expression at all. "I know you think you're all kinds of resilient. And maybe you are in the normal run of things. But that twat was afraid. Scared on a deep - bone-deep - level. I don't think I've ever seen anything like it. And I've been around. So believe me when I say you need to think very carefully if this is a case you want to continue with."

***

Even as they were talking, Kelvin Kregg lay in his own room, staring at the ceiling with bloodshot eyes. His once pristine apartment had become a squalid hole, littered with the remnants of broken furniture, his shattered ego and the stench of blind terror.

He hadn't moved from the spot on the bed where he'd collapsed after Hel left him. His mind churned with paranoia, each creak of the floorboards, each whisper of wind through the cracks in the window, sending spikes of terror through his gut.

89

Then the front door creaked open, and Kregg's heart leapt into his throat. He tried to move, to bolt upright, but his fractured limbs wouldn't obey.

His eyes, wild and desperate, fixed on the figure standing in the doorway, silhouetted against the faint light from the hallway. They closed the door with a deliberate, almost ceremonial slowness, and Kregg's breath hitched in his throat, recognition dawning in his eyes.

He tried to speak, but his voice came out as a strangled croak. "I didn't tell her… anything… I swear…" The words tumbled out in a frantic whisper, his tongue tripping over itself to spill the denial. His body shook, a cold sweat broke across his skin as the figure advanced.

The intruder said nothing, its silence more terrifying than any threat could have been. Each step the figure took closer towards him ratcheted up Kregg's panic.

He struggled to sit up, his hands clawing at the sheets, but what Hel had left of his muscles refused to cooperate. His heart thundered in his chest, the blood rushing in his ears drowning out any rational thought.

The figure reached the bed, looming over him like a shadow of death, and still, they said nothing.

Then, without warning, the figure struck. It was methodical, precise, and almost clinical. Its claws gleamed in the dim light as they descended, a flash of bone that caught the last shreds of Kregg's sanity and sliced it to ribbons.

The first cut was quick, severing the tendons in his wrists, a clean slice that left his hands useless, flopping like dead fish.

Kregg screamed, a high, keening wail that filled the small room, but no one would hear him. The figure's hand clamped over his mouth, silencing the scream, forcing the sound back down his throat where it bubbled up as a sickening gurgle.

His eyes bulged, tears streaming down his cheeks, his body convulsing as the blade moved with grim efficiency.

The claws carved into him, slicing through skin, muscle, and bone with ease. Blood sprayed across the bed, splattering the walls, the sheets, and the figure's clothes. His chest was flayed open, ribs cracked apart like a butcher disassembling a carcass.

The figure worked with a cold detachment, the movements almost mechanical as they dug into his chest cavity, pulling apart the flesh to expose the pulsing organs within. Kregg's vision swam with red as his life drained away. The figure reached into his chest, fingers curling around his heart, feeling the last, desperate beats before squeezing.

The final act was almost tender as the heart was ripped free. Kregg's body slumped back against the bed, lifeless, an empty husk.

The figure stood over the corpse, staring down at the ruined body, their face expressionless. Then, its mouth opened, and a river of slime flowed from it, covering the body and immediately beginning to consume it.

By the time the first of the Investigators arrived in the morning, there was relatively little left to question.

# CHAPTER NINETEEN – DEAD MEN DON'T CHARM

*Mental Fortress* was having all sorts of impacts on Lowe's quality of life.

Sure, twenty-four bells was a pretty small sample size from which to draw a conclusion, but he couldn't ignore the fact his day-to-day existence was clearly going through some pretty significant changes since gaining the Skill.

First up, for a passive ability, it was an absolute mana-hog.

At a stroke, half of Lowe's available pool was being constantly drawn away to reinforce the massive walls that had sprung up around his mind.

Not that he was complaining, of course - even in just a day, he was already experiencing huge benefits from its protection - but without all the recent under-the-table boosts to his Intellect and Wisdom, he wouldn't have a drop to spare for anything else.

Because of said improvements, he'd moved away from partaking of Mylaf's manas based consumables, but as soon as his MP dipped below 50% that evening, he'd asked her to focus on producing goodies that could help counteract that.

It seemed that slurping down on a delightful banana and kiwi smoothie that gave him a flat 1000 mana on demand was thus just going to be a price he'd have to pay.

The more he thought about it, the more he wondered whether *Mental Fortress* would be - what he was choosing to describe as - a Rank 2 Skill.

It wasn't just the insane mana demands - though there was no way anyone sub-Level 60 (or without a pet Legendary consumable producer) could even consider it as an option - but he had yet to come across *anything* that could so much as a put a dent into its defences.

And that was the second massive change in his life. Because, suddenly, not a single mental Skill in Soar worked on him.

None of them.

Not the subtle brush of *Munchies!* from the guy hawking toasted nuts from a cart on the corner of his street.

Not the *Sinner's Remorse* from the Preacher bellowing about the benefits of worshipping one god or another from the front of the Celestial Temple.

And not the overpowering sense of "look on my works ye worms and despair" that poured from every mighty fucker that passed him on the street.

It was a remarkably liberating feeling to suddenly see the world of the Soar without any of its forced illusions whatsoever.

"Is this how you feel all the time? To be able to see through all the lies?" he asked Arebella, as he escorted her to work the following morning. She had played her face at his White Knight routine but was snuggled happily against his arm as they approached the Tower of Law.

"Not really," she said. "My Skills are all active and need to be focused on a target. From how you describe it, you're pretty much experiencing the unvarnished nature of the world all the time." Arebella stopped and turned to face him. "I imagine it's not actually a lot of fun, right?"

That was kind of an understatement.

Standing in the middle of the street, the world roiling around him, it felt like every single citizen of Soar was actively assaulting him.

On the plus side, *Mental Fortress* was levelling up like a hamster in a wheel. On the other, though, it gave him a pretty bleak impression of the rest of humanity. He'd had no idea that the world was such a succession of lies, damned lies and showtunes. But now none of them affected him, it was making everything feel a touch . . . drab.

They continued walking, Lowe trying not to be distracted by all the incidental strikes against his mind pinging off his shields.

He was looking forward to catching up with Kregg this morning - the goon squad should be picking him up about now - and watching that smug fucker trying to Charm him with his weak-ass little Skills would be pretty entertaining.

Although not as much as pushing his teeth down his throat. He hadn't been able to sleep after reading the Public Relation Bard's diary.

"Well, this is me," Arebella said, leaning forward to kiss him on the cheek. "Unless you think something terrible is going to happen to me between here and my office door?"

Lowe glanced up at the hulking presences of the Justicars guarding the entrance to the Tower of Law. He had it on pretty decent authority that they were not to be messed with - although Latham was clear he could take any two of them in a pinch - so he was pretty confident nothing Nuroon-inspired was likely to befall Arebella during work hours.

"Nah, it's alright. I'm happy to leave you in the capable hands of these two. Hel will pick you up, though."

"And you're okay leaving me with someone who can, quite literally, sweep me off my feet?"

"Hey, if you want to trade me in for a spicier model, I won't make a big deal out of it. But you have to let me watch, okay?"

Arebella batted him softly on the arm and started running up the steps. "Don't let anything happen to my best girl, though, you hear? Or you'll have me to answer to," Lowe called to the guards.

One the Justicars, the shorter of the two - although, of course, these things were entirely relative. He was still bigger than most bears - put a sneer on his face and pulsed out a wave of *Intimidation*.

The Skill crashed into Lowe's *Mental Fortress* and evaporated away to nothing. He gave a cheeky little wink back. This didn't do very much for cross-judiciary relations.

"What the fuck are you winking at?" the Justicar said, stepping forward, pushing more *Intimidation* Lowe's way.

"Jana, this isn't helpful. I work here!" Arebella said, turning around, hands on hips.

"You hear what the lady said, gentlemen. Thus, in respect of her wishes, I won't be kicking your arses today. But take care of her, do you hear?"

Sighing, Arebella returned to walking up the stairs, muttering under her breath. "As if he needed anything else to make him unjustifiably cocky."

***

Fortunately, though, Lowe still had people in his life capable of bringing him down to size. His boss, for example. "How did someone as fucking dozy as you end up in a position of responsibility?"

"I'm sorry!"

"Yes, well, apology not fucking accepted."

"I wasn't apologising, boss. I was expressing my confusion at all the shouting the minute I walk in the door!."

"Dozy. Fucker." Staffen leaned down and retrieved something from under her desk, which she then tossed to Lowe. "Know what that is?"

Lowe caught the transparent bag of something gelatinous and squishy. "Clear evidence as to why I'm never coming to dinner at your house. I mean, what the fuck Commander? Is this your lunch?"

"Hardly. That's Kelvin Kregg."

Lowe dropped the bag to the floor, where it landed with a heavy squelch. "I don't understand."

"No. And that's because you are a . . ." Staffen gestured with her hand for Lowe to supply the answer.

"A dozy fucker, boss?"

"Precisely. Because, call me a bluff, old traditionalist, but when one of my Investigators comes into possession of evidence of epic sexual misconduct, I expect him to take care of business properly. After what I've read this morning, no one would care if that fucker had taken a long walk off a short tower, but liquifying him with necrotic slime is the sort of thing to cause comment."

"What? I didn't do this, boss!"

Staffen sniffed and leaned back in her chair. "You saying this wasn't you?"

"Of course not! Since when did I get a reputation for this sort of batshittery?"

Staffen looked at Lowe silently, questing out with *First Impression*. It wasn't - strictly speaking - one of her more powerful Skills, but she'd always found it useful when getting a quick read as to whether someone was telling her the truth or not.

She frowned as it bounced straight off Lowe. She tried again. "Tell it to me straight, Inspector, did you kill him?"

Even before Lowe emphatically shook his head, Staffen's Skill had failed for a second time. Which was pretty unusual.

A long and successful career as a Guardian of the Wall had given her access to considerable resources - most of which she had reinvested in her build. In fact, one of the reasons why Soar's Mayor had been so keen to recall her to active service after the Commander Cenorth debacle was that - like or hate her - no one could deny Pernille Staffen was a monstrous powerhouse.

Thus, having a Classless Level 25 bat away one of her techniques was fairly noteworthy—and she guessed it gave her an excuse to bring out the big guns.

"Inspector Lowe, do you deny *any* involvement in the murder of Kelvin Kregg?" she said, triggering *Confession is Good for the Soul*, her Legendary threshold reward from Blurian. Her patron god famously didn't fuck around with niceties, and using this had been known to make hardened Level 50 Juggernauts break down in tears, spilling all their misdemeanours back to being toddlers.

At the very least, the man in front of her should immediately start gibbering. At the worst, he'd probably fully stroke out, but she figured Lowe could take a little stay in the hospital after all the hassle he'd been causing her in the last few days.

That he simply pulled a face and shrugged back at her was . . . unexpected. "Absolutely. He's no good to me dead, is he?!" Lowe bent down and picked up the bag of goo. "Is this really all that was left of him?"

Trying to hide her astonishment at this turn of events, Staffen looked away and shuffled papers around on her desk. "Yep. His front door was open, the place was trashed, blood everywhere, and this was all that lying on his bed. He'd been completely melted."

"Just like the Curators?"

"I don't know, Inspector Lowe. But it would be simply lovely if you were to get the fuck out of here and ask that sort of question back at the museum. You know, before even more of their fucking staff are murdered?"

Lowe, sensing the dismissal, stood, leaving what remained of Kregg on the arm of his seat. "And you are happy if I push it quite hard with the Director? He was pretty punchy when I last spoke to him."

Staffen fixed Lowe with her best glare - irritated that he barely seemed to quail under its pressure. "Somehow, Inspector, I think you'll cope."

Lowe had barely set foot out of her office, before she was activating a Sending Stone - her own, personal one, not the one Cuckoo House provided - and speaking to someone with whom she had not connected for some time.

"It's me. Yes, sorry. I know it's been a while. Yes. I know. I know. And I'm sorry. But can we put that aside for a moment. I need to run something by you. Can you meet me in the unusual place? Excellent. Yes, I'll make it worth your while. Particularly if you bring everything you have on Essence Transmutation Theory."

# CHAPTER TWENTY – WHAT THE CURATOR SAW

Lowe's afternoon at Soar Museum had been far from fruitful.

The atmosphere, already tense after the deaths of two Curators and the vanishing of their Senior Preservationist, had taken a . . . turn following the recent, and rather spectacular, melting of Kelvin Kregg.

By which was meant, of course, that the dusty corridors of exhibits now thrummed with a bizarre and almost festive air. In the shadow of that man's death, the museum had found itself in the grip of a strange, electric joy—a sort of unrestrained celebration.

There was talk, he noted in passing, of an open bar at the funeral. Classy.

Lowe, taking a brief break from a succession of largely unprofitable interviews, wandered into the museum's inner courtyard. He activated *Grid View* as he did so, flicking through the memories of the morning like a tired gambler rifling through losing bets. "I didn't do it, but I'd shake the hand of whoever did." Over and over and over again.

It struck him that it was more than a little unproductive to have had a man like Kregg in charge of public relations. Perhaps the museum's Board hadn't noticed that having a PR lead who could double as a textbook example of a serial predator was, at best, counterintuitive.

Surely, there was someone else in Soar—someone not involved in bullying, abuse, and wide-scale harassment—who could've done the job? But no, Kregg had been Nuroon's choice. And that, in and of itself, was interesting, was it not?

"Can I have a word, Inspector?"

Lowe was pulled from his musings by a polite cough behind him. He turned, seeing a Curator he'd spoken to the day before. Preece. A relic of a man, far too old to be among the fresh-faced recruits that populated the museum. More than that, Preece had the look of someone who'd once been important. Lowe wondered at his story.

"Of course," Lowe replied, though his tone was hardly encouraging. "Although, if you're about to tell me how glad you are that Kregg's dead, can it wait a few minutes? I'm finding the outright joy a touch wearing. And believe me, considering I read that fucker's diary, I'm as surprised at that as the next person."

Preece's face twitched as if caught between a grimace and a smile, then settled on an expression Lowe hadn't seen in years—one that belonged to a different era, when emotions were bottled up, not vomited at every opportunity. It had looked as though the man might actually cry for a moment, but then he steeled himself, the flicker of vulnerability passing as quickly as it had appeared.

"I *was* glad when I heard he had died."

Lowe paused, his hand halfway to Preece's shoulder, and then thought better of it. The gesture might have been appropriate for a distraught young kid. To a teary peer, it felt . . . arch. Instead, he let his hand drop and studied the older man. Far too old to still be a Curator, surely? All of the others he had spoken to were in their early twenties. This guy was probably older than Lowe himself.

"Mate, you're hardly unique in that. I'm amazed no one's choreographed a 'ding dong the handsy tosser is dead' dance routine, to be honest. Trust me, there's no need to get upset about it."

Preece's face crumpled again, then cleared as if he'd decided something. "No, not Kregg. I doubt even his mother will mourn his passing. I'm talking about Isadora."

Lowe took a moment to shift gears.

Isadora.

The first Curator to die. He'd read the reports, though they hadn't been exceptionally detailed—Inspector Wyst had seen to that. Still, he remembered the basics: Isadora had been well-liked, or so it was said.

But then again, people tended to remember the dead more fondly than they ever did the living. Looking at the storm of emotions swirling on Preece's face, there was really only one question worth asking.

"Curator Preece, is this a confession? Did you kill her?"

"No, sir."

"What about Curator Harker? Or Mr Kregg?"

"No, sir."

Lowe ground his teeth. This was like pulling teeth. "Okay. So why don't you tell me what's on your mind?"

Preece hesitated, then, with a sigh, began to unravel his pathetic story.

It hadn't seemed like stealing at the time. It had seemed like a miracle. Money was tight, especially since his career change, his wife was making all sorts of unreasonable demands, and most of his meagre salary was gone as soon as it came in. Then, at the end of an especially long shift, he'd returned to his room and found one of the exhibits from the Ctholnic Exhibition in his pocket.

It was just a small piece of polished stone. He must have absentmindedly put it there whilst cleaning the larger display. He didn't know why, but he'd dropped into a pawn shop on the way home and had been astonished at the amount of gold that had been hastily pressed into his hand.

That had been enough to get his wife off his back for a bit.

"And how long ago was this?" Lowe thought he could see where this might be going.

"Just over two months ago."

"And how did Curator Isadora know you had taken the stone?"

"She said that she'd seen me on the street after our shift and happened to follow me into the pawnshop. Looking back, I'm not sure she didn't plant the fucking thing on me in the first place, but I was too surprised at the time to know what to think. She'd bought the stone and replaced it, would you believe!"

Lowe raised an eyebrow. "When did she first bring it up with you?"

"A sevenday later."

So, the Curator had waited to reveal what she knew.

Lowe wondered why.

If she had dropped the stone in Preece's pocket—obviously interested in seeing what he'd do—it suggested she might not have been the 'good girl' Wyst's reports painted her as. More so if she'd then followed Preece home to see what he'd do with his good fortune.

And why hadn't she tackled him about it at once?

"Was she blackmailing you?"

Preece didn't answer, which, Lowe thought, was an answer all on its own.

"Okay. So she was. What did she ask you to do?"

Preece shuffled around, glancing back at the museum buildings as if they might offer him some protection. "It wasn't just me, you understand? Isadora was . . . she was good at getting people to do what she wanted. Harker will tell you . . . would tell you, I guess."

Harker. The second Curator to have been melted with necrotic slime.

Curiouser and curiouser.

Instinctively, he believed what Preece was telling him, however why hadn't the man shared any of this with Inspector Wyst? Was there something about the later murders that had shaken it free? That had made him anxious to share this morning? Lowe wondered what the final straw was—was Preece fearing he might be next, or was something else at play?

Lowe brought to mind what he had read about Curator Isadora in Wyst's— somewhat limited—report. By all accounts, she had been a popular employee. No one had said anything about her being some sort of mastermind, a secret puppeteer controlling the museum's staff from the shadows. If what Preece was hinting at here was accurate, Isadora had been a dangerous young woman.

And bad things tended to happen to bad people.

Waiting for a sevenday to reveal her knowledge of what Preece had done - until she could be reasonably sure that the money had been spent - was hardly what you did by accident.

The girl had left Preece with no option but to do what she asked. He could scarcely claim then that he had given in to a sudden impulse, felt terrible about it and intended to return the money. It was a calculated move, one that spoke of a mind far more ruthless than her colleagues had described.

"And Harker?" Lowe pressed, feeling the weight of the unanswered questions sprouting up all around them.

Preece glanced around again, as if someone might be listening in.

As well they might, Lowe thought. This was hardly the right setting for this sort of questioning, but he sensed Preece's resolve to confess might not survive a trip to Cuckoo House.

"She had something on him, too. I don't know what, but it was enough to make him do whatever she wanted. I think . . . I think she enjoyed it. The power. Isadora had this way of looking at you, like she knew exactly what you were thinking, and that she could crush you if she wanted. But the thing is, Harker wasn't relieved when she was dead. It was like things had gotten worse. The night before . . . he died, he was falling apart. So much so, if you'd told me he'd killed himself, I would have believed it."

"Yeah, not so much," Lowe said drily. "No one chooses to go out like that."

The silence stretched between them. Preece was rattled, more so than Lowe had initially realised. With its corridors filled with artefacts of long-dead cultures, the museum seemed an odd place for such a sinister game to play out.

But perhaps that was the point—Isadora had used the dust and decay as her cover, hiding whatever game she was up to behind the veneer of a dutiful employee.

A Curator of secrets, as much as exhibits.

"What about Kregg?" Lowe asked finally, curious to see where the thread might lead.

Preece looked down, his voice barely above a whisper. "I don't know. She didn't need to blackmail him, not really. He . . . he was infatuated with her. Did whatever she asked, like a puppy following its master."

Now, that was interesting.

Kregg, the museum's resident sexual predator, reduced to a lovesick fool by a woman more than half his age. Lowe could almost see it—the pathetic image of a man like Kregg bending over backwards to please someone who likely saw him as nothing more than a useful tool.

Lowe shook his head slightly, a gesture more to himself than to Preece. This wasn't just about petty theft or even murder—it was about control.

And if there was one thing Lowe now understood about necrotic slime, it was that it was all about the control. It sounded like Isadora had been playing the museum's staff like a finely tuned instrument, each note perfectly in place.

But in the end, someone had cut the strings.

"And Culloden? Was she involved in any of this? Did Isadora have anything on her?"

Preece shook his head. "No, I don't know anything about that."

Lowe's voice took on a harder edge. "Why didn't you tell Wyst any of this?"

The man looked up, his eyes full of a weariness that seemed to come from a deeper place than just the events of the last few weeks.

"Because I was scared, Inspector. Scared of what might happen if I did. Scared that she might still have some hold over me, even from beyond the grave." Preece gave a sad, resigned shrug, then turned to leave, his footsteps echoing across the courtyard.

Lowe watched him go, his mind turning over the pieces of the puzzle that had just been handed to him. Isadora's shadow stretched longer than he'd anticipated, her influence lingering in the museum like a ghost that refused to be laid to rest.

He would have to dig deeper, but he had more than enough to chew on for now.

# CHAPTER TWENTY ONE – WHERE THE WALLS BLEED

It was a slightly less objectionable version of Trei Levick that Lowe managed to track down in the museum grounds.

After his . . . interesting conversation with Curator Preece, the Inspector had been loath to return to the little room the Director had set aside for him to conduct his interviews.

Lowe had initially thought it was a good thing that Nuroon hadn't insisted Felicitous Gral oversaw things again, but a few hours in, he was rapidly reassessing that view. Other than a general, unrestrained joy at the death of Kregg - and other than Preece's intriguing contribution to proceedings - Lowe did not feel any better informed about the murders than he had before he had arrived.

Thus, he found stumbling across the Estate Manager supervising a small group of Apprentice Labourers somewhat fortuitous.

"You still hanging about here then?" Levick said, then turned to yell at one of the enormous men fumbling about with a handful of bricks. "For the love of all the gods, stop! Put the trowels down before you murder that poor thing any further!" The Estate Manager glanced back at Lowe and gave a shrug. "Just a minute, sir."

"Sure," Lowe was pretty pleased Levick was even acknowledging his existence. From everything he'd heard, the old man was as spikey as Nuroon when it came to people interfering with the running of his domain.

The Apprentice Labourers paused at Levick's yell, their hands hovering in the air. Sweat dripped from their brows, pooling into small, muddy patches on the ground. They were each, gormlessly, staring at the half-constructed wall, a lopsided monstrosity that looked like it was trying to break free from its sorry existence.

"I've told the Director it's a false economy cutting corners to employ these morons. At half the hassle, I'd get twice as much done with some decently trained staff."

As Trei stepped forward, his eyes narrowing at the mess of mortar and stone, Lowe reflected that it seemed odd the museum had cash to spare in some areas but was making savings in others.

He hadn't missed the numbers of the Lower Classed in positions he might expect to have been filled with more expert presences. Of course, there was nothing wrong with keeping costs low, but it was oddly inconsistent with the gold that seemed to be awash elsewhere.

"You lot have the brains of a rock but none of the reliability," Levick yelled, his hands twitching, and with a flick of his fingers, activated *Master Mason's Eye*. In response to the Skill, every crack, every uneven surface in the wall suddenly glowed faintly as if begging for correction. The botched construction shimmered with a haze of errors, and Levick's lips curled into a tight line of disdain.

"Right," he said, his voice dropping to a growl. "Step back and let a professional handle this." As he spoke, he triggered *Structural Reversion*, and the wall sighed in relief as it unravelled, bricks slipping apart with a gentle thrum, the poorly mixed mortar dissolving into harmless dust. The Apprentice Labourers watched, slack-jawed, as the stones they had placed settled back on the ground.

Levick spun around, his eyes narrowed. "I'm not your nanny, and this isn't a sandbox. You're here to learn, so try fucking doing it the way I showed you!" He grabbed a trowel, not that he needed one with his Skills, but he wanted to show them how a proper wall was built. With precise movements, he activated *Perfect Placement*, and each brick clicked into place under his hands like it was born to be there.

One of the apprentices, a lad with arms thicker than Lowe's entire torso, lifted a brick, his hands trembling with effort despite his *Strong as an Ox* passive. It would be the only Skill the poor kid would have, Lowe knew, at least until he was able to catch the eye of one god or another.

By the look of the age of some of these apprentices, though, they'd long since passed the stage where they could reasonably expect to be patronised. Thinking back to his conversation with Preece, Lowe frowned. What was it with this place and employing older people? Nuroon didn't strike him as the sort of man to have an altruistic streak when it came to employment practices.

"Put that fucking thing back down!" Levick barked. "What do you think you're doing? Haven't you ballsed this up enough yet?"

The apprentice dropped the brick in fright, narrowly missing the Estate Manager's foot, but Levick didn't even flinch. Instead, he activated *Reinforced Foundations*, sending a pulse of energy through the ground beneath the wall, stabilising the earth.

"That's how it's done," he said, his voice like gravel. "Now, take those shovels, and fill in the gaps where they belong, not where your fucking idiot heads think they should be."

The Apprentice Labourers moved slower than molasses on a winter's day, but they moved. Levick turned back to Lowe but kept a sharp eye on their work, his *Supervisor's Intuition* giving him a constant stream of notifications whenever one of them even thought about making a mistake.

Every now and again, he barked orders and corrected their errors. "Remember," Levick said, his voice softer but no less cutting, "you're here to build, not demolish. If I have to undo your mess again, I'll be charging you the repair fees out of your hides. Now, where were we?" he said, looking back at Lowe

"We hadn't actually started," Lowe replied, "but before we do, can I ask you about all the unskilled around the place?"

"Bane of my fucking life, sir. Bane of my fucking life. The Director's been on some massive efficiency drive for the last few years, and you should see the fucking idiots -" he raised his voice as he said that, the apprenticeships cringing in response -"I get landed with."

"But why should that be the case? From everything else I've seen, gold doesn't seem to be an issue."

Levick snorted. "Welcome to my world, sir. None of that fucking good fortune has trickled down to us on the ground level yet."

"Good fortune?"

Levick sucked air through his teeth. "Ah, now that would start to wander into areas I'm going to have to refer you back to Mr Gral. Outside my jurisdiction, you see."

Sighing, Lowe made a mental note that he would need to drop by that creepy man's office in the Tower of Law once he was finished here and pressed on. "So, what can you tell me about the murders?"

"Don't rightly know we're supposed to call them that, are we? A falling stone crushed the girl, and the lad and the wanker got themselves melted. Messing with powers beyond their ken and all that."

"Okay. Well, let's focus on the deaths of the Curators to start with. Did you know them?"

"Barely. Paths didn't cross much if you know what I'm saying. They'd be with the exhibits, and me and my lads would be trying to keep this fucking ramshackle show on the road. My two silvers' worth is that I don't think either was popular, if that makes any difference. The lass was one of them sneaky types that listens more than you think, and the lad . . . well, the only thing I know about him is I'd keep finding him places he shouldn't be. Usually, with a confused expression on his face and a fucking useless excuse in his mouth. If you ask me, he was simple-minded enough to be working with these cretinous mouth-breeders!" The Apprentice Labourers cringed as Levick raised his voice once more.

"You'd 'keep finding him in places he shouldn't be'. Was that a recent thing?"

Levick frowned at that. "Now you mention it, yes. I probably wouldn't have even known his name if he hadn't been making such a fucking nuisance of himself in these last couple of weeks."

"What sort of thing was Curator Harker doing?"

"Oh, nothing that I'm not used to those academic twats getting up to. But if I got a notification that a door had been forced or a seal broken, by the time I got there, I'd find him stood, mouth open like a fish, and looking around like he'd been sleepwalking. To hear him tell it, he had no idea of what had happened."

Lowe frowned at that. "And that didn't strike you as unusual?"

"Sir, I have been the Estate Manager at Soar Museum for the best part of twenty years. Nothing the Curators get up to surprises me. The only thing that was even slightly unusual about this was that he didn't stink of alcohol, and there was no half-dressed serving wench to be found in the shadows. It's a fucking colossal site, sir, and - literally - years can pass between my crew maintaining one area or the next. It's famously one of the attractions of the Curator job, provided you can stand Nuroon. There are all sorts of shenanigans and extra-judiciary fun and games you can get up to here without anyone ever noticing. I'm surprised even more stuff doesn't get nicked, to be honest."

Lowe nodded absently at the little rant and then frowned. There was something about Levick's emphasis in that sentence which grabbed his attention. "You say 'even more stuff.' What do you mean?"

"Fuck's sake, sir. I thought that was what you wanted to talk about. Soar knows no one else has been interested. I told the last guy that came around, that Wyst bloke, and he wrote it all down in his little notepad."

Lowe kept his face still, sensing he might finally be getting somewhere. "I'm sure it will all be in a report somewhere. But why don't you give it to me from the horse's mouth, as it were?"

Levick sighed and, having lambasted the apprentices for their slowness once again, turned back to Lowe. "Look, sir, I don't want to make a big thing about this. But I reported it at least a month before that girl came to her end, and I can't believe no one is making more of it."

"Of what?"

"One of our Dreadnaughts is missing."

# <u>CHAPTER TWENTY TWO – ONE GONE, FIVE WATCHING</u>

Lowe frowned at the unfamiliar word, more so that Levick was looking at him like there was a clear expected response to the news.

"Oh no!" he tried, raising his hands in a little show of unwelcome surprise.

"Fuck's sake," Levick shook his head and turned back towards the Apprentice Labourers. "That's it for today, boys and girls. Go and do . . . whatever it is you lazy cretins get up to when I'm not trying to help you better yourselves."

The group didn't need to be told twice, and in moments, Lowe and Levick were stood alone in front of an inexpertly created wall.

The Estate Manager cocked his head, sniffed, and then waved his hand, the bricks instantly correcting themselves into a more uniform position. "Don't get me wrong, they're not bad lads; it's just at my time of life . . . " Levick's voice trailed off for so long that Lowe opened his mouth to speak before he continued. "It's a big site, you get me? And I can't be everywhere. I said to the Director that it was getting to be a bit much for me and do you know what he said?"

Lowe shook his head, sensing he wasn't really needed in this part of the conversation.

"He said I had two choices: I could retire, and he could find someone 'younger', or I could train up a proper maintenance crew and supervise. Think I've doubled my workload."

Lowe let the pause settle for a while until it threatened to become maudlin. "You said something about a Dreadnaught?"

Levick's head snapped up, and eyes that had been in danger of becoming misty cleared. "Yeah, I did. Probably best you see this yourself."

And then the crotchety man was off and Lowe struggling to keep up with the pace he set across the courtyard. Although not an unfit man, Lowe recognised that he could probably stand to do a little more exercise. He quickly found himself channelling *Roll with the Punches* to avoid panting like asthmatic buffalo.

Levick reached a door in a building at the extreme end of the space - directly opposite from the room in which Lowe had been conducting his interviews - and paused to check the Inspector was still behind him. "Are you okay?"

Despite his running Skill, Lowe could feel that his face was flushed. "Yeah, no worries."

Levick frowned at him. "You need to spend a little more time outside, sir. All the desk-jockeying is not good for you. Last thing the museum needs is another dead body on its hands."

The conversation was moving rather too close to a conversation Arebella had with him the other night. The one where she tactfully raised that there was a chance he might have been partaking a touch heavily of some of Mylaf's sweeter consumables. Having no wish to revisit his mortification there, Lowe motioned for Levick to get on with it. "You said you had something to show me?"

Casting a critical eye to the bead of sweat that had appeared on Lowe's brow, Levick pushed a stream of his mana into the lock of the door before them. It made a complicated whirring noise and then shuddered and cracked open.

Levick stood to one side, his face etched with the deep lines that come from years of scowling at things that don't make sense—or, worse, things that do. "Get in, then," he growled, "don't dawdle. This isn't a fucking sightseeing tour."

As the Estate Manager had, quite literally, invited him along to show him something, Lowe couldn't help but feel this was slightly unfair. However, as he crossed the door's threshold - the air inside spilling out a metallic aura, like old blood on rusted steel - he let it side.

The inside of the room was large, far larger than the external look of the place would have suggested, but the low ceiling made it feel smaller, as though the building was hunched over in the shadows, watching those who came in. The exhibits - if that was what you could call things in a room clearly not intended for view - were scattered about in no particular order, like pieces in a puzzle that no one had the time or patience to solve.

The first display Lowe noticed was a case on his left, its glass smeared with what looked like fingerprints, though on closer inspection, they were more like claw marks. Inside, a collection of delicate instruments—brass compasses, astrolabes, and things that looked like they were probably used to explore something more like internal biology—glimmered faintly in the light.

As Lowe leaned in, he caught a glimpse of something moving in the reflection, a shadow that wasn't his own. He pulled back sharply, his heart skipping a beat and looking around, but the shadow was gone, leaving only his distorted reflection in the glass.

Levick snorted. "Don't bother trying to figure those out. They belong to an astronomer who thought the stars could talk. Turns out they can, but he didn't much like what they had to say. They used to be out on display, but there's only so much screaming the Director could countenance. Even that PR wanker couldn't keep smoothing that over. And he isn't going to be doing any of that anymore, is he?"

Lowe nodded, unsure whether Levick was joking. It was hard to tell.

They moved on through the quiet dark, Lowe's eyes drawn to a massive tapestry hanging against one wall. The fabric was heavy, soaking up any available light and keeping it for itself. The scene depicted was chaotic, a battle, or perhaps a massacre— figures locked in combat, but their forms twisted, exaggerated, as though painted in a fever dream. The longer Lowe looked, the more the figures seemed to move, not in the usual way a trick of the eye might play, but as if they were actually writhing against the fabric.

"Careful with that one," Levick said, his voice gruff but laced with something that might have been caution. "It's called 'The Last War.' Every now and then, one of those poor sods gets out, and that's no Sun Day morning picnic, I can tell you."

Lowe tore his gaze away, his nerves beginning to jangle. He was having the same creeping feeling of dread that had almost overwhelmed him in the corridors beneath the museum. Surreptitiously, he checked *Mental Fortress*, but it was running as usual. This wasn't any sort of mind attack; it was just a genuinely freaky room.

Lowe stepped further into the room, his eyes catching on a small, unassuming box on a pedestal. It was plain wood, no bigger than a loaf of bread, with a simple latch. But something about it felt off as if it were vibrating at a frequency just below hearing. He could feel it in his teeth, a low, constant hum that set his nerves on edge.

"That," Levick said, with a disdainful wave, "is a music box. Plays a tune that no one ever finishes listening to, on account of what happens if they do."

Lowe didn't need to ask what happened. The box seemed to buzz with a barely contained menace, which certainly did have *Mental Fortress* performing all sorts of gymnastics. He quickly moved past it, feeling the cold sweat prickle on the back of his neck.

With a lurch, the room appeared to twist in on itself, the exhibits becoming more bizarre, more unsettling the deeper they went. A mirror reflected not their faces but a dark hallway lined with doors, each slightly ajar, with something unseen moving behind them. A table held a clock that ticked backwards, the hands scraping against the glass as they fought against time itself.

The oddities went on. Every corner seemed to hold something just out of sight, a whisper of movement that vanished the moment Lowe tried to focus on it.

"This is basically a dumping ground for everything the powers-that-be can't find a way to explain," Levick said, his tone bitter, like a man forced to babysit a pack of rabid dogs.

"Is it safe?"

"Safe? Who the fuck are you kidding? There's a reason why it's all kept under lock and key. I only have access because someone needs to keep on top of all the damage."

They had reached the far end of the room, where a single, flickering lantern cast long, jittery shadows across six towering figures. Or rather, Lowe assumed, what should have been six.

"Here we are," Levick said with a weary sigh, suggesting he'd rather be anywhere else. "Our Dreadnaughts. Or what's left of them."

Lowe stared, his mind rebelling against what he was seeing.

The Dreadnaughts defied description, their forms shifting and warping with every heartbeat. One moment, they were statues, tall and menacing, carved from some black, gleaming stone. The next, they melted, flowing like quicksilver, only to solidify again as something else entirely—armoured beasts, towering pillars of light, a roiling masses of shadow. As Lowe watched, they were never the same thing twice, as if they were always in flux, trapped between realities.

And yet, for all that mutability, they exuded a terrifying presence, an overwhelming sense of terror that pressed in on Lowe like the purest essence of necrotic slime.

His *Mental Fortress* shivered under the assault, the normally impenetrable barrier quivering like a leaf in a storm and levelling up at an astonishing pace. It wasn't just the sight of them which was so awful - and Lowe was certainly full of awe - it was the sense that these things were alive, aware, and far more dangerous than they appeared.

And there was one missing.

"One's gone," Lowe said, more to himself than to Levick.

"Aye," Levick replied, his tone clipped. "Awhile back now. And if you've got half a brain in that head of yours, you'll start worrying about where it's gone and what it's planning. As I told the last Inspector, these things don't just wander off for some fresh air."

Lowe couldn't tear his eyes away from the remaining Dreadnaughts, their forms flickering and shifting with a slow, relentless rhythm. They seemed to pulse with a silent, malevolent energy, as if they were aware of their missing sibling and were waiting—patiently, ominously—for its return.

# CHAPTER TWENTY THREE – STREETS LIKE BLADES

Following his encounter with Levick - although the Dreadnaughts probably had something to do with it too, of course - Lowe had not been able to bring himself to return to interviewing museum employees.

He had made his excuses to the guard that had been put at his disposal - another oddly low-classed woman in an ill-fitting uniform - and taken to the avenues and roads of Soar for a wander.

During his trials and tribulations of the last year, Lowe had found himself walking these dark and mean streets more and more. Mostly, that was because, post-Classtration, he no longer had an office from which to work, but also because it was difficult to think clearly in an apartment that smelled of desperation, regret and last week's uneaten curry.

However, there was also something about the city of Soar, especially at this time of night, that had always helped him clear his head. And, right now, with *Mental Fortress* whirling nineteen-to-the-dozen, he figured his psyche needed all the support it could get.

Taking in a deep breath, Lowe stepped through the museum gates and into the early evening light, allowing Soar to wrap itself around him like a lover with sharp nails and a smoky laugh. Ignoring the portal stone opposite, he turned left and made his way into the heart of the Cultural Quarter.

Lowe had lived in Soar his whole adult life, arriving as a fresh-faced teenager with hopes, dreams and parents back home in the sticks who were as glad to be rid of him as he was to escape.

What he found on arrival was a city with too many secrets and not enough scruples—a lady of the night who'd steal your wallet and kiss you sweetly while doing it. Lowe winced at that. He would like to think that was a metaphorical flight of fancy, but that had actually happened more than once over the years.

As he walked down a familiar avenue - this street wasn't a million leagues away from his beat when he was first deployed from Cuckoo House - he relaxed into a comfortable stroll, the cobblestones underfoot slick with the recent rain and other - less salubrious - liquids. It might have been his overactive imagination, but it looked as if each of the stones glistened like wet lips under the mana-empowered lights.

Even though it was getting late - exactly how long had he stood and stared at those writhing, moving Dreadnaughts? - Soar never slept; she merely waited, lying in a bed of shadows, her heartbeat a low, persistent thrum that echoed to the distant clatter of hooves and the muted murmur of voices drifting from barely-lit pubs.

If he took a left here - at the crossroads of Hope and Expectation - he would soon be unable to move for places - and people - that could take his mind off what he had seen. There was a time - and not really that long ago, now he thought about it - when this would have been a pretty easy decision to make.

Now, though, Lowe resolutely stalked forward even as *Mental Fortress* positively shook under the assault of sights, sounds and entreaties from the darkness. At times like this, it felt to him like Soar was alive, but only just—like a parasite that thrived on the vices of its inhabitants, feeding off their desperation. This city was, to all intents and purposes, a vampire with a sense of humour.

Or, now he thought about it, just your average, common-or-garden god . . .

Then Lowe staggered slightly, suddenly light-headed. Puzzled, he checked his stats and noted, with alarm, that his mana pool was almost exhausted: both *Mental Fortress* and *Roll with the Punches* appeared to be going gangbusters.

The first made sense after what he'd been through with the Dreadnaughts. He'd have been astonished if it wasn't. The second though... were all these mental attacks actually causing him physical damage?

Figuring this was an issue to ponder another time - and not wanting to see what would happen to his sanity if he no longer had mana to spare - he pulled out one of Mylaf's smoothies from his inventory and downed it in one gulp. Voices called from the side alleys, asking for "a little taste, mate? That looks cracking!" but Lowe had long since learned to keep his cards close to his chest—Soar might've been the kind of woman who could make you forget yourself, but Lowe wasn't about to let her get back under his skin.

His mana refilled, although he noted it began ticking down immediately.

Lowe started to regret his decision to walk home rather than use the portal.

Mana exhaustion was no picnic, and he really didn't want to get caught up in something without *Roll with the Punches* to rely on. Since having his Intellect and Wisdom power levelled by Latham, he hadn't had to worry about that happening.

But now?

Well, he just wanted to be safely tucked up in bed. He was getting old . . .

Dipping his head to avoid eye contact with anyone, Lowe passed by a narrow alley, its entrance framed by the flicker of glowing signs that seemed to beckon with a finger only the desperate could see. Even as he had that thought, he made out a group of figures loitering in the shadows beneath the words, eyes gleaming with a hunger that only came from wanting something you knew you'd never have.

Soar attracted this type of lost man - and woman! - like moths to a flame, and she burned them all up just as easily, leaving nothing but ashes and regrets behind.

A soft breeze stirred, carrying a discordant burst of music—a minor-key tune that drifted from a hidden doorway, its notes curling around the group and pulling them towards it. Lowe recognised that sound, the melancholy hum of one of the innumerable Sirens that patrolled the riverside.

They knew how to break a person's heart and make you thankful and - even protected as he was against the allure of their music - Lowe felt himself taking a hesitant step after the group as they left. Then his defences snapped back into place, and he soon gained control over himself, turning the other way with alacrity. Soar wasn't a city to offer easy solace; she'd take what you had left and laugh in your face for thinking you could keep it.

Lowe's mana dipped alarmingly again - what was going on! - and he downed a second smoothie. With alarm, he saw his inventory was starting to run low of the consumable.

Mylaf would, of course, be delighted to whip up another batch, but that wouldn't help him if he ran dry before he got back. With an uncharacteristic burst of pace, he walked on, past shuttered windows that watched his progress with feigned disinterest, like a woman who'd seen it all before and wasn't impressed.

The cracks in their facades were evident in the mana light—wrinkles in the skin of a city that had long since stopped caring about appearances. Soar didn't need to be beautiful; she had style, which was far more dangerous.

Lowe's undignified haste brought him to the main thoroughfare - Displacement - which would pass by his apartment. Here, the street widened into a boulevard lined with hawkers selling trinkets, consumables and promises. The crowds here were thick, bodies pressed close together, seeking a last vestige of something significant to make of their day. Lowe straightened his coat and started down the street, knowing that no matter how quickly he walked, Soar would be right there with him, her hand in his pocket and a smirk on her lips.

And then words swam across his vision.

*Skill: Mental Fortress available to progress to Rank 2*

*Do you wish to Proceed?*

He shook his head as much to clear the confusion in his mind as to answer the question. More of this Rank 2 bullshit? Skills didn't move to Rank 2. They had four tiers - Common, Rare, Epic, Legendary - everyone knew that. They didn't 'rank up.' *And, as far as anyone else knows, neither do attributes*, a little voice said in his head.

Considering the power of *Mental Fortress*, Lowe was forced to conclude it was probably his own brain supplying the narrative commentary. He was glad it was good for something.

*Do you wish to Proceed?*

"I don't know! What does Rank 2 mean?" In any other city, passersby might have commented on a slightly dishevelled, middle-aged man talking plaintively to himself in the middle of the street. In Soar - and at this time of the evening - such behaviour was so common as to be almost mandatory.

*Rank 2 Skill: Mental Fortress allows selection of one of the following options:*

1.  ***Reflective Barricade:*** *Any mental assault directed at the Fortress is reflected back at the attacker, magnified by the strength of [Lowe's] Willpower.*
2.  ***Thought Amplification:*** *[Lowe's] mental processing speed and cognitive abilities are vastly enhanced, allowing for instantaneous problem-solving or the rapid learning of new Skills.*
3.  ***Shared Bulwark:*** *[Lowe] can, temporarily, share their mental protections with an individual or with a group.*

*Do you wish to Proceed?*

He needed to stop by Latham's house.

# CHAPTER TWENTY FOUR – THE MIND'S EDGE

"Yeah, there's no fucking way you're coming in here."

Lowe tilted his head back, taking in the Temple Warder who loomed over him like a thundercloud given flesh. She wasn't quite 'Latham-big,' but neither was she likely to be mistaken for a garden gnome. Her arms were crossed over her chest, biceps flexing against the confines of her uniform in a way that suggested they had their own opinions about his presence. "Why not?" he asked, managing to sound only mildly put out.

"'Why not,' he says," drawled the second Warder, leaning lazily against his halberd. He was older and his belly had long since declared independence from the rest of his physique. "What possible justification could there be for you being on the 'no entry' list?"

Lowe considered this.

Off the top of his head, he could think of at least half a dozen reasons why he might not be the Celestial Temple's favourite visitor. There was the murder of Gianna d'Avec, the late High Priestess of Gravalk—a case that, while technically solved, had left enough scorched earth behind to grow suspicion for a generation. Then there was that misunderstanding with the Harbinger of Oulian, which had ended in both literal and metaphorical fireworks.

And, of course, the less said about his dealings with the Avatar of Blurian, the better.

Still, he was pretty sure he'd racked up enough goodwill with at least one of Soar's gods during all of that to avoid outright excommunication. Or so he had thought.

However, he was saved from further debate by the sudden, looming presence of Warder Latham appearing in the Temple doorway.

"It's okay, Ferok. I'll take it from here."

It was childish, but Lowe felt a little burst of pleasure as the other two Warders visibly quailed in Latham's presence. *Yeah, you better run*, he thought as they retreated into the main building. *That's my mate, that is.*

"What the fuck are you doing here, little man?" It seemed the Warder was less delighted to see him than might have been hoped. "I told you to steer clear of this place until some of the bad feeling dies down."

Lowe tried a 'what did I do' gesture. "I stopped by your house first, but Hel said you were on the night shift. And it does seem pretty harsh to say I'm banned from this place!"

"We're still sweeping up the dematerialised ashes of supplicants murdered during your last visit. I'm not sure 'harsh' is entirely justified."

"Hang on. All of the deaths were hardly my fault!"

"Little man, how about I explain this to you via the method of analogy? Say, for example, a man is being pursued by a ravenous tiger - a tiger, let's make clear, that this man has gone out of his way to piss off royally - and, in the process of his escape, he leads said angry big cat into a crowded room whereby all of the occupants are torn to pieces allowing the man to escape. Now, how do you think the friends and relatives of the rendered and consumed will likely feel towards that man the next time he rocks up for a chinwag?"

"Okay, so you have a point."

"Indeed. I have a point. Come on, let's see if we can get out of fireball range before a lower floor avatar decides to make a name for themselves."

***

Over eighteen muffins, ten bacon sandwiches and a vat of coffee, Lowe filled his friend in on developments, mainly focusing on what Levick had shown him of the Dreadnaughts and the subsequent 'ranking up' of his *Mental Fortress*.

"Never heard of it," the Warder said, motioning for the Waitress to refresh his plates.

"No," Lowe said, dropping yet another gold coin on the table. "By the way, at what stage did we decide it was my responsibility to pick up your tab?"

"Oh, I don't know. Probably somewhere in between the third or fourth time I saved your life? Or, it might have been around when you asked my ladyfriend - a very expensive and highly sought-after mercenary - to beat up a Public Relations Bard for you. A Bard who, it should be noted, has since been murdered, bringing all kinds of undesired heat her way. It's likely to be one of them, I'd have thought."

"Ladyfriend? What are you, an eighty-year-old maiden aunt?"

"Fuck you, Lowe."

They sat together in comfortable silence for a moment whilst Latham consumed his way through the last of the food.

"How is your 'ladyfriend', by the way? She didn't seem to be in the mood to chat. If it puts minds at ease, tell her that we haven't seen any sign of her presence in Kregg's apartment. And he was too badly melted for anything she did to him to show up to the Deathcaller. She obviously got in and out clean."

"Well, some of us are professionals, little man, and others -" Latham looked around, searching for the Waitress who reappeared at a run with a new plate of pastries -"Ah, excellent!"

"Others are... "

"Largely only good for picking up the bill. Now, where were we? Ah, yes. Your increasingly broken build. Talk me through again how this Skill initially appeared."

Lowe did so, adding in what Hel beat out of Kregg.

"Fucking necrotic slime. Can't stand the stuff," the Warder said, swallowing a croissant whole.

"No, I can't say I'm much of a fan either."

"Okay, so what do you have? Three deaths at the museum, a member of staff who went missing at the time of the second murder and necrotic slime everywhere."

"And a missing nasty that got loose from its cage a few months before any of this happened," Lowe added.

"And you've not only got a new Skill out of the whole thing, but it's 'ranked up' too. You know, as far as I can tell, if we're looking at who benefits from this whole thing, you're the only person coming out ahead. A less self-assured man might think he was being manipulated in some way..."

111

Lowe shifted uncomfortably at that. His mind returned to the case that had first brought him into contact with Latham - he'd been used by the powers that be there, too.

"Come on then," Latham said, wiping his mouth with the back of his hand. "Let's have a look at these 'rank up' options."

Lowe shared the notification with the Temple Warder, who leaned forward, his broad face tightening into a frown as he read. The silence stretched long enough to grow roots. "Do you need me to explain any of the longer words?" Lowe asked.

"Fuck you, Lowe."

"Just trying to be helpful."

Latham dismissed the notification with a huff and leaned back. His expression grew thoughtful, a rare stillness settling over him. "I've not come across anything like this before."

Lowe opened his mouth to speak, but the Warder silenced him with a sharp gesture, his palm out like a barricade. "The appearance of a new Skill itself is strange enough. People don't just spontaneously gain Skills by tinkering with the ones they've already got. But this has happened to you twice now, in less than a year."

Lowe nodded, recalling the first time. *Medic!* had manifested after Hel's friend had been hurt dragged him out of captivity, bleeding like a butcher's apron. He'd barely thought about it at the time, but *Medic!* had branched from *Roll with the Punches*, hadn't it?

"If I were laying down gold on this," Latham continued, "I'd bet it's tied to you being Classless. Without a pre-set roadmap to follow, your progression seems a bit more . . . flexible."

"Flexible?" Lowe repeated.

"You know, stretchable. Like a blob," Latham said, gesturing vaguely with his hands. "Without a rigid mould to force your Skills into, your progression has more room to—what's the word—shift? Reshape itself? It's like you're working with an amorphous ball of potential instead of a standard, cookie-cutter build."

"And in this analogy, I'm a blob, am I?"

"A blob with potential. Don't knock it."

***

Having spent more time than he might have hoped looking at melted, amorphous blobs of late, Lowe couldn't help but think Latham's choice of words was somewhat pointed. "And you've never heard of anyone else doing this before?"

"Little man, with the best will in the world, the life-expediency of Soar's Classless is about as long as it takes to say 'XP Farming.' If your old boss hadn't been pushing to keep you around until you were a useful card to play, I doubt you'd have survived a week. Guys in your situation usually don't live long enough to get a chance to manifest new Skills this way."

Memories of the immediate aftermath of his Classtration tried to rise to the surface of Lowe's mind, but he pushed them down. Now was, very much, not the time. "So, what, I might be able to develop more Skills?"

Latham shrugged, his shoulders rising and falling like tectonic plates shifting. "No idea. Not a fucking clue, to be honest. But you've pulled it off twice now, and in quick succession. So, yeah, it's not unreasonable to think it could happen again. Just don't let it go to your head."

He leaned forward, resting his forearms on the table, his tone growing pointed. "The rest of us? We've got Class perks and patron gods tossing Skills at us like it's our nameday. You? You're out here brewing up your own bespoke abilities from scratch, cobbling together what the rest of us get handed on a gilded platter. Sure, it's impressive—cool, even—but don't start thinking you're going to make me lose sleep over the rise of some terrifying new powerhouse. Not yet, anyway."

Lowe nodded at that. He would need to generate a whole host of Skills this way even to get close to the range of what he had had at his disposal before . . . the incident. "But the rank up?" he asked, tentatively, oddly disappointed about the news thus far.

"Ah, now that is more interesting. What's your thinking on which to choose?"

"I like the idea of the *Reflective Barrier*. As far as I can tell, just by opening my front door, I'm under constant mental assault. It would be nice to give a little back."

Latham was shaking his head. "Oh, diddums! Are all the nasty men and women trying to influence your mind? Poor you. It's almost like you're living in a fucking modern age of grifters, charlatans and hustlers. What do you think will happen if you rank up with this bad boy?"

"I don't know, maybe people will learn to stop forcing their thoughts inside other people's heads?"

"Fucking hell, little man! Were you always this wet behind the ears?" Lowe was about to reply, but Latham raised his voice and continued. "I've got about nine - no, it's ten - mental passives running right now. Most of them are versions of '*I will fuck you up*' intimidation Skill, but there are a couple of others doing more subtle information gathering about the world around me. What do you think would happen if you start mentally slapping me about over coffee?"

"I'd hurt you?" Lowe suggested.

"Like fuck you would. Even with all the under-the-table bollocks you've got going on, I'm still so far above your level you should be licking my shoes for me deigning to speak to you without ripping your fucking arm off. No. You fucking wouldn't hurt me. All that would happen is that, eventually, I'd realise what the irritating buzzing in my ears was and, if I was in a good mood, I might just restrict myself to putting you into a coma."

Latham leant forward as he said that, which made Lowe realise that Level ?? didn't just need mental passives to be intimidating.

"Yeah, Reflective Barrier's tempting. Real tempting. But let's face it, you'd end up turning Soar into a war zone every time someone gave you the hard sell. That's fine for the little fish—blow up a few con artists' brains, put the fear of whatever into street-level grifters—but the big players?" He tilted his head. "You'd have your guts for garters before the ink dried on the incident reports."

Lowe nodded, swirling the dregs of his drink and setting it down with a soft clink. "So, not Reflective Barrier. That leaves two options. Which do you like?"

The Warder's grin widened into something that was almost feral. He tapped the notification floating between them.

"Now, this is where it gets interesting…"

# CHAPTER TWENTY FIVE –
# REFLECTIONS IN A CRACKED SHIELD

Latham surveyed the empty plates on the table.

He was still working his way through what seemed like the last stack of buttered crumpets the Waitress had brought, and though his fingers were slick with grease, his expression was suddenly serious.

Across from him, Lowe nursed a lukewarm cup of tea, untouched for a while now. The chatter of the coffee shop around them—clinking cups, murmured conversations, the hiss of the steam wand—provided an oddly serene backdrop to the tension bubbling between them.

If it wasn't for the panic of their server, it might even have been restful.

"The obvious choice," Latham continued between bites, his voice almost lost in the low hum of the room, "is *Thought Amplification*. You've got, especially for a Classless, pretty high Intelligence and Willpower—enough to make most people nervous. That upgrade can only add to it. In your job, with that freaky memory power of yours, it'd make you pretty fucking astute."

Lowe raised an eyebrow, sensing the direction of the conversation as one might anticipate an approaching fist. "I'm sensing a 'but' coming here…"

Latham paused, his giant hand reaching out to cradle a half-empty cup of coffee. He stared into it like a Diviner peering into the dregs of an ill-omened future. For a moment, Lowe wondered what the man was thinking. Whether the sudden introspection was due to the weight of his words or the sheer volume of food he'd consumed, Lowe couldn't tell.

Finally, Latham looked up, his eyes sharp with an intensity that belied his casual tone.

"For me, it's all too perfect. I think you're being played."

Lowe blinked, the straightforward declaration taking him off guard. "What do you mean?"

"Look, little man," Latham began, "I don't know a better way to put this, but everything you've told me thus far feels a bit too fucking coincidental for my liking. You're on a case knee-deep in necrotic bloody slime—oceans of the stuff washing about, right? And then—oh, how convenient—your OP healing Skill suddenly evolves to block out mental attacks. That's pretty fucking situationally useful, don't you think?"

Lowe couldn't argue with the logic. It was like Soar was handing him precisely what he needed, right when he needed it. "Okay…"

"And then," Latham continued, leaning forward slightly, his voice dropping to a near-whisper as if the walls themselves had ears, "not only do you end up with this ridiculous new Skill that largely negates any and all mental attacks, but it then, almost immediately, 'ranks up'—which again, if anyone is keeping score, is more colossal bullshit—and offers you three stupidly useful new upgrade abilities. And let's not forget, the Council has expressly limited you to three Skills. So, not only have you broken through that barrier twice, but your newest fucking Skill can now become even more powerful."

Lowe felt a pit forming in his stomach. The way Latham laid it all out made it sound pretty unlikely. "What are you saying?"

"I'm saying, little man," Latham replied, "that for someone who, famously, does not have a patron god, you're getting offered some pretty nifty toys lately. And that brings me back to *Thought Amplification*."

The Waitress appeared next to him, replacing his cup, which Latham downed in one gulp, his Adam's apple bobbing as he swallowed. "It's the perfect upgrade for you, particularly in the middle of a case that's proving to be a bit of a stumper. Choose that, and I'll put my left ball on you being able to pick your way through whatever tangled web Grackle Nuroon is spinning down at the museum."

"Sounds pretty good to me," Lowe said cautiously.

"Yeah, it does, doesn't it? So why don't you be a good little pawn, pick it, and get on with doing the bidding of whoever is fucking dangling useful baubles in front of you?"

Latham's bluntness landed like a punch to the gut. And Lowe had plenty of context of that occurance to feel like the simile had merit. He let those words sink in, the implication gnawing at the back of his mind. "You think I'm being manipulated?"

Latham nodded, his expression grim. "Don't get me wrong, *Thought Amplification* would be a massively beneficial enhancement for you. It's just . . . too useful—too coincidentally useful—right now. You get what I'm saying, little man? This is Soar. No good deed goes unpunished, and no gift is entirely without strings."

Lowe leaned back in his chair, the worn leather creaking under his weight. He took a deep breath, letting his eyes wander around the room as he processed Latham's words. The coffee shop was full of life, oblivious to the existential quandary unfolding at their table.

The world of Soar outside the fogged-up windows carried on as usual, blissfully unaware of the cosmic chess game Latham suggested he was a piece in.

He thought back over the last few days. Since being assigned to the museum case, his luck had indeed been uncanny. The appearance of *Mental Fortress* had the potential to be a game-changer—a seismic leap forward for him.

Complete protection against mental attacks was invaluable, particularly in a city as treacherous as Soar. And now, to be offered *Thought Amplification* on top of that? Something that could push his mental faculties to new heights . . . It was everything he could ask for. It would make him formidable again, maybe even close to what he had been before the Classtration.

But Latham's words hung in the air like, coincidentally, the bitter scent of burnt coffee. The Waitress was back, swapping out cups and plates. Watching her low-level panic at being in the presence of such a powerful being, Lowe recognised her feelings of helplessness.

He knew what it felt like to have everything stripped away, to be left with nothing but the hollow shell of what he once was. Despite all the gains he had made recently, the wounds of losing his Class had never fully healed, and the thought of going through it again was almost too much to bear.

"I'm not going to belabour the point here, Jana," Latham said, his voice softer now, tinged with an uncharacteristic note of concern. "I'll say this once and leave it up to you. You've had everything taken from you once, and most people don't bounce back from that. I doubt I would. But you did, and you're still here. I respect that. But I'm worried that by hook or by crook, you're having all sorts of new goodies given to you that are just ripe for being taken off you at the worst possible moment. Do you remember what I told you in the Dungeon?"

Lowe didn't need to trigger *Grid View* to recall the words. They were etched into his memory, a mantra repeated in the darkest hours. "Skills are temporary; Stats are forever."

"Damn straight," Latham said, nodding with approval. "You're a Level 25 with the stats of a Level 50. And you've achieved that without being artificially boosted by any god-given Skills. That's solid, and it'll only get better. And, crucially, they can never take it from you. You could be called in front of the Council tomorrow, and they could strip you of all your Skills, and you'd still be in a decent place."

Lowe wasn't so sure about that. "Without *Roll with the Punches* . . ."

"Fuck it," Latham interjected, waving away the concern as if it were nothing more than a minor inconvenience. "It's a nice healing Skill, but by the time you're Level 30—with the various Threshold Bonuses you'll pick up on the way—you'll have enough Progress Points to move at least Strength and maybe Constitution to Rank 2. At that point, you'll be tanky enough that just with normal HP regeneration, you'll make that Skill pretty redundant on a day-to-day basis. Sure, you'd still need it if I decided to kick your arse, but not against anyone close to a normal Level. So yeah, *Thought Amplification* would be awesome for you, but—given enough time—it won't do anything for you that you won't be able to do yourself."

The words were meant to be reassuring, but they had the opposite effect. Lowe's thoughts drifted back to his post-Classtration cell, the cold emptiness of it, the way the world had felt like it was collapsing around him.

Losing all but three of his Skills had been like losing a part of himself, and the idea that it could happen again—that his new powers could be ripped away just as he was beginning to feel whole again—was terrifying.

"So… *Shared Bulwark* then?" he asked, his voice almost a whisper.

"Put it another way," Latham said, standing up from the table and stretching his massive frame, "I've always wondered what a few of the gods look like without all their glamours in place. Think of it as just scratching one of my itches as payback for all the times I've saved your life!"

Lowe watched as Latham prepared to leave, the Temple Warder's presence as imposing as ever, even amid a crowded coffee shop. He knew that Latham was speaking from a place of genuine concern, but that didn't make the decision any easier.

He felt the weight of it pressing down on him like an unseen hand, the choice between power and safety, between risking everything for the chance to be more than he was or playing it safe and potentially living with the regret of never knowing what could have been.

As Latham pushed open the door and stepped out into the misty Soar afternoon, Lowe moved to follow him, not noticing - as he was deep in thought - the various eyes that tracked his progress and the hands that dropped into pockets to retrieve Sending Stones.

# CHAPTER TWENTY SIX – NO GLOW, NO MERCY

"You going to do anything about all the gold blinking lights, little man?" Latham asked as the two of them made their way through Soar streets. "I mean, I'm no hot-shot Security Service Inspector, but I imagine there are probably all sorts of downsides to being quite so fucking noticeable."

Lowe raised his hands, grimacing at the glowing manifestation of a still-yet-to-be-chosen Skill. "I don't know how to switch it off without choosing the Skill, and I don't want to do that yet."

Latham sighed theatrically. "I'm going to get a migraine today, aren't I?"

"Look, not that I don't appreciate all the help, but don't you have some sort of day job you should be doing?"

"No. Not at all. Temple Warders are famously louche, what with Soar's gods being so chill and all."

"In that case, please don't let me keep you . . ."

Latham reached down and cuffed Lowe on the back of the head. The blinking lights seemed to increase in intensity at the impact. "Look, ask me no questions, and I'll tell you no lies. I am unwilling to either confirm or deny that a certain interested party would like me to ensure you don't end up as a blob of liquifying goo."

"A god has commanded you to protect me again? Fucking hell, Latham, I'm not sure about that! It didn't work out so well for me last time, did it?"

"Well, fuck you very much, little man. I have a distinct memory of going balls to the wall for you against an Advanced Class motherfucker. Maybe I won't bother next time."

Lowe shook his head. Or he may have been ducking in advance of another, teeth-jarring clout.

It was undoubtedly one of the two. "I meant more that the gods taking an involvement in my life was hardly beneficial for my general wellbeing. Your protection was, of course, much appreciated. And you did get a *ladyfriend* out of it all, didn't you?"

"Okay, okay. No need to emote all over me." Latham suddenly stopped, turning around to face back the way they had just come. "I'm sure you all are just coming this way as a coincidence, right?" he bellowed down the street. There was a pause, as if the mass of bodies trailing them were momentarily stunned by the power of the giant's voice, then people started to, slowly, pass by them.

Lowe made to continue walking, but Latham reached out and grabbed him, holding him still. "We'll let all these pass by, I think. Can you try to do something about the fucking glow? It'd be easier to move you covertly around Soar without, you know, you acting like a bloody lighthouse."

"Are we being followed?" Lowe asked, trying to twist in Latham's grip and look behind them.

"No idea. I don't have any sort of counterespionage Skills. Temple Warders are more your classic 'punch you in the face, ask questions later' builds. But it never hurts to make them think you might do, though."

"The 'them' being…?"

"No fucking idea. But there's been three murders and a disappearance at Grackle Nuroon's museum, and you're insisting on sticking your beak in. I don't think I'm going to go out on a limb by assuming you're being followed. Which, coincidentally, is much easier to do with you flashing gold. Sort it out, little man." Latham raised his voice again and pointed, entirely randomly, back up the street. "Come on, hurry up! I fucking see you skulking back there!"

Lowe left Latham to his intimidation of random commuters and focused on the notifications that had sprung up around his new Skill. He wasn't sure what was making him reluctant to choose one of the three options to evolve *Mental Fortress*.

Any of them would be a significant improvement and, after Latham's advice, he felt sure that the third was the most obvious thing to select. However, Lowe was bothered by the Temple Warder's commentary around the coincidental nature of the way these upgrades had come about.

Before the loss of his Class, Skills had come thick and fast to Lowe. He knew there might be a bit of rose-tinted glasses thinking going on, but looking back, it had felt like barely a week had passed without him passing some Threshold or other or picking up a useful reward for a well-done job. Indeed, he had been so overloaded with abilities that, when they were taken from him, he was sure there were a few he'd never actually used.

Thus, the experience of suddenly developing new Skills was - rather than an alien feeling - rather like coming home. Latham's advice that his good fortune might be all part of a plot he had become swept up into was profoundly disappointing. He knew it was a silly reaction, but - just for a little while - it had felt like he was back to business as usual.

But no, Latham had punctured that dream. It seemed Lowe was back to being a pawn, and someone was throwing baubles his way to make him more useful in whatever game they were playing.

And it wasn't a role he was interested in taking up.

He was not, he realised, going to pick an upgrade. At least, not yet. Fuck his hidden benefactor. The only time any of the powers-that-be in Soar wanted anything to do with him was when they planned on making his life harder than it needed to be.

So, no, he wasn't going to do what they wanted. But he did need to stop the glowing that indicated he had recently Skilled up. Latham was right; it was pretty noticeable.

*Do you wish to proceed?*

"No. Not yet. Can I pause the upgrade?" Lowe hazarded, feeling a touch foolish for speaking aloud to an unseen presence.

There was a pause.

*Upgrade to Skill: Mental Fortress is to be rejected?*

"No. Well, I'm not sure. Maybe. I just don't want to do it yet."

*Confirm rejection of upgrade to Skill: Mental Fortress?*

Well, no one could accuse his notification of lacking a single-minded focus. "What would happen if I rejected the upgrade?"

"Just in case you were wondering, the addition of 'talking to yourself like a loon' is adding to your noticeability quotient," Latham growled. "Any chance you could pick a lane?"

"Hang on, I'm trying to sort out the glowing!"

*Restriction Breaker Title active. Redistribution of Skill: Mental Fortress upgrade possible. Do you wish to proceed?*

"Latham? It's letting me 'redistribute' the upgrade rather than accepting one of those three options. Should I go for it?"

"Little man, I have no idea what 'it' is, much less what 'redistribution' might mean. Why, what are you thinking?"

"Not sure I am."

For several long moments, Lowe hesitated. There was being an independent maverick, refusing help from shadowy sources, and then there was not only looking a gift horse in the mouth but climbing all the way down its throat and setting up home in its stomach.

Somebody wanted to give him a shiny evolution to *Mental Fortress*, and he was planning to not only reject it but also strip it down for parts? That seemed a tad ungrateful, no?

But, then again, no one asked him if he wanted it in the first place.

"Yes, I wish to proceed."

This led to a flurry of activity in his notifications

Upgrade to Skill: Mental Fortress rejected. Boost of equivalent gains to focus on both primary and secondary attributes active:

1. Primary Attributes:
- **+30 Intelligence** (Mental prowess in resisting mental manipulation ties to Intelligence, so this boost emphasises mental sharpness)
- **+20 Wisdom** (Wisdom governs decision-making, insight, and understanding—attributes linked to resisting mental influence)
2. Secondary Attributes:
- **+25 Willpower** (Increases resistance to mental and emotional attacks directly)
- **+15 Perception** (Enhancing awareness of surroundings, which indirectly aids in resisting manipulative influences)
3. Special Stat Buffs:
- +5 Luck

Lowe staggered as the change took place. Latham reached out and steadied him. "Well, the glowing has stopped. You did it then?"

"I think so."

"Fuck me. I hope it was worth it!"

Lowe shared his stat screen with the Temple Warder

**Name:** *Jana Lowe*

*Level: 25*

*Class: ***Removed****

*Primary Attributes:*

MALORY

- *Strength: 120*
- *Dexterity: 90*
- *Intelligence: 295 (+30)*
- *Wisdom: 238 (+20)*
- *Charisma: 60*
- *Constitution: 75*
*Secondary Attributes:*
- *Perception: 95 (+15)*
- *Willpower: 99 (+25)*
- *Luck:** 63 (+5)*

**Health Points** (HP): 1150 - *Regeneration Rate: 2 HP/min (natural); 15 HP/sec (via Roll with the Punches)*

**Mana Points** (MP): 400 - *Regeneration Rate: 1 MP/min (natural); 2 MP/min when Mana falls below 10%*

**Stamina Points** (SP): 550 - *Regeneration Rate:** 5 SP/min*
*Skills:*

*1. Roll with the Punches (Passive) - Rare - Level 32*
*Converts 10 MP to heal 15 HP per second.*
*- Activation depletes 5% of the maximum mana pool.*
*- Cooldown: None.*

*2. Grid View (Active) - Rare - Level 27*
*Records events with perfect recall of details.*
*- Mana Cost: 50% of total MP.*
*- Cooldown: None.*

*3. Slugger (Active) - Rare - Level 23*
*Next melee attack deals triple damage.*
*- Cooldown: 10 minutes.*

*4. Medic! (Active) - Rare - Level 12*
*Heal a companion at a 2:1 MP to HP ratio.*
*- Cooldown: None.*

*5. Mental Fortress (Passive) - Legendary - Level 50 (Rank Up Rejected - balanced stat bonuses granted in place of upgrade.)*

- *Grants heightened resistance to mental manipulation and emotional attacks.*
- *Mana Cost: 10% MP cost each successful defence*

**** Skill slots 4 and upwards are blocked as per Council decree ****

Latham whistled. "Yeah, that'll do, little man. That'll do."

# CHAPTER TWENTY SEVEN – WHAT THEY LEFT BEHIND

It turned out that having a glowering Temple Warder standing behind you when you were conducting interviews significantly increased the quality of answers museum employees were prepared to give.

Whereas before, there had been a sullen, resentful taciturnity in response to his questions, the various Curators, Gallery Attendants, and Conservation Technicians Lowe reinterviewed now had all manner of observations to offer.

None of it was especially helpful to his investigation, but at least they had opened up somewhat.

"What can I say, little man? I'm a nice guy. People instinctively feel the need to tell me things."

Lowe wasn't sure about that. Although it might well have been the Warder's winning personality loosening tongues a touch, he wasn't sure that told the whole story. Or maybe it was the Warder's habit of drawing his sword and looking at it affectionately when there was some hesitancy in their answers.

Either way, his presence was proving to be effective. The Warder's narrowed eyes could sweet-talk a confession out of a rock if it didn't crack from the pressure first.

When they had returned to Soar Museum, Lowe had passed off Latham's presence as a "consultant" to the disinterested Level 14 Unaffiliated Security at the front gate. Mind you, as the spotty youth manning the post didn't even lift his head from his scroll, Lowe didn't think the subterfuge was worth it.

He thought the lad barely looked old enough to be trusted with a whetstone, let alone security for an entire museum. He would have expected—three murders and a vanishing in—there would be a ramping up of protective measures. Maybe a ward or two, at least an angry guard dog with a taste for intruders. Instead, they were greeted with a wave so indifferent it could have been a light breeze.

Lowe wasn't sure if that lack of concern was a good sign.

Perhaps Nuroon had nothing to hide, or maybe it was just another display of the Director's overbearing arrogance. A man with too much to hide often compensates by acting like there's nothing to find. That's the thing about arrogant men—they always think they're clever enough to keep everyone else in the dark.

Three bells of interviews later, Lowe was feeling the weight of tedium pressing down on him.

As helpful as the museum employees were now being, none of what they had to tell him was particularly useful. And under Latham's glare, they were now enthusiastic in their unhelpfulness, a feat of human nature Lowe had never quite appreciated until this moment.

Fear was a fantastic motivator, but it didn't necessarily improve quality.

Lowe had been interested in testing his newly allocated stat boosts—nothing like a murder investigation to put those to use—but so far, nothing glaringly new had popped up.

It was all the same script: "We don't know anything. We saw nothing. It must've been Martha Culloden." It was like being trapped in a room with a malfunctioning echo charm.

If any of them had thoughts as to why a hitherto meek and mild Senior Preservationist - a middle-aged woman with no history of serial sociopathy - had suddenly gone off on a whole-scale slaughter-fest, none of them felt able to offer it.

"What about Harker? Did he seem off the night he died?" Lowe asked, for the umpteenth time, over and over again, hoping for a shift in the wind.

"No, sir, Curator Harker seemed his usual self," came the predictable, dreary replies, multiplied across a variety of faces as dull as their answers.

When the last of the scheduled interviewees had left, Lowe had turned to the Warder. "They must save their creativity for exhibit displays. Sounds like Nuroon has them well drilled."

Latham gave a smile at that. "Short of asking them outright if they thought Harker might have known his murderer, you couldn't have put it much plainer. They had every opportunity to offer alternative theories, but they seem pretty settled that this woman is the big bad. They don't know why, of course, but they seem happy to throw her - on mass - to the sharks. No one who works here has got ideas of their own?"

"At least they're consistent with the various timelines," Lowe said. "I don't for a moment believe Martha Culloden is behind all this, but... well, all the evidence does suggest she's the most likely suspect. And she's been off grid ever since—during which time someone whacked Kregg. It's not going to be easy to convince anyone she isn't at the heart of this. Especially now she's gone missing herself. Convenient, really."

"Convenience doesn't murder people," Latham replied. "But it sure makes for an easy case for the powers-that-be to wrap everything up nice and tight. Nothing to see here. Just a little workplace snafu. Still, it's odd. No one here's even remotely interested in why the blasted woman might have gone on a killing spree. Most folk who go around massacring their colleagues at least have some sort of personal vendetta to work out. Here, they're shrugging it off like it's a blip in payroll. And why necrotic slime? There are easier ways to earn XP if that's what is at the heart of it all. And why wipe out Kregg *after* the other two?"

Lowe leaned back in his chair, frowning at the thought. "I'm sure someone here must know more than they're saying, but with the memory wipe around the events that led to Isadora's death and the way everyone's closed ranks around Harker's death, it's like we're looking at shadows on a foggy night. If it weren't for Preece and Levick hinting that something more is happening, I'd think we needed to close the whole thing down. And I'm not sure their motives in speaking to me are all that pure, either."

Latham raised an eyebrow. "So, we're chasing ghosts again, are we?"

Lowe smiled at the big man's use of 'we' in that sentence. He hadn't realised how much he had missed having the Temple Warder about to bounce ideas off. Throughout his career, he'd never put too much truck with working with partners, but he was beginning to see the point.

And it wasn't just not having to worry that someone was going to randomly kick his arse. It was nice to be able to speak aloud and have someone answer. "Not ghosts, exactly," he replied, "but I'm certainly wondering how much the missing Dreadnaught might be involved."

Lowe stood and began pacing the small room, pulling threads and snatches of statements from *Grid View* as he did so. He felt doing this was a little easier since his upgrades. It still wasn't quite to the level of insight he was able to reach before his Classtration, but he was definitely within touching distance. A broad smile broke out on his face at that thought. Yeah, fuck you, Council of grey faces. How do you like me now?

"Okay. Let's break this all down a little. We've got three deaths, but something is telling me the first is the key. Considering all the upgrades I've recently had, I'm comfortable going with my gut here. The death of Isadora is the only one anyone has tried to do anything to properly hide. The night she vanished, Harker was left as a blob of rotting flesh in Culloden's office. And then Kregg was murdered in his own room just after he'd spiked me with necrotic slime. Someone wants us to read more into those events than I think is there. Let's put those two aside for the moment. I think we'll need to reconstruct what happened around Curator Isadora's death if we want any hope of shaking something loose about why the later murders were needed. You never know; maybe reconstructing what happened a month back will break through someone's memory wipe. I've heard that such things can happen."

"Well, with that boost to your Luck, little man, you never know."

Lowe grinned again, though it was a touch thin this time.

He'd rather not rely on Luck to solve murder cases. If he had little trust for gods, he had even less for a stat that seemed to have little or no impact on his daily existence. "We can start with what Wyst pulled together about the day the sarcophagus was opened, along with Lant's notes on the injuries to the girl. It's not exactly an ideal way to reconstruct a scene, but it's a start."

"Hey, as long as you don't end up with another corpse to add to the exhibit, I suppose it'll be worth it."

Latham opened the door for Lowe, checking the corridor beyond.

It was empty. The museum was quiet in a way that only places filled with the past can be—echoing with the silence of things long gone. And maybe, just maybe, the sound of someone preparing their next step to keep their crimes hidden from notice.

"This bloody place does seem to be touched with ill luck," Latham added, "but I doubt the killer will have another go while we're around."

That, as it turned out, was a remarkably unprophetic remark.

# CHAPTER TWENTY EIGHT – SILENT WITNESSES

Karolen tilted her head, trying—yet again—to get a read on the somewhat crumpled man issuing orders in front of her.

In the unforgiving light of the earning morning sun, Lowe had the look of a man who had lived too many lives on too little sleep. He seemed to generate his own cloud of weariness, like he'd been born tired and just kept going out of sheer spite.

And, beyond that, he just looked liked he needed a good wash.

Arebella always maintained that her boyfriend had "hidden depths," but Karolen had never seen it. Maybe it was because Arebella had a soft spot for men who looked like they might collapse under the weight of their melancholy, or perhaps it was a quirk of her friend's unending optimism.

After all, this was the same Arebella who had once believed in the redeeming qualities of a Necromancer with "a lovely smile." For someone with a Class that could see unfailingly to the truth, her friend had terrible taste in men.

Ever since their first day together at school, Arebella had the reputation of taking home every waif and stray she'd encountered, like a walking Guild for Broken People. Their little friendship group had hoped she'd eventually outgrow it before getting her heartbroken. However, she'd graduated from lost kittens and birds with broken wings to full-grown men who seemed to attract trouble like flies to honey—case in point: Jana Lowe.

"And this was how it looked when you came into the Great Hall, was it?" Lowe said, turning to face her, eyebrows raised like punctuation marks at the end of a question he wasn't sure he believed.

Karolen didn't immediately answer. Not because she didn't know what to say—oh, she had plenty to say—but because she was currently weighing the merits of slapping him versus just walking out and pretending this whole charade was not happening.

For one, her firm was less than thrilled she'd been pulled off her latest assignment to attend this little farce. Reliving a scene that had been, to say the least, a professional embarrassment wasn't high on her list of things to do today.

Actually, it wasn't even on the list.

It wasn't anywhere near the list.

It was somewhere far beyond the horizon of lists, in the dark realm of "things best forgotten."

Whilst none of the Partners had been gauche enough to outright suggest accusing Director Nuroon of complicity in a massive cover-up was unwise, it was clear the prevailing opinion leaned towards *not accusing one's clients of murder* if it could at all be helped.

They hadn't even let her finish her audit. The excuse? Trauma. Because apparently, when one witnesses something truly horrifying, the best course of action is to shove the inconvenient employee into a quiet corner and hope the problem sorts itself out.

Especially if said witness was a terribly fragile member of the female persuasion.

She'd been patronisingly replaced before she'd even had the chance to file her initial findings. As if that wasn't insult enough, the Museum's accounts had been accepted without alteration, and no further audit was scheduled.

To top it all off, Liando Verlan had blocked her Sending Stone. When the Chair of the Museum Trustees starts ghosting you, it's a fairly solid sign that everyone involved wants to forget the whole sordid affair. It was the kind of thing that would give anyone the urge to throw in the towel—or, in Karolen's case, the urge to throw a punch at a childhood friend's reignited flame.

So yes, she felt quite justified in not immediately answering Lowe's question. She had a rapidly growing suspicion that whatever Lowe was up to here, it wasn't going to end well for her.

Or anyone, for that matter.

"Auditor Mehin?" Lowe prompted, his voice dry enough to suck the moisture from the air.

Karloen triggered one of her memory skills, pulling up a mental image of the layout of the Great Hall as it had been that day. The problem with memory skills, though, is they're often too accurate. Every detail was etched in her mind: the smell of ancient stone, the cold draft that never quite left the room, the eerie silence just before everything went wrong.

As the only person present who hadn't wiped their memory, she could understand why Arebella's boyfriend had insisted she be here. But that didn't mean she had to like it. Not at all.

She scanned the room, her eyes flicking to the older man standing next to a sarcophagus, flanked by two Security Service personnel playing the parts of the dead Curators. Although now she thought of it, maybe someone else could be more reliable in their recall . . .

"Not quite," Karloen said, pointing to the sarcophagus lid suspended in the air, covered in ropes that looked a bit too flimsy for the job. In fact, the whole thing looked more like an elaborate prank than a reenactment of a tragedy. "That wasn't like that when we arrived. The Curators had only just broken the seal."

Lowe frowned and turned to Felicitous Gral, performing the dual position of legal advisor and stand-in Grackle Nuroon in today's "charade," as the Director had called it earlier.

Gral, true to form, was managing to play both roles with the minimum amount of effort.

If there was a Threshold reward for looking bored while being professionally insufferable, Gral would've had more Progress Points than anyone in Soar.

"The report I have says the lid was already in the air when the Director and Auditor Mehin entered the Great Hall," Lowe said.

Gral barely moved, managing to shrug without disturbing even his tie. "I am working from the same report, Inspector. Let me remind you, I was not here. And—the young lady apart—no one who was present can remember what occurred. Whether the lid was already in the air or not seems a peculiarly pointless thing to become hung up on, as it were. Especially as, within moments, it will be crashing to the ground with . . . unfortunate side effects."

"Unfortunate side effects," Karolen said to herself. Right. That's what they were calling it these days. The way Gral said it, you'd think someone had accidentally spilt tea on a carpet rather than . . . well, a violent death.

Lowe frowned and indicated that the lid should be lowered onto the sarcophagus. "This is a reenactment. The whole point is that we actually re-enact what took place, not just live out whatever version of the truth Nuroon sold to his insurers. So, the lid was in place?"

Karolen nodded. "Yes, the, erm, older gentleman there was just prising it open when the Director noticed. The other two Curators were stood on either side. That's when the Director, myself, Bard Kregg, and the Senior Preservationist arrived."

"And where was everyone else?" Lowe asked, pacing as if he wanted to shake the truth out of someone. Anyone.

Karolen closed her eyes, getting a sense of the room as it had been. Unlike what she understood from Arebella about Lowe's *Grid View*, she didn't have an instant visual recall of events, but more of a spatial awareness, a sense of how resources had been allocated. "Most of the others here were on the outskirts of the Hall. They were not really paying attention to the exhibit. At least, not until the Director began shouting."

"A rather loaded term, my dear," Gral interrupted, clearing his throat in an expensive way. "I think it would be better to note that the Director was eager to ensure Health and Safety protocols were followed. Indeed, had Director Nuroon arrived earlier, any loss of life might likely have been avoided."

"Even though the lid was down and only raised in his presence?" Lowe asked, eyes sparkling mischievously for the first time that morning. In that, Karolen caught a glimmer of wit there, the kind that made her understand what Arebella saw in him.

Gral smiled thinly in response. "A minor detail, Inspector."

"Okay," Lowe clapped his hands together, shooing the various Curators to the edges of the Hall like a ringmaster herding reluctant circus animals. "So, this is the scene. We have you three attempting to open the sarcophagus, no one else is particularly interested, and then the big cheeses enter on their grand tour. What happened next?"

"The Director was... unhappy to see the seal being broken."

"Without appropriate safety procedures in place, no doubt," Gral muttered, more to himself than anyone else.

For some reason, the lawyer's tone rubbed Karolen the wrong way, irritating her into saying more than she'd planned. "Actually, after his initial anger, he seemed more interested than annoyed. After bawling out the three Curators, he wanted to see what they'd found. That was when the other woman—"

"Senior Preservationist Culloden, who is currently on the run from the Security Services on suspicion of the murder of Curator Harker and Public Relations Bard Kregg?" Gral asked, his tone mild, almost bored.

"Yes. Her. Well, she used a Skill to raise the lid, at which stage the ropes were used to secure it."

"Oh. Martha Culloden raised the stone, did she?" Gral raised an eyebrow. "Well, that is most interesting. Inspector, do you not find it intriguing that a woman now suspected of two murders was the one who raised the stone? A stone which, I should remind you, would soon crash down and crush a poor Curator to her death. This doesn't sound like an accident to me."

Lowe's frown deepened, clearly unimpressed with Gral's theatrics. "Perhaps, but—"

"And," Gral continued as though Lowe hadn't spoken, "was it not the Senior Preservationist who insisted all museum employees wipe their memories via *Clean the Canvas*, Ms Mehin?"

Karolen bit back her annoyance at his failure to use her title. "Yes, she was the one who told the Curators it was expected, but she was only delivering the Director's orders."

"Although, of course, we only have her word for that, don't we?" Gral's smile was infuriatingly smug. "You didn't hear the Director tell her that, did you?"

Karolen shook her head slightly, wishing she could disappear into the floor.

"My apologies for belabouring the point, Ms Mehin," Gral pressed on, "but can you confirm that it was Martha Culloden whose Skill raised the sarcophagus stone, that she ordered Curator Isadora to climb inside, shortly before—what?—her Skill failed, bringing the lid crashing down on the poor girl, and then commanded all museum employees to wipe their memories to cover up her crime?"

It was at this point Karolen lost her temper. "I think you're forgetting the part where the girl was melted to death before the lid fell!"

Things were quiet for a bit after that.

# CHAPTER TWENTY NINE – WHAT THE ARMOUR CONSUMES

Lowe didn't know why, but he'd never quite hit it off with any of Arebella's friends.

Well, that wasn't strictly true.

He knew precisely why that was.

It was because every single one of them terrified the life out of him, and it made him appallingly awkward in their company. There was probably a moment in his life—back when he was young and foolish—when he hadn't been utterly intimidated by smart, independent, competent women.

But if there was, it was long gone, buried under layers of insecurity and whatever passed for his personality these days. He sensed he could search his *Grid View* for the rest of his life but still never found it.

Karolen wasn't quite the scariest of the pack—at least she'd acknowledged his existence since his Classtration—but even if he hadn't known the devastating carnage a pissed-off Auditor was capable of, he still wouldn't have chosen to further involve her in this mess.

Still, as Latham had pointed out, she was literally the only person with any memory of what had occurred when Curator Isadora had met her untimely end. So, reluctantly, Lowe had called in a few favours—he preferred to think of it that way, rather than admitting he'd asked his girlfriend to help him out—and had thus found himself met by a very irate Auditor at the gates of Soar Museum on this bright and shining morning.

However, now, standing in the chilly, echoing expanse of the Great Hall, Lowe was glad he had.

For his part, Gral seemed determined to turn Karolen's outburst into some kind of intellectual sparring match. He raised an eyebrow, giving her a look one might reserve for someone who had just announced they believed in unicorns.

"I know that's what you *think* you saw, my dear," Gral continued, "but all the formal reports I have read on the event make it very clear that the poor girl was crushed to death rather than . . . anything more fanciful, so let's stay within the realms of reality if we can."

"Are you calling me a liar?" Karolen said back.

"No, not at all." Gral's best condescending smile stretched once again across his face. "I merely think the trauma of the event has exacerbated matters in your mind. Memory is a tricky thing, as I'm sure you're well aware. I've read several studies that suggest high-stress situations can—"

"—distort the perception of reality? Right, because, of course, us silly little girls tend to overreact in high-stress situations!"

Lowe winced. He didn't know how Gral was managing it, but he seemed to have a supernatural talent for saying precisely the wrong thing at exactly the worst moment. So much so, Lowe was starting to wonder if he might not be doing it on purpose.

There were surely easier ways to sabotage this re-enactment than annoying an Auditor primed to explode.

Gral continued in using his conversational shovel. "I would never imply such a thing, Ms. Mehin. I'm merely suggesting that we consider the possibility that your recollection may not align perfectly with the facts." He glanced towards Preece, who was standing awkwardly by the sarcophagus, trying very hard to blend into the background. "After all, no one else present remembers the event."

Karolen's eyes flashed at that. "No one else remembers the event because *someone* had everyone wipe their memories. Convenient, isn't it? Let's all just forget the part where a young woman was melted alive before the stone fell on her."

"Melted. Hmmm," Gral said, moving the word around in his mouth as if it tasted bitter. "That's an exceptionally colourful description, my dear, but not one supported by the official autopsy conducted by Deathcaller Lant."

Lowe felt the tension crackle like an Elemental Mage at a light show. Karolen wasn't just angry—she was livid, and Gral's dismissive manner was exacerbating things. "So, it is your opinion that I am being hysterical, and my memory is incorrect?"

"It is your contention that the Curator was melted. Now, if we explore that, it is an intriguing word choice. Are you talking about some form of magical reaction? Or perhaps—"

"You weren't there. You didn't see it!"

"And neither did anyone else, Ms Mehin. Thus, I am inclined to trust the evidence rather than one angry young lady's opinion."

Preece cleared his throat softly. It was a sound that should have barely registered in the Hall, but it caught everyone's attention. All eyes turned his way, making the poor man blush and look like he wanted to crawl into the sarcophagus and pull the lid over himself.

Lowe couldn't blame him. If the Auditor got any angrier, he'd be looking to join him.

"She's telling the truth."

Gral rolled his eyes and sighed theatrically. "I am sure we all appreciate the chivalry, sir, but how can you possibly know that?"

I . . . I didn't wipe my memory," Preece's voice was quiet, and yet was strong enough for everyone to hear it. There was a pause, long and heavy, like the moment before a thunderstorm breaks.

"I knew it!" Karolen's voice raised several octaves. Gral, for once, said nothing, though Lowe could see the faintest flicker of surprise on the lawyer's face.

"I . . . I didn't wipe my memory," Preece repeated, a little louder this time, as if he needed to convince himself as much as the others. "I was supposed to. Everyone was supposed to. Ms Culloden made sure of that, had the mana potions in place and everything. But I didn't go through with it."

Lowe could almost feel the cogs turning in his head. This was big. Huge. It immediately justified all the shit he was sure Nuroon was going to have flung his way for going ahead with this re-enactment. The fact that there was someone else who had managed to avoid the memory wipe, who had info on the first death changed everything.

"Why not?" he asked, careful not to spook the older man.

Preece shifted nervously, clearly uncomfortable with the attention, but pushed forward anyway. "Because . . . because I knew something was wrong. I couldn't bring myself to forget. Not when . . . not after what I saw."

Lowe watched Karolen's expression shift as she stepped towards Preece, her posture slightly softening as if coaxing him to reveal more. "And what exactly did you see?" she asked quietly.

The Curator hesitated, his gaze flicking between Lowe, Karolen, and Gral, before settling back on Karolen. "I . . . I saw Isadora. I saw what happened to her before the stone fell."

Gral seemed to realise the importance of the moment, standing up straighter, his previously smug expression tinged with alarm.

"And?" Karolen pressed gently, her eyes locked on Preece. "What did you see?" Lowe had a moment of annoyance that she seemed to be leading the questioning but then decided to get over himself. Who did it matter was the one to get the information.

Preece swallowed hard, his voice barely above a whisper. "She was . . . she was eaten alive."

Lowe couldn't help himself. "And did you see what ate her?"

Preece's face paled. He opened his mouth as if to speak, but no sound came out.

Gral seized the moment to try to get control of the conversation. "This is all very interesting, Mr. Preece. But, if I may, this all seems very convenient. If what you say is true, why didn't you come forward with this information sooner? Why wait until now to make this revelation?"

Preece's gaze flicked to Gral, and for the first time, Lowe saw something else in his expression—guilt. "I didn't want to remember," Preece admitted. "But then I found that I couldn't forget."

The confession hung in the air like the heavy scent of something rotten, and Lowe didn't miss the flicker of fear that darted through the man's eyes.

It wasn't just that he hadn't wiped his memory—there was something more, something worse, that he was holding back. Lowe could feel it in the way the man's voice trembled, the way he couldn't quite look anyone in the eye for more than a second.

Whatever Preece had witnessed that day was still clawing at him from the inside. He needed to get this off his chest.

"Mr. Preece," Gral said, the words oozing out of him. "You say you didn't want to remember, yet you chose not to go through with the wipe. That's a rather significant decision to make, don't you think? And one that is not very consistent. Especially given the . . . pressures of the situation. Come now, what exactly did you see? You said the poor girl was 'eaten', but if this is true, we need specifics. What caused it? What did you witness that was so horrific you felt compelled to keep your memory intact? Or are you just seeking a little attention for yourself in the middle of this debacle?"

Preece shifted, his discomfort palpable, but Karolen stepped forward.

She knew how to read people—how to find a way to get them talking—and she wasn't about to let Gral bully the Curator into silence. Whatever Preece had seen, it was more than just Isadora's death. She triggered a Skill that kept its target calm. This was always useful during especially difficult audits. "Curator, you don't have to protect anyone anymore. If you know something, it's time to tell us. You saw what happened to Isadora before the stone fell. What caused it?"

Preece looked at her, then at Lowe, his eyes pleading for some kind of escape. But there was no way out. Not now.

"It was . . . it was the armour."

Lowe's breath caught in his throat.

Armour?

That was new. His *Grid View* flickered, trying to make sense of the new information, but the connections didn't align. No one had mentioned anything about armour in any of his hours of interviews. "What armour?"

"The sarcophagus . . . the first one we opened. The one from earlier in the day? It wasn't empty. Martha was sure we'd find the same thing in the second if we looked. She pushed us to move, opening it up to the top of the schedule. I don't think she told the Director, though."

Lowe's pulse quickened, but it was the Auditor who spoke first. "What was inside?"

Preece looked at the floor, his voice shaking. "A Dreadnaught's armour."

Gral's expression hardened, obviously wishing the Director was here to deal with these revelations. "You're saying that you and these other Curators, the ones that have died, opened a sarcophagus containing the armour of a Dreadnaught? And it was awake?"

Preece shook his head. "No, the first one, the one in the sarcophagus we opened in the morning, was stable. It was moved somewhere, but I don't know where. And we didn't know what it was at first. It was Martha . . . Senior Preservationist Culloden who told us it was important. She was very excited."

"And the Curator who died?" Lowe's voice was sharp, cutting through the rising dread in the room. "What happened to her?"

Preece's face creased, the memory clearly still raw. "She got into the sarcophagus and touched it. Martha warned us in the morning not to make contact with it; to assess its condition without waking it. But the moment Isadora made contact, something happened. The armour... reacted. It expanded, covering her in some sort of slime and began feeding."

"So, Isadora didn't die from the stone falling on her. She was already dead before that?" There was a sense of finality to Karolen's voice.

Lowe thought it sounded a little bit like vindication.

"The stone falling . . . it was just a coincidence. Or it was Kregg who did it. He was the one who kept going on and on about the blasted stone. But Isadora was dead long before it crushed her. The armour . . . it killed her the moment she touched it. It ate her. And then it vanished."

Lowe felt a shiver run down his spine. All this time, they had been operating under the assumption that Isadora's death was the result of an accident, a tragic miscalculation. But now, the truth was coming to light, and it was fucking dark.

"And what about Harker?" he asked. "Do you know what happened to him? What about Kregg? Do you know where Martha Culloden is?"

But Preece was shaking his head. "Harker was worried about something after Isadora died. But I don't know what happened to him. It could have been the armour, I suppose."

Gral's voice broke the silence, his smugness replaced by something more measured. "Mr Preece, for absolute clarity, are you suggesting that Martha Culloden was aware of the presence of the armour before you and your colleagues opened the first sarcophagus?"

Preece hesitated, then nodded slowly. "Yes. She knew. She knew exactly what they were. She . . . she didn't tell us, but I could tell. She was excited. She wanted us to wake them up."

Lowe exchanged a glance with Karolen. This wasn't just about some museum exhibit gone wrong. However, before he could speak, they were interrupted by a distant rumble echoing through the museum. It was low, almost imperceptible, but it sent a chill down his spine.

"What the hell was that?" he asked, his voice tight with apprehension.

Karolen's gaze shifted, her eyes narrowing. "No idea. But we need to find out."

# CHAPTER THIRTY – CONTROL THE PIECES, IGNORE THE NOISE

Grackle Nuroon sat behind his desk, fingers drumming on the worn leather armrest.

His office was lit only by the cold morning light filtering through narrow windows, but the darkness did little to improve his mood. He scowled, his fingers still tapping, each beat thrumming into the darker corners of the room.

He was bristling with irritation at so many different people that he was struggling to find an appropriate outlet for his rage. Faces moved in and out of focus in his mind like a roulette wheel of wrath.

Liando Verlan.

Yeah, that name made his anger flare. The Chair of Trustees had become too bold of late, pushing him, testing the limits of his forbearance. Her desire to displace him had been apparent for the years she'd circled him.

But she'd miscalculated with that damn audit.

His smirk came and then it was gone. Like an assassin's blade in the press of a busy street. Had Verlan really thought she'd be rid of him with such a simple gambit? That sending an Auditor would cause his grip on things to unravel?

To be scrupulously fair, Karolen Mehin was smart - might even be as smart as Nuroon himself, he thought - but circumstances had not been in her favour.

Another person might have thought twice about describing the horrific death of a woman in his employ as 'circumstances', but Grackle Nuroon had long since let such niceties ooze away from his personality.

And when the Auditor had overplayed her hand— all but accusing him of complicity in that Curator's death - she'd neutralised herself.

That was Verlan's fundamental mistake. She thought she could defeat him on the field of his own domain. That she could use 'process' to erode his authority. She had underestimated the strength of his position and his senior team's loyalty—if not out of respect, then out of fear.

Now?

Well, sources told him that Verlan's power base amongst the Trustees was crumbling. She could hide behind perfect smiles, manicured fingers and bouffant hair, but the fatal damage was done. It was just a matter of time before the inevitable confidence vote, and then he'd be rid of her.

His sixth Chair of Trustees. He wondered if there was some sort of reward for that.

He assumed not.

Nuroon shifted in his chair. He'd won that little war, and yet the pleasure of seeing that bitch falter did nothing to soften the dark knot of anger in his gut.

This was his museum.

His!

He'd built it, piece by piece, clawing his way through decades of bureaucratic infighting, navigating the endless sea of backstabbing academics and pretentious Trustees. And now it was all his—every inch of it. Every whisper in its halls, every brick in its walls and - and this, right now, was the most important thing to him - every artefact stored behind glass cases.

And yet, here he still was, battling the likes of Liando fucking Verlan and her simpering sycophants. It was almost beneath him.

Almost, but not quite.

The roulette of rage span, and the tapping of his fingers ceased, replaced by a slow, deliberate tightening of his grip on the armrest. His knuckles whitened as his mind shifted to that smug bastard, Inspector Lowe.

If there was one thing Nuroon hated more than scheming Trustees - and, to be clear, there were certainly more than just one - it was interference from the Security Services.

Nuroon had thought he was free and clear once he'd gotten his claws into Inspector Wyst. That old fool had backed away from the case faster than the Director could say, 'Do you like how many fingers your wife has?' But this new man? Lowe? There was nothing Nuroon despised more than righteous men—they were the hardest to corrupt, and even harder to get rid of.

The second round of murders had brought Lowe here, of course.

Unavoidable.

The stink of death tended to attract his kind, like flies to a corpse. Nuroon could almost laugh at the thought. The murders were a mess—an annoyance, more than anything—a distraction from his actual work. But what did it matter? Dead Curators and missing Preservationists were hardly worth losing sleep over. They were replaceable. Names on a ledger, dust in the wind.

And as for Kregg . . . Nuroon's lip curled.

Well, he was perhaps more of a loss.

He'd hated the man from the moment they'd met. Smarmy, lecherous, always whispering in the ears of anyone who would listen. The Public Relations Bard was a predator, and Nuroon knew it. He'd known it for years, heard the rumours, seen the too-familiar smiles Kregg threw at the young, naïve museum staff. But there was no doubt that Kregg had been useful. He had a way with words, connections, and an ability to spin even the worst disasters into something palatable. And that was all that had mattered.

Until now.

Kregg's death left a hole in his operations, and that, at this precise moment, was . . . irritating. The man had been a useful shield, and Nuroon didn't like feeling exposed. He wouldn't admit it, not even to himself, but there was a part of him that felt uneasy without the Bard's silver tongue to smooth things over. People were watching, waiting for him to falter.

Kregg had been a buffer.

He exhaled slowly, letting the frustration simmer. There was no use in mourning a man he hated. The real problem was Lowe. The longer the detective and his team stayed in the museum, the more likely they were to stumble onto something . . . inconvenient.

His fingers twitched, and he summoned one of his Skills. A faint shimmer passed through the air, barely noticeable. A subtle thing. *Listening Post.* The whispers drifted toward him, swirling around his head like ghosts—voices from the corridors, from rooms he couldn't see.

"…Lowe's pushing… something about the sarcophagus…"

The words slithered into his ears, half-formed and disjointed. Nuroon narrowed his eyes. Always with that sarcophagus. He wished he'd followed his considerable instincts and told Culloden to leave those two stone coffins in the collapsed dungeon.

Nothing good had come of their extraction.

He closed his fist, and the whispers vanished. Lowe was a problem. One that needed to be solved. He wasn't the kind of man who could be easily bought off or scared away. That much was clear. And the problem with men like Lowe was that they didn't know when to quit. They came in, Skills blazing, waving around their principles and their morals, thinking they could untangle the truth with enough grit and determination.

Nuroon sneered. *Truth.* A luxury for people who didn't have real power. And he knew all about that. It was about control. Control of the narrative, control of the people who mattered, and most of all, control of the pieces on the board.

He'd built his career on that understanding. You didn't have to be the strongest or the smartest—just the one who knew how to move the pieces. And he'd moved plenty over the years. Trustees, donors, politicians . . . they were all just pieces. Some were useful, some weren't. When they outlived their usefulness, he replaced them. It was that simple.

It had always been that simple.

He grimaced, leaning forward slightly as a twinge of pain shot through his lower back.

His body, like everything else, was betraying him. Slowly. Painfully. It was an insult, really. To have climbed so high, only to be dragged down by the wear and tear of age. He could still feel the sharp ache in his knees from standing too long at the last Trustee meeting, where Verlan had pretended to play nice after her audit attempt had crumbled.

She had simpered, smiled, shaken hands like nothing had happened. But Nuroon had seen the look in her eyes, the frustration barely masked beneath her perfect makeup.

The other Trustees were starting to murmur. They hadn't said anything directly—yet—but he could sense it. Smell it, like rot beneath fresh paint. They'd all been too polite, too distant, as if they were giving him space to clean up the mess. And when the time came, when the pressure built up just enough, they'd come for him. They always did.

The trick was making sure they never had the chance.

Nuroon let out a slow breath, his eyes narrowing. He'd have to move fast. He'd need a replacement for Kregg, someone who could keep the lid on the whole affair while the dust settled.

And he'd need to deal with Lowe.

His thoughts drifted back to the murders. It wasn't just Kregg, of course. Two others had died, Curators who had worked closely with the absent Senior

Preservationist. Lowe had latched onto that connection, insisting she was the key to the whole mess.

Nuroon didn't buy it.

Culloden was eccentric, obsessive even, but she wasn't a killer. He didn't believe for a second that she had committed the murders, but if blaming her would keep Lowe off his back, then so be it. Culloden wasn't essential to the museum's operations. She was useful, yes, but not irreplaceable. If Lowe needed a scapegoat, Nuroon would let him have it. He had no interest in protecting her.

In fact, there was something almost satisfying about it.

Culloden had pushed him too far over these dungeon artefacts—demanding more resources, more attention for her precious research on the Dreadnaughts. Nuroon had granted her some leeway, but she always wanted more. More time, more funding, more space for her experiments. It was exhausting.

But now, she was a convenient distraction. While Lowe chased after her, Nuroon could focus on securing his own position. Verlan could watch all she wanted; he'd see her crumble before he allowed himself to be pulled down by this.

The slow burn of satisfaction spread through him. Let Lowe run his investigation. Let him sniff around the museum. In the end, he'd come up with nothing but dead ends. And by the time he realised it, it would be too late.

Then, just as Nuroon contemplated his next move, a low rumble echoed through the museum, faint but unmistakable. His eyes flicked toward the door.

The sound was distant, almost imperceptible, but it sent a shiver down his spine. He knew this museum, every inch of it, every sound it made. That noise didn't belong here.

"What in Soar...?" he muttered, the words barely escaping his lips.

He turned, slowly, and the cold, familiar dread settled in his gut. Something was wrong. Very wrong.

# CHAPTER THIRTY ONE – THE SHIFTING OF SOAR

Latham wasn't the type to worry.

His primary function was to ensure the well-being of those in and around the Celestial Temple. Considering most of the occupants of that building were capable of the sort of violence rarely seen outside of a kindergarten classroom during wet play, stoicism was very much his middle name.

Worry didn't enter into it.

Not for a man built like a fortress, loaded with Skills and rocking the most divine of authorities. People liked to joke (not when within punching distance, obviously) that Latham didn't have blood in his veins, just violence that hadn't happened to other people yet.

Nevertheless, something was gnawing at him.

Ever since being put on 'Lowe Watch' during the investigation into the death of Gianna d'Avec, he'd found himself having this small, irritating thorn of unease in his belly. If he didn't know any better, he'd say it was . . . concern for another person.

That was why, rather than being on post at the Temple Gate, Latham found himself loitering in an alley with a good view of Soar Museum.

He'd rather die than admit it to the little man, but he just wanted to make sure the re-enactment had gone okay. Wherever Lowe went, chaos seemed to follow, and once he'd woken up with a sense that something was about to tip over, he couldn't do anything else than take a different path at the Portal Stone to cast his eye over the museum.

And, as so often seemed to be the case, his instincts were spot on. His fingers tightened around the handle of his sword. Something was brewing inside that museum. He didn't know what it was, but he could feel the weight of it pressing down on the city, like the air before a storm.

Then, without warning, the storm broke.

The ground trembled beneath Latham's feet, the stone of the cobbles vibrating with a low, ominous groan. His eyes snapped to the gates of the museum. It wasn't just shaking—it was *changing*. Columns that had stood proudly for decades began to twist, the marble bending and contorting in ways that defied physics. Walls shifted, warping like wax under a flame.

Latham activated every defensive Skill he had as the museum grew, its structure stretching upward, taller and more grotesque with each passing second. He could see the spires elongating, their shapes becoming jagged, unnatural, like claws reaching for the sky.

"By the gods…" Latham whispered, the words barely escaping his lips.

He took a step forward, instinct urging him to charge toward the museum, to do . . . something. But he stopped. What could he do against this? Against a building that was no longer just stone and mortar? It was turning into something dark. Something alive.

Soar Museum had become a Dungeon. And Lowe was still inside.

***

Hel had to admit that she liked nothing more than the freedom of an afternoon flight. Since her... retirement from active service, she had ensured that, whenever she could, she'd drop everything, summon up strands of wind and soar above the city.

Soar above Soar.

That made her giggle uncontrollably, prompting her to drop just a little lower in the sky, where the air was less thin. When she was flying, she felt like she was the eye of a storm; she loved the thrill of the tempest beneath her feet, the raw power surging through the air. Others never appreciated the sheer violence of nature . . . not until she dropped a building on their heads.

But no. That wasn't her anymore. She was trying to go... if not straight, then less epically bloodthirsty. An image of the battered face of Kelvin Kregg appeared in her mind. Well, some of the time. There were just people who deserved a damn good smiting.

Something caught her attention—a ripple of dark energy more violent than even the tempest she was travelling in. Hel dipped lower, eyes locking onto the source. Soar Museum. It wasn't just shaking; it was *bleeding*.

Walls rippled, twisted, and then burst - literally burst - open. A scream of stone and earth tore through the air, deafening even from her altitude. Hel's eyes widened as she watched deep cracks split open the foundations of the building, blood-red light pouring from the gashes. Despite herself, she dipped lower and what she saw made her skin crawl.

Passersby, tourists, museum guards - anyone standing too close - were ripped apart in the building's transformation. The ground beneath their feet buckled, hurling them into the air. A man walking calmly with a scroll in hand was flung like a ragdoll into the air, his limbs snapping in grotesque directions when he landed, before a jagged fissure swallowed his body. The earth chewed him up without hesitation, the cracks widening to gulp down the screams of others nearby.

Hel swooped lower, seeing the carnage unfold. Stone turned to flesh before her eyes, the museum's walls seeming to pulse, as though alive. A woman stumbled back, desperately seeking safety, but her scream was cut short as one of the grotesque spires above her exploded, raining down jagged chunks of masonry and shards of glass that tore through her body like knives. She crumpled in a heap, her blood painting the cobblestones. Down the street, she saw a mother dragging her child away, both of them covered in dust and blood. They didn't make it far. The street buckled, cracking open beneath them, and a slab of stone rose like a jagged tooth, impaling them both in a sickening crunch. Their bodies hung limp, blood streaming down the stone like a macabre fountain.

Hel hovered above it all, watching in horror as the museum transformed into something far more sinister, more alive. The walls groaned and flexed, the spires twisting into jagged, unnatural shapes.

"Just what we needed. A fucking Dungeon in the middle of the city."

***

Pernille Staffen had seen a lot in her years at Cuckoo House. She'd dealt with inspectors, dignitaries, and worse, the paperwork that followed in their wake. But nothing prepared her for the sensation that ran through the building that day.

It started small, a low rumble beneath her feet, like a distant thunderstorm rolling across the plains. She frowned, her teacup rattling gently on the saucer. Not unusual in an old building like Cuckoo House. Old foundations, old stone—sometimes things just shifted.

But then the whole damn place started shaking.

Her tea, tragically abandoned, sloshed over the cup's rim as the photographs on her wall jittered violently, frames clattering against each other. Staffen stood up, cursing a blue streak, and strode to the window, bracing herself against the wall as the shaking intensified.

She pushed open the window and leaned out, scanning the streets below. The city itself looked… normal. Busy, bustling, with people going about their day like the world wasn't on the verge of collapse.

Knowing in her heart that Jana fucking Lowe was at the heart of whatever was going on, she triggered her *Interfering Bitch* Skill - her god really didn't waste time on flowery names for his gifts - and zoomed her vision in on the heart of the chaos.

Soar Museum, the grand old structure that had stood for so long, was shifting, twisting in ways no building should. Its stone rippled like water, the spires bent and cracked, and the entire structure seemed to *grow*, its shadow stretching over the surrounding streets. It was wrong, deeply, profoundly wrong, and it sent a shiver down her spine.

"Oh, for the love of—" Staffen muttered, rubbing her temples. "Bloody Jana Lowe."

She turned away from the window, already knowing what she would find. Chaos. More chaos. People would be pouring into her office, demanding answers she didn't have. And all of it, every single bit of it, seemed to trace back to that damn Inspector. A man she had a rather thick file on now - after an illuminating chat with an old . . . adversary - than had been the case the day before.

She sighed, resigned. "I'm going to need more tea."

***

Atop the First Floor of the Celestial Temple, Arkola drifted between realms, their mind untethered from the mundane concerns of the world below. They observed, they guided, but they rarely intervened. Mortals were amusing in their way, scurrying about, desperately trying to shape their own destinies, unaware of the threads they tangled in their attempts to control their fates.

But today, something tugged at Arkola's attention.

It was subtle at first, a faint ripple in the fabric of reality, like the pluck of a single string in an otherwise harmonious melody. But it grew stronger, pulling them back toward the mortal plane. With a sigh, Arkola allowed themselves to be drawn in, their gaze focusing on the source of the disturbance.

Soar Museum.

It was… changing. Warping. Pulsing with raw, ancient power. The kind of power Arkola had not felt in millennia.

A Dungeon Reborn.

Arkola tilted their head, curiosity piqued. Dungeons did not simply begin again. They were relics of an older time, places of great power and danger, born from the chaos that had once ruled the world. And yet, here it was, a Dungeon manifesting in the heart of Soar.

Interesting.

Arkola smiled, a slow, languid expression. They could feel the ripple of energy spreading from the museum, washing over the city like a tidal wave, changing everything in its path.

And there, at its heart, was the aura of a man who had been delightfully helpful recently.

"Interesting. Very interesting."

# CHAPTER THIRTY TWO - DUNGEON ETIQUETTE

"Don't move!"

Lowe slowly returned to consciousness at the sound of that voice. He thought he recognised it, but it was pretty early in the whole 'waking up' process to be sure. Still, he was long enough in the tooth to recognise that following such a command was usually good business sense.

It got him punched in the mouth much less, for example.

Nevertheless, on this occasion, he did not think it was delivered as an order that would be backed up with physical violence if he failed to listen, so much as an urgent warning of which it would be sensible to take heed.

What had happened? He was at the museum, wasn't he? They had been running through a re-enactment of what had occurred the day Curator Isadora had been killed. Yes. That was right. Arebella's friend was just giving the smarmy lawyer what for with both barrels when . . . something had changed.

Doing his best to stay perfectly still, Lowe's eyes darted around him. Yes, he was still in the Great Hall of the museum. Well, a version of the Great Hall that had been redecorated by a madman with a fire and brimstone fetish. Had there been an explosion? Lowe didn't think there could have been. His mana pool was full, which suggested that *Roll with the Punches* hadn't been needed to stick him back together again. But there was an awful lot of devastation lying around . . .

"I think we're the first to wake up," the voice said again. It came from behind Lowe, so he couldn't see the speaker without turning around. However, now that he was a touch more with it, he thought he had recognised the speaker.

"Preece, is that you? Are you okay?"

"Yep," the Curator confirmed. "Living the dream."

"What's going on?"

"Well, I have two theories," Preece continued. "The first is that I'm still in bed and, for whatever reason, my psyche has decided to inflict a particularly specific nightmare on me."

"Okay, well, as I'm pretty sure I'm not a figment of your imagination, shall we put a pin in that one? What's your other thought?"

"That a Dungeon has spontaneously formed around us, and it's sat there, waiting for us to move and trigger it so that the fucking giant spider hovering just above us can swoop down and feast on our still shrieking corpses."

There was a pause. "So, I'm rooting for this being a nightmare then."

"Me too, Mr Lowe. Me too."

***

Lowe didn't have an awful lot of experience in Dungeons. In fact, other than being boosted through the one in Soar's undercity, he had no context whatsoever for what was occurring. He did remember, though, that Latham had made a big deal about not doing anything to trigger the Dungeon to begin before they were ready.

Unfortunately, in the last few minutes, it seemed that several other members of the re-enactment group hadn't got that memo . . .

"Interesting," Preece said once all the frenzy of activity had come to an abrupt end.

"I mean, sure. If you find visceral, appalling death 'interesting', then that was really, really, *really* interesting. Mind you, if that's your reaction to what has just happened to a bunch of your colleagues, I'm going to be moving you quite a bit higher in the murder suspect pool . . . "

"No, what I mean is that it is interesting is that all those guys running for the exit seemed to do so within their own instance. The Dungeon didn't start for us."

"And that's unusual?"

"Very. This Dungeon isn't treating all of us as being in one giant party. It's creating separate versions of itself for a fresh run each time someone starts it. I mean, I've heard that's possible, but I've never seen it happen. Mind you, I've never witnessed a Dungeon spontaneously generate before, so I think my expertise is pretty limited here."

"I don't know about that, mate; you're seeming pretty fucking well informed from where I'm stood."

There was a scream as the two members of the Security Services, who'd figured they wanted out of this situation and fast, met a grisly end in the Hall's shadows. Lowe winced. Staffen was going to have his guts for garters over losing those two. Providing, of course, he made it out of here with his guts intact. That wasn't seeming too likely right now.

"Wasn't always a Curator, sir."

Well, that answered a few questions Lowe had about the older man: his only being Level 14 if he'd reset his Class made much more sense. "Do a lot of delving in your time, Preece?"

"Sure. Some people might even have described me as pretty hot stuff, once upon a time. Wife didn't like it, though. After I got all torn up by a Werewolf, she made me promise I'd never make another run and that I'd find a safer job. To tell the truth, I wasn't missing it too much until about half a bell ago. Now, though, all my old gear and Skills would be just the ticket."

A soft *ping* echoed in Lowe's mind, and a **Party Up?** notification appeared in the corner of his vision. "You sure?" he asked the man behind him.

"Honestly, I don't think I have much choice. Ideally, you'd be closer to my Level, but you're the only person who hasn't completely lost their head thus far. I mean that metaphorically, of course. A whole bunch of folks have *literally* lost their heads. And, well, beggars can't be choosers. From what I can tell, each newly formed instance is benchmarked to the highest-powered person in each group. Which, again, is pretty damn unusual. I've got no chance against anything your Level, but as I have literally no offensive Skills, I'm not overburdened with options against anything I could theoretically fight. So, if I'm getting out of here, I'm going to need to do it behind someone else. But then again, you're Classless, aren't you? You got anything that's likely to be useful, or are we basically doomed?"

Lowe paused before answering. He didn't love the idea of lying to a guy being pretty upfront about his own position, but Latham had been clear that he shouldn't share anything about his unusual stats. "I've got a decent self-heal, and I can punch pretty hard. Oh, and I've got a flawless memory: when we get out of here, I can relive all this for you, beat for beat, whenever you want. So, we have that to look forward to. You seriously got nothing that will help in a fight?"

"Curators aren't known for their DPS. If - when - I get to Level 20, I was hoping to pick up something useful from my Threshold rewards, but right now, I'm going to be no help at all."

"But you've done a lot of Dungeons?"

"Oh, yes."

"Okay," Lowe said, accepting the party invite. "Consider yourself selected as my Dungeon Consultant. Your job is to plot our way out of here. I'll take the hits and do my best to keep us safe. Deal?"

"Deal."

The chime of the Party forming was overshadowed by a new voice coming from Lowe's right. "So is this Party-thing going to be a sausage-fest, or is there room for a member of the weaker sex?"

"Auditor Mehin? Are you okay?"

"Peachy. You know there's a massive spider right above us, right?"

"Yeah," Lowe said. "It won't do anything until the Dungeon starts. So, don't move."

"Okay. Well, that's not at all terrifying. Are we in a Dungeon? How did that happen?"

"If I were a betting man - which considering my appalling luck, I very much am not - I'd suggest that someone working here might have grave robbed the Core from that exhausted Dungeon on the edge of the city and then done something colossally silly with it. Probably involving necrotic slime and Dreadnaughts. Sound about right Curator Preece?"

There was a brief silence. "I think you'll have to take that up with Director Nuroon, sir."

Lowe blew out his cheeks. "I might just do that. Fuck. Okay," he pushed the party notification to Karolen. "Look, the bad guys in here are coded to match Level. From what I know about Auditiors, you're probably the only one of us who has a chance of actually fighting their way out of here on their own terms. However, if you want company and don't mind punching up . . ."

Karolen let the notification blink for a few moments. Lowe wasn't wrong in his assumption about her capabilities; she doubted there would be much in a Level 20 Dungeon - even such an unusual one as this - that she couldn't handle on a solo run. However, running it as a member of a Level 25 Party would have far better XP rewards and considering her sudden loss of favour with her firm's Partners, this might not be a bad thing. Oh, and if she joined up, she wouldn't have to tell Arebella she'd left her boyfriend to die . . .

"Okay, I'm in." Karolen accepted the invite, seeing the Level of the Spider above them change to a Level 25 as she did so. "So, what do we do?"

"Well, for that, I'm going to defer to our Dungeon Consultant. You have a plan for how we deal with *that*, Preece?"

For the first time since awakening in the Dungeon, Lowe thought he heard a trace of grim happiness in the man's voice. "Actually, I rather think that I do."

# CHAPTER THIRTY THREE – ARACHNOPHOBIA

Lowe had faced down all manner of unpleasantness in his career - and that was even before his Classtration - but the image of the spider hanging from the ceiling, its frozen body filled with murderous anticipation, ranked pretty high on the list of things that made him wish he'd stayed in bed with Arebella this morning. The creature was massive, its many eyes glinting in the sickly light of the transformed Great Hall.

Lowe's skin was trying to crawl away just by looking at it. Soar knew what it would do when the instance actually began, but Lowe suspected it wouldn't be pretty.

"Okay, last final check. Are we sure we've all got a handle on what comes next?" Lowe whispered, keeping his head still, eyes locked on the spider.

"Let you get mauled while I chop it to pieces?" Karolen replied dryly. "Yeah, I've got it. It's subtle."

Preece stood a little behind them, visibly trembling but doing his best to hold his ground. "Look, thinking about it again, I'm sure there's got to be another way of kicking things off . . . "

"Shh!" Karolen hissed, glaring at him. "We don't want to startle it before we're ready."

Lowe took a deep breath and stepped forward, waving a hand at the giant arachnid. "Oi! Eight legs! Fancy a dance?"

The Dungeon instance sparked to life, the spider responding with a low, vibrating hiss, its body swaying from side to side as it dropped from the ceiling on a thick web, landing with a squelch in front of Lowe. Its fangs clicked together; in response, every muscle in Lowe's body screamed for him to turn and run.

Instead, gritting his teeth and missing Latham more than at any time in his life, he spread his arms wide, downed a Mylaf smoothie, triggered *Rolls with the Punches* and offered himself up like an idiot at a buffet. "Come on, then."

With terrifying speed, the spider lunged, its fangs snapping at Lowe. He barely managed to twist out of the way, throwing out *Slugger* in an attempt to take the thing down in one punch. He'd been vaguely hopeful this might have worked, but the spider's speed was far beyond anything he had anticipated. Its fangs grazed him, sending a searing pain down his side as the creature reared back for another strike.

"Anytime, Karolen!" he shouted, feeling the bottom drop out of his stomach as *Roll with the Punches* kicked in big style, dulling the pain but not nearly enough for his liking.

Karolen moved like lightning. No, that wasn't fair to her. The Auditor moved so quickly she would have streaked past lightning and left it for dust. As she charged, in her hand manifested a glowing Balanceblade—a straight, double-edged sword whose surface was etched with thin lines resembling tally marks. Its hilt was wrapped in dark leather, and it had a guard shaped like interlocking scales— and she lunged for the spider, slicing into one of its hairy legs with a sweeping motion.

The creature released a high-pitched screech, rearing back and thrashing wildly, but Karolen held her ground, using Lowe as a human shield in a way that didn't endear her too much to him. He understood that of the two of them, he was the only one who had a chance of tanking a strike from a Level 25 monster, but it wouldn't be fun for him either.

Unfortunately, the spider didn't seem too keen on playing dead just yet. It skittered forward, faster than anything that size had any right to move, and slammed into Lowe, trying to get past him to Karolen. He hit the ground hard, the wind knocked from his lungs.

Lowe's head spun, *Roll with the Punches* doing its best to keep him conscious so that he could stay in what he was laughably choosing to see it as 'the fight.' The spider's fangs came down again, and this time, they found flesh. The sharp, jagged teeth sank into his shoulder, hot venom burning into him. His body spasmed, every nerve screaming in agony as the spider tried to rip into him again.

For a moment, his Mana Pool ran dry, and his flesh tore like wet paper, and blood sprayed across the floor as the creature gnawed at him. The pain was all-encompassing, a white-hot blaze that blurred the edges of his vision.

But then, his smoothie-enhanced mana regeneration kicked in, along with Mental Fortress pushing his mind away from the pain. Lowe went from losing consciousness to being able to feel the agony, but distantly, like a dull throb on the other side of a thick wall. His body was still being shredded, and the spider was still tearing into him, but he felt calm. Detached. He could think again. And mostly, he was thinking, 'Get the fuck on with it, Karolen!'

***

The Auditor was hacking away at the back of the spider, her blade slicing through its carapace, but each cut took more time than she thought Lowe had to spare. The creature was a Level 25, and every hit from her Level 20 sword was barely enough to dent the exoskeleton. In a rising panic, Karolen cycled through every active Skill she had to throw at the thing, and even though she was relentless, she could tell it would take much longer than Preece had planned.

***

Lowe, in the meantime, was hanging on by a thread—both literally and metaphorically. The spider's venom coursed through him, but *Roll with the Punches* was keeping him together, his wounds knitting just enough to keep him alive. He was still trying to throw out the occasional *Slugger*, but eventually he decided it was better to save the mana for healing. The pain was still there, lurking at the edge of his mind, but *Mental Fortress* kept it at bay. He could feel his body healing, the skin pulling tight over torn muscle and shattered bone, but the damage was bad. Worse than he'd imagined.

"Karolen," Lowe grunted, "without wishing to rush you..."

"I'm working on it!" she snapped, driving her blade into the spider's thorax, which elicited another ear-splitting screech. Red fluid gushed from the wound, spraying the floor in thick arcs. The spider shuddered, its legs spasming as it tried to throw her off, but Karolen held firm, her blade biting deeper and deeper.

Then, inevitably, the creature buckled, its body convulsing as Karolen added her *Death and Taxes* Skill to her final blow, driving her sword through its abdomen with a sickening crunch. The spider let out one last shriek before collapsing, its legs twitching in death spasms.

Lowe lay beneath it, his breath coming in gasps as his healing Skill finally began to catch up with the damage. Blood dripped from the gaping wounds on his side and shoulder, pooling beneath him in a spreading crimson stain. He pushed the pain away, letting his body do the work of mending itself, but it was slow. Too slow.

Karolen staggered back, panting as the spider's corpse oozed onto the floor. "You still alive?"

"Barely," Lowe muttered.

"Good. I'm not sure Arebella would forgive me if I let you be eaten on my watch."

Preece stepped forward cautiously, staring down at the wreckage. "I'm so sorry! I never thought it was going to be so bad. That was . . . brutal."

"You're telling me," Lowe groaned, clutching his side.

They barely had time to catch their breath when a low, measured voice spoke from the shadows.

"Well, that was quite the spectacle."

Lowe blinked, wiping blood out of his eyes to allow him to focus on the figure stepping forward into the flickering light. Felicitous Gral adjusted his greasy, stained suit and looked at them with an amused expression. "I hope you don't mind; I took the opportunity to join your party."

Lowe looked down at the spider and swore. Level 33. No wonder it had been such a fucking nightmare

Karolen's eyes narrowed. "You've been awake this whole time?"

Gral smiled smoothly, ignoring the blood and ichor on the floor. "Oh, I've been observing. And I must say, you're quite the team."

Lowe tried to push himself up, but his body protested, and he chose to listen to it. "What do you want, Gral?"

Gral raised an eyebrow. "I want to survive this. And I think we are all aware I probably know things that will be the key to doing that. Let me come with you as you make your little bid for freedom, and I'll tell you everything I know about how this . . . event has come about. I am all for client confidentiality, but not when it puts my own life at risk. Believe me when I tell you, you will want to hear what I have to say."

Preece looked nervously between them. "He's Level 33 . . . If we keep him in the group, the Dungeon's going to scale."

Gral smiled, his eyes glinting. "Well, then. It looks like we're about to have some real fun, doesn't it?"

# CHAPTER THIRTY FOUR – THE FOLLY OF AMBITIOUS MEN

Lowe sighed.

His every instinct told him not to trust Gral. The man was a lawyer, and worse, he was a lawyer who, from what Hel had told him, always operated on the shadiest edges of Soar's judicial system. But the truth was, the man was right. They needed every bit of help they could get, especially with the Dungeon being so unusually aggressive.

But was it worth the eight-level difficulty hike? Especially with the much weaker Preece already being so exposed?

Karolen seemed to sense Lowe's hesitation and gave him a significant look. She appeared to have any number of those at her disposal. "You're not seriously considering this, are you?"

Lowe closed his eyes for a second, taking in the pain, the exhaustion, the dead spider still twitching on the floor. Then, finding no clarity in the self-imposed darkness, he opened them and glared at Gral. "Do you honestly know how this happened? One moment we're in Soar Museum and the next... If you want to tag along with us, you need to start talking."

Gral's smile faltered for just a second, then returned in all its insincere glory. "Of course. If I have a commitment to future cordial relations?"

Reluctantly, much to the audible disgust of Karolen and Preece, Lowe nodded.

"Well, to understand the how, you need to understand the why. As I am sure you are aware, Dungeons do not just appear out of thin air. Certainly not nowadays. Something, or more importantly, someone, has to trigger them. And have the power to be able to do so. And in this case, I dare suggest that it was a very particular someone. A very particular 'someone', indeed."

Lowe sighed, already knew where this was going.

Gral's eyes flicked toward Karolen, then Preece, before settling on Lowe. "Director Nuroon had known about the existence of the Dungeon core for quite some time. Long before today, in fact. How could he not? A dormant power with the potential to change the landscape of Soar's political scene? Of course, he knew about it. And knowing about it, he couldn't resist dabbling. It's in his nature, after all."

Even though there was a crushing inevitability about the revelation, Lowe still found himself wanting to rail against the man. Wanted to shout and hit something, preferably the Director himself. But something restrained him.

The entire museum was now a Dungeon, twisted and reanimated by some malign force. This wasn't a development that he thought was something Nuroon would have countenanced. The man was as ambitious as they came—an old crook who had been manipulating the city's political and academic circles for decades. But this? This went far beyond ambition. There was a depth to this chaos that felt . . . ancient. And would

Nuroon have risked the destruction of his pride and joy? No. That didn't seem quite right.

"And you?" Karolen asked. "Where do you fit into all of this, Gral?"

Gral's eyes sparkled with something that might have been amusement. Maybe. "Me, Ms Mehin? Oh, I'm just a humble legal advisor. My role was simple: ensure the museum didn't face any liability if things went . . . sideways. Of course, I wasn't expecting a Dungeon to spontaneously form around me, but well, that's life, isn't it? Full of surprises."

Karolen snorted, shaking her head. "Surprises. Sure. You're all heart, Gral."

Lowe tried to stand again, this time managing to pull himself upright, though the pain still radiated through his body. *Roll with the Punches* had repaired the worst of the damage, but he wasn't anywhere near full strength. And his Mana Pool would need a good few minutes to fill back up. "And you're saying Nuroon knew this would happen?"

Gral's smile faltered for the second time. He wasn't telling them the full story, but - right now - Lowe would take what he could get. "Not quite. He knew the risk was there, but he was, of course, confident he could control it. That is, after all, the problem with men like him—they always think they can control things that are far beyond their comprehension."

There was something in Gral's tone, something deeper, almost like a flicker of fear. Lowe didn't think it was because of what had just happened. Gral knew more than he was letting on. "And now?"

Gral's smile disappeared entirely. "Now? He's likely trapped in here with the rest of us. Though I doubt he's feeling the same level of regret as you. Men like Nuroon rarely see their own actions as the cause of their downfall. He'll be planning, scheming, trying to figure out how to use this to his advantage. And he will survive. If there's one thing of which I am certain, if only one person walks out of this Dungeon it will be Director Nuroon."

Lowe swore under his breath. So, the emergence of this Dungeon wasn't just a random event. It was the result of Nuroon's ambition, his greed, and now they were all paying the price. But there was something else, wasn't there?

"Come on. There's more. If you want to rage along with us, you need to be honest. Spill."

"Sharp as ever, Inspector. Yes, there is one more thing. The Dungeon core . . . well, there's no easy way of putting this. It's sentient. It's not just some rediscovered artefact of power. It's alive. And, as far as I understand these things, it's been feeding on the museum's energy since it was brought inside a month back."

Preece gasped, stepping back, his face ashen. "Alive? We were never told that!"

Gral nodded. "Oh yes. And now that it's awake, it's very much in control. Every moment we spend in here, it's learning more about us. Adapting. This particular Dungeon isn't just a collection of traps and monsters—it's an organism. A predator. And right now? I rather suspect that we're the prey."

At those words, the atmosphere in the room closed in around them, the walls pulsing with a faint, rhythmic thrum. Lowe couldn't help but feel he'd experienced this before, in the basement beneath the museum. But that had been because of his infection via necrotic slime. This was different. This wasn't an hallucination. It was real.

"Alright," Karolen said, breaking the silence. "We get it. We're screwed. So, what's your plan, Gral? If you're so smart, how do we get out?"

Gral's grin returned, though this time it was more subdued. "Ah, that's the tricky part. You see, the Dungeon's core is located deep within the museum—below even the lower levels. It's buried itself tight down there, and everything is drawn to protect it. If we want to escape, then I rather think we will have to reach the core and destroy it."

Lowe could feel something clicking into place in his mind. "That armour. The armour of the Dreadnaught. It came from the exhausted Dungeon too, didn't it?"

Preece nodded. "Yes. The armour was found in the loot table of the same site. But, like much of the gear we found, it was dormant when we brought it up to the museum - harmless inside its sarcophagus. It was Martha Culloden who thought it would make an excellent exhibit. But the thing about newly uncovered artefacts, especially ones buried with a Dungeon core, is that they have... connections."

"Connections?" Karolen asked. "What kind of connections?"

Gral's eyes gleamed, taking over from Preece. "Well, this is where I suspect everything began to get a touch out of hand. You see the first armour was entirely passive, it appears that the second armour was a little more important. It was made to house the soul of a very particular warrior Dreadnaught. In the wrong hands—or the right hands—the Director posited it could have unimaginable power. Unfortunately, through activating the armour close to an exposed Dungeon core . . ."

Lowe felt a cold lump forming in his chest. "It could trigger something cataclysmic. In defence. Something rather like this."

"Exactly. I think it will help if you consider the Dreadnaught armour as the spark, and the Dungeon core as an especially dangerous powder keg that suddenly felt a touch exposed. Director Nuroon, in his infinite wisdom, brought them both to the surface, believing he could contain their power. He thought he could turn it all into a neat little exhibit, something to showcase his brilliance." Gral's smile twisted. "But it turns out the Core and the armour in concert might have their own agenda. Somethings, my dear Inspector - and I suspect I probably do not need to tell you this - are probably better staying buried."

A low rumble reverberated through the Great Hall, making the floor beneath them tremble. The walls shifted, the shapes twisting into even more unnatural forms. Lowe might be wrong, but it almost felt like they formed into grinning, expectant faces.

Karolen grimaced "This just keeps getting better."

Preece, looking more anxious than ever, pointed toward the far end of the Great Hall.

Two doors stood there, each increasingly becoming warped and twisted by the Dungeon's influence. "We need to move. The Dungeon's changing again. If we stay here, I rather suspect we'll be sitting ducks."

Lowe nodded, his mind racing. "Alright, sold. Which way?"

Preece swallowed hard, his eyes darting between the doors. "Left. We go left."

"Why left?"

Preece hesitated, then said, "Left is usually the safer option in Dungeons. Fewer traps. Fewer surprises. Of course, the other side of that is there tends to be more... confrontations, but lesser of two evils and all that."

Lowe raised an eyebrow. "Interesting logic. Though I'm beginning to think we're well beyond the 'safe' part of this journey." He turned to Karolen. "What do you think?"

She shrugged, her gaze never leaving Gral. "We're in trouble either way. I've done some delving, but nothing serious. If the Curator knows his stuff, I have no issue following his lead. Might as well go left."

Lowe licked his lips. When you only had bad choices, you cling to any lifeboat offered. "Alright. Left it is." He took a step toward the door, his newly rebuilt skin and muscles protesting with every movement. "Let's get this over with."

He pushed the door open, the hinges creaking with a sound that made his teeth grind. Beyond the threshold lay a narrow corridor, twisting and turning into the darkness, the walls lined with grotesque, pulsating growths that seemed to have as many eyes as teeth.

Preece swore under his breath. "It's getting worse. I don't want to be the voice of doom here, but the deeper we go, I'd suggest the more it will change. I've never seen anything so... aggressive."

"Welcome to Soar," Karolen muttered, stepping in behind the Inspector in a defensive position.

Lowe couldn't argue with that. The twisted, living wall made it feel like they were walking through a throat that could close on them at any moment. If he'd ever seen anything more representative of life in this city, he couldn't recall it.

"Welcome to Soar, indeed."

# CHAPTER THIRTY FIVE – A FORTUNATE CHANCE TO GEAR UP

The left-hand corridor beyond the Great Hall stretched before them, a long expanse that was less stone passage and more fleshy tube pulsating with growths, the walls warping like the inside of some colossal, breathing beast. It could not have been clearer that the Dungeon was alive—watching, waiting.

Which was more than anyone could say about the other museum employees they walked past. Although in their own, separate instance, the Dungeon seemed keen for Lowe and his party to see how poorly everyone else was doing in negotiating it.

"How come everyone is wiping? If the Dungeon is balancing itself to the individual delver - or, at worst, to the Level of the highest person in the party - shouldn't at least a few people be doing okay?"

Preece shook his head. "You've got to remember the audience here. I wouldn't be surprised if I was the only person who worked here who had ever been down a Dungeon in their life. Mind you," the Curator said, looking down at the headless corpse of a Level 12 Contract Cleaner, "even then, you do have a point. Most noobs can usually struggle their way through a Level 10 solo Dungeon. People are dying within seconds of the place starting."

Lowe's instincts were screaming at him to stay on alert. With Gral in the party, the Dungeon had already spiked its difficulty, and every creak, every shift in the shadows felt like a prelude to something cataclysmic about to arrive. Even after two more of Mylaf's smoothies, he was conscious that his mana still hadn't fully regenerated yet. It felt less than ideal for the party's tank to be relying on pure grit to keep moving forward.

"Is it just me, or are we moving downwards?" Karolen muttered. "Feels like it's getting colder."

"That's because it is," Gral said, his voice tight. "These walls—they weren't like this before. They're... evolving."

"Dungeons feed on fear and death," Preece said. "This one is brand new, and it's hungry. And it knows we're in here."

Lowe rolled his shoulders and stopped short. "I appreciate you are the one with the expertise here, but if you could stop being quite so doomful about it, I'm sure we'd all appreciate it." He turned his attention back to the corridor, body still aching from the venomous bite. He wasn't sure how much further they had to go - the geography of the museum had totally transformed since it had become a Dungeon - but the more they walked, the deeper they seemed to be going.

Suddenly, Karolen stopped, raising a hand. "Hold up."

"What is it?" Lowe said.

The Auditor squinted ahead, and then pointed. "Look. The floor. It's uneven."

Lowe followed her gaze, and sure enough, a section of the floor ahead seemed to dip slightly—a subtle shift in the stone that was barely noticeable. Barely, but not enough for the sharp eyes of a Level 20 Auditor to miss.

"If I were putting money on it, I'd say that was some sort of trap."

"Awesome. Any idea what kind?" Lowe asked Preece.

The older man shook her head. "No, but whatever it is, it won't be pleasant. Level 33 and all that," he added, glaring at Gral.

"Great. Look, I don't want to be a whiner here, but if we could figure out a way forward that didn't involve me just walking into it and seeing what happens, I'd really appreciate it."

Karolen bent down, studying the trap for a moment before stepping carefully around it. "Looks like it only triggers if you step directly on it. Just follow my lead."

Lowe nodded and followed suit, carefully avoiding the trap. Gral pushed past Preece to follow, but his foot slipped, and he stumbled forward.

As the lawyer's foot hit the plate with a dull *thunk*, the entire corridor rumbled in response. Lowe's heart skipped a beat as he lunged forward, grabbing Gral by the collar and yanking him back just as the walls on either side exploded with spikes, jagged metal spears shooting out at terrifying speed.

Lowe barely managed to pull Gral clear, the spikes missing him by inches. His heart pounded as he stared at row upon row of spears jutting from the walls. Fuck. Where was Latham when he needed him?

For once, Gral seemed genuinely affected by what had happened, his eyes wide with shock. "I—I didn't see it—"

"You almost got wiped!" Lowe snapped, his voice sharp with adrenaline. "Pay attention!"

"Just stick close and don't wander off. I can't keep pulling your ass out of the fire every five minutes. It's this deadly because you are with us. The least you could do is carry your own weight."

Karolen chuckled softly. "Perhaps we should invest in a leash for our esteemed colleague."

Lowe shot her a glare. "Not helping!"

"Merely offering a practical solution."

They continued down the corridor, the traps becoming more frequent and potentially deadly with every step. It became clear that the only practical way forward - in lieu of a party member with *Disarm Traps* - was for Lowe to go first and be the most blundering delver in the history of Dungeons.

This was doing little for either his physical or his mental health.

"How the fuck are you still alive?" Karolen asked him in a recovery pause after he had led with his chin into a swinging pendulum of rock. "How good is your heal Skill!"

Lowe just shook his head and popped a 500 HP cookie in his mouth. Having the equivalent Intelligence and Wisdom of a Level 50 was letting *Roll with the Punches* bounce him straight back from damage that should be zeroing him, but it wasn't doing anything to stop him from feeling every cut, burn or crush injury. He was pretty sure it was only *Mental Fortress* working overtime that was keeping him stubborn enough to keep taking step after step forward. Even then, he was starting to struggle.

"Let's just hope the next room isn't too bad," he replied.

Less than half a bell of torture later, the party reached a heavy, iron door at the end of the hallway. Lowe's gut - or it could just have been recent, appalling experience - told him whatever was behind this door wasn't going to be pleasant.

"We could go back?" he asked hopefully.

Preece shook his head. "I don't want to be *that* guy, but I'd be pretty sure all the traps would have rearmed. Going back would be about as much fun as coming through . . . "

Lowe snorted and put his hand on the door. "Ready?" he asked, glancing at the others.

Karolen nodded, manifesting her Balanceblade and triggering enough active Skills that the corridor stank with the mana use. Preece, massively under Levelled for whatever was coming, looked like he was going to be sick, but he gave a shaky nod. Gral looked unfazed, but Lowe could hear that his breath had quickened.

With a shove, Lowe pushed the door open, the heavy iron creaking loudly as it swung inward. "Oh, for fuck's sake!"

The room inside was vast, a cavernous space that seemed far too large to fit within the museum's structure. The walls were lined with more of the grotesque, pulsating growths, and the air was thick with the stench of decay. But what caught Lowe's attention immediately was the sight of what lay scattered across the floor.

Gear.

Weapons, armour, supplies—everything they could have possibly needed for the rest of their journey. It was all there, strewn haphazardly across the ground as if dropped by someone—or something—in a hurry.

"Well, that seems fortunate..." Preece said.

Karolen stepped forward cautiously, scanning the room for any signs of danger. "I don't see any traps, but, you know, this is the reddest of red flags."

Lowe didn't disagree. However... "Look, I don't know about anyone else, but I need gear that can help me weather all the damage. I hadn't exactly packed for a Level 33 Dungeon." Cautiously, he stepped into the centre of the space.

Straight in front of him, he saw a set of armour—Level 25 (of course it was. Almost like it had been left for him) scale mail. It looked lightweight but durable, perfect for someone like Lowe who needed mobility as much as protection. There was also a sword—a well-crafted, Level 25 blade that practically hummed with latent power. He reached for it, feeling its weight in his hand.

"Careful," Karolen warned. "Don't touch anything that feels . . . off."

"It's weird, but this actually feels the opposite," Lowe said, inspecting the blade. It wasn't enchanted, but it was sharp, and - more importantly than anything else - it felt like it would hold a charge of *Slugger*.

As Lowe strapped on the armour, Karolen knelt beside a pile of supplies, rifling through the gear. She pulled out a set of throwing knives, each etched with runes that glowed faintly in the dim light. "These will do."

Preece, meanwhile, was staring at a staff leaning against the wall. It was ornate, made of dark wood and inlaid with silver filigree, but it had an air of menace that made Lowe uneasy.

"You sure about that?" Lowe asked, eyeing the staff warily.

Preece hesitated, then nodded. "It's a Curator's Staff. It'll help me with my identification Skills. And . . . look, I think I might need it."

Gral watched all of this with a sly grin. "A veritable treasure trove, isn't it? Almost as if the Dungeon is offering us a gift."

Lowe didn't trust the bounty, but the way he saw it, they didn't have much choice. They needed this gear if they were going to survive whatever was waiting for them deeper in the Dungeon. He finished strapping on the armour, feeling a little more secure with the steel plates covering his chest and shoulders. Mylaf was going to kick his arse when she saw the state of his suit.

As they prepared to move forward, a low rumble echoed through the room, followed by a faint, rhythmic thumping sound. Lowe tensed, gripping his new sword tightly.

"What now?" Karolen said, her eyes scanning the room for the source of the noise.

The floor beneath their feet began to tremble, the thumping growing louder, more insistent. Lowe could feel it in his bones, a deep, primal rhythm that seemed to pulse through the very air.

"It's coming from beneath us," Preece whispered, "Something's coming."

Lowe started running for the exit on the opposite side of the cavern. "Fucking move. Now!"

The party hurried across the room, their new gear clinking softly with every step. The door to which they were heading was a large, arched doorway, but as they approached, the rumbling intensified. As they ran, the walls around them began to shift, the pulsating growths twitching and expanding.

"Well, this is going well!" Karolen yelled, turning to look behind her as they reached the exit. Then, the floor beneath them erupted in a shower of stone shards. Lowe barely had time to react before a massive, hulking figure emerged from the ground, its body covered in jagged armour.

"Go, go, go!" Lowe shouted, pushing Preece forward as whatever the creature was roared.

They sprinted through the door, slamming it shut behind them. The monster simply exploded through it and stayed hot on their heels, lumbering forward. Fortunately, the corridor beyond them was narrow, the walls closing in around them as they ran, making it harder for the creature to move as easily as them. Although, as this was because it was at least twice their size and fixated on their imminent demise, this was very much a good news/bad news situation

"We need to lose it!" Karolen shouted, her breath coming in short gasps.

"You think?" Lowe replied, caught between leading the way down the corridor in case of danger and putting himself at the back of the group so the monster chasing them reached him first.

"There!" Gral shouted, pointing to a side passage, an even narrower tunnel that branched off from the main corridor.

Lowe didn't hesitate. "Take it! It won't be able to follow us down there."

They veered off into the side tunnel, the sound of the creature's pursuit growing fainter as they moved deeper into the narrow passage. The walls here were closer, the air colder, but for the moment, they were safe.

For now.

# CHAPTER THIRTY SIX – FIRE AND BOURBON

Lowe peered through the narrow gap at the monster, sucking in his stomach as he did so. Arebella had tactfully - and Mylaf rather more untactfully - suggested he needed to ease up a little on the baked good consumables. However, if anything was going to persuade him to reconsider his dietary choices, it would probably be being slightly too big to comfortably escape what appeared to be a huge, oozing undead werewolf.

"Is it still out there?" Gral asked from, Lowe noticed, the very front of their little group. The lawyer was about as far away from danger as it was possible to get and considering Gral was the highest level of any of them - and was the reason their pursuer was quite so powerful - this did not feel exactly value for money.

"No. I think it got bored and wandered off."

"Really?"

The creature howled and scrabbled at the entrance to the side tunnel again, claws very nearly reaching Lowe's chest. "No, not really, you fucking moron."

"Can you see what it is?" Preece asked.

"Other than terrifying?"

"If we know what it is, I might be able to help with how to fight it. There's precious little in the Dungeonverse I haven't come across. Knowledge is power and all that."

That made sense to Lowe, and he craned his neck a little further out. "I can't make out the text from here, but it appears to be some sort of giant zombie wolf."

"Ah."

"Is that an 'excellent. I have encountered many of this species in my Dungeon Delving days and have a step-by-step plan for you on how to defeat the creature' ah, or . . ." Lowe let the silence hover in the air for a moment. "This is where you come in with some reassuring words."

"Is it?"

"Come on, Preece. This is your time for your underpowered ass to shine. How do we take this down?"

The monster let out a low, rumbling howl, which sounded worryingly like it was letting its fellows know that meat was back on the menu. Lowe did his best to back off down the tunnel, noting how very tight the fit was the further he went. "Look, we really don't want to be stuck here if it summons any others. It only needs one of these things to be a touch smaller, and we're done. Anyone see where this tunnel leads?"

"I don't want to play fast and loose with the words 'dead end' here," Karolen said, her voice tight. "But as far as I can tell, it just keeps getting narrower and narrower. The more I look at it, the more I'm not convinced it isn't just a trap to get us all wedged in."

"Excellent." Lowe twisted slightly to face the gap to the corridor face-on. "So, real rock and a hard place, stuff."

"Well, undead werewolf and a hard place, certainly," Gral added, somewhat unhelpfully to Lowe's mind.

Stooping slightly, Lowe risked slipping his head forward a little further to catch the words floating above the monster's head a little clearer. "Level 31 Corrupt Fenrir. Any good to you?" he called back to Preece.

"Shit. Okay. Well, that's not great. Could be worse, certainly, but I've not got many good memories of fighting against those fuckers. Although . . . "

"Although what? Fuck!" Lowe jerked his head back just in time to avoid losing his nose to a raking claw. "Preece, mate, make with the exposition!"

"It's just one of them, you say?"

"Sure. It keeps howling as if calling others, but it's just the one at the moment. I'm not being funny, though, I think it can probably take us."

"Okay. Well, when isolated, it'll be running under a *Lone Wolf* debuff. So, basically, when not in a pack, a Corrupt Fenrir will move into a berserk state and have no real sense of self-preservation. Its attack patterns will become predictable, which usually means you can exploit its blind rage to make a fairly easy kill." Preece's voice had the biggest 'but' of all time, hovering just beyond expression

"Anything else useful other than it's fucking out of its mind with anger? Because I'm not seeing that as much of an upside."

"Sorry. I know of a bunch of group formations that would be killer against such a foe, but - well - we're lacking a bit in most of the suggested team members. I doubt it would even know I was attacking it."

Lowe took a moment to let the problem percolate through his mind. This was too early on in the Dungeon for them to be this outclassed. He only really had his experience of being power levelled by Latham to call on, but each of the Dungeons he had done with the Temple Warder had followed a fairly benign difficulty curve.

Sure, because of Gral being in their party and the Dungeon scaling to him, they were batting way above their average, but - then again - so was Lowe himself. In real terms, he was basically a Level 50. A Level 31 wolf - all on its lonesome and debuffed - really shouldn't be this much of a head-scratcher.

Lowe shut out the snarling and did his best to think. Over the last year, he'd become so used to being Classless - the literal runt of any litter he ran across - he'd stopped looking at problems as if there was any other outcome than him trying to survive being hosed. What did he have on his side here. Well, according to Preece, this thing was stupid. Strong, violent and vicious, for sure, but it sounded like its debuff made it thick as mince. If he couldn't figure out how to take it down, he really wasn't trying . . .

There was a pause as he ran a hand through his sweat-damp hair, his fingers catching on the clumps of grit and blood. He would never admit it out loud, but all he kept thinking was, 'What would Latham do?'

Lowe squinted at the entrance to the side tunnel—just wide enough for him if he sucked in his gut, but certainly not wide enough for the massive, clawing beast trying to wriggle through. Its claws were getting frantic now, scraping up flecks of stone as they gouged and scrabbled with a manic desperation that told Lowe the creature's patience was running out.

Yeah, he could do something with this level of manic, frantic devotion...

"All right, ladies and gentlemen, I think I have a plan."

"Please tell me it doesn't involve heroic self-sacrifice," Gral muttered from his safe spot. "Or if it does, at least not by me."

"Tempting, but no." Lowe said as he checked through his inventory. He was sure that somewhere in here, he had just the thing. Ah, there it was—an old, half-empty bottle of 'Inferno Bourbon'. Arebella had banned the stuff from her house - and that had been during their first time on the relationship merry-go-round. The label was faded and peeling, but it probably had matured splendidly during that time. Lowe grinned, already feeling the gears whirring in his head.

He tossed the bottle to Preece, who fumbled it like it was a live demonic imp. "Lowe! What—"

"Keep it steady. On the count of three, we're all going back the way we came."

Gral blinked. "Seriously?"

"Seriously. I'm going to grab him, you all slip past as he - doubtlessly - rips me a new one and then I'm pulling him back in here."

"Right..." Karolen clearly did not think much of this plan.

"Because if this tunnel's too small for us, then it's damned well going to be too small for it. And we'll make sure it's too flammable for him, too." Lowe spoke fast, hand gripping and regripping his newly earned blade.

The Fenrir's claws raked closer, catching the leather strap of Lowe's belt as he backed up a step. Was he really planning on grappling with this thing?

"Right, listen," Lowe knew he was babbling, but he couldn't stop. If he did, he figured he'd lose his nerve. "I'm not going to fight it directly. I'm just going to pull it in. It's stupid. Predictable, right, Preece? All I need to do is trigger it into berserk mode, and then—"

"It'll just fight blindly," Karolen finished, her eyes gleaming as the plan came together. "Trapped in a bottleneck. You're going to light it up, aren't you?"

"Exactly, the Fenrir's stuck, I torch the tunnel, and we avoid being clawed to death by a very angry wolf. Simple, right?"

"Define simple," Preece muttered, but he was already prepping the bottle, pulling off the cork. "I have a flint," he said, passing it up the line to Lowe.

Gral cleared his throat. "Loathe as I am to offer a counterargument here, and whilst I am very much on board with the plan to cook the wolf, is there not a danger of you being similarly incinerated? Not that this is a deal breaker as far as I am concerned, but I do feel the need to bring it up. Morally, you understand?"

The creature howled again, this time louder, its head starting to wedge into the tunnel. Its crimson eyes locked onto Lowe, who felt the feral heat of its gaze like a physical force.

Perfect. It was furious now.

"I'm going to be working on the principle that one of us has an overpowered healing Skill, and the other is a monster covered in hair. I'm not loving the idea, but I'm not hating my odds, either. We all good?"

With no one having a better plan, it seemed to Lowe that Operation Cook-off was a go.

With no further ado, Lowe dashed forward, crashing into the beast and doing his best to lock its arms to the side. He saw the others run past and, headbutting the Fenrir on the snout, he let go, backing off into the tunnel again. The creature responded with a maddened snarl, lunging forward, wedging itself millimetres from Lowe's face.

"Now, Preece!" Lowe shouted, ducking back.

With a regretful sigh, Preece lobbed the bottle at their feet. Lowe felt the liquid wash under him and was already striking the flint against the side of the tunnel. Sparks caught the liquid. There was a moment of sickening silence as the fiery alcohol met flesh. Then, the explosion ripped through the tunnel.

Both the Corrupt Fenrir and Lowe howled, in fury as fire spread across them, igniting necrotic tissue and skin like dry tinder. Its claws flailed, smacking against Lowe in a frenzy, trying to force itself back, but it was too late. The creature's berserk rage had driven it too deep into the tunnel to escape.

It was stuck. As was Lowe.

Karolen watched, chest heaving as the fire consumed the two figures in the tunnel from the inside out. The smell was beyond foul—like burnt meat and rotting carcasses—but it was done. The monster's movements slowed, then finally, mercifully, stopped.

There was the longest pause any of the rest of the group had ever experienced. And then there was a dry hacking cough.

"Well," Lowe said, voice low and gravelly. "I think that counts as well-done. See, Mr Lawyer. No heroic self-sacrifice required. Or not a permanent one, anyway."

Gral, looking slightly ill from what he had just witnessed, gave a hesitant thumbs up. "For the record, I, uh, prefer plans when they don't involve people melting."

"You're welcome," Lowe replied

"You're insane," Preece added, but there was admiration in his tone.

"Insanity's just another word for creative problem-solving. Now," he continued. "In the interests of preserving our Auditor's blushes, I don't suppose any of you happen to have any clothes in my size?"

# CHAPTER THIRTY SEVEN – NO REWARD COMES FREE

"Anyone else picking up unusual rewards?"

Preece's question brought Lowe out of his reverie. He was staring at his hands, trying to stop them from shaking, and he didn't think that was just because of *Roll with the Punches* working overtime to heal his skin. The Corrupt Fenrir was hardly the first life he had taken - but then again, was it even a life? He wasn't wholly sure of the status of the creatures a Dungeon generated. Latham had said they were constructs of pure mana, no more alive than a reflection in a mirror, but right now, Lowe wasn't so sure about that. He'd been forced to look into that wolf's eyes as the blaze had consumed it, and he didn't think he'd simply watched a mana construct splutter and die.

"I don't know what you mean. I didn't get anything," Gral said.

"Shocking. And you did so much to help, after all. You should sue!"

"I think not, my dear Inspector. You know the old saying, *A man who is his own lawyer has a fool for a client.* I would imagine that, being the same level as that poor animal, my XP gains were substantially less than the rest of you. Why, at his underdeveloped level, Mr Preece probably has never seen so many gains in one go in his life."

"I wasn't always a Curator, Gral!"

"And we will not always be in this Dungeon, *Preece.* I would recommend you watch your tone."

"Can everyone just be quiet for a moment!" Karolen said, eyes unfocused as she checked her own stat sheet. "Lowe, are you seeing this?"

Lowe brought up his Core sheet and frowned. "What the fuck is a Remnant when it is at home?"

Preece shook his head. "No idea. I've not seen anything like it before. As . . . *Mister* Gral said, I would have expected a fairly substantial XP surge from that fight. But all I got was a 'Remnant of Memory'."

Karolen snorted. "'Remnant of Skill' for me. Lowe?"

Lowe looked at the strange notification flashing on the corner of his Core. He had long become used to his stats sheet looking a touch unusual. In the year since losing his Class, he'd avoided looking at it at all, so depressed did it make him. Even after being power levelled by Latham and with all the weirdness that Essence Transmutation Theory had wrought on him, he still found himself scared to contemplate it too much. But it would be hard to miss the red glow that blinked in the top right corner now. He mentally pressed down on it, and its name became apparent. Remnant of Essence.

"Preece, this is your area of expertise . . . "

"As I said, I've never seen anything like it before!"

Lowe narrowed his eyes. There was something about the tone of the Curator's voice that suggested he knew more than he was saying. 'Look, I don't need it to stand up in the Middle Court. But if you have any ideas, now would be a good time to share. I did just burn myself alive to save your ass."

Preece wiped a hand over his face. "Look, at best I'm just going to be guessing, right?"

"Understood."

"This is a new Dungeon, right? But we think it's based on the Dungeon Core from the exhausted one on the outskirts of Soar."

"Okay..." Karolen had moved to stand next to Lowe, her eyes scanning the corridor for sign of any other monsters.

"So, we don't really know where Dungeon's get the XP they reward delvers with. But as most of them are so ancient, it's widely theorised that they are simply focal points for recycling energy from those that die in their completion. You know, real 'circle of life' stuff. Power from the fallen is taken and then given back to those who are successful."

"Right." Lowe had never heard this before, but both the Auditor and Gral were nodding sagely along. "How's that linked to these . . . these Remnants?"

"This is just a theory, right?"

"Fucking hell, Preece!"

"Sorry, I've just gotten used to Director Nuroon needing every 'i' and 't' dotted and crossed before saying anything. Right. So, we think this Dungeon has manifested from an exhausted Core. That means it probably does not have any spare XP sloshing around as rewards. I mean, once we're all dead, that situation might change, but right now, I'd guess it might be running on empty."

"So, Remnants?"

Preece shrugged. "I could be wrong, but if I were a betting man, I'd say they're probably fragments of past challengers. Mine is sitting above my Core, so it has to be a temporary effect rather than anything permanent like a new Skill or an XP gain. I reckon they will be unique abilities that don't directly affect core stats like Strength or Dexterity but offer creative and situational advantages. You know what, fuck it." At that, Preece's eyes unfocused, and a yellow glow infused his body.

"Ha. Nice to be right on occasion. Maybe I'm not such a lousy Curator after all. So, a Remnant of Memory is a fragment of knowledge left behind by previous challengers. I've got a couple of choices here for what I turn this one into - what's your pleasure?"

"What are the options?" Lowe was itching to check out what his own Remnant would give him but sensed that might be a touch rude.

"I can either 'unlock secret passages that aren't visible to regular perception', 'grant hints to counter specific traps or bosses' or 'reveal past mistakes made by previous adventurers, giving the delver foresight into upcoming challenges.'"

"Traps," Karolen and Lowe said together.

"Sold." The light around Preece increased, then abruptly faded. "Cool. So, everyone should take two quick steps to the right." He smirked as they did so. "Just kidding."

"Hilarious. So, it didn't work?" Karolen asked.

"Oh, no, I think it is working fine. I'm having, for example, the very strong inclination that we take the middle corridor in the branch ahead. Try your own."

"I must say, it does seem rather unfair that you three are getting all sorts of new abilities whereas I, who am in no less danger than the rest of you..."

"My heart is bleeding," Karolen interrupted. Her own body glowed a neon pink as she accessed her own Remnant. "Hmmm, nothing so useful as a spot trap ability. Of the options, I think I'll grab the third one. 'A half-formed teleportation ability, allowing a short-range blink movement, but only in areas of deep shadow." I guess that might help?"

"If you think that is best." Lowe hardly felt qualified to advise on such things. It certainly couldn't hurt the rest of their time in the Dungeon for her to have something that made her a touch more deadly in the shadows.

Interested in the properties of his own Remnant, Lowe touched on the deep red shadow above his core.

**Remnants of Essence** offer temporary, unpredictable boosts or changes to physical or magical capabilities that last for a limited duration during the Dungeon delve. You may consume one Remnant of Essence in order to create the following effects.

- **Essence of Giant's Wrath:** Increases physical strength by 50% for ten minutes, but during that time, your body grows unwieldy, reducing Dexterity.
- **Essence of Silent Thought:** Sharply increases Intelligence and Mana regeneration for five minutes, but during that time, you are unable to speak, communicate telepathically, or use vocal spells.
- **Essence of Spectral Veil:** Temporarily grants partial invisibility, but only if you're standing still and breathing slowly.

Well, thought Lowe, that was something of a shit sandwich. Each of those abilities could be temporarily helpful but also had severe limitations. He didn't think there would be much benefit in the extra strength. *Slugger* already gave him a pretty powerful punch, and dropping his Dexterity would hardly make that more likely to land. Likewise, as he was acting as the tank for his group, he didn't think being able to temporarily go invisible would be all that endearing to those he left exposed. And Arebella had always said she went for the strong, silent type . . . Essence of Silent Thought it is, then.

"Well, if we are all finished luxuriating in our gains, perhaps we can move on?" Gral drawled when the red glow around Lowe faded. "I'm sure the next thing intending to kill us is just around the next corner."

"Sure. I'm going to go quiet for a moment, though. Don't mind me. Just trying something out." It occurred to Lowe that 'sharply' increasing an Intelligence that was already - effectively - Level 50 was likely to be pretty illuminating. With *Silent Thought* sharpening his mind, he was about to think a whole lot clearer—and not just about the Dungeon. There was a lot more to figure out. Like how in Soar they'd ended up here in the first place, and who had been pulling the strings.

# CHAPTER THIRTY EIGHT – FRAGMENTS OF GENIUS

Over the last year, Lowe had – by necessity – become used to experiencing the world through something of a haze.

When you had become accustomed to having access to the wide range of Class Skills that had been his bread and butter throughout his career, the drop off in his sensory experience had been sizeable.

Indeed, he had spent much of the last year feeling as if he'd taken the sort of blow to the head that *Roll with the Punches* couldn't do very much about. Colours were dimmer. Smells less intense. Even something as mundane as working out his *per-hour* rate for the vanishingly small number of clients his abortive Private Investigator business had been able to muster had needed him to use paper and pen.

Then, the murder of Gianna d'Avec had taken place.

He had, in the early stages of that investigation, come across Mylaf and her talent for producing Legendary quality consumables at the drop of a hat. That the Drudge had agreed to move into his apartment had, at a stroke, removed any need to continue to conserve his mana, meaning he was able to go back to using *Grid View* in the casual, reckless way which had been his trademark.

He'd known, intellectually, that he'd missed his perfect memory and the ability to revisit events in his mind at will, but until he'd had that talent back whenever he wanted, he had truly no conception of how crucial that Skill had been to his sense of self. And then, of course, in short order after that, there had been his first Dungeon delve with Latham and the resetting of his Progress Points...

Even that massive boost, though - giving him the 'pure' Intelligence and Wisdom of someone double his Level - still hadn't quite returned him to what he had been before. Nevertheless, those changes supplemented by Mylaf's smoothies, cookies and afternoon snacks, the Lowe that had walked through the door of Soar Museum at the outset of this case was much closer to what he thought of as 'normal' than at any time since his Classtration.

Sure, he might not have all the bells and whistles that had come with his original Class, but the core of him – the bit of him that was better at seeing to the heart of the matter than anyone else in Cuckoo House – felt like it was largely back in place.

And then he had activated the Essence of Silent Thought, and he realised how much he had been kidding himself

Whatever else his reward for burning alive the Corrupt Fenrir did, it gave him access to the sort of white-hot insight that he'd forgotten he had ever possessed.

Half-formed, idle thoughts about the deaths of Curators Isadora and Harker blazed into focus and either were discarded as pathetic, logical fallacies he was ashamed ever to have entertained or gained traction as new possibilities as potential theories formed and developed.

"What's so funny?" Gral asked, glancing sidelong at Lowe as they moved their way down the latest – mercifully trap-free – corridor that Preece was leading them.

Lowe simply shook his head in response.

He wasn't sure he could have explained how he was feeling, even if the Essence had not temporarily removed his ability to speak. On the one hand, there was such joy in his brain ticking over in a way he had feared he would never experience again, but then there was also the agony of knowing that all this was just a buff that would shortly expire.

One of the major downsides of suddenly being a certifiable genius again was that there was no place for comforting lies to hide. As soon as this reward ran out, he'd be back to being plain old Jana Lowe. Not the stupidest man in the world, but certainly not the sharpest. And, having had this taste again of who he used to be, he knew that was going to suck the big one.

No time for that now, though. Self-pity was a luxury for a future, more stupid Lowe. Bless him, and his dull conception of the world. Right now, though, the 'him' that might have moments left to figure out what had happened to the dead Museum employees, plot a way to keep them all alive in this newly formed Dungeon and then work out how to pull everything together into a nice bow for Pernille Fucking Staffen once they'd escaped, had other things to concern him.

*Grid View* sparked into life around him, overlaying the walls of the corridor down which they walked with flashing scenes of everything that had happened since he'd first been called into his boss's office and told to get his arse down to this Museum.

Kaleidoscopic images looped, flared and raced across his mind: millions of details that had not even registered to his consciousness settled and resolved into a coherent narrative he'd not even been aware was being told. Keywords of conversations were cross-checked, lies flagged, and indisputable facts pulled into columns of details that flowed and twisted around that central question: who – or what – was the murderer?

Fucking hell, this was how he used to make sense of the world, wasn't it?

No, no more of that.

Focus.

For some reason, the supercharged part of his mind kept playing and replaying that desperate, panicked hunt Lowe had gone through in the bowels of the museum. His brain kept showing him the liquified body of Curator Harker, his subsequent, typically bad-tempered, conversation with Lant and then the start of his necrotic slime-fuelled hallucination.

But as soon as past-Lowe started walking through the dingy corridors, it paused, reversed and started playing out his first sight of the body again . . .

Lowe leaned into the memory – if he could use as physical a verb as that to explain what he was doing - trying to understand what his mind wanted him to see. The taste of his own frustration was almost tangible – he *knew* what was important here, but he couldn't quite seem to see it. It was quite a vibe to have your own psyche stick the dunce's hat on you and push you to the corner . . .

Standing over Curator Harker's liquified remains.

Deathcaller Lant being his normal, joyous self.

Then Lowe slips out of Culloden's office, and in moments, he was labouring under the effects of the necrotic slime and running scared beneath the museum.

Over. And over again.

What was it that his Essence of Silent Thought enhanced mind was fixating on?

Harker.

Lant.

Lowe walking down the passageway.

The same scene played, then reversed and then played again to him. Lowe felt that if his subconscious mind could have reached out and slapped him, it would have, so great was its irritation with his ongoing stupidity.

Harker.

Lant.

Lowe walking . . .

Then it hit him. He knew what his subconscious mind had noticed, and his sudden excess of Intelligence had finally brought to the fore.

And it was fucking irritating because this wasn't a spectacular leap of intuition; it was something utterly banal that had been staring him in the face all along. Lowe had been labouring under the illusion that he had, somehow, managed to get a blob of necrotic slime on him. Maybe when examining Harker's body?

Or – and if he was honest, this was what he had assumed had happened – Lant had, for shits and giggles, spiked him on his way out of from examining the crime scene. Not enough to cause him real harm – he was a dick, not a psychopath - but enough to cause the nightmarish hallucinations that had followed.

But no. Watching the scene play out over and over again, it was clear nothing like that had happened at all. Lowe had not accidentally transferred any slime off Harker's body.

Nor had Lant done anything vindictive to put a dent in Lowe's day.

Whatever had happened to Lowe beneath the Museum on that day was clearly *not* a necrotic slime-induced nightmare.

Which immediately begged any number of wider questions.

For example, if what Lowe had experienced had been 'real' and not a hallucination, what exactly had hunted him through the twists and turns of the exhibits? And what about all that bollocks with the candle and the writing? His excess of Intelligence surged to offer suggestions but then – abruptly – put all of its attention on a suddenly pretty important question.

When exactly had the Dungeon core that Director Nuroon retrieved from the outskirts of Soar become sentient? Was it earlier than they were all assuming?

That realisation sparked more supercharged neurons firing in Lowe's mind, and he staggered against the wall. Karolen looked his way in alarm, but he shrugged off her concern. If his experiences beneath the Museum that day had actually happened – and it now seemed clear to him that it absolutely had - then a whole host of other dominoes could start to fall into place. And they did. One after another.

So many aspects of the mystery that had baffled him suddenly all began to resolve into far greater clarity, causing him to reach some pretty important conclusions.

The sort of conclusion that made him suddenly not being able to speak to the rest of his party pretty fucking inconvenient...

# **CHAPTER THIRTY NINE – NO WAY IN**

Latham's fists were raw, knuckles split wide from repeatedly smashing them against the portal that had shimmered into being in front of Soar Museum.

The pain didn't register. At least, not anymore. In fact, he hadn't felt anything from his hands for the last half a bell, not since the red mist descended and he'd started to launch blow after blow.

"Feeling better yet?"

Latham didn't answer Hel, throwing another massive punch against the glowing shield. However, just like all of those he'd landed earlier, it seemed to do nothing. Just like every other strike. The door to the Museum simply glowed a touch brighter, as if absorbing the huge amount of kinetic energy the Temple Warder had summoned and drank it in.

Realising he'd reduced his left hand to mush, Latham tapped into the torrent of divine power surging through him, ignoring the 'tut' from some god or other as he – technically - misused one of his Skills to heal the injury, and then power up a punch again, energy thrumming along his veins.

As soon as his fist was full, he unleashed another earth-shattering blow, but the shell that encased the portal didn't even tremble. It was unmovable. Untouchable.

To be honest, he sensed it was – if anything – getting stronger.

Hel sighed, leaning back against the wall, arms crossed. She'd summoned a fairly impressive thunderstorm to drench the street around the museum entrance, and - thus far - no one had risked breaching the localised downpour yet.

Even so, interested crowds were gathering just beyond her impromptu cordon, and she worried it wouldn't be long before someone official took charge of the situation. "Yeah. You keep at it. I'm sure one more punch should do it. If there's one thing I've learned over the years, it's that esoteric magic responds really well to brute force."

"At least I'm trying to get us in."

"You're trying something, certainly. And here was me thinking it was just my patience."

Latham flexed his hand and wiped the pouring blood from his knuckles onto his tunic. "What would you have me do? Stand around and wait? That's working out so well for you, isn't it?"

Hel gave him a long look. "I didn't say I had any answers. I'm just not sure that hammering your fists into dust is much of a net benefit." Her eyes flicked to the gateway, its surface shining with a rainbow glow as if it was mocking them both.

She didn't like being kept away from the centre of the action any more than he did. And wasn't that the worst part of it. Neither of them were used to this... this being shut out. Of all of the terrible situations in which they had found themselves over the years, being unable to act was not one of them.

Especially with Lowe still inside.

Neither Hel nor Latham were the type to sit outside and wait. They certainly didn't let someone else take on all the risk. And yet this fucking Dungeon had separated them, locking Lowe inside the museum while they stood on the wrong side of a seemingly impervious wall.

Latham didn't stop to think about how long Lowe had been in there. How long he'd been trapped. No point in dwelling on that. That was a path to panic, and panic wouldn't help anyone. Especially not now. He had no idea why this strange little Classless man meant so much to him.

But he did.

Latham didn't have friends – terrified acquaintances, certainly – and he wasn't prepared to countenance something bad happening to one of the few he had. "We need to get in there," Latham said, more to himself than to Hel. His hands itched to punch the barrier again, even though he knew it wouldn't make a difference.

Hel raised an eyebrow. "You don't say. Care to share *how* you plan to do that? We've tried brute force, we've tried Skills—well, *I've* tried my Skills. You've been more focused on punching things—and still nothing. So, unless you've got a trick hidden up your sleeve, I suggest you take a breath and actually start thinking."

Latham turned away from her, staring at the entrance to the Dungeon that had taken over Soar Museum. His mind raced through options, strategies, anything that might explain what was happening. But every theory he came up with hit the same dead end.

It didn't add up.

Dungeons didn't just manifest out of thin air; they were ancient things. They certainly didn't just casually spring up in the centre of cities and trap people inside them at random.

But this one had.

"Why this place?" he asked, something significant scratching just on the edge of conscious thought. "Why Soar Museum? Why now?"

Hel pushed off the wall, her boots scraping against the stone as she walked up beside him. "No idea. But it's here now, and it's clearly not going away anytime soon."

Latham clenched his jaw, fists still trembling. It wasn't just the Dungeon that bothered him—it was the timing. The scale. "It doesn't make sense," he said, his voice low. "There's always been rumours about Director Nuroon and Soar Museum, but nothing solid. Nothing that would explain a Dungeon just popping up out of nowhere."

Hel's lips tightened into a thin line. "You think it's a coincidence Lowe was inside when it happened?"

"You think it's not?"

Hel didn't answer immediately. She stared at the entrance, her fingers twitching, lightning flickering beneath her skin. "I know you've been in a lot of Dungeons, Latham. But this—" She gestured at the barrier with a jerk of her head. "This feels like a trap. Not for everyone. For him."

Latham's gut twisted. It wasn't the first time that thought had crossed his mind, but hearing Hel say it made it feel more real. He turned back to the museum, eyes narrowing. A trap. If this was targeted, then that meant someone—something— wanted Lowe in there.

Alone.

And that made it worse.

Lowe was smart, and tougher than he looked, but he wasn't built to do this sort of thing solo. He wasn't supposed to be cut off from support, forced to face whatever was inside without backup. That wasn't what he did best.

"We've got to find a way in," Latham said, the words coming out harsher than he intended. "There's got to be something we missed. Some trick, some backdoor we haven't tried yet."

Hel crossed her arms again, tapping her fingers against her elbow. "We've been here for nearly a bell. If there's a backdoor, we would have found it by now. It's a Dungeon, Latham. You know how these things work. One way in, one way out. And it's not recognising either of us as having the requirements to enter."

Latham's mind raced, trying to ignore the creeping sense of helplessness that had been building since the moment they'd arrived. Hel was right—they'd tried everything they could think of. He'd pounded on the barrier until his fists were bloody. She'd tried every arcane trick in her book. And still, the portal stood between them and Lowe.

But there had to be something. Some angle they hadn't considered. He refused to believe they were locked out.

"I'm a Level ??. There's not a Dungeon on this continent I couldn't solo if I put my mind to it!"

"Yeah, all hail you!" In a burst of frustration, Hel let a mini-tornado appear and then swirl forward to strike against the dungeon entrance. "I hate this," Hel suddenly shouted, breaking the silence. She sounded angrier than he'd ever heard her, and that was saying something. "I hate that we're just standing here while he's in there, doing who knows what."

Latham glanced at her. She was pacing now, her usual cool, detached demeanour cracking under the weight of their situation. He wasn't used to seeing her like this—frustrated, anxious. But then again, none of this was normal. Not for them.

"We'll get him out," Latham said, though even he could hear the uncertainty in his voice. "He's got to know we're out here."

Hel stopped pacing, her eyes locked on the portal. "Neither of us is used to being helpless, Latham. But, on this occasion, it might be Lowe needs to sort it out himself."

Latham didn't respond. He couldn't. The idea of leaving Lowe behind, of not being able to reach him—it wasn't something he could process. Not yet. Not until he'd exhausted every possible option. Until he'd thrown every punch, every spell, every damn thing he had at that portal.

Hel sighed, rubbing the back of her neck. "I've been in a lot of shitty situations. But this is worse. Not being able to help is . . . Fuck. This sucks."

Latham's fists clenched again, his knuckles aching. "It won't be for much longer. We'll figure a way in."

But even as he said it, he wasn't sure if he believed it.

The doorway shimmered again, its surface rippling as if smiling at their impotence. Look at me, it seemed to say.

Still there.

Still immovable.

Still locking you out.

"Maybe," Hel said quietly. "But right now, we're on the wrong side."

And for the first time in a long time, Latham had no idea how to fix that.

# CHAPTER FORTY – CHARADES IN THE DARK

"Look, I have no idea what you're trying to tell me!" Karolen's voice whispered in the dark of the Dungeon.

Her patience had worn thin ages ago, and every additional gesture Lowe made was another fray to her nerves. He was, subtly, waving his hands about like a deranged puppet master, conducting some absurd pantomime that only made sense in the labyrinth of his overworked mind.

"Can I ask, how long is this silence debuff supposed to last? It's a bloody pain in the arse trying to communicate like this."

Lowe shot her a grimace, the tension visible on his face.

His eyes darted to Preece and Gral, who were walking a few paces ahead, seemingly oblivious to Lowe's desperate performance. Then, with barely a moment of hesitation, he started up another round of gestures—this time pointing at Preece with exaggerated care, then flexing his arms dramatically like a bodybuilder mid-pose, and finally saluting before mimicking a punch to the air.

Karolen blinked, utterly bewildered. "Whatever buff that Essence has given you, it hasn't made you any good at charades. I get it. You're worried about something to do with the Curator. But what about him?"

Lowe's eyes were wild with frustration, which she completely understood. For the umpteenth time, Karolen looked around the corridors for something the Inspector could write on. They were in a museum! Surely there had to be any number of bits of paper lying around.

But no.

The route Preece was leading them down seemed to be the exception to that rule. It was just an epically long, empty passageway stretching ever downwards towards the museum's cellar.

To be honest, Karolen was already thoroughly on edge without Lowe pawing at her sleeve and gesturing like a madman.

Lowe, growing more frantic, started a new series of movements—this time, he mimed pulling something heavy over his head like a hood and then suddenly jerked his hands forward as if revealing something grand.

His eyes darted toward Preece again, then back to Karolen.

She threw her hands up in exasperation. "Okay, so Preece is hiding something. Am I supposed to guess what it is now? Is this a game of fucking Twenty Questions?"

Lowe stomped his foot, and if he had the ability to speak, Karolen had no doubt he'd be cursing her out right now. Instead, he slapped his forehead, then frantically gestured downward as if pulling something invisible toward the ground.

"Okay, okay. Let me think. Preece is hiding something... below us?" She raised an eyebrow, hoping for a nod, but Lowe shook his head. "Preece... is pulling something down?" Another shake.

Lowe groaned and, in a fit of desperation, pantomimed lifting something heavy again, only to fall into an exaggerated fighting stance, fists raised like a boxer. He then mimicked stomping, as though driving something into the ground with tremendous force.

Karolen stared at him, blinking rapidly. "Preece... is... a fighter? No, that doesn't make sense. Preece is... oh!" Her eyes widened in a flicker of understanding. "You think he's stronger than he's letting on?"

Lowe's frenzied nod nearly dislodged his own head.

"Well, we know that don't we?" she said, eyes narrowing as she glanced at Preece ahead of them. "He's been open and honest that he was a Dungeon Delver before he changed his Class into being a Curator. But he's not lying about his Level, is he? If he was stronger, we'd have known that when we partied up and the monsters would be higher levelled. What exactly are you trying to tell me, though? Is he dangerous?"

Lowe mimed an explosion with his hands, eyes wide in warning.

Karolen felt the hairs on the back of her neck prickle. "An explosion? You think he's going to blow up? Or that he's something big?" Lowe nodded again, his urgency clear, though the gestures were growing increasingly erratic.

They walked deeper into the Dungeon, the narrow corridors becoming more constricting. The strange, hollow silence that filled the space gnawed at Karolen's nerves. Normally, Dungeons thrummed with life—or at least the constant lurking presence of things waiting to tear you apart—but this place was eerily still, like a tomb waiting for its last visitor.

Preece's voice rang out ahead of them, pulling Karolen out of her thoughts. "From what you know of things, are we getting closer to the Core? This place just keeps winding down."

"Probably not far now," Gral replied smoothly, his tone controlled and even. Too controlled, if you asked Karolen. Gral was always a wildcard—a lawyer who played both sides, always too polished, too poised. She didn't trust him either.

Lowe pulled at her sleeve again, forcing her attention back to his dumbshow. This time, he pointed toward the ground, mimicked slow, deliberate steps, and then pointed to Preece, making the same walking gesture.

Karolen frowned. "A trap. You think he's leading us into a trap." Lowe's exaggerated nod and urgent pointing drove the point home. She could practically feel the heat of his unspoken frustration.

Her thoughts were swirling now. Lowe, who had been blocked from speaking thanks to the Essence of Silent Thought, had been trying to warn her for the past half-bell that something wasn't right. But Preece? The idea that he was more than he seemed—that he was leading them into danger—didn't just sit wrong, it screeched wrong.

"You're telling me he's hiding something," Karolen said, more to herself than Lowe now. "And that whatever it is, it's big enough to put us all in danger. What else am I missing?"

Lowe mimed pulling a hood over his face again and then threw it back with the kind of drama reserved for actors on a stage.

"A disguise," Karolen muttered, her eyes narrowing. "He's hiding behind a disguise?"

Lowe's eyes gleamed with silent desperation. Finally.

Karolen took a steadying breath. It wasn't that she trusted Preece to begin with, but this... this had the potential to be huge. She glanced at Gral, who seemed as unreadable as ever. It felt like they were walking into a trap, and if Preece really was the one leading them there, they were in deep.

And there was nothing Lowe could do to tell them more. He had already played his hand, and now Karolen felt the burden of that knowledge alone.

However, before she could act on any of it, the floor beneath them trembled violently. A deep, shuddering rumble that made the stone walls groan in protest. Karolen's hand was immediately filled with her manifested blade.

Preece froze, turning back toward them, his face carefully composed. "Did you all feel that?"

Lowe nodded, his body tense, pointing frantically toward the ceiling as dust and loose debris began to fall. Karolen's mind raced. Was this it? Was this the trap Lowe was trying to warn her about?

"We need to move—" Gral began, but his voice was drowned out by a deafening *crack.*

The wall beside them exploded inward

Karolen ducked, dragging Lowe down with her as chunks of stone crashed through the corridor like shrapnel. The sound was overwhelming—stone grinding against stone, the thunderous echo of whatever force had just blown a hole through the wall. Her heart raced as thick dust clouded the air. For a few moments, she couldn't see anything, only the sound of debris settling and the distant rumble of the Dungeon's shifting mass.

Lowe coughed beside her, his grip tight on her arm as they both pulled themselves up. "What—what the hell was that?" Karolen yelled, brushing dust from her face. The hallway had collapsed inward, revealing an opening in the wall. No. Not just an opening—a hole large enough for someone - or something - to have forced its way through.

And that's when Karolen saw it: a figure emerging from the smoke, still obscured by the swirling chaos. Cloaked, hood drawn low, striding through the debris projecting an aura of immense power. The ground seemed to ripple beneath each step, and a strange, all-encompassing energy pulsed around it as it moved. Karolen's stomach sank. Whoever this was, they were more than just another Dungeon monster. This was the kind of power that warped reality itself.

The figure moved with the precision of someone who knew they had already won.

Preece and Gral stood frozen, eyes locked on the new arrival. Karolen wasn't sure if they were terrified or in awe—either way, it wouldn't matter.

The cloaked figure didn't hesitate. With a wave of their hand, a bolt of raw, crackling energy shot from the palm of their hand, obliterating... a series of lurking Dungeon beasts that had been hiding in the newly revealed passage. The creatures barely had time to shriek before they were vaporised, reduced to ash and scattered dust.

The figure stepped forward, the shadows around them swirling like a living thing, clinging to their form. Another flick of the wrist, and more creatures were reduced to smouldering ruin. There was no hesitation, no mercy. Whoever this was, they weren't just strong—they were beyond strong. Karolen's pulse pounded in her ears. She couldn't take her eyes off the figure. She needed to see their face, to know who had just torn through the Dungeon like it was made of paper.

The figure paused, standing tall in the centre of the wreckage, surveying the destruction with a kind of grim satisfaction. Slowly, with an almost theatrical motion, they raised their hands to the hood that concealed their face.

The air in the corridor seemed to still, every breath hanging in the silence.

With deliberate care, the figure lowered their hood.

Karolen's breath caught in her throat.

It was Director Nuroon.

# CHAPTER FORTY ONE – MEMORIES OF CLASSTRATION

"Fuck a duck!"

Lowe's exclamation disturbed the silence that had descended following the Director's sudden appearance. "Where the fuck did you come from?"

Nuroon cocked his head towards Lowe, looked him up and down, then dismissed him, turning to face Gral. "I assumed I would come across you in here somewhere, Felicitous. I imagine there are armoured cockroaches that are easier to kill."

"Too kind, sir. If I may say so, it looks as if you have been making short work of the Dungeon's various challenges?"

Nuroon waved a hand negligently towards the remains of the fallen monsters. "All low-level trash. To be honest, I haven't enjoyed myself so much in years. It is easy to forget the thrill that comes with a genuinely involving delve."

"Can't say I share your enjoyment, sir. Although, I am anticipating – with relish – putting in my bill for hazard pay . . ."

The realisation that he could speak let the stilted badinage fade from Lowe's ears. The Essence of Silent Thought had expired, and after all the frustrated dumb play, he could finally tell Karolen . . . what? He caught her by the sleeve, pulling her towards him and opened his mouth to speak.

"What?" she hissed at him, trying to keep half an eye on the suddenly extremely threatening figure of Grackle Nuroon.

"I . . . I don't know," Lowe said, a look of consternation flashing across his face. "I had it! It all made sense. It was... Shit. I can't remember."

So vulnerable did Lowe look at that moment, that Karolen felt herself turning away. "Well, don't push it. It happens sometimes to me at work. The harder you try to remember something, the more difficult it is to summon up. Think about something else for a bit like, I don't know, the sudden and dramatic appearance of a supervillain. It'll come."

But Lowe wasn't listening, not really. He was suddenly bereft – not just of the deductions he'd made about the case (something about Preece, right?) but in mourning for that renewed ability to make such links. He felt. . . hollowed out. Like he was back to those first few seconds following his Classtration.

Lowe felt Karolen's words drifting past him, lost in the surge of panic and loss flooding his mind. Her advice, though sensible, barely registered as he was carried away by a memory he'd done his best to repress. But the sharp, dizzying void that now filled him was all too familiar, tugging him backward, dragging him to somewhere he never wanted to revisit. Not least in his waking moments.

The day he lost everything.

The process had started with a blinding pain, like his core had been set on fire from the inside out. The kind of pain that doesn't come from wounds but from something deeper, something more fundamentally crippling. Every fibre of his being, every thread that held 'him' together had been snapped at once. Intellectually, he knew it wasn't a physical assault he was experiencing, but his muscles had locked, his bones had screamed, and all the power that had once surged through him—his Skills, his bonuses, his Class—was yanked away by an invisible, pitiless hand.

And in that instant, the world had gone dark.

At first, he had thought that blindness was temporary, that his vision would return, that the sharp ringing of tinnitus would fade, that the tightness in his chest would loosen and allow him to breathe deeply again. He had waited for the sensation of the individual parts of his body to return, for the warmth of his power to flood back into screaming limbs.

But it didn't. Not then. And not ever again.

He remembered stumbling forward, hands outstretched, grasping at nothing but the cold, empty air before him. The floor beneath his feet had felt suddenly unstable and uneven like he was standing on shifting sands. His legs had wobbled as if they were suddenly too weak to support his own weight, and he had collapsed, his knees hitting the mosaic tiles with a crack that he hadn't even heard. But it didn't hurt. That he remembered. The impact hadn't registered at all. He couldn't feel the pain. It was as if he couldn't feel anything at all.

It was like being erased. That was how he had explained it to Arebella, later.

His once sharp mind, so brimming with ideas and possibilities and deductive leaps, had been scooped clean. Everything that made him who he was—his thoughts, his insight, the web of connections he could always see in his head—had vanished. His Intelligence, his Wisdom, his Spirit, even his Strength and Agility, had plummeted into nothingness. He was deaf, dumb, and blind all at once. It was as if someone had taken a knife and severed the strings of his consciousness, leaving him dangling, unmoored in his own mind.

Standing here, in the Dungeon that used to be Soar Museum, Lowe could remember the voices around him that day—distant, muffled, like echoes in a vast, empty cavern. Cenorth had been there, shouting his name, but Lowe hadn't been able to process the words. Couldn't even find his voice to answer. The faces of his allies had been blurred, indistinct, as though viewed through a fogged window. He knew them, of course, but there had been no spark of recognition, no sense of connection. Just… blankness.

And then the fear had hit.

Real, primal fear.

Not fear of pain or death. He'd faced those a thousand times. This was the fear of being nothing. Of having no place in the world, no purpose, no identity. Without his Class, without his Skills, he wasn't an Inspector. He wasn't *Lowe*. He was an empty suit, an absence, a man who had been reduced to a husk, stripped of everything that gave him meaning.

He remembered the way his fingers had twitched on the ground, desperate to grasp at anything, at *something* that could anchor him to reality. He had tried to speak, to make a sound, but nothing had come out. His throat had felt paralysed, locked in silence. He had never realised how much of his own voice, his thoughts, his mind he had taken for granted until they were gone.

Time had passed in fits and starts after that—days, maybe weeks of stumbling through the wreckage of his former self. His senses had returned slowly, but nothing else had. Not his sharpness, not his insight. Not the clear mind that had once allowed him to see patterns others missed. He had become dull, sluggish, like a blade blunted by time and misuse. His world had shrunk to the basics: breathe, eat, sleep. Anything beyond that had felt impossible, unreachable.

Lowe's mind snapped back to the present as Karolen's voice reached him again, more distant now as she addressed Gral. The ground beneath his feet felt too solid, too steady compared to the swirling disorientation of that memory. But the sense of loss still clung to him like a second skin.

He glanced at his hands—steady now, but they had once trembled uncontrollably after the Classtration. Back then, he couldn't even hold a quill, much less wield a weapon. His own body had betrayed him, refusing to respond as if each extremity had forgotten they were supposed to follow orders. And his mind... His brilliant mind, the one thing he had always relied on, had felt like a dead weight, dragging him down into the abyss.

It had been Cenorth who had first found him, lying on the cold floor. Cenorth, who had knelt beside him, his face creased with concern and confusion. Lowe had looked up at him, desperate to speak, desperate to explain, but no words had come. Just the empty feeling of a man who had lost everything.

"I'm nothing," Lowe had managed to choke out, his voice barely above a whisper. "It's all gone."

Cenorth, the man he had thought of as his best friend in the world, had stared at him, the disbelief in his eyes giving way to something far worse: pity.

"You're not nothing," the Commander had said, his voice firm, but the words had rung false in Lowe's ears. "We'll fix this. We'll prove this was all a mistake."

But Lowe had known, even then, that there was no fixing this. No going back to who he had been. The Classtration hadn't just taken his Skills, it had taken *him*. It had stolen the core of who he was, leaving him adrift, unmoored in a world where he no longer had a place.

And that was how he felt again now, standing beside Karolen in the Dungeon's echoing halls, the memories of that day flooded back, raw and unrelenting. His hands curled into fists at his sides, the old fear threatening to rise again. The fear of losing everything, of being reduced once more to that hollow shell.

He shook his head, trying to banish the memory, but it clung to him, insistent. The silence that had once trapped him, the numbness that had seeped into his bones, all of it still haunted him. And now, even with his voice restored, even with some of his Skills slowly returning, he couldn't shake the sense that it could all vanish again, just as easily as it had the first time.

Karolen looked at him, her brow furrowed, but she didn't press him. She didn't know—couldn't know—what it had been like to lose everything that day. And he didn't have the words to explain it to her.

But the fear remained, gnawing at him in the dark corners of his mind.

What if it happens again?

And then Director Nuroon was in front of him, wizened face creased into something akin to a grin. "So, Mr Lowe. I see from your haunted expression you have partaken in one of those Essences. Was it everything you hoped it would be?"

Lowe punched him full in the face.

# CHAPTER FORTY TWO – NO HONOUR AMONG DELVERS

"You broge by fugging dose!"

Lowe yelped and shook out his hand, *Slugger* fading away even as *Roll with the Punches* took charge to rebuild a considerable number of fractured fingers.

Say what you will about Grackle Nuroon – and there was certainly plenty that could be said – the guy could take a punch. Lowe didn't really feel much better for unloading – even in his prime, he'd never been someone who worked out his emotions with his fists – but there was something about the outraged shock on the Director's face that, even if momentarily, cured what ailed him.

"How did you do dat! You're a fugging Lebel 25!"

Lowe turned his back on Nuroon and walked instead to Preece, prodding a mangled finger into his chest. "I don't know what it was I realised about you with that Essence running, but you need to tell me how you're involved in all this. Now!"

The Curator held up his hands in supplication. "I've no idea! Honestly! I've told you everything I know. About Isadora. About the blackmail. About her and Kregg. There's nothing else!" Preece's eyes strayed, with horrid fascination, to the bones visibly rearranging in Lowe's hand, the twisting, rotating finger of which was resting on his breastbone. "I'm doing everything I can to help you out here! Honestly."

Lowe swore under his breath. Every instinct he still possessed said the man was telling him the truth. Which made no sense at all. He couldn't remember what his revelation had been about Preece, but he was absolutely certain he was not what he seemed. And, more than that, that he was dangerous. "Tell me again about your friend. The other Curator, Harker."

"Sure. What do you want to know?"

"Insbegdor! I wan' do dalk do you!"

Lowe felt a brief, painful pressure on his mind – presumably, Nuroon had activated some sort of command Skill to bring him to heel? – but *Mental Fortress* batted it away. Without turning around, he flipped the Director the bird – his broken finger still not quite upright – and concentrated on Preece.

"When we met before, you said you wouldn't have been surprised to have heard Harker had killed himself?"

"Yeah. Isadora had something over him, and it was making him sick…"

"But Curator Harker died a month after her. Why would he still be so depressed – so much so that you genuinely feared he would take his own life – if the person blackmailing him was dead, cremated and gone."

Preece shrugged. "I don't know. Guilt? Fear of being blamed for her death?"

But Lowe was already shaking his head. In other circumstances, he could imagine Harker's low mood would make sense. His extraordinarily successful clear-up rate for murders was as much down to his former brilliance as it was to the utter stupidity of most criminals.

No blinding leaps of deductive logic had been required, for example, when he charged the wife of a slain wealthy industrialist with pushing him in a vat of his own solvent.

That she'd taken a selfie on her Sending Stone of her stood over said machinery with the caption "Well, I did promise I'd help you dissolve our differences" hadn't exactly hindered his investigation.

Lowe had a million such stories. The average bad guy in Soar was – almost to a fault – spectacularly dumb. Thus, it would be totally reasonable for Harker to be going out of his mind with worry that his crime in offing his blackmailer was going to be uncovered.

If, that was, Grackle Nuroon hadn't successfully closed down the investigation. Inspector Wyst had written it up as an accident far before Harker himself shuffled off this mortal coil. There was absolutely no reason in Soar for Curator Harker to be anything other than gleefully smug at getting away with murder; if that was what truly had been bothering him.

So, if it wasn't fear of discovery that had that man in such a state the night before he was murdered, what was it? He'd been murdered in Martha Culloden's office. A woman obsessed with Dreadnaughts and who had one who had not been seen since... Pieces of the puzzle continued to move in Lowe's head, but it didn't feel like these were the same revelations the Essence of Silent Thought had led him to.

No, *they* had been more about Preece...

"Inspector Lowe, on the instructions of my client, I am issuing you with notice of an intention to prosecute."

Lowe turned to look into the wide-set eyes of Felicitous Gral. "I'm sorry?"

"I rather think this has gone too far for a simple apology to be acceptable. In full view of witnesses, you casually, and with no provocation, struck Director Nuroon in the face. You have caused him considerable distress and we intend to lodge a complaint with the highest of authorities. You will never work in Soar again. I will be needing your witness statement," Gral said first to Karolen and then nodded towards Preece. "And yours too, sir. Nothing fancy, just confirmation you witnessed the assault will do for now."

Karolen pulled a 'Who me, guv?' face. "I have absolutely no idea what you are talking about."

"Oh, my dear," Gral tutted sadly. "I really would not encourage you to risk your promising career by doing anything as silly as this. You already have one rather significant strike against you for going up against Soar Museum. Do you really think anyone will employ an Auditor that has, not once, but twice, needed to be taken out to the woodshed and shown the error of her ways?"

"Honestly, I have no idea what you are getting at. We're in the middle of a Dungeon! Pardon me if I wasn't looking in the right direction when your 'client' took the beating he so richly deserved."

The two glared at each other for a moment. Lowe was pretty impressed that it was the greasy lawyer who broke away first. He could grow to like this girl.

Maybe all of Arebella's friends weren't wholly without merit.

"Well, be that as it may. Alongside my testimony, we will only need the evidence of one other person who saw the event to secure a prosecution. Ms Menin clearly cannot comment either way as she 'wasn't looking' so the word of Mr Preece will be all that is required. Can you confirm you witnessed the assault, sir?"

The colour leached from the Curator's face, and he gave a nod. "I saw Lowe hit the Director."

Gral smiled widely and made an 'ah, well' gesture. "And that's all she wrote. I am very sorry, Mr Lowe, to say that I cannot see someone even of your redoubtable resilience coming back from this one."

Preece gave a little cough. "I said I saw Lowe hit the Director. But as the Director is in a different Party, I'm not sure why that would be a problem."

"What?" Gral's voice was irritated.

"Director Nuroon is in a competing Dungeon Party. I absolutely saw Inspector Lowe strike him, but such an attack is not just viewed as lawful under Dungeon law, it's actively encouraged."

"Whad do you dink you are doing, Mr...?" Nuroon clearly cast around in his memory for Preece's name and came up blank. He pressed on regardless. "I would suggesd you dink bery garefully aboud whad you're saying here."

Preece, if possible, went even whiter. "I'm absolutely happy to testify anywhere you want that Lowe hit you, Director. No problem at all. Saw it clear as day. But it's not against the law to hit another delver."

Nuroon glared at Gral who shrugged back. "Not my area of expertise, I'm afraid, sir. However, that does sound familiar."

"Mr. Lowe," the Director snarled, stepping up close to the Inspector, blood still dripping down his ruined nose. "It may surprise you to know this isn'd the first dime someone's seen fid do lay hands on me. My life's been rich, full of experiences, afder all. Bud one thing's always been drue—those who dared do do so lived do regred id. Nod long, of course. Bud helbless, blubbering sorrow for their imbosidion? Yeah, that was alwags their final emotion."

"Mate, I'm going to be honest, I'd be trying to use fewer plosives until you get that damage buffed out. I don't have a clue what you just said."

There was a moment of stretched tension as the two of them stared at each other, during which Lowe could feel mental Skill after mental Skill crashing against his defences. So much psychic energy was sloshing about that the other three party members were brought to their knees, clutching their heads in agony. Lowe simply stood bolt upright and winked back.

"You are… an unushual man, Mr Lowe. I've always been drawn do rare and curiush things—like a cragged vase, or a piece of art that defies classivication. I like do dake by dime with shuch pieces, study dem, unbick ebery thread until I undershtand preshisely whad makes dem sho... unique. You, Mr. Lowe, will be no different. When I finish, I'll know exactly how do dismandle you, down do the lasht tick of your clockwork soul. And believe me... I dake by dime."

"Nope. Nothing. Sorry. Still not getting it. Is it possible you are offering to bake me a cake?"

Nuroon glared and then turned to stride down the corridor. "Felishidus, cub. Led's see how well these low-lebel non-endidies do widdoud the brodection of their bedders."

Gral glared at them, but scurried after his master without another word.

**'Felicitous Gral has left your Party'**

Preece, Karolen and Lowe stood in a silence for a minute before the Inspector broke the mood. "That true?" he asked. "About there being no laws about PVP in a Dungeon?"

"Fuck me, not at all!" Preece said, grinning. "Can you imagine if there were rules like that? It'd be carnage on every run. Violence against other delvers is actually more strictly enforced in a Dungeon than it is on the outside."

"He's going to be pissed when he realises you lied to him," Karolen cautioned.

"To be honest, it sounds like he's really looking forward to dealing with me personally, so I doubt he'll much miss taking me to court. Thanks for having my back, though," Lowe said to Preece.

"Don't mention it. Glad to help."

Was there an odd expression to Preece's face when he said that? Lowe wasn't sure. Maybe he was just becoming paranoid. It would hardly be the first time "Come on," he said, stretching out his newly repaired hand. "We need to get moving if we want to beat them to the Dungeon core."

But Karolen was shaking her head. "We've got no chance of keeping up with those two. You saw how Nuroon massacred those monsters. He's going to be unstoppable"

"Ah," Lowe said, beaming, "you seem to have forgotten that this Dungeon scales to members of each individual Party. And whilst Nuroon is going to be, pretty much, soloing his way there, our little party has just lost its Level 33 dead weight . . ."

The race was on.

# CHAPTER FORTY THREE – WHEN THE RULES DON'T APPLY

As races go, Lowe thought - a little more than a bell later - it was a remarkably slow one to the Dungeon's Core.

Almost as soon as Nuroon and Gral were out of sight, the Dungeon appeared to properly distance all of the delvers away from each other in a relatively suspicious manner.

It was almost as if it had been hoping for some sort of explosive confrontation between the different parties and, now that it had not come to pass, it was sulkily enforcing its proper rules.

Lowe wasn't sure if it was healthy that he was anthropomorphising a Dungeon, but he couldn't think of many other ways to explain what was going on.

Especially as it had, at the same time, significantly ramped up the number of mobs. There were suddenly so many bad guys dogging their steps that Lowe was very grateful indeed that the worst of them were now benchmarked to his more modest Level 25.

After the emotional turmoil of his experiences with the Essence of Silent Thought, he did not think he had many more voluntary incinerations of Level 33s in him. As it was, the combination of him tanking and Karolen supplying the damage was more than enough to deal with the succession of common-or-garden Dungeon bad guys that came their way.

"That's my fourth level-up," Preece called out, somewhat sheepishly. Lowe assumed that considering his previous occupation, he felt a bit of a heel passively being power levelled in this way.

"Good for you! Just the two for me," Karolen said, wiping her gore-stained blade on the corpse of a Level 24 Moleman. "Not to mention an absolute shedload of gold."

"Careful," Lowe said, "you'll start sounding like Gral."

Karolen shot him a look. "That's uncalled for."

Lowe checked his own stat sheet and was pleased to see that he'd hit Level 26 himself.

That wasn't exactly completely great news, though. Especially as it probably meant that enough people had now died in the Dungeon for it to have started doling out the XP rewards. Lowe didn't think that said anything good for the rest of the employees in the Museum. Nevertheless, he sensed they might need every last bit of XP they could gather if they were going to have a chance once they reached the Dungeon Core.

He was pleased for Karolen and Preece, who were talking excitedly about the new Skills their Classes were offering them as they ranked up.

Unfortunately for Lowe, there were no extra threshold bonuses for reaching Level 26, so he only had one new Progress Point to play with. He was aware that people spoke about the painfully slow climb from Level 25 to Level 30, which was where all sorts of exciting evolutionary options manifested.

That thought gave him another hit of sadness - he wouldn't be getting any of the traditional Level 30 Class goodies, would he? - but he squashed it down. Lowe recognised that his experiences with the Essence were making him feel more than usually raw about such things.

Without really thinking too much about it, he dropped his Progress Point into Intelligence, bringing it up to 296. He didn't think he'd get anything especially noteworthy when it hit 300—not like when he Ranked it up at 200—but you never knew.

He was just about to close the screen down when the slight change to the description on *Roll with the Punches* caught his eye.

**Name:** *Jana Lowe*
**Level:** *26*
**Class:** ****Removed****
**Primary Attributes:**
*- Strength: 120*
*- Dexterity: 90*
*- Intelligence: 296 (+30)*
*- Wisdom: 238 (+20)*
*- Charisma: 60*
*- Constitution: 75*


**Secondary Attributes:**
*- Perception: 95 (+15)*
*- Willpower: 99 (+25)*
*- Luck: 63 (+5)*
*Health Points (HP): 1150 - Regeneration Rate: 2 HP/min (natural); 15 HP/sec (via *Roll with the Punches*)*
*Mana Points (MP): 400 - Regeneration Rate: 1 MP/min (natural); 2 MP/min when Mana falls below 10%*
*Stamina Points (SP): 550 - Regeneration Rate: 5 SP/min*
**Skills:**
*1. Roll with the Punches (Passive) - Rare - Level 50 (Rank-Up Available)*
   *Converts 10 MP to heal 15 HP per second.*
   *- Activation depletes 5% of the maximum mana pool.*
   *- Cooldown: None.*
*2. Grid View (Active) - Rare - Level 43*
   *Records events with perfect recall of details.*
   *- Mana Cost: 50% of total MP.*
   *- Cooldown: None.*
*3. Slugger (Active) - Rare - Level 42*
   *Next melee attack deals triple damage.*
   *- Cooldown: 10 minutes.*
*4. Medic! (Active) - Rare - Level 15*
   *Heal a companion at a 2:1 MP to HP ratio.*
   *- Cooldown: None.*
*5. Mental Fortress (Passive) - Legendary - Level 50 (Rank Up Rejected)*
   *Grants heightened resistance to mental manipulation and emotional attacks.*

> *- Mana Cost: 10% MP cost each successful defence*
> **** Skill slots 4 and upwards are blocked as per Council decree ****

His most overused Skill had reached Level 50—which was hardly surprising considering he was tanking all sorts of crap in this Dungeon—but it seemed like he was being offered an opportunity to rank it up, which was a surprise. Mind you, as he was glowing again, it probably shouldn't.

As both *Medic!* and *Mental Fortress* had evolved directly from that Skill, he had not really anticipated there could be anywhere else for it to go. To have gained two new Skills—especially considering his Skill slots were functionally blocked—felt like a pretty OP reward already.

He mentally pressed down on the Skill, and nothing happened.

It was as he had thought; it must be a leftover artefact from his Class. He probably should have been able to evolve the Skill when it hit Level 50, but Classtration had removed—as with so many things—that possibility.

Well, you didn't miss that you'd never had.

"Erm, Lowe. Everything okay?" Karolen's voice was strained, surprising him.

"Yes, why?" he said, turning to face her.

Both she and Preece were staring at him, eyes wide, but it was Preece who cleared his throat and tried to answer.

"You're, erm, I don't really know how to say this . . ."

"What?"

"You're glowing," Karolen supplied. "Like properly flashing on and off. Lighthouse-style."

Lowe sighed and re-opened his stat sheet. And yes, as he had feared, there was a new message.

*Restriction Breaker Title active. Skill: Roll with the Punches Rank-Up available. Do you wish to proceed?*

"Hang on. I think I've ranked something up. Give me a moment. I just need to choose an option for it and it'll fade. This has happened before. It's not a problem."

"I don't glow like that when I rank up," Preece murmured to Karolen. "You?"

"Not that anyone has mentioned. I think it might have come up otherwise."

"And how can he rank-up his Skills anyway? Isn't he supposed to be properly locked down, or something like that? That's what Classtration means, isn't it? That he cannot progress anymore."

Karolen gave Lowe a long look. What Preece had said was right.

After Arebella had made clear that she had no intention of turning her back on Lowe after his punishment at the hands of the Council, Karolen had looked into what her friend could expect from the man she seemed so determined to tie her wagon to.

Available information on the Classless wasn't high, but all of it was pretty consistent on one point. They weren't long for this world. Without many legal means to level-up their Skills, and without the capacity to get any more, it was just a matter of time before the fundamental order of Soar applied itself.

Dog eats dog, and the canine smorgasbord was especially tasty where the weak were concerned.

As a Classless Level 20, she'd given Lowe a month at best. And had told Arebella much the same. The fact he was not only alive and kicking but still able to progress through the levels was not just extraordinary, it pretty much defied Karolen's way of looking at the world.

"You okay?" Preece said. "You have the weirdest look on your face. What's up?"

Karolen let out a slow breath, weighing her words. "You ever have the feeling everything you think about how things work might be wrong?"

Preece snorted. "I'm a Curator who, up to last year, spent his life battling bosses in Underground Dungeons for cash. I think it's fair to say I'm familiar with moments of profound self-reflection and doubt."

Karolen half-smiled, though her thoughts were elsewhere. She had never expected this outcome—Lowe, of all people, defying the odds, pushing back against a system designed to crush him. "I did some digging, you know," she said, her voice dropping. "On the Classless."

"Oh?"

"Yeah. Lowe shouldn't have lasted this long. None of them do. The system's not built for them. It's built to chew them up."

Preece raised an eyebrow. "And yet, here he is. Still kicking. I think you might need to adjust your assumptions."

"Maybe," she replied, her tone softer than before. But even as she said it, her mind was racing. *What the hell is going on with him?*

They went back to watching Lowe attempt to choose a Rank-Up option that would finally diffuse his flashing light.

# CHAPTER FORTY FOUR – BLOOD OF THE PHOENIX

Lowe did his best to ignore Karolen and Preece's whispering, closing his eyes and taking a breath that felt heavier than it should.

His stat sheet was still open in front of him, the glowing notification blinking obnoxiously at the centre of his vision.

*Roll with the Punches.*

Since his Classtration, that had been his absolute lifeline. Quite literally. It was a Skill that had let him survive any number of absolute pastings during his year of exile and, more recently, it had been the basis for both of those new Skills he had somehow developed: *Medic!* and *Mental Fortress.*

And now it had reached Level 50 and, what, had become available to 'rank up' to a level he'd never thought he'd see on a stat screen?

**Mythic**.

He stared at the word as it pulsed redly on his screen.

People like him didn't get access to Mythic Skills.

He didn't even think Latham, for all of his other considerable attributes, had anything of that level. If you had enough gold, then bringing all your skills to Legendary was entirely possible.

Mylaf's previous employer, the High Priestess of Gravalk, Gianna d'Avec, had ensured her former nanny had access to the very best of Skill upgrades that money could buy. But even she – with access to almost limitless funds – hadn't been able to bring her Skills to the Mythic level.

It wasn't an upgrade you could gain through normal means. It was a reward, apparently. And yet the key emotion Lowe was feeling right now wasn't triumph. It felt . . . like fear.

The offer to upgrade remained there, waiting in front of him like a trap with its jaws wide open. His instinct, obviously, was to accept it, to take the power and hold it close to him. But something—something deep inside him—held him back.

He glanced over towards Karolen and Preece again, both of whom were now watching him closely, though trying not to make it too obvious. Karolen was ostentatiously sharpening her Auditor's blade, but he could see her looking at him from the corner of her eye. Preece, meanwhile, was pretending to fiddle with his own stats, but the tension in his shoulders gave away his own interest in what was going.

They were worried about him, which he appreciated.

Maybe not openly, but the flickers of concern were there. And he had a momentary pulse of satisfaction at actually having people in his life who showed such care for his wellbeing. Add them to Arebella, Latham, Hel and maybe even Staffen . . . well, he certainly wasn't the lone wolf anymore.

Lowe flexed his hands, remembering the feeling of that first punch he had tried to deliver after his Classtration.

He had been reduced to nothing—stripped of his Class, his identity, all of his Strength. Sure, *Slugger* had still been able to come through in a pinch, and *Grid View* was always helpful as a memory aid but *Roll with the Punches* had been the Skill that had kept him tethered to something. It had evolved as he had adapted, becoming more than just a passive Skill to him.

It had been the difference between being found dead in a gutter or still standing here, glowing on and off like some absurd beacon of uncertainty.

But to upgrade it to Mythic? That was a whole world of difference. Like a doorway to a world he wasn't sure he wanted to step through.

**Mythic**.

That word echoed in his mind, growing heavier with each repetition. Mythic quality Skills weren't just stronger versions of what came before—they were game-changing. They twisted the rules, rewrote the laws of how Classes worked, how abilities functioned. They closed the gap between humans and the gods . . . People who had developed Mythic Skills were rare enough in Soar, but Lowe had seen one or two in action to sense such abilities were as much a curse as a blessing. Power like that didn't come for free.

And when those with Mythic Skills broke, they broke bad. He had, for example, a pretty vivid memory of Arkola descending from their home at the top of the Celestial Temple to bring a particularly appalling Mythic-inspired rampage to an entirely abrupt conclusion.

Did he really want to be in possession of a power that put him on Arkola's 'to squash' list?

Thoughts of that god led Lowe's gaze to flick to the side, towards where his Restriction Breaker title glimmered faintly at the edge of his stat screen. That title had been hanging over him like the spectre at the proverbial feast ever since he had gained it, and yet it was the key that unlocked this upgrade.

Without it, he wouldn't even have this current choice.

*Restriction Breaker.*

The name felt almost mocking. Lowe had broken no restrictions—he had been trapped by them, nearly broken by them. And yet, and yet, and yet... In all the reading he'd done since Latham had opened his eyes to Essence Transmutation Theory, he'd never come across mention of anything like it. In fact, if he had to put money on it, it occurred that this title might have been some sort of reward for his efforts in the d'Avec case from the supreme being in Soar.

Which was an absolutely brain-shredding thought to contemplate...

Especially considering the consequence of that title, was – apparently – the option for this upgrade. Which had the potential to change who he was. Again. Gritting his teeth, Lowe scrolled through the options that he was being offered, each one leaving him more overwhelmed than the last.


*Roll with the Punches (Mythic Upgrade):*

*1. Indomitable Flesh (Mythic)*

*Your body becomes a conduit for damage absorption, converting all incoming damage into health regeneration at a rate of 50%.*

*- Side Effect: All healing is delayed by 10 seconds, forcing you to endure accumulated pain before it dissipates.*

*- Cooldown: None.*

### 2. Unyielding Spirit (Mythic)

*Damage heals 75% of lost HP immediately, while your Intelligence fuels a defensive aura that negates 25% of all magical damage.*

*- Side Effect: For every minute spent under attack, your Wisdom will temporarily drain by 10%, reducing your ability to resist mental effects.*

*- Cooldown: None.*

### 3. Blood of the Phoenix (Mythic)

*Upon falling to zero HP, your body is consumed by flames, and from the ashes, you are reborn at full health after a five-second delay.*

*- Side Effect: The resurrection ignites a residual flame within you. For the next hour, your regeneration abilities are suppressed, and any attempt to heal you instead inflicts a portion of its intended benefit as burning damage. However, this flame grants you a temporary increase in Strength and Willpower during the duration.*

*- Cooldown: One use per twelve hours.*


He stared at the three options, the flavour text glinting with both promise and threat. Each upgrade came with enormous potential—but also carried commensurate risk.

Certainly, it was the consequences of each upgrade that stuck with him. *Indomitable Flesh* would apparently let him tank practically any hit, but the idea of accumulating pain, stacking it up until it burst through his body in one agonising wave . . . well, that reminded him too much of his Classtration.

Of the way the pain had built and built until it consumed him. He wasn't sure he would be able to relive that, even in short bursts.

*Unyielding Spirit,* on the other hand, was more tempting, offering not just healing but protection from magical attacks, which would be certainly useful against the Dungeon Core. But the thought of his Wisdom draining over time felt dangerous. He had spent too long shoring up his mental defences after the Classtration, fortifying his mind against the creeping despair that came with being stripped of his identity.

And then there was *Mental Fortress.* For that to lose its potency? To have it slowly chipped away in the heat of battle? After everything that this case had shown him about necrotic slime, that terrified him.

Finally, there was *Blood of the Phoenix.* Resurrection. A second chance right when he would need it most. The ultimate backup plan. But the cost in the aftermath? Losing all regeneration for an hour meant he'd be wholly vulnerable. Defenceless. A sitting duck once that miraculous revival wore off. In a protracted battle, that hour could mean the difference between life and death.

A second life at the cost of being unable to defend the first one...

Lowe clenched his jaw, feeling the weight of the decision. Any of these upgrades would fundamentally change how he approached being 'him'.

They were all game-changers, and the pressure of picking the right one pressed down on him like one of Latham's meaty shoulder taps. He looked again over at Karolen, still sharpening her blade with deliberate, rhythmic strokes. Preece was still pretending not to pay attention. Each of them was both moving forward during this Dungeon, both gaining levels and becoming more of who they had the potential to be.

But Lowe wasn't like them anymore, was he?

He didn't have a Class.

He didn't really have a future.

Not one set in stone, anyway. This choice wasn't just about which Skill would keep him alive longer. It was about who he wanted to be.

Lowe tried to calm his thoughts, but his mind was replaying every battle he'd survived, every scrape that had brought him this far.

Each time, *Roll with the Punches* had been there, absorbing the hits, healing his wounds, giving him a lifeline. But it had also been a crutch. A safety net. Maybe that's why he was hesitating. He wasn't sure he wanted that safety anymore. He wasn't sure he wanted to keep patching himself up, just to survive the next fight. He wanted more than that.

More than just getting by.

The blinking message was still there, waiting for him to make a decision. The glow from his body had dimmed, but it was still there, pulsing faintly, a reminder that this moment mattered.

Lowe scrolled back to *Blood of the Phoenix*. A second chance. A burst of life when everything seemed lost. It wasn't perfect. It came with a downside in that golden hour following his return. But maybe that's what he needed. Something with risk.

Something that didn't just keep him going, but gave him the chance to rise when all seemed lost.

He pressed down on the option, feeling the weight of his choice settle into place.

*Roll with the Punches has been upgraded to include Blood of the Phoenix*

The glow around him intensified for a moment before fading completely. He felt it settle into his bones, an odd sense of peace washing over him. He had made his choice.

Karolen glanced over at him, eyes sharp. "You done?"

Lowe nodded. "Yeah. I think I am."

"Time to move on?"

"Sure. Let's roll."

But as they continued down the corridor toward the Dungeon Core, a small, quiet thought lingered in the back of his mind, whispering: What have I just become?

# CHAPTER FORTY FIVE – PLANS WITHIN PLANS

"So, we do have a plan, right?" Preece yelled, circling around the cavern, trying to keep as much as possible to the shadows.

"Oh yeah," Lowe replied, "an awesome one. All sorts of easy-to-follow practical steps, plenty of redundancy built in and a cool victory dance for when it's all over. I'm really proud of it. One of my better ones."

Preece cocked his head. "And are we following that plan right now?"

Lowe was spared answering via the medium of all the air being forced from his lungs by being slammed back against the wall.

Unfortunately, without him being front and centre, the giant Octopus - whither an Octopus? Who knew - defending the Dungeon Core could focus its tentacles on Karolen. The Auditor barely dodged its attack in time, sprawling on the floor as multiple swishing blows flailed above her.

"Fuck's sake, Lowe. Less chat, more tanking!"

"On it!"

Shaking his head to clear his blurred vision, Lowe stood and grabbed hold of a tentacle as it whipped passed him. He was jerked back off his feet but clung on, riding the momentum of the slash back to the centre of the cavern, where he landed a solid *Slugger* into the middle of the creature's face.

The impact momentarily stunned the monster, allowing Karolen to scramble back to her feet and begin pounding on it from behind again. It had been about half a bell since they'd begun engaging the guardian of the Dungeon Core, and – as far as Lowe could tell – they'd made very little progress thus far.

"Look, I'm all for a 'if you don't succeed, try, try again' vibe, but are you sure this is the best approach?"

Lowe glanced over his shoulder at Preece, which was a mistake, as the guardian beast caught him with another crashing blow into the side that sent him flying again. "Do you have any other – motherfucker, that hurt – ideas? You're supposed to be our resident Dungeon expert!"

Preece did his best to ignore the sight of Lowe's broken arm snapping itself back into place. The *click* of the bone reconnecting was harder to miss. "Maybe. In a 'normal' Dungeon, we'd need to defeat the Big Bad in order to complete the quest line. But that's not the case here, is it?"

"Lowe, will you fucking hold the aggro!" Karolen danced under and over tentacles in an entirely balletic and kick-arse way. "I can't attack it and have to focus on staying alive at the same time!"

"Sorry! Preece, what are you getting at?"

"We don't have a quest, do we? The Dungeon spawned around us, and we've not actually been given anything we're supposed to be doing, have we? If you ask me, I'm not even sure if this encounter has even officially started."

Lowe took another stinging, glancing blow to the face as he re-engaged the monster. "I don't know, mate. It's feeling pretty fucking active right now!"

Karolen let out a shriek as she was dragged off her feet by a tentacle wrapping around her leg. Preece fired off a bolt from a looted crossbow and skewered the squirming appendage, letting the Auditor retreat back again. "What are you suggesting we do?!" she called across the cavern.

"Let's fall back to the entrance and see if it resets."

"I've not got a better idea." Lowe absorbed another stinging flap to the face. "And this is all getting a bit old. After you, Karolen."

"Damn straight 'after fucking me'. Seriously, Lowe, have you never tanked before?"

Lowe let that one slide, staggering back as the Octopus lashed out again.

Preece was right, wasn't he? This *wasn't* a normal Dungeon encounter. Not that he had all that much experience with such things. But there was no quest. No objective. Just this endless, maddening brawl with a creature that refused to go down. And that couldn't be right. Could it?

Preece, crouched low and darting from shadow to shadow, waved them back towards the cavern entrance. "Come on! Fall back. It's time to bail, guys!"

Karolen didn't need another invitation. She leapt over a final thrashing tentacle and sprinted for the entrance with Lowe following close behind, taking blow after blow on the back. His ribs repeatedly broke and reknitted back together, but the lingering pain gnawed at him as it always did. First Preece, then Karolen and finally Lowe skidded back into the corridor leading to the final encounter just as another tentacle shot toward them, slamming into the ground with a thud. However, once they were out of range, the creature let out a low, furious roar that echoed throughout the cavern and then settled itself back down again. Almost calm in repose.

"Well," Karolen said, breathing heavily, "that was... not ideal."

Lowe leaned against the wall, wiping blood, sweat and tears from his brow and down the front of his shirt. Mylaf was going to be *pissed*. Then he remembered, his own clothes had already been burned to ash. Kind of a good news, bad news thing there. He decided not to dwell on it. "No kidding. Okay, so we're not going to get anywhere against that thing by brute force. Tell me you've got something better than running away and hoping it doesn't eat us, Preece."

The Curator's brow furrowed as he poked his head around the edge of the corridor, making sure the creature hadn't tried to follow. His face was pale, but there was something of gleam in his eyes. "You know what? I actually think I do. Look, I've been wondering about this since Gral first told us about the Core. You see, I don't believe completing this Dungeon is going to be about any sort of final Boss fight at all. It's about the Dungeon itself. You've noticed how everything feels... off, right?"

"No shit!" Karolen said, pacing around to do something about all the adrenaline racing around her veins. "But it's a Dungeon; they're all a bit messed up. Olly in there isn't exactly unusual!"

"Olly?" Lowe asked.

"The Octopus."

"And you named him 'Olly'?"

"I can call him fucking 'Kenneth' if it makes you happy."

"No. Olly's fine. It's just some of us were a bit busy to come up with cutesy nicknames for the giant fucking monster trying to kill us."

"Ah, is that what you were doing? Being busy. You should have said. It looked like a lot of lying around and getting stomped on."

Preece cleared his throat. "Sorry to interrupt, but would you like me to continue to outline my theory, or are we done with that now?" Lowe gestured for him to go on. "From the very start, we've noticed that the Dungeon has sought to tailor itself to whoever is running it. It's a Level 26 Dungeon because that's the highest level person in our party. And this boss—well, it feels like it's just there to keep us busy. The more I think about it, the more I think it's a distraction."

Lowe almost smiled at that. "A distraction? It's a fucking effective one, then. What do you think it's distracting us from?"

Preece gestured toward the swirling, shimmering globe of light just behind the beast. "The Core. I don't actually think this Dungeon is designed to be beaten in the usual way. No quest, no objective to kill the big bad. No nothing. It's all about the Core. I think, if we want to get out of here, we need to get to it without engaging the boss at all."

Karolen paused in her pacing. "And how do you propose we do that? In case you missed it, every time we so much as blink near that thing, it goes full murderhobo."

"Exactly!" Preece said. "Every time *we* try. But I reckon it's dialled in to react to threat levels. And it's geared to Lowe's strength."

Lowe's mind raced as he processed the Curator's words. Preece was right, wasn't he? From the very start the Dungeon was benchmarking to their levels, responding to the most powerful among them. But Preece . . . Preece was far lower levelled. Maybe low enough that the creature wouldn't react to him . . . "Let's cut to the chase. You think because you're a lower level, you can sneak past it and claim the Core?" Lowe asked. "That's a hell of a gamble."

Preece shrugged. "I've been getting power-levelled the whole way through here because I'm so much weaker than you. It's worth a shot, at least."

Karolen was clearly unconvinced. "That's a dangerous assumption, Preece. If you're wrong, that thing is going to turn you into paste the second you step foot in there."

"Yeah, well," Preece said, rubbing the back of his neck, "I'm not thrilled about the idea, but it's better than getting nowhere. Look, we can't beat this thing the normal way. It's too strong, too fast, and whatever we throw at it, it just adapts. This is the only shot we've got. Eventually, it's going to wipe the pair of you, and then my outcome is going to be the same. If you look at it that way, we might as well roll the dice."

Lowe stared at the glowing orb visible just beyond the boss: the Dungeon Core. It shimmered like some kind of miniature universe suspended in space. He felt the pull of it, the same tug he had felt ever since they entered the place.

That Core was the key to escaping from here. It always had been. And he felt the explanation for all the murders lay with it, too. But something else was bothering him. His brain was trying to bring forward a lingering worry that had been at the back of his mind ever since they had started this last fight.

"What about the Dreadnaught?" Karolen asked. "It's supposed to be here, isn't it? We've seen nothing—no necrotic slime, no trace of it. If that thing's still out there..."

Preece shrugged. "We'll deal with the Dreadnaught when we have to. For now, the Core's the priority."

Karolen glanced back toward the cavern, her expression grim. "Maybe that's why we're not seeing the usual signs. The Dreadnaught might be tied to the Core in ways we don't understand. But until we know more, we have to assume that getting to that Core is the only way to shut it down."

They all turned towards the space containing the Boss.

The faint glimmer of the Core was barely visible behind the hulking form of the octopus-like beast. Lowe clenched his fists, staring down the long stretch of stone that separated them from their goal. Every instinct in him screamed that this was not the right way forward; that he was still missing something important. But, try as he might, he couldn't quite put his finger on it. He sure could do with an Essence of Silent Thought, right now. However. as far as he could tell, Preece was right. And they had no other options.

"Alright," Lowe said finally. "Let's do it. But Preece, you better be right about this, or you're going to have a lot more than a tentacle to worry about. Die out there and I am going to be pissed!"

Preece grinned. "No pressure, then."

They gathered at the entrance of the boss chamber once more, their eyes trained on the beast as it shifted and writhed. It had reset entirely from their previous attack and wasn't on full alert anymore.

It was waiting.

Almost frozen. However, once Lowe took a step into the chamber, the beast immediately reacted, its tentacles whipping up in the air in a defensive posture. He stopped. "Yep. Still very much awake." Karolen tried next, darting quickly across the floor. The creature's eyes followed her instantly, its hulking mass shifting toward her direction: she quickly retreated back to the entrance.

Preece stepped forward, swallowing hard. "Well, I guess that's our answer. It's going to be down to me."

# CHAPTER FORTY SIX – IN THE GRIP OF THE DREADNAUGHT

The cavern trembled as Preece approached the Core, its swirling energy casting kaleidoscopic patterns on the stone walls. Lowe and Karolen stood at the threshold, watching him warily. Lowe didn't think either of them could reach him in time if this went wrong, but he knew they'd do their best.

"Preece, slow down," Lowe called. "No sudden moves. That thing's still watching. The second it looks like the monster notices you, you need to get the fuck out of there."

The octopus-like guardian tentacles undulated lazily, as Preece approached, though, as if it were simply biding its time before striking. Its glowing eyes tracked Preece's every movement, but it still didn't attack.

So far, so good.

"I'm fine," Preece said, and his voice carried an unusual steadiness that prickled at Lowe's instincts. "It's not reacting. I think... I think we're good."

Karolen shifted uncomfortably, her hand hovering near her manifested blade. "Lowe," she said quietly, "this doesn't feel right. After everything, this feels all too calm. I get that he's weaker than us, but it makes no sense that a Dungeon Big Bad is letting him just walk past and take the prize. It's like it's accepting him."

"Yeah," Lowe said. He triggered *Slugger*, his eyes darting between the guardian and Preece. Something about the entire scene was gnawing at him too—it was a dissonance he couldn't quite quiet.

Preece was past the guardian now and reaching for the Core, standing before it with an almost worshipful stillness. The swirling light bathed the Curator in a glow that seemed to amplify his presence, casting his features into sharp relief.

Slowly, he raised a hand.

As his fingers brushed its surface, the Dungeon Core flared with blinding light, flooding the chamber in an instant. The guardian creature let out a roar, its tentacles lashing wildly, but it didn't attack Preece. Instead, it froze, its massive form quivering as if held in place by unseen chains.

Then, to Lowe and Karolen's shock, the guardian began to dissolve, its mass crumbling into motes of light that scattered and vanished into the air.

"What the fuck?" Karolen whispered.

"Stay back," Lowe warned, holding out an arm to stop her. His gaze locked on Preece, who now stood alone with the Core, his hand resting on its surface.

Something was wrong.

The glow surrounding Preece intensified, warping the air around him like heat rising from a flame. When he turned to face them, Lowe felt the first pangs of dread claw at his chest.

The man before them was no longer the Preece they had traveled with. His face, once timid and uncertain, was now suffused with confidence—a cruel, mocking smile twisting his lips. His eyes burned with an unnatural light, their depths brimming with malice.

"Thank you," Preece said, his voice filled with mocking amusement. "I couldn't have done it without you."

Karolen's blade was in her hand, "Preece, what the fuck are you talking about?"

"I don't think that's Preece anymore," Lowe said.

Preece chuckled, the sound low and venomous. "What I was always going to do. You're just realising it now, aren't you? All that trust. All that camaraderie. How quaint."

The air around the Curator rippled, and his form began to shift. His features elongated and twisted, his slight frame bulging with muscle and sinew. His skin darkened, veins pulsing with blackened energy, and his grin widened, revealing jagged, inhuman teeth.

"You..." Lowe's voice was barely a whisper as all the pieces fell into place. His mind raced through every interaction, every moment they'd shared since entering the Dungeon. The murders. The manipulation. It all led to this. "You're the fucking sixth Dreadnaught."

The creature that had been Preece laughed, a sound like grinding stone. "Very good, Inspector. I was beginning to think you'd never figure it out. But then, I suppose I gave you just enough rope to hang yourselves with."

Karolen charged across the space, her blade aimed for the Dreadnaught's throat, but he moved with impossible speed. One massive clawed hand caught her sword mid-swing, stopping it effortlessly. With a flick of his wrist, he sent her flying into the cavern wall.

She hit with a sickening crack and crumpled to the ground.

The Dreadnaught's glowing eyes locked on to Lowe movements, its smile never faltering. "Oh, don't worry about her, Inspector. She'll live—if only so you both can hear what I have to say."

Lowe stepped forward, letting *Slugger* fade away. He didn't think this was anything he was going to be able to punch his way out of. "You see, I couldn't give a fuck what you want to say. It's going to be some version of 'You fools! You've meddled where you shouldn't have!' or maybe 'You'll never understand my true purpose!' Or, if you're really feeling yourself, a classic 'You're too late to stop me!' Well, spoiler alert: you're not the first oversized munchkin with a god complex I've had to deal with, and you won't be the last. So can we just skip the monologue?"

"You don't want to know why I did it? No curiosity at all? Typical of your kind—charging in without seeking the greater truth."

"Alright, fine. I'll bite. Why'd you do it? Revenge? Power? Mommy didn't hug you enough? Come on, give me the bullet points. I've got a busy schedule of not dying today."

"Oh, Inspector. I do this because—"

"Wait, wait," Lowe interrupted, holding up a hand. "Let me guess. You do this because mortals are ants, or because destiny demands it, or, oh! Because someone *wronged* you centuries ago, and now you're making *us* pay for it. Do I have it? Close enough? No? Tell you what, you keep the speech. I'll just skip to the part where I punch you in your big metal face."

The Dreadnaught's smile vanished, replaced by a snarl. "You insolent—"

"Oh, here it comes," Lowe said. "The part where you call me 'insolent' and something about my 'puny mortal arrogance.' Honestly, you guys should unionize. Get a scriptwriter. Spice it up a little."

The Dreadnaught's roar of rage shook the room, and Lowe grinned, stepping into a defensive stance.

"There we go. Now that's more like it. Let me tell you what I think happened, and feel free to correct me if I get anything wrong. You freed yourself when fucking Grackle Nuroon brought in a sarcophagus containing Dreadnaught armour which was opened the day before this all kicked off. There was a Dreadnaught armour in there, and when the seal was broken, you just slipped right inside, didn't you? Suddenly, you were more than just a dusty relic. You became functional. That's why you could move, think, and, oh yeah, *murder*. Unlike the rest of your mates all still stuck on display. I bet they fucking *hate* you right now."

The Dreadnaught nodded. "Correct. The one they called Harker was the first to realise I was free. That was after I consumed the woman. He figured out what had happened. He saw the signs."

"The poor bastard pieced it together before anyone else," Lowe said. "And that, naturally, made him a liability. Let me guess, though—he didn't tell anyone, did he? Classic mistake. Never hesitate when you're dealing with eldritch horrors. You guys aren't exactly big on forgiveness."

The Dreadnaught chuckled. "Indeed."

"So, you gave him a thorough sliming," Lowe continued, "and then kept Kregg around for a while. What was he for—PR? Maybe he was the handsome face of your little murder operation?"

"Access," the thing that used to be Preece interjected. "Kregg had connections and could move around the museum without raising suspicion. But he screwed up when he lost the necrotic slime to, presumably, someone you sent to question him."

"Hel," Lowe confirmed with a shrug. "And yeah, I can see how that would have been a dealbreaker for you. That slime wasn't just a murder weapon, was it? It's a mental conduit. A way to feed power back to you. Without it, Kregg became… what's the phrase? Oh yeah, dead weight. Literally."

The Dreadnaught didn't deny it, which was, Lowe supposed, the closest thing to confirmation he was going to get.

"And then," Lowe said, jabbing a thumb toward the possessed Preece, "you moved on to this poor sod. Why him?"

"He was convenient," the Dreadnaught said, its tone dismissive. "The weakest link I could find. No one would question him acting strangely during the re-enactment. Not when everyone else had already wiped their memories. And…" it gestured around them with a gauntleted hand, "I needed him for the Dungeon."

"And there it is," Lowe said. "The Dungeon. That's the real game here, isn't it? The Great Hall was primed—enough death, enough power swirling around, enough artefacts hoarded by a Director who should have known better—and the Dungeon was almost ready to form. Almost."

"And I couldn't get close to it," the Dreadnaught said. "Not in my true form. Too powerful. The safeguards in a Dungeon's formation stop entities like me from going near the core until it's fully established. For precisely this reason."

"But as Preece?" Lowe said, "No problem. A low-level Curator wandering around? Nothing suspicious there. You used him to finish what you started. Get close enough to give the Dungeon the final nudge it needed to form. And now, it's got what it wanted—a bloody fortress to keep itself safe while it powers up. But you had slid inside."

"That's… about the size of it, yes."

"So, let me recap for the slow learners at the back. A walking tank with murder on its mind hijacks a hapless Curator, uses him to kickstart a Dungeon it can't otherwise get into, and now we're all trapped in here, fighting for our lives while it gets cozy at the core. Brilliant. Just brilliant"

"But I couldn't have done any of it without you, Inspector. The Dungeon is a means to an end. But you've missed one crucial detail, Inspector."

Lowe raised an eyebrow. "Oh? Enlighten me."

"The Dungeon's formation required a final sacrifice. Not just death— something… significant. A nexus of conflicting energies. And you, Jana Lowe, are uniquely positioned to provide exactly that."

Lowe froze. "I'm sorry, what?"

"You are an aberration," the Dreadnaught said, "A man with no Class, yet still alive. You are an anomaly, a paradox. And your essence will complete the Dungeon in ways no ordinary life force ever could."

Lowe backed away. "You've got to be kidding me. I've been killed enough times today. Find someone else."

"I think not," the Dreadnaught said, raising one gauntleted hand. "You've been a delightful distraction, Inspector. But now it's time to serve your purpose."

Lowe turned, ready to run, but the Dreadnaught moved faster than he could have imagined. Its hand shot out, grasping him by the throat and lifting him off the ground. He struggled, clawing at the unyielding metal, but it was no use.

"You will be the cornerstone of something greater than yourself," the Dreadnaught said, "Take comfort in that, if nothing else."

And with that, it crushed the life from him.

# CHAPTER FORTY SEVEN: KNIGHTS HAVE NO MEANING IN THIS GAME. IT WASN'T A GAME FOR KNIGHTS.

Being dead was nothing like being Classtrated.

That was the first thing Lowe realised.

Classtration had been a kind of *unmaking*—a tearing apart of his very sense of self. Every piece of him that had once fit together so seamlessly had been ripped apart and scattered, leaving only fragments where there had once been cohesion.

The pain of it wasn't just physical, though that had been unbearable enough. No, it was a deeper, existential agony. A constant ache that whispered, *You're broken now, Lowe. You're not whole anymore. You never will be.*

This, though? Death?

Death was… quiet.

He could get used to it.

Honestly, it wasn't what he'd expected. Not that he'd ever spent much time expecting death. He'd faced it often enough in his line of work to know it could come at any moment, but like most people, he'd always filed it under "tomorrow's problem."

Yet here it was, not waiting for tomorrow at all. And it wasn't pain, or fear, or regret. It was just… *release.*

He wasn't sure if he was floating, standing, or lying down, but - to be honest - it didn't seem to matter. He felt weightless, unburdened, as if all the chains he'd carried through his life had finally snapped.

The worry was gone.

And that worry had always been there, hadn't it? Even before the Classtration. That gnawing, endless anxiety, chewing at the edges of his thoughts. Worry about making rent. Worry about solving the case. Worry about losing Arebella. Worry about who he was and who he might become.

Worry about being enough.

Now, there was none of that.

The constant hum of tension that had threaded through every moment of his existence had gone quiet. No more *Grid View* offering him a thousand paths, most of which he couldn't take. No more Skills to balance, Progress Points to allocate, choices to second-guess.

No more climbing, falling, or clawing his way forward.

Just… peace.

And that was something he didn't really think he'd ever experienced.

It had always felt like something for *other* people. It was a luxury he couldn't afford.

He'd always been so busy running, fighting, surviving. But, right now, he though he understood the attraction. Peace wasn't something you earned; it was just something you *found*.

Or maybe something that found you.

When a Dreadnaught had finished crushing you to death, of course.

Was this what he'd been missing all along? He wasn't sure. It was hard to be sure of anything in this space, wherever or whatever it was. But for the first time in what felt like forever, he didn't feel the need to figure it out.

There was a strange comfort in the finality of it.

No more battles to fight. No more wrongs to right. No more wondering if he was living up to some expectation, whether his own or someone else's.

He was done.

Finished.

Complete.

Lowe had never thought of death as a gift, but now, he was starting to wonder if that's what it was. An end to pain. An end to trying. An end to everything that had ever weighed him down.

And yet…

Even as he floated in this perfect stillness, he couldn't shake the faintest flicker of a thought. A small, stubborn ember buried deep within him, refusing to go out.

Was this really how he wanted it all to end.

The idea of returning to life—of going back to all that chaos, all that pain— should have felt like a nightmare. But somehow, it didn't.

Because as much as Lowe hated the pain, the worry, the struggle, it was also what had defined him. It was what made him who he was. And even in death, he couldn't quite let go of that.

Maybe that was the joke, the cruel twist at the end of it all.

Even here, in the perfect silence of the void, Lowe couldn't stop being Lowe. The man who couldn't let sleeping dogs lie. The man who had to see the case through to the end.

The man who, even in death, wasn't ready to rest.

The void was serene—quiet, peaceful, and utterly free from the noise of life. Lowe had just started to appreciate the calm when the silence shattered.

*Oh, you are a dramatic one, aren't you?* A voice Lowe thought he recognised filled the space around him. *Floating here in the ether, basking in your existential freedom. Very poetic.*

Lowe blinked—or at least thought he did. Did you blink in a void? He wasn't sure. "Who the hell—?"

*Not hell,* the voice interrupted. *Close, though, depending on how you measure things. Arkola, Supreme Being, Architect of Reality, Arbiter of the Cosmos. Pleased to meet you. Or did we meet before? I have a somewhat fluid relationship with time.*

"You're kidding me."

*I assure you, I am not. And before you ask: no, nothing is sacred. Least of all this.*

"So even death doesn't come with a little privacy?" Lowe said. "Seriously, mate, I just died. Can't a guy get five minutes without some omnipotent busybody sticking their celestial nose in?"

*Touchy,* Arkola said. *You mortals really do take dying too seriously. You're acting like it's a permanent condition.*

"Maybe I want it to be."

*Oh, Jana Lowe. Always the contrarian. Tell me, is that really what you want? To drift here in the void, unburdened, untethered, and utterly… irrelevant?*

"You don't know what I want."

*Oh, but I do.* Arkola's tone was maddeningly smug. *I see your soul, Lowe. And you know what I see? The mark of the Blood of the Phoenix. People don't get Mythic Skills like that when they're planning to shuffle off this mortal coil permanently. That's not the mark of a man looking for peace. That's the mark of someone who plans to bounce back.*

"Maybe I don't want to do it," Lowe said, "Maybe I'm tired."

*Don't be a whiny cunt, I never give anyone more than they can handle. And you, Inspector, are nowhere near your limit.*

"Funny," Lowe said, "because from where I'm standing—or floating—it sure feels like I've hit it."

Arkola sighed. *Oh, I could argue with you all day, Lowe, but let's skip the tedium and get to the good part, shall we? I'll make going back more worth your while. How's that?*

"I'm not interested in bribes."

*Oh, but you'll want this one,* Arkola purred. *How about you go back and sort out this messy Dreadnaught business and I tell you who the Black Knight really was?*

The name hit Lowe like a fist made of bad decisions, square to the jaw of his consciousness.

It didn't knock him out, though. No, it woke him up in the worst way possible. Memories sparked like a broken engine coughing to life, throwing up smoke and bile as they roared back to the forefront.

*That case.* The one that had chewed him up, spat him out, and then went back for seconds just to be thorough.

The one that had led to his Classtration.

The botched operation. That delightful little circus where everyone wore blindfolds and threw knives at each other.

The ransom money that had evaporated faster than good intentions, leaving nothing but death, the stink of failure and career suicide.

The note. The Black Knight. Laughing at him from the smudged parchment.

The Council's judgment, as warm and compassionate as a snake bite. A room full of grey-faced statues, handing him all the blame

And then, the final hammer blow: his incompetence, they'd said, had left the child dead.

That failure—it wasn't a weight. No, weights could be dropped, shrugged off, set aside.

This was a shadow, a second skin, a whispering ghost that had followed him into every alley and stared back from every whiskey glass. It had gutted him long before the Council had gotten around to finishing the job.

And when they'd stripped him of everything, left him Classless? That wasn't punishment. That was just punctuation.

"You're lying," Lowe said, his voice hoarse. "The Black Knight was a ghost. A myth. Nobody knows who they were."

*Not nobody,* Arkola corrected, his tone smug. *I do. And I'll tell you—if you go back.*

Lowe hesitated, his mind a storm of conflicting emotions.

He'd spent a year burying the pain of that case, the anger, the questions. But now, standing—or whatever—in this void, it all came roaring back with a vengeance. The answers he'd always told himself didn't matter suddenly felt like the only thing in the universe worth knowing.

"What's the catch?" he asked.

Arkola laughed, a sound like rolling thunder. *Oh, Lowe. You're smarter than that. There's always a catch. But I'll make it simple for you: go back, and I'll give you what you've always wanted. The truth.*

Lowe clenched his fists, the peace of the void suddenly suffocating. His mind raced, weighing the offer, the risks, the price.

Because Arkola was right. He wasn't ready to rest.

Not yet.

Not with this unfinished.

Not with this one last thread hanging loose.

"Fine," he said, the word tasting like defeat. "I'll go back."

*Good choice*, Arkola said, the smug satisfaction practically radiating from the void. *And, Lowe? Try not to fuck it up this time.*

Before Lowe could retort, the void dissolved, and he fell.

# CHAPTER FORTY EIGHT - RESURRECTION IS A HELL OF A WAKE-UP CALL

Lowe sat up with a sharp gasp, like a diver breaking the surface after forgetting oxygen was a thing.

His eyes darted around, wild and unfocused, before settling on Karolen.

For her part, she was looking like she'd seen a ghost—or more accurately, like she'd seen a corpse suddenly decide it had better things to do.

His sudden movement had startled her. Karolen had been kneeling over his lifeless body, tears carving streaks through the grime and blood on her face. She flinched violently, recoiling as though from a ghost, her hand brushing against her blade. It clattered against the cavern floor, the metallic sound echoing briefly before the weapon dissipated into nothingness.

"What the—Lowe?" she stammered. "You were—"

"Dead. Yeah, got that," Lowe said. "It didn't take."

Carefully, he turned his head left, then right, testing for any lingering stiffness or surprises. Next, he flexed his fingers, opening and closing his hands slowly. So far, so good. Everything seemed to be in working order, no sudden pangs or ominous clicks—just the faint, surreal sensation of having recently been dead.

Which, on its own, was quite a vibe.

A small, glowing countdown ticked in the corner of his vision: 59:55. The bell-long healing lockout. Right. That was the trade-off for not staying permanently dead. A bit stingy, sure, but when you're gambling with house money, griping feels like an ungrateful waste of breath—especially when you've just been given a second shot at using it.

"To be honest, I'm feeling surprisingly chipper," he said, swinging his legs around and rising to his feet. The motion was startlingly smooth, almost unnervingly so, considering he'd been a corpse all of two moments ago. "Turns out dying's the best nap I've had in years. Who knew?"

Karolen stared up at him, her face a mix of shock, relief, and the faintest hint of irritation. "You—you were gone. I thought—" She shook her head, as if trying to shake loose the memory of his lifeless body, then paused, her expression shifting as something else clicked. "Wait. How the hell are you cracking jokes? You just—Lowe, you died."

"Yeah, yeah, tragic stuff, I'm sure," Lowe said, brushing non-existent dust off his coat with exaggerated nonchalance. "But I'm back now, so let's stick to the highlights: How much did I miss? Where did the Big Bad wander off to while I was . . . otherwise engaged?"

"You're impossible."

"Damn right I am," he said, dismissing the countdown in his vision. "Also, just a heads up: no healing for the next hour. So, if you were planning on any tender, heroic moments where you slap a potion in my hand and save the day, maybe pencil that in for later."

"I don't understand?"

"Yeah, me neither. Just don't try and heal me for a while—clock's still ticking on that one. Come on, up you get. We've got a fully armoured Dreadnaught with a stolen Dungeon Core to deal with. How about you? Need any boosts, or are you good to go?" Lowe pulled a pastry and a smoothie from his inventory, holding them out like peace offerings. "Here, eat up. Trust me, these'll sort out anything that ails you. Mylaf's finest. Practically a breakfast miracle."

Karolen stared at him, blinking as if her brain hadn't quite caught up to events. A minute ago, she'd been bracing herself to tell her best friend that Lowe had died in a Dungeon. Now, he was casually offering her snacks.

"Go on," Lowe said, waggling the croissant at her. "It's a chocolate one. Best thing you'll put in your mouth all week." There was a pause. "Yeah, don't tell Arebella I said that. Blame that on the resurrection."

Resigned to the absurdity of it all, Karolen took the croissant (+30% to Critical Hit) and the raspberry smoothie (flat 200 on HP). One bite of buttery, chocolate-laced bliss and a sip of tart sweetness later, she was chewing in stunned silence. Whatever she'd been about to say was effectively neutralized by the pastries' sheer brilliance.

Lowe grinned. "Told you."

When she was finished, Lowe extended a hand. Karolen hesitated for a moment, then took it, allowing him to haul her to her feet. She shook her head as if trying to clear it, muttering under her breath.

Lowe didn't catch every word, but he was fairly certain "insufferable bastard" made an appearance, wrapped in a tone that teetered somewhere between exasperation and reluctant admiration.

"Flattery will get you everywhere," he said, "And I missed you too. Now did you see which way the Big Bad went?"

***

According to Karolen, the instant Lowe had exhaled his last, shuddering breath, the Dreadnaught had wasted no time. It had dropped him like last year's fashions, let out an earth-shaking roar, and with a swing of its massive arm, it had torn a hole straight through the Dungeon wall. Then, without so much of a backward glance, it had disappeared into the night beyond.

"It didn't even pause," she said as they carefully navigated the fractured remains of the wall. "One moment it was gloating over your corpse—because, you know, ancient Dreadnaughts just *have* to get in a last word—and the next, it's all 'so long, Dungeon, time to see the world.' It didn't hesitate, didn't look back—just straight through the wall like a wrecking ball in full sprint."

Lowe stumbled slightly on a chunk of fallen debris, still trying to shake off the strange, unmoored feeling that came with being yanked back from the dead. "Places to go, people to see, I get it. But didn't it occur to you to, I don't know, try and stop it?"

Karolen shot him a glare. "Oh, sure, Lowe. I'll just whip out my *Stop a Rampaging Dreadnaught* Skill next time. You know, right after I finish not dying while mourning your dramatic, heroic death. My bad for not keeping up. Preece might have been low Level, but that thing was at least Level 60."

"Fair point," Lowe said, stepping cautiously over a piece of shattered masonry. The cool air of Soar was a bit different here—thicker, almost humming with residual energy. The destruction of the museum's wall had left more than just physical damage; it was like the very fabric of reality had been pulled thin and stitched poorly back together.

If he looked closely, he could see where the Dungeon' Core's influence had imposed itself on the structure of Soar Museum. The wall they were passing through hadn't just crumbled under the Dreadnaught's assault, it had shifted and stretched, lines of glowing mana hovering midair like frozen lightning bolts. They twisted and warped, forming incomplete patterns that fizzled and sparked before vanishing.

The place where the Dreadnaught had struck the wall gaped open like a festering wound, spilling remnants of magical containment. Grackle Nuroon was going to have a conniption.

The two of them stepped through the hole in the wall, and the moment they crossed the threshold, Lowe felt the subtle, electric snap of their delve coming to an abrupt end.

It was like a taut thread had been cut, leaving the air around them suddenly lighter, less charged. The shared notifications in his periphery—the ones linked to Karolen's XP, stats, and progress—flickered and disappeared, leaving an odd emptiness in their wake as their party dissolved. It was almost strange after what they had recently been through, like losing the hum of background noise you hadn't realised you'd gotten used to.

"Yeah, that's about right," Lowe said.

"What's about right?"

"No rewards," he said. "We went through all that—death, resurrection, Dreadnaughts busting out into the city—and we get jack-all for actually completing the Dungeon. Where's the loot? The XP? The celebratory 'you did it' fanfare? Obviously, I'm pretty new at this whole delving thing, but I'm fairly sure I got all sort of goodies when I finished my previous run in the Undercity."

"Lowe, you *died*. That is the literal opposite of finishing a Dungeon."

"Pfft, technicalities," he said. "I came back, didn't I? That's got to count for something."

"Oh, absolutely," she said. "It counts as you *not* finishing the Dungeon. It's not my fault the Dungeon Core - a Core that incidentally has been stolen by a monster we apparently helped break in - wasn't up for rewarding sheer bloody-minded stubbornness."

"I'll have you know that stubbornness is a heroic quality."

"It really isn't," Karolen said. Her gaze shifted back toward the city, where the distant skyline still seemed to tremble from the Dreadnaught's escape. "Heroics or not, there's an armoured Dreadnaught stomping around out there now—with a stolen Dungeon Core for dessert. If we thought that thing was bad news inside the Dungeon…"

"You know what?" Lowe said, "I'm not sure that's going to be a problem."

"Why not?"

"Because, by the sound of all that fighting, and a bit of familiar swearing, I'd put good gold on it that the Dreadnaught's just run into a few friends of mine."

# CHAPTER FORTY NINE - WHEN TITANS BLEED

"Friends? You have friends?"

"You know, there are people that might find such a comment rather hurtful," Lowe said. "Especially the newly resurrected. I'm not completely unlikable, you know."

"I didn't say you were. I just don't picture your 'friends' being the type to take on a rampaging Dreadnaught."

"Well," Lowe said, jerking his thumb toward the increasingly loud noise of shouting and very insistent explosions from just beyond the grounds of the museum, "I do. And these particular friends of mine aren't really the *hug-it-out* kind of folk."

The noise of... whatever was happening escalated significantly. Booming impacts, each on their own sounding like the end of the world, sent tremors rippling through the ground beneath their feet.

The keening whistle of wind slicing through stone shrieked in eerie harmony, with the explosions, the sound so sharp it felt as if it might rip through the air itself. And layered over it all was a metallic screech of steel-on-steel.

Karolen squinted through the destruction, her eyes stinging as smoke and dust clung thick to the air, muting the fractured light and shrouding the world beyond into a shifting haze. Her hand tightened instinctively on the hilt of her reconstituted blade and she triggered all of her offensive Skills. She knew it was pretty pointless if they were planning to mix it up with a Dreadnaught but she was damned if she was going down without a fight.

"What in Soar is causing all that racket!" she whispered.

Lowe, for once, said nothing.

Moving shapes suddenly resolved ahead—blurred, figures moving, too fast to seem real. A gust of wind blasted through the street, scattering debris and clearing the worst of the haze, and for a moment, Karolen saw it.

No, them.

The Dreadnaught, now showing no trace of Preece's form, stood at the epicenter of a circle of annihilation. Encased in its ancient armour, it was like a titan ripped from legend. Its fists swung with the raw force of a living siege engine, every impact capable of reducing a city to rubble. Yet there was a noticeable sluggishness to its movements—an unnatural hesitation that betrayed its burden.

Clutched protectively against its chest, the glowing Dungeon Core pulsed erratically, its light flickering in panicked bursts as if aware of its impending peril. The energy radiating from it was almost pleading, the rhythm of its pulsing quickening like a trapped heartbeat. The Dreadnaught shielded the Core with almost parental care as if anxious to keep it safe from any danger.

And, boy, was there some danger about . . .

"Yeah," Lowe said. "I've got some pretty great friends."

A streak of lightning carved through the sky above, slamming into the street at the Dreadnaught's feet with a force that ignited the cobblestones. From the explosion of scorched and shattered rocks emerged Latham, his massive blade already arcing toward the Dreadnaught's head.

The impact of their clash was colossal, shattering the glass of the surrounding shop windows and toppling what few walls were still standing. But the Temple Warder didn't pause for a moment, continuing to hack away at the retreating monster like he was chopping wood.

"Is that—" Karolen started, but her voice faltered as the ground shuddered beneath them once again.

The air screamed again, the clouds twisting into entirely unnatural spirals and, at the eye of the storm, Hel hovered, her hair a wild corona of energy.

With a clap of her hands, she guided the wind around her into slicing gales and deadly whirlwinds which harried the escaping monster. Each gesture brought destruction raining down on the Dreadnaught—a spear of ice here, a sudden column of air that hurled debris at impossible speeds there. Her attacks hammered the creature relentlessly, stopping it from being able to properly respond to Latham's relentless advance.

Then, the Dreadnaught opened its mouth impossibly loud and *screamed*, a noise that seemed to come from some deep, primal abyss. Its free hand slashed out, catching Latham mid-stride and sending him flying back and away, vanishing through a wall. However, before it could look to press its advantage, more of Hel's targeted wind attacks struck, carving a deep gash into its armour and forcing it to stumble back.

"She's doing all *that*," Karolen said faintly, staring at Hel. "And it's still standing."

"Ha, that's nothing. She chopped off my arm once and I barely gave it a second thought."

Karolen opened her mouth to respond and then obviously thought better of it.

Latham suddenly burst out of the wreckage, his own armour singed but his blade already swinging and there was the glow of any number of triggered Skills around him. Lowe hadn't been present for the Temple Warder's epic throwdown with the Advanced Classed Bright in the reception plaza of the Celestial Temple. But he'd heard stories.

Watching Latham now—moving like pure, unbridled force—Lowe decided those wide-eyed witnesses had been soft-selling it. Latham wasn't just good, he was *good*. Level ?? good. Every swing of his sword left trails of crackling energy, and each strike landed with the sound of a world tearing itself apart.

The Dreadnaught, for all its power and bulk, struggled to match him. It was no slouch—it countered with devastating swings of its own, its massive fists smashing into the Temple Warder time and time again. But Latham just took each blow and kept coming and the monster ended up tanking hits more than it probably wanted—Latham's cuts and slashes crashing into its armour, each one carving deep, glowing scars that oozed molten light.

Lowe winced as a particularly brutal clash sent sparks and debris flying past him. "Guess even ancient murder machines can have bad days."

And that day just got worse.

Hel swooped low, a blur of motion as she hurled a tempest at the Dreadnaught's legs, toppling it over. Latham was there in an instant, abandoning his sword to bring both fists down with an almighty crunch.

The Dreadnaught howled, dropping the Dungeon Core to the ground where it rolled away. There was then quite some smackdown put on the monster.

Without a moment's hesitation, Karolen and Lowe broke into a sprint, weaving through the battlefield. Masonry rained down around them, each crash sending up clouds of dust that clung to the swirling smoke. Magical blasts tore through the air, streaking the shattered street with bursts of searing light and deafening cracks that sounded like the world itself was splitting apart.

Karolen spotted the discarded Dungeon Core first, its glow seeping through the rubble. The ancient artifact seemed alive, each pulse of light rippling outward in waves that made her skin prickle. She didn't pause, didn't think—her hand shot forward, gripping the Core and pulling it free.

The second it touched her skin, a jolt ran through her, as if the Core was trying to imprint its desperation onto her. It burned with frantic energy, its chaotic rhythm matching the pandemonium around them. She clenched her jaw, steadying herself as its heat threatened to overwhelm her.

"Got it!" she shouted over the din.

"Do you want me to hold it," Lowe called, seeing the pain on the Auditor's face.

"Your healing cooldown over?" she replied, taking out a Health Potion and downing it. The Core was burning the skin off her hand.

Lowe cursed. "Not yet," he said and then cast *Medic!* on Karolen.

"Then probably best I hold it for now, don't you think?"

Then they ran, trying to put as much distance between the Dreadnaught and the Core, which burned hotter and hotter in Karolen's grasp with every passing moment—but they didn't stop. They couldn't.

"You know," Lowe said, breathing heavily as they ran, "it's true what they say?"

"What?" Karolen managed through the agony of her burning palms. Lowe's Skill was helping, but all it was doing was repairing the damage. It didn't do anything about the pain.

"That cooked human smells like pork."

"Fuck off, Lowe."

Unfortunately, freed from the burden of seeking to protect its prize, the Dreadnaught was able to turn its full attention to the fight with Hel and Latham. This turned out to be fairly decisive as it effortlessly tossed the Temple Warder away from it.

Hel, her body all electric, tempestuous fury, dove from the sky at the creature, unleashing a torrent of Skills. But, sadly, it was ready this time. A massive, clawed hand shot up, grabbing her mid-dive as if plucking a bird from the air. A single brutal punch to the head followed and then her unconscious form was sent spiralling away, before her body crashed into the ground, leaving her motionless.

Latham roared in furious response, his fists glowing as he pummelled the monster. But for the first time, the Dreadnaught seemed almost... grinning. It shifted, feinted, and when Latham's focus faltered for the briefest moment—his eyes flicking to Hel's prone form—it struck.

The punch came like a meteor. It slammed onto the top of Latham's head, driving him downwards with an apocalyptic force. The cobblestones beneath Latham's feet shattered, the ground caved in, and the Temple Warder vanished into a smoking crater, as dust and shards of stone cascading into the yawning pit.

The street fell deathly still for a moment, as if even the air was holding its breath.

Karolen clutched the Core even tighter, despite the burning agony, as the Dreadnaught's massive frame turned toward them.

No longer beset by Hel and Latham, it moved with predatory grace, unhurried, its steps almost balletic as it charged towards her. Lowe stepped in front of her instinctively, *Slugger* armed and fists raised though they both knew it wouldn't do a damn thing.

"Well," Lowe said to her, "this is probably not ideal."

Then, there was a sound.

A low rumble of metal grinding against metal, growing louder with every second. The Dreadnaught froze, its head turning to the source.

It appeared that the Senior Preservationist, Martha Culloden, had finally resurfaced.

And she was clad head-to-toe in Dreadnaught armour of her own.

# CHAPTER FIFTY - CATASTROPHIC UNMINED MANA EXPLOSION

"Are you—are you *fucking kidding me?* You're telling me—no, no, let me get this straight—you're telling me that you died, Lowe? *Died?* Like, heart-stopped, brain-shut-down, body-went-rigor-mortis, *died?* And now you're sitting here, cracking wise, like *that's* the part of this story I should be focusing on? Are you *actually* fucking insane? Because, here's the thing, Lowe—*that's not even the worst part!* Oh no, you dying? That's just the opening fucking act. Let's talk about the *millions* of gold worth of damage to the street outside the Museum! MILLIONS, Lowe! Cobblestones blasted apart, walls collapsed, storefronts levelled, businesses eradicated! Do you know how long it's going to take to rebuild that? Neither do I, but I guarantee the Mayor's going to be taking that out of my budget."

Staffen slammed her hand on the desk for emphasis, making her pens rattle. "And speaking of the Museum—oh, yeah, that's mostly just fucking *gone!* Poof! Vanished into the gods-damned ether! Do you know what it takes to remove a building that old from this plane of existence, Lowe? No? Well, apparently you and your little shit-show found a way. And don't even get me started on the giant, headless, armoured corpse you've left sprawled out in front of the district portal. Do you have any idea the kind of traffic chaos that's causing? No one can get in or out! Trade's at a standstill! People are screaming bloody murder because they can't fetch their fucking luxury cheeses or whatever the fuck rich idiots buy these days!"

Her eyes widened, little sparks of electricity spiralling out to incinerate several stacks of reports before her "And that's still not the worst part! The *worst part*, Lowe, is that somehow, somehow, you've managed to make this entire disaster MY FUCKING PROBLEM! Because when the Mayor finally stops freaking out over this shitstorm, you know what he's going to say? He's going to pick up his Sending Stone and ask 'Pernille, how did you let this happen? Pernille, why weren't you on top of this? Pernille, didn't I ask you to drop the case at Soar fucking Museum'!"

"To be fair, boss, you did ask me to properly look into it . . ."

Staffen pointed a trembling finger at Lowe, her face flushed with rage. "Don't you be coming here with any of your *facts*, Lowe. I don't want to hear it! Do you have *any* idea the paperwork this is going to cause? The explanations? The ass-kissing I'm going to have to do to keep the Mayor from nailing my fucking arse to a wall? Because I sure as shit do, Lowe, and let me tell you, it is going to be *monumental*. So, no, Lowe. I don't want to hear about how you came back from the dead or how you 'heroically' stopped the Dungeon from fully forming. All I care about is how the *fuck* you're going to clean up this *absolute clusterfuck* of a mess, because if you don't, I swear to every god in the pantheon, I will personally stuff that headless Dreadnaught corpse up your arse and leave it there."

The Commander of Soar's Security Forces had been monologuing in this manner for the best part of a half a bell.

Whilst Lowe was the first to admit that he didn't always pick up the nuance of interpersonal relationships, he sensed his boss was a touch narked with him.

He let her furious anger wash over him - he sensed he'd be getting plenty of repeats of this little rant from various sources in his near future - mind returning to the last moments of the Dreadnaught. Activating *Grid View* to watch again as the Senior Preservationist of Soar Museum simply walked up to the Dreadnaught and tore its head off.

He reversed the sequence and replayed it over and over again.

Yep.

That was still all there was to it.

After all the sound and fury, all that chaos, all that heroic sacrifice and effort, the key moment in the whole caper was a short, blonde, middle-aged woman, clad in shining ancient armour, literally ripping a monster from the netherworlds in two.

Using her bare hands.

A monster that had taken everything Hel and Latham could throw at it and came out the other side grinning, was casually torn in two.

"Don't you fucking tell me you're fucking ignoring me, Lowe!"

Guilty, he switched off the Skill. "Sorry boss. Trauma, you know. What with dying and all."

If Staffen felt a moment's sympathy, it didn't show on her face. Or in her voice. Or in the cavalcade of mental Skills she kept, impotently, throwing Lowe's way. "Do you have any explanation for all of this?"

"Catastrophic unmined mana explosion," Lowe said automatically, reaching for the cover story they'd all agreed to go with.

Staffen stared at him, unblinking. "Catastrophic. Unmined. Mana explosion," she repeated slowly, as if tasting each word and finding them each rather rancid. "That's the best you've got? That's the story you're going with?"

Lowe shrugged. "It's plausible. Mana's volatile, right? Boom, bang, ancient artefacts, and—ta-da!—sudden architectural makeover. No one's fault. No harm. No foul. All the insurance payouts in the world."

"'Plausible,' he says," Staffen said. "Lowe, the *entire street* looks like it's been chewed up and spat out by an angry Elemental. There's a headless giant monster blocking a portal. Half the museum is fucking *gone*. And your answer is: 'Oops! Mana go boom'?"

"Well," Lowe said, scratching his chin thoughtfully, "when you put that silly voice on when you say it, it does sound pretty bad. But technically, none of it's inaccurate."

"None of it's—are you fucking listening to yourself?" Staffen nearly exploded herself, her hands flailing like she was trying to physically strangle his words. "'Mana go boom'? What, did that giant fucking headless monster spontaneously generate as a side effect of the explosion? And where has that Dungeon Core gone in the middle of this . . . unexpected explosion"

"Dungeon Core? I don't think I remember seeing any—"

"I swear to every deity ever worshipped in Soar if you finish that sentence, I will personally write the Mayor a report blaming this entire disaster on you and have them strip you of whatever sliver of dignity your Classless arse has got left!"

Lowe's expression became steely at that. "You know what, ma'am? I don't think there's a single thing the Mayor or the fucking Council have left to do to me, is there?"

They sat in silence for a moment.

Eventually, Lowe held up his hands in mock surrender. "Alright, alright. Catastrophic unmined mana explosion *might* not cover all the bases. But it's concise, right? People love concise."

"Lowe," Pernille said, "concise doesn't cut it when the entire city is asking why the museum looks like a bloody war zone and half the nobility can't get their carriages past a giant corpse. Do you think anyone's going to buy your half-assed excuse for even a second?"

"Well, I bought it, and I was there, so everyone else can get in line. Oh, and considering I also cleared up three murders whilst I was doing it, I reckon I should earn some credit from the Council there."

Staffen sighed and dismissed the Skills she was desperately using to try to pry open Lowe's mind. "Why don't we start all this again? Explain to me what went down at the Museum."

"And you promise no shouting this time?"

"Lowe!"

"Fine. So, moments after the catastrophic unmined mana explosion . . ."

***

With a complicated gesture, Martha Culloden dismissed the armour she was encased in and stepped, carefully, away from the body of the now decapitated Dreadnaught. "You can probably put that down now," she said to Karolen.

The Auditor was stood, slack-jawed, staring at the Senior Preservationist. "Put what down?"

"The Dungeon Core burning a hole through your hand."

With a startled yelp, Karolen flinched and let the sphere slip from her hands. Its fall to the ground stopped just shy of impact, halting mid-air as if it had a mind of its own. Its slow descent continued before it finally settled amidst the shattered cobbles of the street, as if perfectly content to nestle there.

"Now, doesn't that feel better?"

Lowe, after unloading all of his mana on Hel and Latham via *Medic!* crossed to stand in front of the Senior Preservationist. "How in Soar did you manage that? No, hang on. A more pressing question is where the fuck have you been?"

The woman gave a tired smile. "I think the answer to both of those questions are probably linked."

Karolen, her hand now healed, joined Lowe. "You went missing the night the second Curator - Harker - was killed. Everyone thinks you did it! No one has seen anything of you since then!"

"Poor Josep," Martha said, and to Lowe's mind, she did really seem sorry. "He came to see me just before I left for the evening. He was in a terrible state. His role was to catalogue the more exotic exhibits from the collapsed Dungeon on the edge of Soar and he was sure there was a discrepancy in the records of recovered Dreadnaught armour. It seemed, on the day of Isadora's death - when we were all commanded to *Cleanse the Canvas* - one of the suits went missing. He'd been searching the Dungeon high and low for a month and hadn't been able to find it, and he was sure the Director was going to blame him for its loss. He was sick with worry. Being a Curator was his whole life. I, of course, realised there was a far bigger concern."

"That the missing Dreadnaught had found a home."

"Well, quite. I'd told the Director over and over again that it was ridiculously dangerous for us to keep untethered Dreadnaughts on site - especially once we started bringing in all sorts of new Dungeon artefacts. But, well, as I imagine you have noticed, you cannot tell Nuroon anything. Even presented with evidence that one of them escaped its binding, he remained blithely unconcerned. After all, a Dreadnaught without its armour is little more than a shadow."

"But then," Karolen said, "the museum began bringing new Dungeon artefacts on site - including Dreadnaught armour. Didn't anyone think that might be a massively dangerous thing?"

"I'm sure we did, my dear," Martha's voice was cool. "But then, unfortunately, we all wiped our memories after Curator Isadora's *accident*."

"Allowing the Dreadnaught complete freedom to act."

"Indeed. It was only when Harker came to me that I started to piece together what was likely to have happened. The Dreadnaught was able to access The Great Hall when the Director was showing Ms Mehin around and took advantage of the . . . escalated tension to enter the open Sarcophagus and claim its armour. It would have consumed Isadora to complete the binding process."

Karolen thought back to that morning. Had she noticed any unusual . . . shadows around her? And, if she did, would she have thought anything much of them?

"With our memories wiped," Culloden continued, "the Dreadnaught had all the time in the world to secure itself to this realm. In fact, if it hadn't been for Harker, I would have been none the wiser anything was going on before that Dungeon reformed itself."

"And you think that was the Dreadnaughts plan?" Lowe asked, "to claim the Dungeon Core?" They all dropped their eyes to look at the glowing sphere still happily nesting on the ground.

"Of course. A Dreadnaught is powerful, but this was a newly formed one. If it had the opportunity to drain a Dungeon Core? Well, that would have been a whole different kettle of fish. Its immaturity was the only reason I was able to escape when it attacked Harker and I in my office that night. That poor young man took the brunt of its necrotic slime attack, and I had just enough time to escape through a passageway to the Chapel of Rest and used a Skill to lock the door behind me."

"But where did you then go? You activated the portal and didn't go through it?" Lowe said.

"I didn't know what was best. After the kerfuffle over the audit," Martha grimaced at Karolen, "Nuroon was pretty much invincible. I couldn't go to him and say what I thought, that because of his insistence on secrecy, he'd allowed an ancient horror lose on Soar. He'd scared off the Security Service from investigating Isadora's death, so there was no point going to Cuckoo House. And the Trustees had made it clear they had no appetite for hearing any more bad news."

"So, what. You just hid out in the museum?" Lowe said.

"Yes," Culloden replied with a shrug. "We'd uncovered a second set of Dreadnaught armour in another sarcophagus the day before Isadora's death, and - after Harker's research had brought that to my attention - I assimilated my core with it. A rather delicate undertaking, I might add. And it's not like I didn't try to warn you about what was going on," she added, casting an accusatory glance at Lowe.

"It was you, then?" Lowe said. "You were the one following me in the corridors beneath the museum?"

"Well, yes. Of course, it was me," Culloden said, as though the answer were obvious. "Unfortunately, at that stage, I was in the early phases of integrating with the armour, and controlling the necrotic slime was... challenging. I assume that's why you ran off like a scared little girl?"

Lowe offered no response to that jab.

Karolen stepped in. "So, what made you show yourself now? Not that we're not grateful, of course," she added hastily, glancing at the headless Dreadnaught lying amidst the rubble.

"Once the armour fully accepted me, I had nothing left to fear," Culloden said. "That's the thing about the bindings we had in place on those monsters—they were calibrated for extremely powerful beings. The Dreadnaught that escaped was far from whole and its connection to its core was tenuous at best, which is why it was able to break free. But if it had managed to consume that Dungeon Core?" She paused, letting the gravity of the statement hang in the air. "That would have been an entirely different story."

"What now?" Lowe asked. "This is going to be a hell of a thing to explain."

"Well," Culloden said, leaning forward, "how much do you know about catastrophic unmined mana explosions . . ."

# CHAPTER FIFTY ONE: BLOOD ON THE LEDGER, SMOKE IN THE AIR

Grackle Nuroon stared at the man sitting opposite him.

The room was quiet. Horribly quiet. The kind of quiet that crawls under your skin, opens a can of itching powder and just *goes to town* all over your histamines.

Overhead, the hiss of a cracked mana light added its own flavour of unease to the atmosphere, flickering like it had a stutter. After all the carnage wrought by the Dungeon's abortive attempt to root itself in his Museum, most of the passive Skills the Director had built - with his own hands - into the walls were on the fritz.

The usual comforting buzz of complete arcane stability was now a series of loud and discordant clicks as the damage slowly - and far too slowly for the Director's liking - repaired itself

Grackle Nuroon tapped a finger, slowly against his chin. Although his face was frozen in its usual, belligerent, expression, he was feeling far from secure. He hated this unusual experience of vulnerability, particularly within the context of having added five whole Levels during his own experiences in the Dungeon.

With his newly acquired Skill—*Temporal Archive*—he should have been feeling like a million bags of gold right now. The ability to transform the Museum into a time-fractured version of itself for one minute, overlaying the past onto the present, was nothing short of extraordinary. The Skill allowed him to temporarily manifest objects and entities from bygone eras—legendary artefacts humming with dormant power, spectral echoes of past visitors, allies, or enemies—all brought to life within the Museum's walls.

That said, there were caveats. The mana cost was obscene—an almost parasitic drain that threatened to leave him crippled for hours afterward. And, right now, with his Museum so badly compromised, he couldn't afford to properly explore its possibilities.

Especially as, sitting across from him, like a crumpled monument to all that had recently gone wrong, was Jana Lowe, hands rested loosely on the armrests, but his eyes were anything but relaxed.

Nuroon resisted the urge to shift in his seat.

A bead of sweat rolled down Nuroon's temple. He told himself it was just the light—the room was warm, after all. But Lowe's gaze didn't give him an inch.

He cleared his throat, a sound that felt embarrassingly loud. "Was there something you wanted, Inspector? As you may imagine, I have an awful lot to be getting on with."

"I'm sure you do, mate. I'm sure you do. Can't be every day a Dungeon establishes itself in the middle of your Museum?"

"No," Nuroon said, resisting the urge to nervously smooth out the papers on his desk, "it has all been very traumatic for everyone who works here."

"Yeah, it's been quite a month for you, hasn't it? Bunch of murders, bit of random mayhem and I see you also managed to hit your Level 70 threshold. Congratulations! You must be feeling very proud."

"What I'm feeling isn't remotely your business, Mr Lowe. Now, if there's nothing else?" Nuroon stood, pushing out with a mental Skill - *Executive Egress* - that had never failed to cause subordinates to scuttle from his presence. Lowe just looked back at him with the same, intense expression.

"Isadora. Harker. Preece. You've lost three Curators in a very short space of time," he began, "For the completion of my report on all that has occurred, could you clarify the arrangements you've made for their families?"

"Mr Lowe, not that it is any of your business," Grackle said smoothly, "but Curators are all independent contractors. Their deaths are, of course, regrettable, but they are due no recompense. I trust that satisfies your curiosity?"

Lowe's brow shot up in exaggerated surprise. "Independent contractors, you say? No recompense? Oh, that's fascinating. Truly. Let me make sure I've got this straight—three people die, *in your museum*, under *your roof*, while working on *your behalf*, and you think that's just… what? A footnote? A 'whoops, my bad' situation? A shrug and move on?"

He leaned forward, his hand glowing as *Slugger*, almost unconscious activated, the faux curiosity in his tone giving way to something darker. "That's the play you're going with? Because let me tell you, Grackle my old mate, that's a *bold* strategy. I mean, sure, why not? You're Level 70 and are probably feeling pretty chipper right now. Let's just ignore the glaringly obvious part where this is entirely your responsibility and focus on the real issue here—your complete and utter lack of shame. But hey, who am I to judge? What would I know about accountability, right?"

"The terms of their contracts were clear. It's hardly unusual in—"

"In what? Exploitative corporate practices?" Lowe said, voice rising. "Let me tell you, Grackle, Soar loves a scandal. Imagine the headlines: 'Museum Director Leaves Families Penniless After Tragic Deaths.' You think the Trustees are going to love explaining that one to the public?"

"Their contracts…" he started, but Lowe was already cutting him off.

"Oh, I'm sure their contracts were airtight," Lowe said. "But here's the thing: the court of public opinion doesn't give a flying fuck about contracts. They care about how it looks. And right now, Grackle, your optics are looking pretty damn bleak. So how about we skip the part where I leak this to someone with a sharper quill than me and jump straight to the bit where you do the decent thing?"

Nuroon's jaw folded his hands together as if to physically stop himself from wringing Lowe's neck. "What exactly are you suggesting?"

"I'm suggesting," Lowe said, his tone casual but his eyes like steel, "that you make a gesture. A big one. Something that says, 'Hey, I'm not a completely heartless bastard.' Let's call it… a hundred thousand gold per family. Sounds fair, doesn't it?"

"A hundred—" Nuroon choked, his composure slipping for the first time. "That's preposterous. It's—"

"Doable," Lowe finished for him. "Oh, don't look at me like that. You've got a whole museum full of priceless junk. Sell a vase or two. I hear the city's elite will pay absurd amounts for a little cultural enrichment."

Nuroon's expression stayed frozen, but he was already mentally inventorying the artefacts he could part with as well as the potential profits he could wring from his newly developed Skill. Three hundred thousand goal wasn't nothing, but he could probably make that work . . .

"Very well. I'll arrange something for the families."

"A hundred thousand," Lowe reminded him.

"Yes, yes," Nuroon snapped, waving a hand dismissively. "I'll have to convene with the Trustees, of course, but it will be done."

"Excellent. Now," Lowe reached into his pocket and withdrew a bloodstained notebook. "Do you know what this is?"

Nuroon recoiled slightly. "No idea at all."

Lowe gave him a hard look, and then nodded. "I actually believe you. Okay, well at least you have that going for you. This is Kelvin Kregg's little diary of . . . interactions. I assume you know that your employee was a colossal piece of shit?"

"Bard Kregg was..."

"Don't. Just don't," the glow in Lowe's hand increased substantially.

Despite the disparity in their levels, Nuroon found himself flinching slightly. How was he being intimidated by this man? A Classless non-entity with three Skills? "I don't understand what you want from me here, Mr Lowe."

"There's a whole book of women here that, in the very near future, are going to receive some good news. Fifty thousand gold each feels about right. It won't make them forget what he did to them but, considering the one good thing the Dreadnaught that escaped from *your museum* did was to literally tear this guy a new one, I figure the cash will be a welcome second act of appropriate contrition."

Nuroon picked up the book and flicked through it, disgust on his face. "There must be a hundred odd names in here!"

"I know. Terrible isn't it? Imagine employing someone that predatory and not doing anything about it! Thinking about it, sixty thousand gold is probably appropriate."

"I don't know what leverage you think you have in these negotiations, Mr Lowe . . ."

Lowe reached into his other pocket and, from within, he retrieved a small sphere—much smaller now than it had been when the Dreadnaught had clutched it. The object's surface was slick with some unnatural sheen that shimmered like oil on water. He placed it on Nuroon's desk with a wet *thunk*, leaving behind a smear of charred skin that hissed faintly against the polished wood.

The smell hit the Director first. It wasn't just the reek of scorched flesh but something far worse: the smell of mana corruption laced with the unmistakable stench of cooked meat. Nuroon's stomach churned as his eyes flicked to Lowe's hand, and his bile rose further.

The Inspector's hand was a ruin. Skin blistered and blackened, the flesh cracked open to reveal raw, angry tissue beneath. Patches of his palm looked like overcooked parchment, peeling away in thin, jagged strips, while the tips of his fingers still smoked faintly. Blood mixed with the burnt remnants, dripping sluggishly onto the desk as if unwilling to acknowledge the mess it had come from.

"Thought you might want this back."

Nuroon didn't move, his gaze torn between the grotesque damage to Lowe's hand - already repairing itself - and the pulsating sphere now sitting on his desk.

"What do you propose I do with that?" he asked eventually. "That thing nearly destroyed my whole museum!"

Lowe shrugged. "I couldn't give a flying fuck what you do with it. I imagine you've got plenty of secret little hidey-holes in this place for your very special exhibits. Stick it in one of those. Or, if it's too much trouble, I can always haul it over to the Celestial Temple. See if anyone there's got a use for it—or better yet, a taste for the kind of trouble it brings."

"No. No. No. We'll take it," he almost leapt across the desk to prevent Lowe taking the Dungeon Core back. "It is only right, after all, that an object of such importance is maintained for posterity inside our walls." Nuroon already knew exactly the spot in his . . . private collection this piece would sit in. "Sixty thousand gold each you say? Done."

"See? That wasn't so hard, was it? Who knows, Grackle, maybe this'll be the start of your redemption arc."


"If there wasn't anything else, Mr Lowe?"

Lowe stood, brushing the charred remnants of his ruined skin off his lap like dandruff. "No," he said, "I think that's my lot."

He turned and strode toward the door, his footsteps echoing in the uneasy silence of the room. His hand reached for the handle of the office door, and for a moment, it seemed like that was it.

Business concluded.

Then he stopped and gave a sharp intake of breath, just audible enough to make Nuroon flinch. Lowe tilted his head slightly, as though something had only now occurred to him. "Oh, uh… just one more thing. You know, Director, it's funny," he said. "I've been noticing all the upgrades around here. Quite the budget you've been working with lately."

"The Trustees have been very supportive of my vision. They understand the importance of maintaining Soar Museum's standing as the crown jewel of this city."

"Supportive, you say?" Lowe said. "Fascinating, then, how that vision aligns so neatly with the sudden *flurry* of auctions I've been hearing about. Unusually rare artifacts hitting the block, fetching eye-watering sums. A Blacksmith's Codex from the First Age? That was in your inventory during your last audit. Oh, and wasn't there a legendary Tome of Binding that mysteriously found its way into a private collection in the south?"

Nuroon's smile didn't falter. "I am, of course, always looking to ensure the museum's sustainability, Mr Lowe. Some lesser pieces are occasionally deaccessioned to make room for—"

"Lesser pieces," Lowe said. "Interesting term for priceless historical artifacts that just so happen to vanish without a trace. I'm sure the Trustees will find that definition fascinating when I bring it up. What do you think? Do they even know you've been flogging off the family silver? Or is this a little side hustle of yours?"

Lowe pulled the door open with a flourish, stepping aside as Karolen filled the doorway, resplendent in her full Auditor regalia. Her polished armour positively gleamed, and the sigil of her station glowed on her chest. Behind her stood Liando Verlan, arms crossed.

Nuroon's smile faltered for the first time, his composure cracking just slightly as Karolen stepped forward.

"You know what, Director Nuroon?" Lowe said, slipping past her and out the door, "I think you're going to want to make sure all of that compensation gold comes from your *own* accounts. I imagine the Museum's books are about to be… rigorously monitored moving forward."

Karolen didn't say a word, but the glint in her eye and the faint upturn of her lips said plenty. Liando remained silent, his gaze locked on Nuroon.

Lowe tipped an imaginary hat, "Have a great day."

The door clicked shut behind him, leaving Nuroon alone in the office with Karolen and Verlan.

# <u>EPILOGUE</u>

Lowe leaned back in his creaking chair, flipping through the final pages of his report.

It was a masterclass in bullshit. It perfectly balanced the tightrope of bureaucratic survival—a blend of half-truths, artfully crafted omissions, and just enough verifiable facts to discourage anyone from digging too deep.

The perfect cocktail of plausible deniability. An almost textbook Cuckoo House report.

No one would be happy with it, but no one would be angry enough to pull at the threads. And in Soar, that was often the best you could hope for.

A lot of people were dead, and while a few of them had it coming, far too many hadn't. But that was Soar, wasn't it? A city that thrived on grinding people up and spitting out what was left. If you let yourself care too much, you'd never make it out of bed.

With a tap of his finger, Lowe activated the cuckoo sigil embossed on the cover of the file—a silver emblem of a bird mid-dive, its wings outstretched. It quivered once, twice, and then rose from the desk in a wide spiral, as if testing its newfound freedom. Tiny, glowing feathers sprouted from its corners, and the pages rifled with the faintest 'coo', like a real bird waking from slumber.

Lowe watched as the file darted toward the open window, weaving around his lamp and narrowly missing a tower of precariously stacked case notes. It hesitated at the frame, flapping softly as though sniffing the air, before shooting off with purpose, leaving a trail of fairydust in its wake.

Off to Central Filing—wherever in the gods' name that actually was.

Almost immediately, another file, dull and heavy, thudded onto his desk, spat back through his window by the same Skill that had taken the first one away. Its edges were frayed, its corners scuffed, but the sigil on its cover burned bright and angry, as if demanding attention.

Lowe sighed, his fingers brushing the cracked leather.

A return file.

Great.

He wasn't done for the night after all. How had he offended the admin trolls this time?

The file was thick with worn edges and scuffed corners. It looked exactly like hundreds of others he had handled during his career. But something about it gave Lowe pause.

His hand hesitated above the cover, and then he saw *Unsolved* stamped across it in faded ink.

He knew this file.

And he knew the case that remained *Unsolved*.

And with that, the pit opened in his stomach and, without any conscious thought, *Grid View* activated, dragging him unwillingly into the scene that had haunted his nights for the past year.

Smoke curled through the air, thick and choking, curling around the overturned furniture and shattered glass of the room like a giant, constricting serpent. Somewhere in the distance, alarms blared, their wails distant and distorted, as if he were swimming underwater.

The stink of burned mana clawed at his throat, mingling with the stench of blood.

A scene frozen in time, etched into his soul.

The body lay crumpled on the floor.

Small.

Too small.

The fine fabric of its clothes was torn, the rich colours dulled and smeared with grime and darker stains he refused to name. The child's arm was flung out above its head, and one shoe was missing, as though they'd tried to run.

Or maybe fight.

Lowe had no idea which thought hurt worse.

His breathing came sharp and fast as the steel trap of the image locked in his mind. Smoke swirled around him, painting shadows where none should be, twisting into cruel shapes. The alarms rang on, each one a hammer to his heart.

And then the laughter started.

Low, cruel, and echoing.

It wasn't real—not here, not now—but *Grid View* dragged it from his memory in perfect replication anyway. That horrible, mocking sound, spiralling into his ears and parasitically latching onto his mind.

The Black Knight.

That failed ransom handover.

His fuckup that had caused the death of a child.

The case that had ruined his life.

He retched, and that action broke the hold of his Skill and forced him back into the present.

Lowe blinked the vision away, returning to the dim light of his office. His hand trembled as he reached for the file again, and he cursed under his breath as he saw it.

A slip of paper, neatly tagged to the front of the file, stark against the dull manila cover. Lowe's fingers hesitated before plucking it free, his other hand wiping at his eyes in frustration at the sudden and unwelcome moisture there.

The handwriting was precise, almost elegant.

*I feel our previous game ended a little early. What do you say about a rematch? Yours, as ever. The Black Knight.*

And then every alarm in Cuckoo House erupted into life.

Shrill. Insistent. Every system designed to catch the tiniest ripple of a threat now howled in unison. Lights flared red along the walls, the polished floors gleaming like blood. The whole building seemed to lurch with purpose, like a beast waking from slumber.

Lowe stared at the note in his hand, his jaw tightening as the cacophony around him intensified.

"Fuck me," he said, his voice lost in the wailing alarms.

Inspector Lowe will return for the conclusion of The Soar Chronicles in *The Cuckoo's Last Call*

End Of Book One.

# **<u>Thank you</u>**

Hi everyone! I hope you've enjoyed the second installment of the Soar Chronicles? The third, and for now, final case for Inspector Lowe will be coming up soon. We get to see the disaster that led to his Classtration and also an insight into the worst of his foes. I hope you'll check it out!

A big shoutout here to everyone on Royal Road that has offered thoughts and comments on these stories as they've been developing. The fun thing about writing a serial murder mystery is that you get to see, in real time, how people are responding to the clues and the hints you are leaving out there. Hopefully you feel the outcome here has been satisfying!

As always, a huge thank you to everyone involved in Legion. I could not hope for a group of people offering better advice to a newbie author. Cheers, guys.

Cheers,

Malory

17/5/2025

# THE CUCKOOS LAST CALL

## Book 3 Soar Chronicles

## By Malory

No Class. High Stats. Deadly Skills.
Jana Lowe is back in action, badge in hand, but still a man without a Class.
When the ruthless serial killer, the Black Knight, resurfaces, leaving Lowe's colleagues dead in the streets, it's personal. Driven by revenge and armed with unique abilities, Lowe must dive headfirst into the dark heart of Soar City, where only levelling up will mean he can survive.
But the Black Knight is just the tip of the iceberg. The trail leads Lowe to a high-security Vault, a priceless artefact vanished into thin air, and powerful players—including the Mayor and the Warden of Reserves—wielding influence from the shadows. And, of course, behind it all stands Arkola, a manipulative deity pulling strings that threaten the city's very existence.
As Lowe's Skills evolve, unlocking dangerous new abilities, he's forced to confront not only shapeshifting assassins but also ghosts from his own past. The deeper he digs, the clearer it becomes: the Black Knight isn't just an enemy; he might well be someone Lowe once called friend . . .
In Cuckoo House, the coffee's burnt, the boss bites, and the corpses never stop coming.

Coming soon!

# JOURNEY TO THE DARK TOWER

By Malory

**Nothing ruins your day like a quest with a ransom note.**

Especially when you're a fake wizard with real problems.
I was supposed to be dead. Instead, I'm stumbling through medieval Britain
with Merlin's ghost backseat-driving my magical education.
And now? Princess Guinevere's gone missing, and everyone's looking at me like
I'm supposed to know what to do about it.

Fantastic.

Nothing says "qualified wizard" like leading a rescue party of misfits—a prince
with anger issues, a berserker who thinks diplomacy means hitting people slightly
less hard, and me, still trying to figure out which end of my sword shoots fire.

Between dodging Saxon war parties, navigating the Enchanted Forest, and
searching for a Dark Tower that's playing hard to get, I'm starting to think death
might have been the easier option.

**Welcome to the Dark Tower, where the quests are impossible, the magic
is unreliable, and historical accuracy is someone else's problem.**

Order Now!

# RISE OF MANKIND 6 : AGE OF GLASS

By Jez Cajiao

**The Age of Glass dawns, a fragile era balanced on the edge of oblivion. Will it shatter beneath the relentless hammer of fate?**

From the depths of despair to the pinnacle of power, Matt's ascension to Dungeon Lord has been a crucible of blood and terror. But the higher he climbs, the more precarious his perch becomes. As winter's icy fingers close around his hard-won domain, Matt and his beleaguered allies yearn for respite. Instead, they face a nightmare beyond imagining.
The Coronaught infection sweeps through the land like wildfire, twisting human flesh into abominations that defy sanity. Grotesque mutations stalk the shadows, their hunger insatiable. In this maelstrom of horror, Matt must be more than a leader – he must become a legend.

With each agonizing decision, the weight of command threatens to crush his spirit. Can he salvage the humanity of the infected, or will the price of compassion be too steep? Nuclear fire looms on the horizon, a cleansing inferno that promises annihilation. How much of his soul will Matt sacrifice to shield his people from the coming storm?

In the bowels of the earth, Matt labors to transform his dungeon into an impregnable fortress. But in a world where loyalty shatters like spun sugar, yesterday's allies may become tomorrow's executioners. Survival exacts a terrible toll, paid in blood and betrayal.

**Step carefully into the Age of Glass, where every triumph balances on a knife's edge, and a single misstep can leave you bleeding in the dark.**

**Preorder Now!**

# **THEFT OF DECKS**

By Lars Machmuller

When the deck is stacked against you? Change the game!

In the frontier town of Isarn, Chase will never be more than the lowly Darkborn thief he is. Banned from training, banned from acquiring better cards, if the Lightborn had their way, he'd be banned from life itself.

He's not alone though, and the one thing he and his friends have is determination. Losing a hand to a brutal punishment only fueled his obsession to get access to his own amazing, reality-bending cards.

That is the path to power and a future for them all. Nobody cares where you came from when you're rich enough. For now, though, they're facing both established powers, churches and age-old prejudices. It's time to get to work, and if the Lightborn won't share and play nice?

Sometimes the only way to get dealt a better hand is to steal the whole damn deck!

**Buy on Amazon**

# QUEST ACADEMY

By Brian J. Nordon

*A world infested by demons.*
*An Academy designed to train Heroes to save humanity from annihilation.*
*A new student's power could make all the difference.*

Humans have been pushed to the brink of extinction by an ever-evolving demonic threat. Portals are opening faster than ever, Towers bursting into the skies and Dungeons being mined below the last safe havens of society. The demons are winning.

Quest Academy stands defiantly against them, as a place to train the next generation of Heroes. The Guild Association is holding the line, but are in dire need of new blood and the powerful abilities they could bring to the battlefront. To be the saviors that humanity needs, they need to surpass the limits of those that came before them.

In a war with everything on the line, every power matters. With an adaptive enemy, comes the need for a constant shift in tactics. A new age of strategy is emerging, with even the unlikeliest of Heroes making an impact.

**Salvatore Argento has never seen a demon.**
**He has never aspired to become a Hero.**
**Yet his power might be the one to tip the odds in humanity's favor.**

**<u>Buy on Amazon</u>**

# **WANDERING WARRIOR**

By Michael Head

*A divine quest to deliver justice.*
*One year to accomplish his mission.*
*After nineteen planets, there's something different about this one.*

James Holden has reached the maximum level there is for a human. That's perfect, since he's the only one of his kind. A wandering warrior, without control of his destination, tossed between universes by gods who've failed to tell him why. James is the lone Judge on a new world in need of someone to balance the scales. He isn't afraid to do so with extreme prejudice. As the Chief Justice, he has to right the wrongs the innocent can't fix themselves.

As James quickly discovers, the roots of corruption run deep. Guilds choose to protect themselves rather than the people. Monsters roam the wilderness unchecked. Judgment is usually a decision between right and wrong, but nothing is ever that simple. This time, being the strongest human won't be enough to punish the guilty. James might have to recruit some new blood, even if he prefers to work alone.

On his twentieth world, he is going to win, no matter the cost. James will have to find a way to break past the limits of the system if he's going to have a chance at making a difference.

**Buy on Amazon**

# **KNIGHTS OF ETERNITY**

By Rachel Ní Chuirc

***When Zara awoke in chains she thought she'd gone mad.***

She was Zara the Fury - mistress of flame and fear. Her name was whispered across the land, from ramshackle taverns to the royal court. Even the heroic Gilded Knights thought twice before crossing her path.
She was feared—*respected.*
Now she was curled up on a dirt floor on her fiancé's orders. Valerius, leader of the Gilded, mocks her cries for help. And the kingdom is on the brink of war over the missing Lady Eternity…
But that wasn't why Zara thought she had gone mad.
The reason why is that the last thing she remembered was blood, an arcade screen, and the gun that changed everything.

**But no chains can hold the Fury, and when she gets out?**
**The world is going to *burn.***

**<u>Buy on Amazon</u>**

# <u>SCARLET CITADEL</u>

By Jack Fields

Gormon Hughes is 19, thin as a broom, and has—not for the first time in his life—been swept into the path of trouble. Poor, recently heartbroken, and indebted to the sort of people who file their teeth into needle points and devour wriggling bloated spiders for fun, Hughes sets his sights on salvation.

That salvation is the Scarlet Citadel, a wealthy organization of pageant fighters, monster hunters, and secret keepers. With the aid of strange oracles, rare good fortune, and a unique power that bubbles like champagne in the core of Hughes' being, he must join the Citadel and advance himself.

But the ladder of progression is harsh and dark. The rungs are slippery.

*And falling means disaster…*

**<u>Buy on Amazon</u>**

# <u>LITRPG!</u>

To learn more about LitRPG, talk to other authors including myself, and to just have an awesome time, please join the LitRPG Group

**<u>www.facebook.com/groups/LitRPGGroup</u>**

# FACEBOOK

There's also a few really active Facebook groups I'd recommend you join, as you'll get to hear about great new books, new releases and interact with all your (new) favorite authors! (I may also be there, skulking at the back and enjoying the memes…)

https://www.facebook.com/groups/LitRPGlegion/

https://www.facebook.com/groups/GamelitSociety

https://www.facebook.com/groups/LitRPG.books

https://www.facebook.com/groups/LitRPGforum/

# MALORY